DAWN STRIKE

a novel

By PHIL GOTHRO

PUBLISHER'S NOTE

This is a work of fiction. Names, characters, places and incidents are products of the author's imagination or are used fictitiously, any resemblance to actual events or locales or persons, living or dead, is entirely coincidental.

A original publication of Early Publishing

Early Publishing,
P.O. Box 8078
Lacey, Washington. 98509-8078

ISBN: 0-9714174-0-7

Library of Congress Control Number 2002103945

First trade paperback printing April 2002
Printed in the USA

Acknowledgments

With appreciation to Dr. Terry Hazen of the Berkeley National Laboratory for taking the time to explained vectors, and for the work of two friends, Randy Bourne and Gerry Mykelbust who kept pushing when I wanted to quit. Finally, to my wife and son who never tired of my endless rantings. Goodnight Brian sleep tight.

Part I: Old Soldiers Never Die...

One

November 30th, 2003
Podgorica, Montenegro

Captain Theo Warner was about to die, or so he thought. He'd been holed up inside the culvert for three days without heat or food and the German pilot wasn't sure how much longer he could hold on. What were his options? He could turn himself over to the Serbians and face public humiliation or he could try to stick it out a little longer. What was it they said in the briefings? "If you go down, just stay put, someone will come for you."

It was the cold and hunger, which tested the good Captain's resolve most. Even the injury to his arm was not bothering him as much as it had earlier. The cold; that was the real test. He could not remember when he had ever been so cold. His once spotless olive drab flight suit was a disgrace. It was wet, torn, bloody and muddy. The underwear beneath his flight suit was cold, clammy and clung to him like a second skin. His boots were so wet from crouching in water that the leather was actually contracting around his feet. The stabbing pains of a hundred needles radiated outwards from his hands, feet, and even testicles, terminating with intense cramps to his gut. Next came the trembling. He had started quivering earlier that day. With the intense cold, the Captain was now continuously shaking; even his teeth refused to stop chattering. He dared not light a fire however, for fear the Serbs would spot it.

At times the hunger pains seemed worse. The agony came in waves, sometimes long, sometimes short, always twisting and gnawing at his insides. The discomfort would never quite go away. Sometimes, it would fade into a low-level ache that remained in the background, reminding him of how hungry he was. The survival rations would only quench his hunger for a few moments, then, with a vengeance, the cramps would return.

Warner could not recall what a decent meal tasted like. Was it three days? Yes! It had been three days since his last decent meal. Jesus, how the days seemed to blend together. Checking to see if his emergency locator was working properly, the German aviator sighed, "At least they can still find me."

Closing his eyes, Warner attempted to control the pain, something he'd been taught in survival school. He tried to occupy his mind with the events that led to his predicament in the first-place. Warner and his wingman, Lieutenant Henri, had taken off from Aviano, Italy. Just another routine flight. Clear weather with a few scattered clouds, nothing special, a simple reconnaissance mission. All they had to do was make a few photo passes over Serbian gun emplacements around the Montenegrin Capital then back home by dinner. Piece of cake.

As the Germans were climbing away from their final pass over Podgorica, his aircraft sucked a seagull into its starboard intake. Milliseconds later turbo fan blades tore through the aircraft's thin titanium skin tearing fuel lines, smashing computer sensors, destroying avionics and rupturing hydraulics. Alarms began sounding! Control panel lights started flashing. The F/A-18 Hornet became sluggish and proceeded to shake violently. She rolled right, Warner tried several times to compensate to no avail. Finally, the fighter pitched forward and became completely unresponsive.

With the dying aircraft in a flat spin and smoke pouring from what was left of its starboard engine, Warner knew his time was running out. With the plane losing altitude rapidly, and Lieutenant Henri shouting over the radio to eject, the Captain decided it was time to punch out, or die! As if he was on autopilot, Warner reached down with his left hand, pulled the yellow and black striped lever between his legs, and in a flash, was instantly propelled from the cockpit. While ejecting from the aircraft, the aviator hit his right arm on the control panel, giving it a nasty cut. The G-forces from the ejection were so incredibly strong, he passed out.

As the parachute deployed, and his chair dropped away, the friendly tug of the shrouds brought Warner back to reality. Regaining his senses, the Captain watched his once sleek aircraft hit the ground and explode. Drifting slowly earthward, Theo was able to inspect his arm, which was bleeding profusely from a jagged gash that ran from just above his wrist to his elbow. Funny, no pain just tingling! Holding his arm with his left hand, Warner tried to stem the flow as best he could while bracing for a landing.

The landing was pure textbook, just the way he'd always practiced. After unstrapping himself from the harness and collecting his chute, the unlucky flyer worked his way towards a drainage ditch he'd spotted on the descent. Looking up through the trees, Warner spotted his wingman making a low pass over his location. He waved to let Henri know he was okay. Following the ditch a short distance, Warner came upon a highway, which had a large culvert running through it. Thankful for the shelter, he ducked in.

The culvert was about five feet high with dry leaves and branches scattered along the bottom. A faint musty smell assaulted his nostrils, a mixture of dead leaves, grass and old fecal matter. Regardless, Captain Warner knew he would be safe there. Stumbling about five or six feet into the shadows to make sure he was well out of sight, the German pilot took stock in his plight. The unlucky aviator was short on rations, had an injured arm that needed immediate medical attention and was in hostile territory. One small piece of comfort was the 9mm Glock that he had been issued.

Warner's flight suit pockets contained a portable medical kit packed with plenty of painkillers, vitamins, some basic dressings, tweezers, safety pins and other accouterments. His remaining pockets contained several packets of freeze-dried survival rations, a penlight, map and compass. Most importantly attached over his right breast pocket, was his personal emergency locator. After switching the locator on, and checking his sidearm, Warner settled down to await darkness. That's when the first wave of pain swept over him.

Beginning as a dull, steady throb, pain began to radiate outwards from his elbow to his wrist. As its intensity grew, the pain became almost unbearable. Taking several painkillers from the medical kit, Warner debated whether he should ration them or not. Another wave convinced him to seek solace in the little white pills. Knocking back a couple, he proceeded to tenderly pin the wound together with the safety pins. Afterwards, to help control the bleeding, the pilot carefully wrapped the arm with sterilized tape. Lastly he fashioned a sling from nylon he'd cut earlier from his chute.

"What a fine mess you're in now!" he thought. *"I can see the papers now, 'German NATO pilot, Captain Theo Warner, is missing due to hostile bird action.'"*

Checking his map coordinates, Warner decided to try and walk out. First he'd need a plan. The Captain spent most of the night working out a route to the sea. He would move by night and hole up by day. If he were careful, it looked like it would be about a four-day trek. By the next morning however, there was a lot of military activity moving along the road overhead.

Warner could hear trucks and personnel carriers passing at regular intervals. Sometimes he could even distinguish voices. Perhaps the Serbs were looking for the pilot of the plane that had crashed nearby. Not wanting to be spotted, he decided to stay put. The pilot spent his daytime hours being as quiet as possible, sometimes napping and sometimes listening to the activity above him.

Towards evening it started raining. A light mist at first, followed by a steady downpour. The once dry culvert now flowed with six inches of water. At least he would not die of thirst!

The following morning there was still too much activity for Captain Warner to leave his hiding place. He spent the second day much like the first, keeping as quiet as possible while waiting for the Serbs to vacate the area.

The rain never let up, and with the rain came the cold. By the second evening, the cold had assaulted his toes and worked its way up his cramped legs. Every few hours Warner would take something for the pain in his arm but his condition was rapidly deteriorating. The pilot could not remember many details of his third day in the culvert. By now he no longer had the desire to walk out; maybe it wouldn't be so bad to give up. At least he would be warm and get medical attention. His arm had started to worry him, it was continually hurting and it was starting to smell. Maybe...

Opening his eyes, Warner thought he heard a noise, a faint clinking sound and some soft splashing. Very soft, almost as if something or someone was crawling along the drainage ditch. Was someone coming? Drawing his side arm, he slowly backed farther into the culvert. Hugging the left wall, the German tried to blend in as best he could. Yes! There it was again, the soft clink of metal and faint footsteps. There was someone there! Was it friend, or foe?

"Did someone send out for Chinese?" a husky English speaking voice asked.

"Was ist?" Warner asked.

"Can you speak English? Are you Captain Theo Warner, 15th reconnaissance wing, Sixth German Air Force attached to NATO?" A dark shape began to materialize in the culvert's opening.

"Ja, yes, yes!"

"Good, then I'm at the right address." All of a sudden a

big grin emerged from the darkness. "Lieutenant Jake Philips at your service sir. United States Navy, SEAL Team Three."

"Thank God!" the grateful Captain exclaimed.

"You can thank him later," Philips responded, "I'm your ticket home." The dark shape instinctively touched a hand to a throat mic and spoke softly. "TM 4, this is TM 1, over... That's a Roger, send a message to Pitboss... Roger that... Acknowledge Pitboss from Black Jack, that, and I quote, "now we have a crap game."..."

In the darkness, Warner could just barely make out the business end of a silenced Heckler & Koch MP5. He recognized the submachine gun by its retractable wire buttstock and forward pointing twin banana clips. Behind the gun was the silhouette of a person crouching in the culvert's entrance. His black and green painted face, camouflaged BDUs and dark watch cap helped to blend him in with the darkness. The SEAL was talking into his microphone again. "...also send up TM 2, to check on the package, he appears to need attention."

Another shape appeared in the opening. The silhouette was almost the same as the first, watch cap, BDUs, face paint and weapon, however, he was just a bit shorter. Crouching down, the second SEAL snapped on a small, red lens penlight. Putting the light into his mouth, the man proceeded to work deftly in its soft red glow. He carefully touched the German flyer all over until he discovered the injured arm. Working swiftly and quietly, the corpsman cut off the makeshift bandage and examined the wound. "That's some pin job Captain. You do this yourself?"

"Yes, yes it was all I could think of."

"Well, you may have saved your arm. Pretty ingenious if you ask me." TM 2 whispered as he redressed the arm in a matter of seconds. Meanwhile the SEAL named Jake Philips stood guard outside.

Sticking his head inside the entryway, Philips quietly urged, "We've gotta git, this place is crawling with Serbs. We're lucky they haven't spotted us yet." The Lieutenant led the flyer and corpsman from the culvert. Due to his injury, cramps and cold the German could hardly walk.

"TM 3, we need your assistance..." Philips ordered. "Fall back and give TM 2, a hand."

In an instant, another SEAL appeared out of the darkness. Slinging his weapon, this new individual put an arm around Warner and practically carried him. Up and over the road they went to a small ditch on the opposite side. It was really a small break in the embankment but was large enough for the five of them.

Removing a Magellan 6000 GPS receiver from his Kevlar vest, Philips checked his position then reassured the German aviator. "We'll follow that path through the woods to a clearing on the other side; there's transportation standing by."

Captain Warner could barely make out the faint game trail, which disappeared into the woods. TM 2 took up the rear while Philips led the way into the dark forest. After walking for about a mile, he held his hand up signaling everyone to stop. Listening carefully to the sounds of the forest, Philips rechecked their coordinates. He determined that they were still on target for the landing zone. Using hand signals, the Lieutenant indicated that it was safe to proceed. Not a word was spoken between the SEALs as they followed the path for another twenty minutes. Visibility was almost nonexistent, and Warner could hardly see his hand when held out at arm's length. A fine mist was lifting from a nearby stream, forming a low ground fog that had tendrils of white mist radiating out across the path. The only sound one could hear was the soft patter of rain as it fell amongst the foliage and the pounding of one's heart.

Finally they came upon a clearing. The one-and-a-half foot high grass growing wild indicated the field had been fallow for a year. Stopping short and staying within the trees, Philips spoke softly into his microphone, "TM 4, send the signal."

"Roger."

Soon a quiet 'wugh-wugh' could be heard over the trees. Out of the dark sky, flying low to avoid radar, appeared a UH-60 Blackhawk helicopter. Its camouflaged boxy shape was hard to pick out against the dark backdrop of trees. The muffled machine was almost completely silent. Philips dropped back and motioned for everyone to move up while he scanned the landscape for unwanted guests.

Unexpectedly the night sky lit up!

"Flare, everybody down!" the Lieutenant whispered, as a phosphorus flare slowly drifted earthward by its parachute. Dropping to the ground, the entire group could see the helicopter, plain as day, it was a sitting duck. A blinding flash exploded a mere thirty meters in front of the Blackhawk, followed by a heavy concussion.

"Get outta here!" Philips shouted into his microphone, as the helicopter rotors were already increasing their tempo. "TM 4, have 'em pick us up at LZ Gold, 0430 hours." Not waiting for a response, Lieutenant Philips slowly backed his charges from the tree line.

After the Blackhawk had disappeared behind the tree cover and the flare went out, Philips donned his AN PVS-14 night vision goggles. He slowly panned the field to see if he could find out where the mortar round had come from. After several seconds the American could make out several bright shapes. About fifty humans materialized from the woods on the far side of the clearing. Fanning out, the Serbs began a coordinated search effort working their way towards the SEAL's location.

"TM 2, and 4 take Warner to the backup LZ. Mike, let's slow these guys down!"

As the two SEALs set up an ambush for the unsuspecting Serbs, the German flyer was escorted back down the trail.

Jake's heart was pounding! He waited about four minutes until he was sure the flyer was safely out of the area. Crawling to stay out of sight, Philips moved left as he spoke quietly into his microphone. "Mike, I make out about forty-five to fifty guys with various automatic weapons working their way towards our location."

"I Roger that."

"I'm about ten meters to your left. You move right fifteen or so meters and maybe we can catch 'em in a cross fire."

"Sounds good to me."

At the precise moment the Serbs were halfway across the clearing, the Lieutenant stood and sprayed an entire magazine from his silenced MP5 into the crowd. The faint popping sounds his weapon made were barely audible. Catching the Serbs in the crossfire, SEAL Mike, with his shortened M-16 and attached M203 grenade launcher, fired a 40-mm fragmentation grenade into the group. The flash and concussion were almost simultaneous as two silhouettes were tossed into the air. Muffled screams and swearing could be heard over the distinct popping of weapons.

The Serbs return fire was ineffectual. Dropping to the ground, Philips could sense rather than feel bullets striking the earth around him. Discarding the empty clip, he inserted a fresh one, rolled to his right twice, stood and fired two, three-shot bursts into the group. He watched as the second burst struck a Serbian in the chest, tearing it apart. A burst from Mike tossed another man about like a rag doll.

Dropping down again, Philips rolled left this time. The Serb's were getting organized, for now the Lieutenant could see rounds striking the very spot he had just vacated. He could actually make out little tufts of dirt flying in the air.

"Damn, that was too close." Philips muttered through clenched teeth. Standing, the big American unleashed a wall of 9-mm lead into the oncoming group, dropping several. Hitting the ground once more, Philips spoke into his microphone. "Mike, these guys are starting to get hot, one more clip then we git, we've a ride to catch. Meet me by the big mossy rock we passed along the trail."

"Roger, this place is getting a little too hot for comfort!"

Reloading his weapon, Philips jumped up and fired three more bursts into the thinning crowd, as his partner did the same. Both SEALs slowly began working their way back towards the woods, unleashing short bursts as they went. When Philips reached the tree line he took cover behind a large fallen maple and emptied the remaining magazine towards the oncoming horde. He exchanged the exhausted clip for a fresh one and started running towards the rendezvous some hundred meters down the trail.

Checking to see that Mike was okay, Philips started off towards the secondary landing zone. Stopping several times, the SEALs tried to ascertain if anyone was following, but it looked like they'd made a clean escape. About an hour later, the pair caught up with the other half of the team waiting at the designated clearing.

"Everyone okay?" the Lieutenant inquired.

"A-okay! All's quiet," TM 4 responded.

"Send the signal."

"Roger."

Again the quiet 'wugh-wugh' was heard through the trees. This time the Blackhawk landed without incident. Lieutenant Philips gave the signal and everyone quietly and quickly moved across the field. Upon reaching the helicopter, a pair of hands reached out from the dark cavern that was the side door and pulled the injured flyer aboard. The SEALs climbed up one by one until Philips was the last one outside.

"All present and accounted for?" the Lieutenant shouted into the helicopter.

"Aye Sir," came a reply from within the darkness.

"Then let's get the hell outta here," Philips ordered as he boarded the helicopter. The Lieutenant then heard the craft power up and lift off.

"That was a close one," the pilot shouted over his shoulder.

"Nothing we couldn't handle." Philips shouted over the rotor noise. Removing his BDU jacket, the SEAL wiggled two fingers through a bullet hole on the upper left shoulder and grinned, "No, this was close!"

As the helicopter sped away and the inside became illuminated in red light, Captain Warner was finally able to see his rescuers. The SEAL called Jake Philips was very tall indeed with a handsome, austere face, piercing icy blue eyes and hair the color of corn silk. Sporting wide shoulders and slim hips, the man looked like he could run a marathon and never break a sweat. There was something about him you had to like, perhaps it was his sheepish grin or his firm handshake, but there was something else behind those eyes, something sad. Warner did not want to find out what could happen if you ever crossed him, for the American looked to be one tough customer.

The Lieutenant reached over with his right hand and squeezed Captain Warner's left shoulder and said with a grin. "Pleased to meet you Captain Warner, and this is Navy SEAL TEAM THREE, and we were never here!"

Beside Philips sat a tall, athletic individual who had to be a pro quarterback! His six foot two inch frame had not an ounce of fat, he was all muscle. His round tanned face was set with twinkling baby blue eyes. His soft brown hair was short-cropped, and he sported a mustache with a one-inch strip of beard that ran from his lower lip to the bottom of his chin. Dimples that would appear whenever McKay smiled set off the entire package. In all, Mike McKay looked to be a younger, leaner, meaner version of William F. Cody.

Beside him, looking bored, was the biggest guy Theo had ever seen. His shaven head was so shiny it looked like an eight ball. Black as night with laughing eyes, he was six foot four and barrel chested with arms and legs as big as tree trunks. But it was his hands that were most intriguing to Warner. It looked to him as if the black man's hands were twice the size of his own and he could wrap one hand around Warner's biceps.

"Meet petty officers Mike McKay and Clifford Wardon," Philips offered, "Cliff's the big ugly black guy..."

Wardon groaned aloud.

"...also known as TM 2, who looked after your injury back there. It was Mike or TM 3, who pretty much carried you along the path." Philips continued conversationally. "Best two friends a man could have. I never leave home without 'em."

"Hear, hear!" chorused the unlikely pair.

"Lieutenant! You have orders home," the helicopter pilot shouted. "I'm supposed to escort you and your team to Aviano with the good Cap'n."

“What about debriefing?”

“Nope! I say again, I’m to escort you to a waiting plane at Aviano, top priority,” the pilot responded in a mock Sergeant Shultz’s voice, then remarked. “I know noth-thing!”

“Now what!” Wardon complained, “I bet this has something to do with the Captain’s motorcycle.”

“I told you no one would ever find out about that,” McKay playfully cautioned, while jabbing Wardon with his elbow.

Staring out the doorway in silence, Lieutenant Jake Philips wondered what was so important that he was not returning to the *U.S.S. Carl Vinson.*

Two

December 1st, 2003
London, England

The opulent Prince of Wales stood at No. 23 Regent Street in the fashionable SoHo shopping district. The twenty-six story golden smoked glass hotel stood in sharp contrast to the stone and mortar edifices of the surrounding blocks. A little out of place, the owners had wanted to make a statement by locating the modern high-rise in an area where the closest competition was all of five stories. The choice had been a good one, with 2500 rooms, 150 executive suites, five restaurants, shopping mall, and recreation facilities, constantly booked up, the Prince of Wales was a money maker.

The hotel also housed convention facilities, which were among the finest in the city. Located on the third floor, the gigantic hall used to host banquets and large gatherings, could be converted into fifteen smaller conference rooms by simply moving retractable walls and doors. A small kitchen was conveniently located at the south end of the building providing bar service and hors-d'oeuvres to the conventioneers. The main course however, had to be shuttled up from the kitchens below by way of a freight elevator next to the service kitchen.

The scheduled meetings for rooms two through eight were a series of workshops on decreasing trade barriers between the European Economic Union and the People's Republic of China. Eighty members of the Chinese delegation, including translators, were scheduled to sit down at 4 P.M. for a series of dialogues with representatives from Germany, France and Great Britain. Most of the middle-aged Chinese delegates were wearing identical drab navy blue suits issued by their government. Each person had a handwritten nametag, in both English and Chinese, affixed on their left breast pocket. Every emissary had an assigned seat at the long tables with their counterparts sitting opposite, working on specific issues.

Conference room one had a podium set up at the far end of the room. Behind the podium hung a dark blue curtain with the red People's Republic flag and the blue European Union flag. A large banner was stretched across the curtain with the slogan 'Free Trade transcends all Boundaries.'

About ninety chairs were set up in a semi circle with a central aisle in front of the podium. In anticipation of the speaker, all chairs were occupied and an additional twenty or so conventioneers were standing along the back wall. Hushed murmuring could be heard about the room as the delegates waited impatiently for the keynote speaker, Minister Dung Xuxu of the People's Republic to make his appearance.

The room went silent as a short slim man, wearing the same government issue suit, entered the room reading from his notes as he carefully made his way to the podium. Clearing his throat and tapping the microphone, Minister Xuxu took a second to glance at his audience. He remembered the paramount reason as to why these meetings had been convened in the first-place. Due to internal and external pressures, China's foreign trade was in a shambles. Premier Xian had replaced Xuxu's post three times in the past eighteen months with little or no success.

Last year, after months of disappointing results, the Premier had appointed Xuxu Minister of Foreign Trade and Economic Cooperation with hopes of propping up the Chinese economy by attracting foreign investment. The results were almost immediate. New foreign investment, encouraged by Xuxu, started pouring in. He offered tax credits and incentives for companies willing to take a gamble on the immense Chinese economy. A moderate, who did not follow the hard-line Communists philosophy of five-year plans and communes, Xuxu understood that if China were to survive in the global economy successfully, it would have to rethink the way in which it did business. He relished the thought that the Premier had given him carte blanche to perform whatever it took to turn China's ailing economy around.

The middle-aged Minister was also president of Shanghai Bank, the largest financial institution in China. A Cambridge educated man; Xuxu had worked his way up from teller to Chairman of the government owned bank through thirty years of hard and diligent service.

Shanghai Bank had been privatized five years previously and he was the logical choice to head up its commercial lending and overseas operations. Within three years, Xuxu had the bank working efficiently and showing a profit. The old hard liners criticized his capitalistic ideas but tolerated him because of his close relationship with Premier Xian.

Xuxu started speaking slowly and carefully about the importance of open trade and the eagerness with which China was willing to embrace the idea. A neatly dressed individual entered the room and hesitated just inside the doorway as he scanned the conventioneers. He was really quite nondescript except for his flaming red hair and handlebar mustache. Appearing to be keenly interested in what the minister had to say, the stranger leaned slightly forward as if intent on catching every word. Without comment, he walked about half way up the aisle towards the podium and pulled a Walther P. P. K. out from under his coat. The assassin proceeded to squeeze off three rounds in as little as two seconds. The first 7.65-mm tumbler struck the unaware Minister right between the eyes, causing the back of his head to explode into a crimson cloud of blood, brain tissue and bone. The blue curtain caught most of the matter as the stricken Xuxu fell to the floor. The other two shots were intentionally fired into the ceiling with the idea of causing as much confusion as possible.

Within the confines of the small room the effect was perfect. The deafening report from the weapon caused the entire room to drop to the floor for cover. The assassin quickly turned and silently walked out the way he had come in. He moved effortlessly to the freight elevator as screams of panic and shouts for help could be heard coming from the conference room. No one challenged the armed gunman as he made good his escape.

five hours later...

Paris, France

Winter rains had come early to the city of lights. Low clouds hung over Paris giving the city a surreal sense of dread. The light rain and slick streets did not dissuade the early evening traffic. Small cars were beeping and darting in and around slower cars, pedestrians, sightseeing buses and trucks. Even pedestrians along the boulevards and avenues had an extra spring to their step as throngs of people scurried to get out of the evening shower. It seemed as if everyone was in a hurry.

At the Chateau de Charlevoix the atmosphere was quite the opposite. The main lobby was overdone with gilt and large fluted columns. Several guests were silently reading newspapers while seated on Louis XVI couches that faced one another opposite the hotel check-in. Occasionally, a waitress from the restaurant next door would wander through to see if anyone needed their drinks refreshed. Whenever patrons conversed it was in hushed tones, while the loudest sound was the ring of the bell at the reception desk whenever the bellman was summoned.

The Chateau was an obese, baroque style, six-story edifice constructed during the latter stages of the 18th century.

It's sixty-two suites all faced outward with large balconies that offered various views of the boulevards below. Located about a mile from the Arc de Triomphe on the corner of the famed Champs-Elys'ees and Rue Lebouteux, the Chateau de Charlevoix was a popular rendezvous spot for unfaithful executives and out-of-town dignitaries who required discreet liaisons. The Chateau presented large plush sitting rooms decorated in the French impressionist style of the early '20s. Each suite offered such amenities as thick carpeting, oversized beds, well-stocked minibars, gilded bathroom fixtures, and discreet room service. Knowledgeable bellmen only required a subtle nod, or a modest tip with a note of requirements inside a match book, and the suite's occupant would spend many hours in the loving arms of a high-priced prostitute. This made the Chateau most popular with the jet set.

Room 502 was a two-room suite rented by Minister of Agriculture Wu Wei of the People's Republic of China. Wanting a respite from his hectic schedule, Wei had arranged a private liaison with a very discerning service. Following a day of meetings with French scientists who had perfected an efficient way of growing rice, the fortyish Wei was looking forward to an evening of pure unadulterated sex. The service had indicated that the flaxen haired Brittany would arrive at 10 P.M. In the past, his dates had always been punctual, so, by 10:15 Wei was starting to worry.

A moment later, a light tapping at the door interrupted Wei as he was about to call the service and complain about his missing date. Wei set down the brandy he'd been enjoying, adjusted his silk robe and checked his hair in the mirror before answering the door. He did want to look his very best this evening.

"I was starting worry..." Wei exclaimed in halting French, as he swung the door wide, only to be surprised by a red-headed stranger dressed in a long dark wool overcoat. The stranger extended a leather-encased hand, which held a silenced Walther P. P. K. pointed directly at Wei's chest. "Wh-what you w-want? If money, here take wallet," Wei stuttered.

His comments did not elicit a response from the gunman, who merely motioned with the gun for Wei to back slowly into the room. Never taking his eyes from Wei, the stranger took three steps across the threshold into the suite and quietly shut the door.

"Do you know who I am?" asked Wei, with a hint of terror in his voice, as his eyes narrowed, then grew wide with alarm.

Only silence.

Pointing towards the dressing table, Wei pleaded, "Please, please, whatever they pay, I double!"

His answer was three soft puffs as the Walther coughed death. Three neat holes magically appeared in the center of Wei's silk robe. Looking down in disbelief, the Minister had enough time to utter, "Why!" With a final parting look towards the smiling red head, Wei was dead before he hit the floor.

Acting swiftly, the assassin unscrewed the silencer from his weapon as he checked the bedroom to ensure there had been no witnesses. Holstering his pistol, the gunman gave the suite one last look while stepping over the still bleeding Wei. "Nothing personal, just business," he muttered.

Pulling the door securely shut and fixing the 'do not disturb' sign to the handle, the foreigner strolled down the carpeted corridor towards the elevators.

Pausing to wait on the elevator, he started humming an indistinguishable tune. Glancing down at his shoes, a spot of blood had somehow gotten on the tip of the left toe. Without a second thought the gunman rubbed the spot off by running the soiled shoe up and down behind his right leg a few times.

When the elevator arrived, a radiant blonde about five foot seven stepped from the car. Her hourglass figure was encased in a red silk evening gown with a plunging neckline that accentuated her breasts. She had an overcoat folded neatly over her right arm while carrying an umbrella in her left. Her brown eyes danced in the hallway's subdued lighting, while her high cheekbones had a hint of blush from the evening's cool weather.

"Pardon," she stylishly quipped as she eased past the

redhead.

"Merci," he answered and stepped into the car. As he pushed the button for the lobby, the assassin took a long look after her form as the elevator doors closed. Upon exiting the elevator, the executioner briskly left the Chateau and was easily lost in the crowds mulling about on the Champs-Elys'ees.

Three

Chief Inspector Rolf Heinrich had just gotten his tan trench coat and was locking up his corner office, in preparation for catching the underground home, when he spied a trim figure approaching him. Amanda Braxton, the duty dispatcher, was working her way through the crowded room towards him. Heinrich was aware that she had a crush on him and tried to duck out of sight, but was stopped at the last instant.

"Inspector, oh, Inspector!" Amanda shouted across the room as she waved what looked to be a manila folder. "I have something for you." The young lady was constantly making excuses to be around the Inspector. Being some thirty years her senior, Heinrich tried to shun Ms Braxton's advances.

Frowning, the Inspector stood for several seconds pondering the idea of ignoring her. It wasn't that Amanda was hard on the eyes. In fact, she was one of the most beautiful women in the office. Her soft honey-blonde hair fell to just below her shoulders, and her green eyes had a sparkle to them that captivated every young male in the office. Her shapely figure was constantly poured into some revealing, yet tasteful, business suit and today was no exception. She wore a peach colored silk blouse that gave just a hint of cleavage and a short skirt that drew attention to her long shapely legs. Though Amanda had many offers to dinner, as far as anyone knew she had politely declined them all. The problem was the Inspector's ethics. Even though he was flattered by all the attention, Rolf didn't date people with whom he worked.

Right now, Heinrich just wanted to go home after a long day. Moreover, to top it all off, all afternoon he had been in the mood for some of Mrs. Flannery's fish and chips. If he answered, the idea would have to be put on hold. On the other hand, he did not become Chief Inspector in ten years by ignoring duty. Crushing out his cigarette the Inspector answered back, "What?"

"Th-There's been a shooting o'er ta SoHo," said the perky dispatcher.

"So, call a cop!" the impatient Heinrich said out of the side of his mouth, still thinking of fish and chips.

"I wager a pint you'll want to take a peek at this one, In-spec-tor!" she fired back, putting special emphasis on Inspector, and slapped his chest with the folder.

Sighing, Heinrich sat his five foot seven inch frame back into his chair, "Why is it you always get the better of me Amanda?"

"Because you can't put an unread book down."

"And just what's that supposed to mean?" he hesitated then continued, "Oh, skip it, let's just begin, what have you got?"

"It seems some poor bloke got himself shot at the Duke of York."

"Then, why call Interpol?"

"Well, it looks like he's some mucky-muck with the Chinese government, got himself shot in front of a hundred witnesses."

"Lovely! They have the chap that popped him?"

"That's the strange part Inspector, he's gone like a London fog in July."

"Is that the way with it?"

"That's what it says here in the dispatch. You're ta see a

Detective Constable Corbet, he's the chap at the scene."

"Right-O... Umh, Amanda... thanks." Heinrich said uncomfortably as he jotted the information down.

"Don't mention it. Now, get your arse o'er there before the Bobbies muck it up." She remarked while standing close enough for the Inspector to get a good whiff of the perfume she wore.

"You're right about that," he responded, "You arrange the car, I'll be ready in a moment."

Forty-five minutes later Heinrich was silently watching the investigation at the hotel. The Bobbies had been quick to secure the scene and were able to acquire statements from about half the witnesses. Because of the possible international repercussions, Interpol had been called. Heinrich made a mental note to brief the Foreign Secretary in the morning.

Detective Constable Boston Corbet, a ten-year veteran of London's famous police force, was wearing the trademark dark blue wool uniform and pointed hat with low visor the Bobbies were famous for. He even had the brass whistle that was made famous in Hollywood movies; very rarely did he blow it however. Though he looked like the traditional Bobbie, Corbet packed a 9-mm Ruger under his great coat.

Heinrich sought out the Constable and introduced himself. "The man at the door directed me here. Constable Corbet?"

"That's correct. Inspector Heinrich?" he responded offering his hand.

"A pleasure. So what have we got?" the Inspector accepted the firm handshake.

"It peer's that a Dung Xuxu got shot," the Bobby said checking his notes.

"Is that who they were taking out back there?"

"Correct."

"Anything special about this case?"

"No, some chap just walked right up to the poor bloke and started firing. One between the eyes, two into the ceiling."

"Why do you suppose he did that?" the Inspector asked as he gazed upwards.

"To confuse the witnesses?" Constable Corbet answered.

"Very good." Heinrich turned and started to scan the room and its contents. "By the way, what did you say this Xuxu did for the Chinese?"

"He was Minister of Foreign Trade."

"Mind if I poke around a bit?"

"No, not at t'all, we've just finished the diagramming."

"Would you mind sending me copies of your report by the morning post?" the Inspector asked, handing Constable Corbet his business card.

"I can do that." Taking the Inspector's card, he glanced at it before putting it into his pocket. "Go ahead, take all the time you need."

"I'll just do that."

After spending ninety minutes examining the podium and searching every corner of the conference room, Heinrich was able to walk away with two important pieces of information. The crime lab had three spent shell casings tagged and by all accounts the assassin had flaming red hair. Most of the Chinese witnesses claimed, through interpreters, that the assassin was male, however, several seemed to think he was a she. The British witnesses all claimed the shooter was a man.

No one seemed to know what happened to the assassin after he left the conference room, and no attempt at pursuit had been made. An all points dispatch to police agencies within the southern half of England was sent out without success. Airports, Railways and the Channel Ferries were also notified with little result. Without a better description, there was little chance of an apprehension.

Heinrich had just settled down for a nightcap and a little telly, when the phone rang. Dispatch had been told not to disturb him unless it was an emergency. *"I'm going to have a way with them tomorrow!"* Heinrich thought as he picked up the phone still sipping his brandy. "Hello."

A familiar female voice spoke up on the other end, "Hello, Inspector Heinrich?"

"Amanda, don't you ever sleep?"

"So-sorry Sir, my night to stay late."

"I left instructions, I was not to be disturbed," Heinrich responded with impatience in his voice.

"I-I understand, it's just that.."

"Now that you've disturbed me, what is it?"

"It-it..."

"Well spit it out Lassie."

"It would seem Sir, that there has been another mu-murder."

"Am I the only one on call tonight?" he queried with anger in his voice.

"Bu-but Sir, you don't un-understand..."

"What don't I understand?"

"It would seem that this homicide has something to do with your previous case."

"Okay, I'm listening." Heinrich said with curiosity gaining the upper hand.

"Another body has turned up, this time in Paris."

"How long?" he began taking notes.

"About an hour now."

"Go on."

"And the victim is another Chinese government official."

"And?" Heinrich could feel the anger leaving him as his mind started working over details of the earlier murder.

"They have a witness!" Amanda blurted out.

"Good god!" Heinrich explained, "Why didn't you say so in the first-place?"

"I-I tried..."

"I'm on the next plane, have a car collect me in fifteen minutes."

"Right Sir," she responded with relief.

"By the way Ms. Braxton, thank you for calling."

"Thank you Sir." Not waiting for Heinrich to respond, the dispatcher hung up.

Observing the French investigators search the sitting room of suite 502 for clues, Heinrich, the son of German refugees, ran a hand through his coarse brown hair. His weather-beaten face was lined with premature crow's feet around pale blue eyes from countless years of long hours and little sleep. Looking a little disheveled from the hectic pace of the past six hours, the Chief Inspector stood in the sitting room area of the suite with his threadbare overcoat across his right arm wondering if his soiled black pinstripe suit showed. He had mistakenly donned the wrong suit in his haste to get to the airport. He was hoping the Paris police would prove to be as efficient as the British. The Minister's crumpled form had been draped with a white sheet by the Coroner's department. A photographer was kept busy snapping photos while a uniformed officer bagged spent shell casings.

A Paris homicide detective was interviewing a visibly shaken young woman. As she retold her story for the umpteenth time, Heinrich couldn't help but to notice her long tan legs extending below the hem of her red dress. Her body language suggested that she was a person of refinement. *"Obviously a very well paid call girl."* Heinrich concluded, as he lit a cigarette and inhaled deeply.

The detective checked his notes, and approached Heinrich. He noted the cigarette with disdain but refrained from saying anything. Speaking in heavily accented English he addressed Interpol agent. "Inspector Heinrich, Oui? Detective Maurice LaPonte."

Nodding, Heinrich exhaled the smoke towards the ceiling and gave the French detective a cursory inspection. Dressed in a somewhat out of style brown tweed suit, LaPonte had slightly askew brown hair and bright blue eyes with rosy cheeks. He looked to be a likable chap. The Inspector noticed with satisfaction, that the Frenchman referred to his ever-present notepad often. *"How alike we are,"* he thought.

Folding his arms across his chest, Heinrich asked in his own tangy Cockney accent, "So can the lass shed some light on the doings here?"

"I'm afraid not Inspector."

"Was she the one who found the body?"

"That is correct, it seems the lady had an appointment with the deceased for 10 P.M. She was running a little late because of a rain shower we had earlier in the evening."

"I see there was a 'Do not disturb' placard on the door, how'd she get in?"

"She checked in with the front desk, they gave her a key."

"And she saw nothing?" Heinrich questioned, his eyes narrowing. He was trying hard not to show his disappointment over the course of events.

"Madame did see someone waiting on the elevator as she got off."

"Now we're getting somewhere. Can she describe the bloke?" Heinrich asked with renewed interest.

"According to Madame Brittany he was a well dressed man humming to himself in the hallway."

"That's it?" Heinrich was crestfallen. "Not what you'd call a witness, is she?" he said to no one in particular, taking another drag from his cigarette and exhaling towards the ceiling.

"One moment." The Paris official crossed the room and spoke swiftly in French to the young prostitute. Retracing his steps, the detective shook his head and said, "The only other information she can recall was his hair."

"Which is?"

"Flaming red."

Heinrichs eyebrows raised an inch, "Ah, there is a connection." Stepping over to the end table and putting out his cigarette in the ashtray, "So detective, check ballistics. I'll wager you'll find the slugs are 7.65-mm." Handing the detective his business card, "Could you send me a copy of your report?" It was more of an order than a request.

"Oui, I can have the report for you later today. I will fax a copy to your office."

"Good, now I've a plane to catch." When Heinrich left the room he paused in the hallway to collect his thoughts. "*Two*

Chinese ministers assassinated the same day by probably the same man. Looks like I will have a go at this after all."

"Maurice, who was that man and what did he want?" Asked one of the uniformed officers who had been idly standing by watching quietly.

"That was Inspector Heinrich from Interpol, Philippe." Inspector LaPonte said as he turned his attention back to the sobbing Brittany.

Four

December 2nd, 2003
Hong Kong

Exotic Hong Kong was as busy as ever. It's storerooms and warehouses were full to capacity to meet the world's demand for goods manufactured by the city's cheap labor force. Business had not suffered a significant slowdown since the British handed the colony to the Chinese in 1997. In fact, as many as a hundred ships a day now passed through Hong Kong harbor.

Dockside facilities were teeming with stevedores working twenty-four hours a day just to keep pace with shipping orders destined for countries all around the Pacific Rim. Dozens of ships waited at anchor for their turn at the loading quays. The harbor was so busy that small steamers were loaded at their anchorages by barges called lighters. The lighters would come out laden with crates, and then cranes aboard the ships would lift the cargo with huge nets into waiting holds.

The Regents of the former colony had struck a deal with the Chinese government allowing semi-independent rule for at least fifty years. Because of this, the city was flourishing despite

Communist authority. For Hong Kong, it was business as usual.

There was only one exception to the hands off policy. The Chinese military now occupied the former Naval, RAF and Army facilities. This policy allowed the Communist government to 'protect' Hong Kong in case of a national emergency. Government troops could also be used to augment the police force if need be.

The city is divided into many different districts, each one having its own identity and character. Shopkeepers and residents alike rarely venture far from the districts they call home. It is not unusual for someone to live on the sixteenth floor of a thirty-story tower and work in the shops on the first or second floor.

The "Crown Jewel of the Orient", Hong Kong has one of the most photographed skylines in the world. The fifteen hundred-foot Victoria Peak dwarfs the city's towering skyscrapers, while lush tropical foliage ascends the mountain from the city's financial district. On hot, muggy afternoons, many a local resident can be found enjoying a leisurely stroll along trails that meander about the slopes of the peak.

Spread out along the base of Victoria Peak is the district known as Admiralty. Admiralty is a paradox. Along the shore, modern skyscrapers and broad avenues are juxtaposed between ramshackle huts that line both sides of narrow streets that wind endlessly up the mountain. Along the alleys, shopkeepers have set up outdoor bazaars that sell everything from live chickens to wristwatches. Throngs of people crowd the sidewalks looking into shops, examining goods and speaking rapidly to proprietors. In a ritual as old as man, patrons and shopkeepers alike can be seen haggling over mundane details, such as the high price of an item or how much it's needed. Along the boulevards and avenues is a harmonious barrage of restaurants, banks, gemstone exchanges and seedy girlie bars with gaudy neon signs.

The district gets It's name from the former British naval base once located there. Now occupied by the People's Liberation Army, the base has remained essentially intact. All the shore facilities and workshops are being put to hard work by China's struggling Navy. Tied up to pier thirty-six was China's most recent acquisition from Russia, the Saryts missile destroyer *Hangzhou*.

Aboard the destroyer, Captain Zen Tong was putting the finishing touches on a report detailing his movements from Shanghai to Hong Kong. With his paperwork complete, the Captain was finally able to relax. The *Hangzhou's* fifty-four-year-old master was always on edge whenever his beloved destroyer entered a busy port such as Hong Kong. Fearing a collision within the tight confines of the harbor, the close proximity of civilian ships always made him uneasy. Pushing back his chair, the Captain interlaced his fingers behind his head, leaned back, and let out a sigh of relief and spoke loudly through the open hatchway. "Yeoman!"

A Chinese sailor, dressed in white, instantly appeared at the Captain's stateroom door. Saluting, but never entering the quarters, the sailor responded, "Sir."

"Could you get me a cup of tea."

Quickly and efficiently the sailor disappeared and returned in less than ninety seconds with a silver tea service. Putting the tray on the occasional table in front of an old vinyl sofa, the Yeoman quietly put a slice of lime into the cup then poured the steaming tea over it. He silently exited the compartment, never once looking at his Captain.

Captain Tong preferred to be alone whenever he was off duty. A single person who had never married, the Captain preferred peace and quiet to idle conversation. Wanting to stretch his legs, he paced about the quarters. Taking the cup and stirring his tea, the Captain's gaze went from the wood panel bulkheads to the open porthole where the sounds of Hong Kong drifted in. Sipping the tea, Captain Tong crossed the wardroom to the porthole. Gazing out upon the harbor, he thought, *"Hong Kong never changes."* He curiously watched one of the double-decker Green Star ferries plowing sluggishly across the harbor carrying it's human cargo to the Kowloon Peninsula. A thin smile crossed his face as he thought of how much the ferry's master and himself had in common.

Wanting to stretch his legs further and maybe get some

fresh air, Tong set his empty cup down and donned his Captain's cap, then exited the compartment. Following a companionway to a watertight hatch, he opened the dogs and stepped out onto the starboard bridge wing. Immediately he could feel the change from the air-conditioned superstructure to the hot, humid, sticky air. His ears were instantaneously assaulted by the sounds of beeping cars, throaty motorcycles and the clang of bells from various ferries. Over all of this could be heard the din of humanity as it went about it's daily routine.

Leaning on the starboard gyro repeater, the Captain watched for a score of minutes as ships of different sizes, types and shapes, from containers to sampans, came and went along the waterfront. He took special delight in watching a wooden junk, with a roaring lion figurehead, untie from the quay not more than a thousand yards from where his beloved *Hangzhou* was moored. Aboard the junk, an elderly gentleman was barking orders at two eager individuals who seemed to jump whenever a command was uttered. Upon clearing the pier the junk's main sail, which appeared to be made of woven bamboo, was hoisted and the ungainly craft made headway westward towards the Pearl River.

Captain Tong turned his back to the waterfront and slowly inspected his charge from stem to stern. Launched in 1989 and purchased by the Chinese government in 2000, the *Hangzhou* was China's largest warship. With an overall length of 513 feet, she was almost as large as, and faster than, most World War II battleships. From the forward and rear mounted dual 130-mm turrets, to the helo pad located aft, the *Hangzhou* was a cross between traditional naval firepower and a modern weapon systems platform. The ship still sported a main mast; however, instead of sails, it now supported several arrays of radar dishes and communications antenna, including a front dome for the Orekh anti ship weapons system.

The *Hangzhou's* main batteries were no longer the traditional naval guns. Instead, located amidships, were two quad cylinder launchers for the Moskitt SSN medium range anti-ship missile system. Additionally, located forward and aft were single vertical launchers for the SA-N-7 Shitil SAM system. With four torpedo tubes and the capability of carrying up to forty mines the *Hangzhou* was the most powerful ship in the Chinese Navy.

Assigned to the East Seas Fleet, the *Hangzhou* spent most of its time patrolling the waters of the Formosa Strait and the seas off Taiwan. With a bow mounted Platina sonar unit, most of *Hangzhou's* duties consisted of hunter-killer games with the Republic of China's submarines.

As the warship rocked gently pier side, Captain Tong took in the sights and sounds of Hong Kong from the bridge wing. The Captain lost in his reverie, failed to notice his third junior officer approach him. Coughing politely, Ensign Yi let his presence be known.

"Shi, what is it?"

"Begging the Captain's pardon," the ensign stated while saluting, then continuing. "We have a communication from Beijing."

Returning the salute, Tong took the communication and waited for the Ensign to leave him in private. Taking one more glance at Hong Kong harbor, he opened the envelope and read his new orders. The Hangzhou was to begin patrolling an area known as the Spratley Islands off the Brunei Coast. Proceeding onto the bridge, Captain Tong picked up the ship's phone and dialed the engine room. After a brief pause, the chief engineer answered. "Chief! How soon can you have the evaporators working again?"

"About thirty-six hours Sir."

"That will be fine. Keep me posted."

"Shi Sir, you'll be the first to know," responded the chief as he hung up.

Putting the phone back in its cradle, Captain Tong was satisfied with the progress the chief was making on the continually malfunctioning evaporators. "At least I can get a little rest before our next patrol," he said aloud to the deserted bridge.

Aboard the junk, an unseen passenger was curiously observing the Chinese warship from the primitive luxury of the

Captain's quarters. Through a porthole, the observer was afforded an unobstructed view of the white painted destroyer. The only modern convenience aboard the junk was a video set-up that included monitor, cameras and recorder, all directly connected to a mini-cam mounted atop the main mast. The elderly Asian was recording every foot of the destroyer as the junk sailed past. The entire box of tricks was powered by a series of batteries sitting on the floor next to the bunk. Leaning back in an old wicker chair the mysterious passenger sighed, "She'll do just fine." Picking up his cup of tea he stirred it a couple times then took a sip, "Yes, she'll do just fine."

Five

December 2nd, 2003
Nagano, Japan

The sleek black Mercedes limousine moved effortlessly along the snow blanketed streets of Nagano. In back sat a lone, well-dressed Chinese passenger. Lying on the seat beside him was a black patent leather briefcase, from which a small steel chain ran to a handcuff encircling the man's right wrist. He watched in silence as the car negotiated the narrow streets.

Eventually the limousine worked its way from the quiet city streets onto a freeway, which led, away from the downtown area. After a time, the Mercedes was able to pick up speed, leaving houses, high rises and factories behind. Along the highway, buried under a heavy blanket of snow were farms, fields and orchards in their winter slumber. The distant mountains crept closer with amazing speed. The lone passenger could hear the engine start to pull as the freeway worked it's way into the foothills.

After an hour of negotiating winding roads, switchbacks and narrow tunnels, the car came to rest in front of an old wrought iron gate. Strangely out of place, the gate had a design that was more Western European than Far East. A gilded coat of arms with lions and roses adorned both sides, while the initials "H.Y." embellished the center of the coat of arms. The French fleur-de-lis topped every bar.

Twelve-foot high sandstone walls went off in either direction from the gate. A remote security station, with video camera and keypad, stood on a post next to the right side of the gate. The passenger noticed additional cameras along the top of the wall monitoring road traffic in both directions. His driver spoke quickly into the intercom.

The heavy gate slid opened silently allowing the car to proceed. Another ten minutes was required to reach their destination. The limousine worked its way through a dense pine forest, followed by an idyllic alpine meadow. Finally, the car slowed. Nestled below the peaks, in the center of the meadow, stood a fifteenth century English Manor house.

The Manor house, or castle, was complete with turrets, draw bridge, water filled moat, leaded stained glass windows and tall square towers flying red and black banners. The walls were constructed of pink granite and gray sandstone topped with a steeply gabled green patina-colored copper roof. Guards could be seen walking the battlements watching the car's approach. Lofty mountains totally surrounded the estate giving it a fairy tale appearance. To add to the storybook ambiance a light snow began falling. If the stranger hadn't known better, he'd swear he was in Austria's Northern Alps.

To gain entry onto the castle grounds, the car had to cross a drawbridge and pass through the Gatehouse which contained a portcullis or gate. A guard who was standing watch in one of the old fighting chambers, which surrounded the portcullis, waved the limousine through. When the vehicle stopped in the center of a courtyard, it was quickly surrounded by a security detail. The security people were dressed in suits and armed with Ingram Mac-10's, their ever-watchful eyes scanning about. When the passenger exited the Mercedes he was escorted up a dozen steps to the Manor's main doors.

The heavy oaken doors pierced with iron studs, opened as he approached. A beautiful Japanese maiden in a traditional gold silk kimono admitted him into the residence.

"May I take your coat and briefcase?" She greeted him in his native tongue, bowing and keeping her eyes downcast to the floor.

"No!" He barked back "I'll only be a few moments; make sure my car is waiting."

"Yes, he asks that you please wait in the study. He'll be but a moment," the maiden replied with a bow.

The expansive entryway was nothing more than an oversized hallway. Dark oak doors barred opposite ends of the room and a gray stone staircase ascended to a mezzanine level balcony that overlooked the entryway. Strange dancing shadows were emitted from two dozen large candles mounted in an enormous pewter candelabrum suspended by a chain from the ceiling. The room was unfurnished, except for a single wall table next to the entryway. The stranger's gaze shifted from one Fifteenth Century tapestry to another, each depicting different hunting scenes. Suits of armor stared blankly back from their sentry posts on either side of all the room's doorways. Another pair, with crossed lances, stood guard at the top of the stairs. Ancient weapons hung over a huge fireplace that occupied the far wall.

As the maiden pulled the door to, the stranger, being familiar with the castle, ascended the stone staircase to a study that overlooked the reception area. The room's high wooden ceiling was cris-crossed with large heavy beams. An oversized mahogany desk dominated one end of the room. Keeping the winters chill at bay was a large blazing fire made up in an equally large marble fireplace installed along the opposite wall. Large, cathedral-type windows gazed out upon the courtyard and offered unobstructed views of the surrounding countryside. The final wall was taken up with bookshelves from floor to ceiling. *"This place always unsettles me."* He thought.

An eccentric millionaire had purchased the Manor house from an estate in northern England some years past.

Disassembling and relocating the house had been a monumental chore. Brick by brick the numbered stones had been carefully crated and transported by ship to their present location. The house was then painstakingly reconstructed over a natural hot spring that bubbled up in the center of the lowland.

The dungeon had been renovated into a private gymnasium. This gym was equipped with swimming pool, sauna, indoor track and various exercise devices. This was the private domain of Heidiki Sawada.

The wealthy industrialist was enjoying his morning ritual. He had just finished an hour and a half workout; stretching, weight lifting, a five-mile run and two dozen laps in the pool. This was all followed by a good soak in the 110-degree water of the hot spring. The head of Nipton Foods, one of the world's largest distribution empires, never varied his routine 365 days a year. Whether he was home in his beloved castle or in Kobe at the command of one of his gigantic food operations, Sawada never failed to start his day with an invigorating workout.

Glancing at a floor length mirror Sawada was pleased with the reflection. His sixty-five-year-old frame was in excellent shape. He was as strong as an ox, and could still run a marathon in record time. A strict regimen of exercise, diet and mental discipline gave Sawada a physique that was years younger. A little dye to his temples once a month and most strangers thought he was but forty-five.

Yoshi, an unpretentious elderly footman, entered the room after lightly rapping. The manservant, who had been with the family for years, bowed to Mr. Sawada. "Sir. Your guest is in the study."

"Good."

"Your coat." Yoshi handed Sawada a light brown silk smoking jacket. He then bowed and exited the room without further comment. Sawada checked his reflection once again, smiled to himself and proceeded towards the study.

Upon entering the room, Sawada observed his guest gazing out one of the windows towards the distant mountains. He addressed his visitor in perfect Chinese, "Ah, Minister Chan, a most magnificent view." Sawada bowed and inquired, "I hope your trip was most satisfactory?"

"Winter weather, snow, wet and cold, how I hate this time of year." Chan remarked, as he returned the bow and then turned his attention back towards the window.

"This won't take long, you can be out of here in an hour and back in Hong Kong by six. However, I was hoping you would dine with me tonight. I have your favorite room ready." The soft-spoken Sawada said.

"A most gracious offer, but I have pressing matters at home. My absence would be noticed. Are we still on track?"

"Everything is fine. I suspect time is the least of our worries."

Chan turned and approached the desk. Setting his briefcase down, he opened it, and turned it towards Sawada. Nestled in a Styrofoam-protected cup was a vial of clear liquid. The only other item in the leather case was an official looking document. "Your man did a wonderful job with my problem."

"Ah, shi! He is most efficient. I was hoping that was your reason for being here. Now we can begin the next phase." Sawada said as he reached for the briefcase and nodded in approval while examining its contents. "Everything is as planned. Is there anything else we need to take care of before we proceed? Would you care to inspect our preparations?"

"No, no." Chan replied. "My business is with the Spratleys."

"It's a shame, we have come so far..."

"I hope you are right."

Opening a drawer in the desk Sawada extracted a large yellow envelope and set it on the desktop. He then set the contents of the briefcase onto his desk. "A little something for your endeavors, Minister."

"Is it all there?"

"250,000 as requested." Said the Japanese businessmen as he removed the vial from its protective casing and held it up to the light for a closer examination.

"You could have had the bank transfer the cash."

"Ah, but Minister, you know I'm old-fashioned and besides, computer transfers can be traced. Sometimes, the new ways are not necessarily the best way. How did you convince the General Secretary to sign the agreement?"

"I just slipped the document in with others to be signed; the old fool is so feeble he doesn't read them anymore."

"Would you be interested in inspecting our laboratories and workshops before you leave? Our preparations are really quite fascinating." Sawada offered with a wave of his hand.

"I'm not interested in your pet projects! I have other concerns. I trust you will produce the Spratleys and keep the Americans busy as promised."

"Of course."

"And the other item, is it still set for delivery in December?"

"I have my man working on the final details as we speak. Delivery will be in Hong Kong, as agreed."

"Things are almost set in China. Now, I must go." With that, Chan deposited the envelope containing the cash back into the briefcase and snapped it closed. As he turned and walked towards the door, he reminded Sawada, "You now have your exclusive rights; I need that treaty! And, one more thing, my Washington source has informed me the Americans are looking into the matter." With that Minister Chan bowed and walked out the door.

Sawada did not pursue Chan. Instead, he put the test tube back and then inspected the document for the necessary signatures and seal's. He was impressed; Chan had actually pulled it off. Nothing could stop him now. All he had to do was locate a long lost treaty. He already believed he had a pretty good idea where it was located.

After studying the document, Sawada secured it in a wall safe concealed behind an old painting of a Japanese warlord. Thinking about his distaste for the Minister, Sawada thought, *"I would love to sacrifice him to my sword. Maybe someday I'll get the opportunity."* A thin tight smile crept across his otherwise inscrutable face.

Sitting down to his desk, vial in hand, Sawada picked up the phone and spoke in English. “Could you come to the study? We must now begin our final preparations.”

An hour later Sawada entered one of the ‘clean rooms’ he maintained in the basement. A portly, balding Englishman in a white lab coat, who was busy preparing a solution, greeted him.

“Nigel I’ve something for you.” He teased.

Turning to face his benefactor Nigel looked up over his spectacles and questioned. “Really? You have the vector?”

“Yes, it was delivered an hour ago.” Said the Japanese magnate holding up the glass vial for Nigel to see.

Nigel Smyth, formally a microbiologist at Cambridge, had been seduced by Sawada’s promise of instant wealth. He had overseen renovations of the wine cellar into rooms where experiments could be conducted. The labs were constructed to fit his exacting specifications. Now, in the room where he was currently working, several clear five-gallon jugs were filled almost to capacity with oil and one was filled with a milky solution. Taking the vial provided by Sawada, Smyth held it up to the light and inspected it. Opening the stopper, he carefully poured its contents equally among the jugs.

“And now we wait,” Smyth sighed.

“That is all?”

“Yes, within the hour the vectors will attach themselves to the bacteria within the oil. The resident bacteria will then be injected with the vector’s DNA signature. Following an incubation period, the infected bacteria will start producing an enzyme that will degrade appetite...”

“Appetite?” Sawada interrupted.

“Yes, appetite. Appetite is a highly insoluble form of phosphate. Once the phosphate is released, other bacteria...”

Holding up his hand, Sawada indicated for Smyth to desist with his explanation. “Will it do what I want?”

“Most definitely,” answered Smyth.

Sawada wasn’t interested in how it worked; all he wanted was results. Turning abruptly, he left Smyth to continue with his own designs. Now that the agreement and vector were on hand, there were arrangements to attend to.

Six

December 4th 2003
The Pentagon

Lieutenant Jake Philips was wearing out the carpet in the Pentagon waiting room of Rear Admiral Charles Stinson. A dark headed male yeoman sitting behind a plain metal desk, watched in silent amusement as Philips paced to and fro muttering to himself. The young pimple faced sailor loved to see the panic-stricken expressions on officer's faces when they had to report before the Admiral.

His hurried flight from Italy had been hectic. A quick change of planes at Ramstien, where the Lieutenant was allowed enough time to shower, shave and acquire a fresh uniform. Next, a top priority flight directly to Andrews Air Force Base where a naval staff car was waiting to whisk him away.

"*What's with the cloak and dagger stuff?*" he wondered.

"Lieutenant, get in here!" the admiral bellowed, after making the Lieutenant wait fifteen minutes.

Phillips entered the Admiral's office as composed as possible, considering the circumstances, still pondering his fate.

He observed the admiral was not alone. The Lieutenant front and centered himself to Admiral Stinson and smartly saluted the gold braided officer. "Lieutenant Jake Phillips reporting as ordered, Sir."

"At ease," the Admiral quipped, returning the gesture.

Philips took all of ten seconds to reconnoiter the office. The admiral was sitting at what had to be the biggest oak desk that Jake had ever seen. He was a short, squat man, with a head of thinning gray hair. His face had the look and texture of weather-beaten leather, showing many years at sea. The gold on his uniform and a chest full of medals confirmed he didn't get to be an Admiral by sailing a desk.

Behind him, a large window with blinds looked out over the frozen Potomac River. To the admiral's left stood a beautiful, chocolate brown, tuck and roll leather couch, which was occupied by a pair of individuals. An oversized painting of a World War I 'Four-Piper' destroyer hung on the wall behind them. Opposite the couch was a matching chair. Behind the chair was a glass-encased model of the battleship *Missouri*.

"Sit down young man," the admiral said, though it sounded more like an order.

"Aye Sir." Philips sat in the only place available.

"I bet you're wondering what all the hush-hush is about?"

"Aye Sir! I have been pondering that point exactly."

"It was nothing you did, I assure you," Stinson responded. "However, I do have a couple of people here that would like to have a word with you. Under Secretary of the Navy Darnel Parsons..." The shorter of the two persons nodded. Jake gulped.

"...And National Security Adviser Jack Kelly." The heavier individual nodded.

Philips started to sweat, just a little.

"Jake, I can call you Jake can't I?" Admiral Stinson asked conversationally.

Not knowing what else to say Philips used the old "Aye, sir!" meekly.

"Good. I've had a chance to look over your record, and

for an officer of your age, I would have to say you have done quite well for yourself. After enlisting, you applied to and were granted permission to attend OCS and graduated second in a class of 92. Seventeen missions, no losses, Navy Cross for not leaving a wounded crewman behind while under fire in Afghanistan..."

"Everyone comes home, Sir," the Lieutenant interrupted.

"...Yes, son, I know the SEAL motto..."

For a moment the young Philips was back in Kabul, with gunfire all around him, as he dragged a wounded team member to safety.

"...It's just how you did it; holding off a superior force of Taliban guards until extraction could be covered with a gunship. I hear you even have your own team. Impressive, very impressive! I think that you're just the person we're looking for..."

While the admiral was going on, Philips came back to the present and took a second to size up the National Security Adviser and Under Secretary. Jack Kelly was a big man; he looked to weigh in around two hundred and fifty pounds. Despite his size, his powder blue suit was as neat as a pin. Nothing was out of place, his red hair was neatly combed, shoes highly polished, tie perfect. On the other hand, Darnel Parsons looked as if he had been up for days. There were bags under his eyes and his face had an ashen look. His brown suit looked as if he slept in it the previous night. His thinning gray hair was awry and there looked to be a small spot on his pale green shirt. "*What a pair of opposites!*" he thought.

"May I interject here?" Parsons impatiently asked.

"Sorry, I kinda lost myself in Jake's file," the admiral admitted, clearing his throat.

"Lieutenant Philips do you know anything about Mischief Reef?" Parsons asked.

"Mischief Reef sir?"

Kelly shifted his weight and spoke up. "It's a worthless piece of shoal in the South China Sea, part of a group of islands collectively known as the Spratleys, to which the Philippines have a legitimate claim."

"No Sir, I can't say that I have ever heard of them."

"Well, it seems that China may have some designs on them of late," Kelly resumed, "And we would like to have someone take a closer look into the matter."

"I still don't see what that has to do with..." Philips responded.

"I'm coming to that..."

"Coffee anyone?" Stinson interrupted, as he punched a button on his phone.

"Grand idea," Kelly spoke up first. "And could you manage some sandwiches or something? Now, where were we..."

"We think the Chinese are making a new push at taking Taiwan," Parsons added. "With a Military presence on the Spratleys, the South China Sea would be like China's private lake. The island of Taiwan would have the Communists well situated for an assault without having to worry about foreign intervention from the West."

"...However we have an agreement with the Philippines. It's called the Visiting Forces Agreement or VFA II. It's a mutual defense agreement. The Filipino's have asked us for joint exercises within the area. A sort of saber rattling affair. Something to help contain the situation..." Kelly hesitated.

"Is this bad?" Philips asked in the conversation's lull.

"No, not really," replied Kelly

"So that is why a carrier battle group has been ordered to the area," the admiral interrupted.

"Yes, yes," the adviser admitted. "I'm sure you remember the EP-3 Aries fiasco a couple of years back?"

"Yes Sir, we were put on notice of a possible rescue mission but negotiations released the crew," the Lieutenant answered.

"This time we want a lower profile operation." Parsons was quick to add. "Something sort of behind-the-scenes, not so public."

"And I'm to be your low profile!" Philips reasoned. "*This outta be interesting,*" he postulated. "*At least it wasn't my ass they were after."*

"Depends," Kelly replied. "We could have real problems over there. It goes something like this. In 1992 the U.S. was asked by the Aquino Government to leave the Philippines..."

"...And they really don't want us back," Parsons finished, then added. "They were less than enthusiastic when we went after the al-Qaeda cells in the jungles of Basilan. So we decided to do something a little less obvious."

His dialog was interrupted by a knock on the door. "What is it?" the admiral bellowed.

"Coffee sir," said a voice from out in the hall.

"Great! Couldn't have come at a better time," Kelly declared.

The same yeoman from the waiting room entered the office and without hesitation pushed a serving cart into the space. Centered on the cart was a silver coffee service, accompanied by two trays heaping with sandwiches. Stopping short of the coffee table the yeoman stood at attention.

"I can manage," the admiral offered, "you're dismissed."

"Aye Sir," the yeoman saluted and left the office. True to his word, Admiral Stinson poured coffee and passed around trays of sandwiches.

With a sandwich in one hand and a cup of coffee in the other, Kelly complimented "Now this is what I call service." Taking a mammoth bite he continued, "Where was I? Oh yes, since 1992 our relationship with the Philippines has been tenuous to say the least. With a lot of negotiating we have come up with the Visiting Forces Agreement. It's a treaty which allows yearly maneuvers with the Philippine Navy, within Philippine territorial..."

"...If you don't mind me interrupting," Philips began again. "What makes you think the Chinese are interested in these Spratleys?"

It was Parsons' turn to shift into gear. "We have satellite photos that clearly show the Chinese building some sort of military compound, barracks, command structures and possibly an airstrip. A pier has been constructed, which is large enough to accommodate warships or whatever."

"But, Sir, that doesn't mean that China has taken over the islands," Philips reasoned.

"Yes true. The Chinese claim that the structures are just a safe haven for wayward fishermen and the pier to accommodate their vessels. The real question is why have naval ships been spotted patrolling the area, and why do the Chinese keep running the Filipinos off?" Kelly finished between bites of ham and cheese.

"So you're sending in a carrier group six months early for maneuvers," Philips replied.

"Yes, and we would just love to warm up relations with the Filipinos again, perhaps, even reopen Subic." Parsons pointed out. "However, this is a very delicate matter, the Filipinos have a lot of national pride right now and it wouldn't take much to upset the apple cart."

"Right now the Filipinos are really gun-shy about outside intervention," Kelly reiterated.

"Still, I don't see what this has to do with me," the Lieutenant remarked.

Clearing his throat, Parsons spoke up, "We believe that the Chinese have something or can get something to make the Filipinos not want us back."

"And that would be disastrous for everyone involved," Kelly added.

"We have come by some information that indicates the Chinese are doing just that." Parsons continued, "this information is so sensitive that only a few people even know of it. The White House wants someone outside normal channels to look into it."

"So why is it, then, the White House wants Lieutenant Philips? Couldn't they have gone to the CIA or something?" the admiral queried, not comprehending what the young Lieutenant's assignment was.

Clearing his throat again, Parsons looked nervously towards the National Security Adviser, then spoke up. "It would seem that Lieutenant Philips has a certain connection which could prove to be most valuable; and, like I said, he is most certainly outside normal channels."

Standing and stretching Kelly walked over to the Missouri model and studied it for a moment. "Son, the United States in its past has done a few things that are not very honorable. One of those things occurred during the opening days of World War II. Something happened, that if brought to light even today could turn the Filipinos against us."

The Lieutenant looked puzzledly at the National Security Adviser. "I'm not sure I follow you, it's not like the Philippines is a world power."

"Let's put it like this," Under Secretary Parsons said. "If a certain piece of information was to be leaked to the Filipinos, they might ask the United States government to leave the area. This could adversely affect the security of Taiwan. If Taiwan falls to the Chinese, I don't have to tell you what kind of ripple effect this would have on the American economy, not to mention the free world. We're just getting back on our feet again after the World Trade fiasco, and don't need another kick in the shins."

"We believe this information is either presently or about to be in the possession of someone who intends to do just that, for reasons unknown to us at this time." added Kelly.

"And you believe that I have some knowledge of this, this something, whatever it is?" Philips gulped, not believing his ears.

"Ah, but you do, my boy," Kelly said, handing him a file folder. "You just don't know it."

"Could you give me some idea?"

Avoiding the question, Parsons stood and walked towards the door. "Well, gentlemen, looks like that about wraps things up. Lieutenant read this file; if you have any questions call the number attached. It's time to brief the President… Jack."

Lieutenant Philips stood to attention as the unlikely pair headed towards the door. "May I ask one more question?"

"Go ahead," Parsons turned and responded.

"Am I in this alone?"

"No, I think it best you choose a couple of your shipmates to assist in the investigation," Kelly offered. "Anyone in mind?"

"Aye, Sir. I would like petty officers McKay and Wardon

to assist me."

"Done. Lieutenant Philips you have your orders. You work for me now, however any inquiries you may have direct them through Parsons here. Don't hesitate to call if you need anything, that number goes directly to the Under Secretary's office. Admiral, Lieutenant, good day gentlemen," Kelly said as he walked through the door.

Lieutenant Philips looked to the admiral for some sort of answer. The admiral looked just as puzzled and offered none.

"Lieutenant, I'll have the yeoman get you a vacant office so you can get down to work. Looks like you've been grounded for awhile."

"Aye, Sir. Begging the admirals pardon, but would it be okay if I took some time to make some personal calls about my gear?" Philips responded.

Stinson thought this over for a moment then replied. "I don't see why not. Report back here by 1500."

Philips saluted his superior and exited the office.

After the Lieutenant was gone, Admiral Stinson punched a button on his intercom. "Yeoman, get me SEAL Command!"

At 3 P.M. Philips settled down in the office provided by the Yeoman. The spartan workspace contained a metal desk with two folding chairs and a couple of pictures on the walls. Philips held the faded brown bellows file folder that had been given to him by the Adviser. Closing the door and getting as comfortable as the chair would allow, he got down to business.

First he examined the outside of the file, nothing special, just some old red lettering: **CONFIDENTIAL**. He broke the seal and dumped the folder's contents onto the table. Sorting through the pile, Philips set the photographs aside. He then picked up the first document and started to inspect it. It looked to be some kind of debriefing towards the end of World War II. On the top of the first page in bold letters was:

THE JANSON REPORT

William A. Janson Lieutenant General, U.S. Army
former Commanding Officer 14th Philippine Scouts

The report outlined the preparedness and status of the Philippine Scouts units prior to, and during, the 1941 Japanese invasion. Some pretty boring reading. The report took up about three-quarters of the documents within the file. Philips could not see how they had any bearing on the present situation.

Inspecting the faded photographs Philips looked for anything interesting. All the photos appeared to have been taken on Corregidor Island, the guardian of Manila Bay in the Philippines. The first photo was a group of soldiers stationed at Fort Mills, posing beside one of the huge ten-inch disappearing rifles. Another was a panoramic view of the mile long topside barracks. Four or five more photos, all taken on Corregidor with different personnel and different locations, nothing interesting. Upon inspecting the second to the last photo Philips did a double take.

The photo showed five men standing behind a pile of crates. One man, obviously a Filipino, was dressed in a dark suit with top hat. The other four were American army officers. Turning the picture over the caption confirmed what Philips saw in the picture. It read, *'Left to right President Quezon, MacArthur, Wainwright, Janson, and Philips inspect first shipment of Mills Transfer Feb. 5th 1942.'*

Shuffling back through the papers, Philips looked for any reference to the Mills transfer. Under a sub caption titled *'Conduct of the Campaign,'* about fifteen pages from the bottom, he hit paydirt! An entry on the 2nd of January 1942 outlined how Janson and his aide Captain Philips were ordered to witness a treaty signing between President Manuel Quezon of the Philippines and General Douglas MacArthur for the United States. Another notation on the 6th of January was about $5 million in gold bullion being put aboard a submarine for safe transport to Australia. Further examination of the documents could shed no more information or explanation of the transfer.

"So what's this Mills Transfer?" he thought. Taking the

picture and stuffing it inside his breast pocket, Philips returned all the documents and photographs back into the file folder. After five hours of careful studying he was no closer to understanding the situation. What the Lieutenant really wanted to know was how the Mills Transfer was tied to the Spratley problem. He did, however, know someone who might be able to shed some light on the whole affair, General Murdoch J. Philips, U.S. Army (Ret). Lieutenant Philips didn't like it but, after a fifteen-year absence, he was finally going home.

Seven

December 5th 2003
Seattle, Washington

With an overcast sky and light rain falling, dusk was settling quickly over the Emerald City. The skyscrapers and Space Needle appeared to be supporting the grayish mantle of clouds, which hung low over the city. The flight from Washington D.C. had been long and boring so the Lieutenant used the time to catch up on some must-needed rest. He awoke just as the plane touched down.

The cab ride from the airport was arduous. As traffic crawled along the interstate; Philips had a chance to go over what he knew. It still made no sense. *"The Mills Transfer, could it have been more than what the file suggested? Was his grandfather part of some sinister plan all those years ago?"* He mulled over these ideas carefully. *"But why me? And where do I go from here?"*

As Jake Philips stood at the base of Capitol Hill looking over a dock area on Lake Union's east shore, he pulled up the collar of his old Navy peacoat to give himself some protection against a brisk northerly wind. He could see a dozen or so boathouses tied up to the dock, facing each other. Some houses were newer than others, but most were in need of a fresh coat of paint. Every conceivable type of architecture was present, from ultra modern to traditional. The single thing they had in common was the fact they floated gently on the lake just north of Seattle's financial district. It was the houseboat second to the end on the left that concerned Phillips most. This was the very place he had grown up.

Walking slowly down the dock as if to prolong the inevitable, Philips finally made up his mind. It wasn't that he was afraid to go home, it was the memories. Walking slowly, he eventually stopped in front of an unkempt, gray two-story contemporary structure. Jake started to wonder if this was such a good idea. Even with cracked paint and a thick layer of green moss growing upon the roof, there was no mistaking home. Suppressed images came flooding back, sailing, swimming; even the floatplanes coming and going were fond memories. It was the dark memories, the sad ones that had kept him away all these years.

It had been a day much like this when he had enlisted into the Navy. The arguing, his father yelling, Philips storming out of the hotel room vowing never to see his parents again. The plane crash, all the pain. It seemed like only yesterday. As the memories came flooding back, Philips fought back the urge to turn and walk away. Snapping back to the present, he mustered up enough courage to go inside.

Built onto the front of the structure was a small porch with flower boxes at each end. The spare house key was always kept under the flower box next to the door. Checking carefully, Philips discovered the key was no longer under the weed-choked box. Wiping away years of grime from the door's window, the Lieutenant put his nose to the glass and peered inside. With the approaching twilight everything was dark, he could only make out a few details. Natural instinct made him try the doorknob. To his surprise there was a soft click and the door slowly opened.

Stepping inside, Philips tried the light switch and was

surprised for the second time when the living room was illuminated in soft light. Glancing about, Jake stepped back in time fifteen years. The living room to his right was just the way he remembered, modestly furnished with couch, recliner and TV. At the far end of the room in front of the bay window stood an artificial Christmas tree decorated with all the trappings. Standing boldly in the center of the room with a large bow and ribbon, was a red and white Honda XR400R off-road motocross bike, complete with dealer tags and owner's manual sitting on the saddle. Philips slowly proceeded to the bike and read the small card attached 'To: Jake, with love, Dad'. Tears started to well up in his eyes. Glancing at all the still wrapped presents under the tree he again asked himself. *"Damn-it Dad, Why me?"*

He turned and walked from the room, following the hall down past the dining room into the kitchen. Again the room was just as Philips remembered, painted in pale blue with a black and white checkerboard floor. The small window above the sink was yellow with grime. He walked directly to a mahogany liquor cabinet and was surprised to find it stocked. Philips found a glass and poured himself a generous portion of rum. "Here's to you Mom and Dad, I've finally come home!" he said to the room, then drank it down.

Taking the bottle with him, Jake retraced his steps back to the living room where he sat down in the recliner. Taking another drink, this time directly from the bottle, he savored the comforting fire as it worked its way downward. Half an hour later the sailor was passed out in a drunken stupor. Later, in the middle of the night, two figures entered the residence and silently took in the situation. Without saying a word they helped the drunken SEAL to his feet and carried him upstairs where they put him to bed.

Philips slowly regained consciousness. He'd been having the same dream that he had had countless times over the years. He's on an airplane with his Mom and Dad. Suddenly there's an explosion, lots of noise and a rush of air. The aircraft starts dropping, with people screaming and debris flying all around.

Panic is all around him. The Lieutenant looks over to his Mom and Dad and they seem strangely calm considering the situation. He starts to say something, but his mother interrupts him by putting three fingers to his lips.

"It's okay Jake, everything is fine." She softly says.
"But mom, if only I had not argued."
"It had to be this way, it's the only way."
"Mom, I wasn't ready, you were right..."
"I have to go now..." The scene slowly fades out.

As Philips regained his senses, the first thing he became aware of was a pounding headache. "Way too much rum!" he muttered. Then a strong aroma of bacon cooking assailed his nostrils. There was the friendly bang of pans coming from the kitchen with the familiar sounds of someone preparing breakfast. Jumping to his feet, Philips barely registered the fact he'd been sleeping in his old bedroom. Then the realization struck, he was not alone in the house! How had he gotten into his room? His last recollection had been sitting in the recliner drinking.

Now he could hear voices and laughter emanating from the kitchen, it sounded as if there were two of them. Philips proceeded cautiously down the stairs, making sure he had the element of surprise. *"Come on, am I a SEAL or what?"* He thought as he tried to psyche himself up. Being outnumbered and without a weapon, Jake reconsidered. Just as quietly, the SEAL retraced his steps back to his room where he grabbed his old Louisville slugger. Stealthily, with the bat ready, Philips made his way to the hall where he could peer carefully into the kitchen. "What the! -- Mike, Clifford, what you are guys doing here?" he asked excitedly when he spotted his shipmates in the kitchen.

Surprised, the two whirled about at the same time, bumping into each other and knocking a pan of bacon to the floor.

"Yo, Moe! Lookie what we have here!" Wardon exclaimed in his heavy New York accent.

"So that's what the cat drug in!" McKay remarked.

Stooping, he picked up the frying pan and started to clean up the mess. “We thought you’d be out till later in the day.”

“How… how did you guys get here? How did you get in? What are you doing here?” Philips rapid fired his questions.

“In time Jake, in time! Is it okay for Moe here to finish with breakfast? I’m starving!” Wardon remarked as he sat down at the kitchenette. “Nice place by the way, never been on a houseboat before...”

“You left the door open.” McKay interrupted. Turning to his shipmate “...and would you stop calling me Moe!”

“Aw, c’mon Moe, you know it don’t mean nothin.” Wardon defended himself.

“I’m just tired of you calling me Moe, the name’s Mike.” Setting the pan back on the stove, McKay started a new batch of bacon. “And where’s the Jackson you owe on your share of the food?”

“Jackson? What Jackson?”

“You said... Aw skip-it, I should have known better.” Said McKay as he went back to his cooking.

A thin tight smile spread across Philips face; he was more than relieved to see his friends. “Excuse me, but what’s going on here?” he asked the room.

“Sit down man, you make me nervous standing there with your bat like that.” McKay ordered, “It goes something like this, Admiral Stinson put in a call to SEAL headquarters. He requested a couple of team members to work with you...”

“And I got you guys?” Philips interrupted. “Incredible.”

“Go figure, having the two of us to work for you.” remarked Wardon. “Does this mean we still have to call you Sir?”

Ignoring the remark, the Lieutenant crossed the kitchen to the window. He leaned the bat against the wall and watched as a floatplane taxied to the middle of the lake. Turning and looking at his two shipmates Philips said, “I don’t know what’s going on, it looks to me like a bit of research. Why do I need you guys?”

“The Admiral thought maybe you could use some assistance.” McKay spoke over his shoulder as he turned the bacon over. “And according to Stinson, you put in a request.”

“I did, but then I discovered it was just a research project on the Philippine islands.”

“Maybe the Admiral knows something you don’t,” Wardon added, “he insisted we get out here.”

Changing the subject, Philips rubbed his hands together and asked, “Well, when do we eat? The rest of this can wait till later.”

“Ready when you are,” McKay exclaimed as he set two heaping platters of food on the table. “Dig in or I’ll be forced to eat all this myself.” Turning to his friend he added, “Jake, you have some explaining to do. Whose place is this? What’s with the Christmas presents, you expecting relatives?”

Philips filled his plate with scrambled eggs, bacon and toast. Taking a bite, he paused savoring the food, then remarked, “Not bad,” between bites. “I didn’t know you could cook.” Taking another bite, he complemented McKay, “Mmmm even this grub is better than what they serve up in the galley.” Hesitating as if to collect his thoughts, he continued. “I guess I’ll start at the top; this is the house where I grew up. Mom and Dad got the houseboat as a wedding present from Mom’s Dad.” His voice began to tremble. “The lake was my back...”

Wardon started to say something but McKay touched his arm and motioned for him to keep quiet. “Go on,” he urged.

“My backyard…” Philips went on. “I had a lot of happy times in this place. I learned to swim just out that kitchen door. My father’s office was right across the lake. During the summer he used to kayak to work..” He paused.

“And...” McKay encouraged.

“You must forgive me if I get a little mushy on you guys,” cautioned Philips. Taking a deep breath, he began again. “It was the fall of 1988, I had gotten out of high school the previous spring. Mom thought...” A tear developed in his right eye. “Mom thought it would be fun to spend the summer in Europe.”

McKay could see his friend was laboring to tell the story. “Take all the time you need, we’ve got all day.”

"It was late November and we had just finished a six-month tour of the continent. Dad wanted to check on some business associates in Britain so we were staying in London. It had been raining all week and I had become bored with the lack of activities, so one day I went down to the U.S. Embassy and decided to join the Navy."

"And?" Inquired Wardon.

"I can remember it so clearly, that night I met my Mom and Dad for dinner at the hotel's restaurant. Dad really exploded when I told them I was going into the Navy. He insisted I join the Army like my grandfather and great grandfather. Said he would fix it, I told him no! I was going to do this, I wanted to be in the Navy. It was a natural choice, I'd always been around water. Dad told me to get out and never come back. Mom just sat there, never saying a thing..." Philips painfully went on, "...so I stormed out and bought a ticket for the States. I did not come home though, I went straight to the Naval Induction Center at Great Lakes."

"Then what?" queried McKay.

"Mom and Dad followed a few days later..." he hesitated, then continued barely choking out, "...on Pan Am flight 103." A few more tears moved down his cheek.

"So what about flight 103?" Wardon asked.

"Isn't that the flight that was bombed by Libyan terrorists at Christmas time?" asked McKay, beginning to understand.

"Shit!" muttered Wardon.

"Yes, Dec. 21st 1988," Philips choked.

After a few moments of silence, the Lieutenant was able to recover his composure, and went on. "That is why I went to BUDS training, to pay back every mother..." Choking back another tear. "I would extract a huge payment for what they did to me. So, for fifteen years I've had a personal vendetta against terrorists, and I've never had the nerve to return home, until yesterday." He added, "The house is exactly the way Mom must have left it. We used to have a maid; she must have set up the tree and added the presents. I don't know who has kept the house up or why. I plan to find out."

"Whew, that's some story," McKay sighed.

"So that's why you've never taken leave or had a girlfriend," Wardon observed.

Getting up and taking his now empty plate to the sink, Philips stared out the window again. "I've never had time. Every spare moment I had was used at perfecting my skills. Extra time in the gym, going over reconnaissance photos, rereading mission reports and such." Philips perked up, "Enough of this for now, I've got work to do; if you want to tag along it's fine by me."

Following dishes and cleaning up, the trio caught a cab to the nearest library, while Philips briefed his comrades on the meeting in the Admiral's office.

Perched atop Queen Ann Hill was the main branch for the King County library system. The library had one of the most beautiful panoramas Philips could recall. From Queen Ann's vantage point, just north of downtown, the 1000-foot high hill overlooked the entire city and Space Needle. The view was as if one were on an airplane. With the city below them and the blue expanse of Elliot Bay to their right, the guys were enthralled by the ferries and cargo ships coming and going along the busy waterfront. Dominating the entire scene was the 14,000-ft. glacier-covered Mount Rainier.

The library itself was an imposing building. Built during the 1930s, the once majestic white sandstone building wore a heavy mantel of gray muck. Large concrete eagles stood as silent sentinels on either side of the main entrance. The entryway was an old-fashioned large copper rotating door. Inside was a cavernous room filled with rows upon rows of books. In the very center of the room was a square counter with a large sign suspended from the ceiling that read: 'Information'.

As the trio approached the desk, McKay turned to Wardon and commented with a grin, "I bet this is the first time you've ever seen so many books at one time? In one place?"

"Now see here Moe, just cuz I's from da Bronx don't mean we don't have books." He poked fun back at his friend. "Why, I read one just last week. '*Fun with Dick and Jane*' I think's it was called." Wardon said mimicking an intercity youth.

All Philips could do was smile and shake his head. *"It is sure good to be together on this,"* he thought fondly as his friends continued to poke fun back and forth.

"See dat-," Wardon went on nodding towards the mammoth desk covered in white linoleum, "dat's wo we gets info-may-shun." He went on, exaggerating the accent.

McKay lightly pushed his hysterically laughing friend aside as he countered, "So, that's why they have an i-n-f-o-r-m-a-t-i-o-n sign," putting special emphasis on spelling out information to Wardon.

Behind the counter sat a typical librarian. She was an elderly matron with glasses attached to a chain that hung down to the middle of her brown sweater. Looking at her nametag Philips spoke first, "Excuse me Ms. Jane." He eyed the still cackling Wardon with amusement. "Could you direct us to the computers, we would like to do some on-line research."

"You must sign up first," Jane offered up a clipboard, "One-hour intervals. The machines are over in the corner," she continued matter-of-factly, not understanding what was so amusing.

Locating the computers, Philips and company sat down and began to browse the Web. "Look for anything to do with the Spratley islands or Mischief Reef, Chinese occupation, rebuilding of structures, and what have you."

"Okay, and what will you to be doing?" McKay asked.

"I'm going to work the Corregidor and the Mills Transfer angle." Philips answered.

After an hour of quiet surfing the three men found an unused discussion room where they could compare notes.

"So what did we find out?" the Lieutenant asked.

"Well, for starters, I got the same rehash about the Spratleys," Wardon offered first. "Seems the Chinese, Vietnamese, Taiwanese and Filipinos all have claims to the islands. The United Nations recognizes the Philippine claim, however. The islands seems to have mineral deposits and oil. More importantly, they have never been fished, so the reefs are just teeming with life. I would think the oil issue would be foremost but the articles all point towards the fishing issue."

"Well?" asked Philips, taking notes and looking to McKay.

"About the same as Cliff. It seems the fishing issue is in the forefront. The Philippine Navy has blockaded the area to Chinese fishing vessels for the past twenty years. They've even gone so far as to arrest trespassers. In an vain attempt to diffuse tensions, there's been discussions between the Philippine Department of Foreign Affairs and the Chinese Ministry of Fisheries. The talks, however, have broken down; and China has sent in several warships to serve as escorts for the fishing vessels. It also looks like the United States has responded by sending in a carrier group." McKay went on, "What'd you get?"

"It's really strange, the only thing I found was the same two references I discovered at the Pentagon. Something about the Mill's Transfer, but no information. What I've figured out so far is that the United States government took possession of sixty million dollars of both Philippine and American assets. This was in gold bullion, silver bars, coins and currency. The idea was to keep it from getting into the hands of the Japanese. Some of the money was actually transferred aboard submarines and sent to Australia for safekeeping. Most of the gold however was abandoned on the island of Corregidor, and the currency was supposedly burned..."

"Burn cash, now that's a crying shame," Wardon chimed in.

"It was done to keep the money from the Japanese," informed Philips. "There's no mention as to the treaty or agreement, it's like it never existed."

"What say we get some chow?" suggested Wardon changing the subject. "We can compare notes over lunch, can't we?"

"I was thinking the same thing," McKay added.

"Right," Philips agreed, "Then we'll go back to my place and decide where to proceed next."

After lunch, as the trio walked back to the houseboat, Wardon asked, "Did you leave the front door open?"

"No, I don't think so. Why?" Philips responded.

"Well I s'pose they must be trespassers, 'cause they don't look like the cleaning service." Wardon nodded towards a pair of black clad men exiting the front door.

Eight

The two interlopers exiting the houseboat hesitated a moment. Sizing up the situation, the pair broke up; the shorter one heading straight for the approaching trio while the taller, red-haired one bolted with the agility of the cat for a speed boat tied to the end of the dock.

Reacting instinctively, McKay dashed after the red-haired intruder.

"Hey! Stop him!" Philips shouted, as the second goon pushed by, knocking the Lieutenant off balance and sending him into the lake. By the time he had surfaced, the intruder was halfway down the dock with Mike in hot pursuit.

The first interloper jumped off the end of the dock into the waiting speedboat. Shouting to the boat's driver, he turned and stared at the approaching SEAL. The driver responded by pushing the throttles all the way to the stops. The green and white Chris Craft jumped ahead in the water and was a hundred yards away by the time McKay had reached the end of the dock. The craft dashed off across the lake and disappeared into one of the numerous Marinas. McKay went back and helped the Lieutenant from the water.

"You okay?"

"Yeah, the w-water sure is c-cold though," responded a shivering Philips. "Wh-what happened to Clifford?"

"Dunno, I went after the red haired guy." Looking about, the pair could not see their companion.

The second intruder had blown by Wardon in an effort to escape. With not so cat-like reactions, Wardon grabbed for him but slipped and fell on the wet dock. Jumping to his feet, the athletic black man discovered the guy was fast, but he was faster. He caught up to the fleet-footed intruder at the end of the first block past the dock, and made a flying tackle. Wrapping his great arms around the guy's legs, the two of them fell into a heap on the sidewalk, with Wardon scraping his knee on the cement.

Kicking and swearing, the short wiry man was not about to be taken. It was all Wardon could do just to hang on. Raining blows upon the black man's head and face, the intruder finally delivered an axlike blow against the big man's temple, stunning him momentarily. The little guy wiggled free and sprang to his feet. He was off in a flash, this time brandishing a pistol. The gunman stopped once and fired into the air, keeping Wardon at bay. Then he turned and disappeared around the corner. By this time McKay and Philips had caught up to Wardon and helped him to his feet.

"You okay?" McKay asked looking at Wardon's skinned up knee.

"Yeah, nothing that a few Band-Aids won't fix."

"Why'd you let him go?" asked a chuckling Philips.

"Let him go? the guy was slippery as an eel, it took everything I had just to hang onto him! I didn't see you guys lending a hand. Where were you, anyway?" he asked incredulously.

"You looked like you were doing fine without us..." McKay explained. "If I'd known you needed help..."

"I was taking a bath..." Philips added grinning. "Mike let his guy go, I thought you were the fast man on the draw."

"And you call yourselves SEALs!" Wardon exclaimed,

shaking his head and smiling.

"You're lucky he didn't shoot you!" McKay put in.

"I wonder why he didn't?" Philips thought aloud. "What's this all about?"

"Dunno, Let's check inside," Wardon urged, brushing off his jeans.

When the trio entered the houseboat they were not surprised to find the place completely tossed upside-down. The place was devastated, pictures were askew, drawers were dumped, dishes and glasses lay in broken heaps on the floor, even the couch and recliner had been ripped open. Upstairs, the three bedrooms were just as disheveled. All the drawers were dumped in the center of the rooms, dressers toppled and beds turned topsy-turvy. Nothing was spared. The intruders had obviously been looking for something.

"Looks as if these guys wanted something you have," McKay observed. "Or your decorator has a strange sense of humor."

"Well Moe, what you gonna do now?" asked Wardon. Kicking at clothing that was laying in a heap at the bottom of the stairs, he added, "You really could use that maid now."

All Philips could do was stand and stare. Even the Christmas presents had not been spared. They had been ripped open and tossed around and the bike lay on its side. *"These guys were very thorough,"* he thought.

"I'm going for the police," McKay offered as he headed into the kitchen to make the call.

About twenty minutes later, a patrolman approached the houseboat. The Lieutenant had suggested they sit outside, not wanting to disturb any possible evidence. Relating the events as they happened, the trio answered the few cursory questions the officer asked.

"Do you know if there's anything missing?" the patrolman asked Philips once they were inside.

The Lieutenant bent over and stood the bike up. "Not that I know of, however, I won't know until we clean this mess up."

"It looks to me as if you scared off a pair of teenagers,"

the patrolman summed up his investigation.

"Listen Moe, if it was just a pair of teenagers, why toss the place?"

"Well you never know what teenagers are up to these days," the officer remarked as he headed out the door.

"I think appearances can be deceiving, those guys were professionals looking for something," McKay added his two cents worth.

"Until you have evidence that says otherwise, I say it was teenagers," the impatient officer informed the perplexed trio.

"What about the gun? How about the boat? This doesn't add up!" Philips shouted after the indifferent patrolman. Shrugging his shoulders and scratching his head the Lieutenant turned toward the house and said, "C'mon guys, we've work to do."

Upon reentering the residence the SEALs stood in the living room and considered their next move. "Clifford, I need you to go to Washington," Philips ordered.

"Wassup?"

"Something's not right."

"Roger," Wardon said, sensing the seriousness of the situation.

"As of right now this is a military operation. I need you to requisition the necessary small arms and equipment we're going to need on this operation, use this number." Philips handed him the phone number Parsons had given him.

"No prob..."

"I'm not finished yet," Phillips interrupted, "I want you to go to the National Archives and look for any information on the Mills Transfer. If there's any information out there, they will have it."

Yes sir! I'll leave at first light."

Philips seemed to get his second wind. He turned to McKay who had been listening quietly, "Mike, I've been putting this off long enough, it's time to go see the General."

"General? What General?" McKay gave his Lieutenant a quizzical look.

"What General? Why, my grandfather of course!" Philips answered with a broad grin on his face. "Now, let's get this mess cleaned up."

Nine

Just north of Mount Vernon, Washington, is Chuckanut Drive, a delightful two lane scenic byway that follows the Puget Sound shoreline northward towards the Canadian border. Hugging the coastline, the narrow road meanders back and forth upon itself with several hairpin turns. Snaking northward, the drive crests several bluffs offering spectacular panoramas of the Sound and the distant, often cloud-shrouded Olympic Mountains.

McKay was in total awe of the passing scenery as Philips drove the rented car through a light mist and narrated like a cheap tour guide. “Chuckanut Drive follows the Puget Sound shoreline from Sedro Woolly to Bellingham.”

“Does it always rain like this?” McKay observed. “The scenery is so, so green.”

“That's because Western Washington is dominated by a coniferous forest. The local forests are predominantly Sitka Spruce, Douglas Fir, Western hemlock and other evergreen trees. And it only rains two hundred fifty days a year here...”

“You're kidding, no wonder everyone's so pale!” he said, referring to the locals’ obvious lack of tan.

Passing a gravel road that ascended a portion of the mountain they were transversing, McKay pointed out an area that was devoid of trees. “Why have all the trees been cut down? Disease or something?”

“Nope, that's a clear-cut,” Philips chuckled.

“A clear-cut?”

“Where are you from anyway?”

“East Jordan, Michigan, why?”

“Don't they have logging there?”

“Nope, not anymore.”

“A clear-cut is an area were a logging firm goes in and cuts all the trees,” Philips explained as he negotiated a hairpin turn. “The timber is used for housing materials and paper products.”

“And what about the land afterwards?” he asked curiously.

“The cut is replanted.”

“Really!”

"Really. Now, as I was saying before, my grandfather has this place in the Chuckanut Hills just south of Bellingham a few miles from here.”

“What's he got to do with all of this?” McKay asked.

“Not sure, but he was stationed in the Philippines during World War II. I have this photograph of President Quezon, MacArthur and a couple of other guys with him on Corregidor Island,” The Lieutenant explained as he handed over the photograph.

“Where did you get this?”

“It was among some papers in the file I was given back at the Pentagon. Check the caption on the back.”

Studying the photograph a moment McKay turned it over and read the inscription. “Here's a reference to the Mills Transfer.”

“Yep, that's why I sent Clifford back to Washington. By checking the archives, maybe he can dig up something that wasn't in the briefing.”

“If anyone can, Cliff will. Do you think your grandfather

will remember anything? After all it's been sixty years!"

"He's eighty-nine now and I've never known him to be less than a hundred percent," Philips proudly stated.

"So, he's not one of these old coots confined to a wheelchair with drool running down his chin?"

"Nope! Let's just say that our visit should be interesting," chuckled Philips as he directed the rental onto a long sloping driveway.

Tall conifers lined both sides of a narrow pavement barely letting the sun through. In short order Philips pulled up to a three-story gray and white Victorian house. The impeccable lawn was well kept, even for the winter months. Manicured shrubs were scattered about the property. Rhododendron and Azalea bushes lined both sides of the house.

The edifice was topped with a square white cupola with windows looking in all directions. Around the cupola was a widow's walk with white ornate railings. A huge porch wrapped around the front and down the right side of the prestigious residence. A porch swing was situated beside a bay window that overlooked Puget Sound. Smoke could be seen rising from a brick chimney, indicating someone was home.

"Whew! Is this the place or what?" admired the Lieutenant's companion.

"Yeah, my grandfather inherited it from his mother who was the daughter of one of Washington's early timber barons."

"Tell me, is there any money too?" asked McKay grinning.

"Nope, just the house and twenty-five acres," Philips responded with sparkling eyes.

"You know Jake, you're full of surprises," McKay coyly stated, "First we've got the houseboat, then I find out your grandfather's a General. Not just a General, but a member of the Joint Chiefs of Staff. Then there's this big old place in the country. How bad can it be?"

Shrugging his shoulders, the Lieutenant gestured towards the house, "After you."

"I hope there's a welcoming committee. You think?"

Exiting the car the duo mounted the steps and Philips banged on the door. “Wait and see.”

A moment later the door opened a fraction and a pair of medium brown eyes peered through the opening. Growing wider, the door was suddenly flung open. Blocking the entryway was an elderly woman who couldn't have been more than five feet tall. With blue white hair and a smiling tanned face, she was a picture of everyone's grandmother. She looked quite athletic in her blue and white running suit and shoes, however.

“My goodness! If it isn't Jake.”

“Grandma, did I interrupt your afternoon run?”

“Not hardly! I needed a good excuse not to run,” the woman stepped up and gave Philips a bone-crushing hug. Encircling his grandmother with his strong arms, he hugged back. Taking his head between her hands she proceeded to plant a very wet noisy kiss on Jake's lips. Breaking the embrace and stepping back, the small woman slapped the surprised SEAL's left cheek. “Where have you been young man? Fifteen years! Never a note or even a phone call, you could have been dead for all we knew.”

Turning a deep shade of crimson Philips silently rubbed his abused cheek. “I meant to write, I just never found the time. If I had died the Navy would have notified you.”

“That's no excuse, you could've called!”

“Guilty as charged,” he gulped, giving up. “No excuses here, could you ever forgive me?” Stepping forward again, the young man hugged his grandmother once more.

“Apology accepted.” A look of tenderness swept across the elderly woman's face.

Meanwhile, an amused McKay silently observed the reunion. When the opportunity presented itself he extended his right hand. “Mike McKay ma'am, you must be Jake's grandmother.”

“That's correct, Phoebe Philips,” she hesitated, “Sounds kind of funny don't it?” taking his hand and shaking it firmly.

McKay was surprised by the strength of the old woman's grip. “Not really, we have a Katie McKay in the family.” He liked the elderly matron at once.

“Well you two had better come inside before you catch your death.”

"Who the hell's at the door this time?” bellowed a deep baritone voice from a room beyond the hall. “Not another god-damned salesman!”

“Look, Daddy, look who's come to see us,” Phoebe spoke to the hallway as she ushered the men inside.

"Daddy?” McKay inquired quietly while shooting an inquisitive look towards his friend.

“Grandma has always called him that,” he whispered while smiling ear-to-ear. Leading the pair down the hallway to a den situated under the staircase, Phoebe presented the duo to the General.

The room was warmly decorated with wooden accents. A Persian rug was tastefully centered on the floor with two Victorian leather armchairs seated in front of a pair of old-fashioned bay windows. White lace drapes hung from either window indicating a female's touch in an otherwise male domain.

Five rows of medals mounted in a walnut shadow box hung on the wall over the Czechoslovakian marble fireplace. The warm glow and familiar crackle of the fire added a sense of coziness to the room. A large, tattered Japanese battle flag hung from a staff pointing towards the chandelier directly over the General. In the opposite corner was a similar staff from which a North Korean flag draped. There appeared to be a Japanese sword and helmet -with a small hole in it- that sat on a small cherry wood table between the chairs.

An elderly man was seated in one of the armchairs with his stocking feet resting upon an ottoman. Smoking a pipe, he was watching a large TV that stood at the end of the room playing some sort of figure skating tournament while reading the *Seattle Times*.

General Philips, even in his elderly years was an imposing man. At six foot four inches with a full head of white hair, he still retained much of his younger physique. His deeply tanned face and sparkling blue eyes concealed any inner emotions he might have. He wore a pair of faded painter pants with a light blanket wrapped about his legs to ward off the December chill. The General was obviously enjoying his pipe. Like a steam engine, clouds of smoke would puff out the corner of his mouth and float towards the ceiling. On the table beside him sat the last remnants of a ham sandwich and a partially consumed glass of rum.

"Come on in, Jake! I was wondering when you would show up."

Philips was beside himself! Not only did the General know he was there, it was as if he were expected. "Granddad," he said cordially, doing his best to hide his surprise. "Nothing much changes here, does it?" He nodded towards the television.

"Hell no! Same rain, same crime, same high taxes and same politicians complaining about not getting their fair share." His voice boomed as he took another drink from his glass. "Grandma still makes me watch this." His tone softened as he referred to the figure skating.

Grinning, Philips walked over to his grandfather and gave him a hearty handshake. Turning, he introduced McKay to the General. "Mike McKay, meet General Murdoch Phillips, former Chairman of the Joint Chiefs of Staff."

"Pleased to meet you sir, although you're not exactly what I imagined."

"And just what was I supposed to be?"

"I was thinking a little more feeble, sir," he responded to the General's question.

"I'll show you feeble! Put 'er there," the General boomed as he extended his hand.

McKay put his hand out hesitantly and discovered the old man had a vice-like grip that tightened when he applied pressure.

"You can measure a man by his handshake and I think you'll do just fine. By the way son, may I call you Mike? Call me Murdoch," said the old General as he let go.

Nodding, the surprised SEAL stepped back while massaging his hand. It was now Philips' turn to enjoy his friends' discomfort.

"What brings you guys to these parts? Umm, Excuse me, where's my manners? I'll just get an extra chair..." Murdoch apologized as he went to rise.

Putting her hand gently on his shoulder Phoebe quietly commanded, "You just sit right where you're at, I'll manage."

"Phoebe dear!" the big man pleaded.

"You know what the doctor says, now stay put!" she said.

As Phoebe turned to leave, McKay offered his assistance. "How long have you and the General been married?" he asked, making idle conversation as they exited the room.

After his grandmother and shipmate were gone, Philips filled his grandfather in on everything that had transpired within the last week. Knowing the General's keen mind for details, he omitted nothing, explaining the assignment and how he was puzzled about the Secretary's statement that he knew something. He also briefed him on the break-in at the houseboat and the Seattle officer's indifferent attitude.

"Well, let me start by saying the police are worthless and if you want something done you gotta damn well do it yourself. It was I who couldn't bear to close down the house so I just left it as I found it the day after the plane crash, hoping that someday you'd return. My gardener went down to open the place up the day before you got here. I'm sorry, son, about all that has happened, but I can't turn back the clock." The General offered those sobering words as Phoebe and McKay returned with a couple of kitchen chairs.

"Jake, this place is huge! Do you know how far it is to the kitchen?"

"Impressive, isn't it! As a child, my parents used to bring me up here on weekends and I'd get lost and had to be rescued by Grandma," he modestly admitted. Turning back to his grandfather, Phillips handed him the photo. "What can you tell me about this?"

The General took a long look at the faded photograph. "This sure brings back memories. I've been waiting sixty years for someone to ask me about this; I never thought it would be my own grandson." Laying the photo down on the table, Murdoch picked up the remote and turned off the television. Taking his glass and draining the last of the rum, the once powerful General's eyes took on a faraway look.

Philips interrupted his reverie. "Can you tell me about it now?"

"I don't see why not." Turning to his wife of sixty-two years, he said, "Honey could you fix the boys a light supper while I answer Jake's questions? This could take a while."

"Would club sandwiches do?" she asked the group.

"Just fine. Do you want some help?" McKay offered.

"No, you just sit right there, you'll be under foot in my kitchen. I can manage," Phoebe said as she left the room. "Now Daddy, don't you get worked up, remember your blood pressure."

After Phoebe had left, Murdoch said, "She's a good woman, just worries a little too much. If the booze and the pipe haven't killed me by now, nothing will. God knows the Japs couldn't!" A sad smile crept over the General's face.

The duo could see Murdoch was about to start his narrative so they pulled their chairs a little closer. They waited in silence for the General to reveal the long ago events. "Go ahead, let's get started." Philips urged him impatiently.

"What I'm about to tell you I've never told anyone, not even your grandmother," Murdoch began.

"The autumn of 1941 had been a pleasant one, the rains had come early that year and by October they had abated. By mid November the heat and humidity had dropped to a tolerable level. I had been transferred from Fort Dix, New Jersey to Fort McKinley in Manila. My posting to General Janson's staff came as a bit of a surprise. The General had taken a liking to me when he was an instructor at West Point, and when he discovered I had been transferred in, he assigned me to his staff. You gotta understand I was in my late 20s, youngest captain of my class and had been married the previous September, so this was quite a coup.

By the last days of November or the early part of

December war rumors were as thick as ticks in a Philippine jungle. Washington helped fan the flames by putting us on a war alert towards the end of November. There was electricity in the air, you knew something was about to happen, you just didn't know when.

General Janson ordered us to intensify training of the 14th Engineer battalion of the Philippine Scouts. We were a motorized unit that was made up of Philippine soldiers with American officers and support staff. Therefore, while the weather was beautiful, the regiment spent its days in constant drill; checking equipment, making repairs and attending numerous strategy meetings. I, myself, was busy working dispatches between Washington and Honolulu. The General didn't want to hear rumors, he wanted facts!

It was 3:30 A.M. on the eighth of December 1941 when we received news of the attack on Pearl Harbor. It was eight hours later when the Japanese first bombed Camp John Hay. Clark and Nichols fields soon followed. I spent the rest of the day and most of that night decoding dispatches from Honolulu, Washington and San Diego.

General Janson ordered his command to be prepared to move out on a moment's notice. I can still remember the excitement, everyone issuing orders, running about like chickens with their heads chopped off. Damned if we weren't running around in circles, but doing absolutely nothing. Until the Japanese actually landed we had little to do. To keep us busy the General had us filling sandbags and fortifying various important buildings around the base.

Later in the day, General MacArthur convened a staff meeting with all his generals. I can remember Generals Moore, Janson and Jackson being in attendance. At the meeting, MacArthur informed us the United States was not the only country attacked. The Japanese had also bombarded Hong Kong, Singapore and Jakarta. He suspected invasion was imminent and we were to prepare for the inevitable. MacArthur outlined which tactics he would employ as soon as we knew where the Japanese intended to strike. Afterward, he assigned various tasks to the division commanders.

On the 22nd the Japanese landed at Lingayen Gulf in Northern Luzon. You could hear their aircraft over the city every day. They attacked the docks and oil storage tanks along the waterfront. Hospitals became overcrowded within a day or two. With Manila in the middle, there was nothing MacArthur could do but implement War Plan Orange or WPO-3."

"What was WPO-3?" inquired Philips.

"WPO-3 was the withdrawal of all U.S. and Philippine forces to the Bataan Peninsula, with a delaying action until reinforcements could arrive. To spare civilian casualties, MacArthur had Manila declared an open city and removed all defensive guns. That didn't stop the Japanese though, they continued to attack the city in earnest. So MacArthur was forced to move his headquarters from Nichols Field to Fort Mills on Corregidor Island.

Fort Mills had a series of bombproof tunnels from which MacArthur could conduct the defense of the Philippines in relative safety, the largest of which was Malinta tunnel. It was so large that a double row of narrow gauge railroad tracks ran down the corridor, with tunnels branching from either side called laterals. Each lateral was assigned a different function such as ammunition storage, commissary and barracks. I can remember one connected to the hospital tunnel under Middleside..."

"Middleside?" McKay interrupted.

"I forgot, you probably haven't been there. The island of Corregidor is shaped like a tadpole, with its head towards the South China Sea, and its tail towards Manila. The island was divided into three sections. The main section, the area with the batteries and headquarters buildings, was 'Topside', the center of the island was 'Middleside' and the tail was 'Bottomside'," he explained.

"Oh."

"MacArthur's headquarters occupied a space next to the communications and switchboard lateral. General Janson and staff, myself included, transferred over on Christmas Day. Other notables who arrived that day were the U.S. High Commissioner

Francis B. Sayer, President Quezon, Vice President Osmena and several other members of the Philippine government. They were all given private quarters within the tunnel complex.

It was on or about the twenty-eighth or twenty-ninth of December that there was some intense negotiating between Commissioner Sayer and President Quezon. At about 3:00 A.M. on the 30th of December I was awakened and asked to proceed to General MacArthur's lateral."

"Excuse me, but supper is served," Phoebe interrupted, entering the room and setting a platter heaped with sandwiches down on the table between the chairs and exiting the room again.

"Great! I'm famished," proclaimed McKay as he eyed the platter hungrily. Taking the sandwich that was nearest to him, he added, "Got anymore of that rum?"

"You know, I'm beginning to like this guy," General Philips chuckled. "If you look under the helmet there might be a little left."

After a curious inspection Philips came back with a fifth of Ed Teaches Spiced Rum. Taking a whiff he drew back, "Oomph, you still drinking that rot-gut?"

"It kinda grows on ya," Murdoch responded with a mock Southern accent. "How's 'bout y'all joining me for a belt?"

Philips looked about and only spotted the General's glass. Pouring it half full, leaving the glass for his grandfather, he proceeded to take a long pull from the bottle. Passing the bottle to his companion the Lieutenant offered, "Have a sip."

"Don't mind if I do," McKay responded. He followed his commander's example and took a large mouthful, wincing as the liquid fire boiled all the way down. "Holy shit! What is this stuff? Aviation fuel?" he choked.

"A homemade brew." The General laughed at the surprised SEAL. "It's a little something that I distill myself. I thought you guys could drink anything."

"You gotta look before you leap!" Philips snickered at his friend's obvious discomfort. Turning back to his grandfather he urged him to continue.

"Umm. Now where was I?"

"December 29th 1941," Philips reminded his grandfather.

"That's right. Now, let me see. Right, it was the morning of the December 30th when I was summoned to MacArthur's lateral. There were several other people in the room at the time. The High Commissioner was present along with MacArthur, President Quezon and a young Oriental gentleman of slight stature, whom I did not recognize.

Their conversations ceased when I walked in the room. After a moment of uneasy silence, MacArthur approached me, shook my hand, and introduced me around the room. Each person nodded as they were introduced. The stranger was introduced as Mao Tse-tung, who had been smuggled ashore by one of our supply submarines.

Commissioner Sayer cleared his throat and informed me I was to witness an extraordinary treaty. The treaty granted independence to the Republic of the Philippines forthwith, with certain guarantees from the United States and China. Men and material were pledged in the forthcoming fight with the Japanese. Furthermore, President Roosevelt would address the nation committing the entire industrial might of America to assure the Philippines' independence. I was not privileged to the intricacies of the treaty until much later.

MacArthur took charge of the proceedings and had everyone sign at the places indicated, I signed last. The meeting broke up and the fiduciaries went their separate ways. President Roosevelt made his speech the next day and we all were excited about the relief he pledged. I was not to see the treaty again for another two years."

"So what about the photograph?" McKay asked leaning forward.

"Ah, the photograph. It was taken the first week of February '42 when a submarine had snuck into the harbor to replenish torpedoes. MacArthur ordered the first payment of six million dollars worth of gold bullion loaded aboard the sub."

Philips had listened to the General's tale spellbound. "The real question is, what happened to Mao? Why was he not in the photograph?" he finally asked.

The General's face lit up with a broad smile "Bright boy! The reason Mao was not in the photograph was a political one. General Chennualt was cultivating Chiang Kai-shek while MacArthur was working with Mao. After several days, Mao was evacuated by submarine. Later, towards the end of February, President Quezon, his family and Commissioner Sayer all left the rock for the safety of Australia.

Things were beginning to look hopeless; rations were short, fresh water scarce, wounded everywhere, dysentery, malaria and beriberi were rampant because medicine was in short supply. It was about this time when President Roosevelt ordered MacArthur to Australia. Morale hit a new low as the men witnessed his departure from the north pier aboard Lieutenant Buckley's motor patrol boats. General Wainwright tried to bolster morale, but without the promised reinforcements it was only a matter of time.

Bataan fell on the 8th of April and I'm sure you know of the Death March. 76,000 Philippine and American troops that surrendered to General Homma were forced to march three to four days without food or water. They marched more than sixty miles to Taralac in ninety-degree heat and very high humidity. Somewhere around 10,000 soldiers died in the march itself with the Japanese bayoneting or beheading anyone who fell from the ranks.

When on the morning of May 6th the Japanese invaded Bottomside with Marines and tanks, Wainwright thought further resistance fruitless. Subsequent to brief negotiations, the General surrendered Corregidors 13,000 defenders and the entire Philippine Islands at twelve noon. That was but the beginning of our ordeal." The old man sighed.

Ten

The retired General sat in silence for a few moments with a distant look in his eyes, as if reliving the events in that long forgotten place. The two SEALs sat with bated breath waiting for him to continue. Noticing that the room had gone silent, the old man shook his head as if to clear the cobwebs and commented, "Now... Where was I?"

"You just finished up your time at Corregidor, just after Wainwright's surrender," his grandson volunteered.

Looking at an old standard regulator clock hanging over the door, the General realized he had been speaking for several hours. "It's getting late boys, why don't we finish up some other time," he stated while standing to stretch his legs.

"If you don't mind Sir, I'd just as soon get this over with," Philips pleaded as McKay watched in silence.

"If you insist. I don't understand what the rush is, my story has waited long enough. Another day or two shouldn't make much difference." The General surrendered to his grandson's pressure. Walking over to the fireplace he stoked up the fire and spoke loudly in the direction of the doorway.

"Phoebe, could you be a sweetie and bring us another bottle?"

As if she had read his mind Phoebe was already rounding the corner with a fresh bottle and three glasses. Without saying a word she deposited her cargo and exited the room. Returning to his chair, the patriarch sat and sighed, then picked up the bottle and started to fill the empty glasses.

About this time the shutters outside the windows started to rattle. "Looks like the wind's picking up," observed McKay.

"At night we get an offshore flow, sometimes it gets quite breezy up here," Murdoch explained, before continuing his narrative. "Our surrender was anticlimactic. We knew it was coming when the Japs had brought up tanks to Middleside, it was only a matter of hours. I was busy burning documents. There was a sense of..." The General closed his eyes. When he reopened them the faraway look had returned. "...a sense of relief. Yes, it was relief! I know it may sound strange but we really were relieved the fighting was finished."

Philips and McKay shot glances at each other wondering about the General's train of thought. They dared not interrupt him.

"When the shelling stopped, for the first time in many weeks, Malinta tunnel was eerily quiet. We had become so accustomed to the noise that the silence was almost deafening. Even the wounded waited quietly for our captors to appear.

Before I could finish my task, an announcement was made informing the entire garrison that terms had been reached. We were instructed to cease and desist with any further destruction of documents, weapons and other surviving equipment. I ignored the order and continued to burn boxes of documents.

Among the documents I was destroying, I discovered a leather pouch. Forgetting the moment, I let curiosity get the better of me, so I opened the pouch and examined its contents. There, I found two copies of the treaty that I had witnessed earlier! I had on idea why they were there. I can remember thinking that these documents should have been hand carried by Sayer to Australia. I did not know the importance of the treaty, just that the documents needed to be spared. Setting the pouch aside, I continued with what I considered was my sworn duty; to protect vital military documents from capture.

Shortly, an officer appeared at the lateral's entrance accompanied by a Japanese soldier. The soldier reacted instantly, pushing me aside and knocking the burning barrel over. He grabbed a nearby blanket and smothered the flames. After the fire was out, he proceeded to strike me several times in my side with the butt of his rifle, all the while shouting unknown curses in Japanese. As I was receiving my punishment, the accompanying officer stood paralyzed in fear of provoking my assailant upon himself.

We spent the next few days tending our wounded and adjusting to receiving orders, while the Japanese considered what to do with us. After many debates, General Homma decided to ship us all off to Camp O'Donnell, which was the terminus of the infamous Bataan Death March. The officer corps, myself included, was trucked to the camp instead of being marched as the enlisted men were.

Conditions at Camp O'Donnell were deplorable at best. When we first arrived there were maybe 50,000 American and Filipino soldiers living in an area that was no larger than ten acres. Barracks had not been constructed yet and sanitation was nonexistent. One lone creek flowed through the center of camp, which served for both drinking and sanitation purposes. Almost half the prisoners were suffering from some kind of disease; either beriberi, cholera, malaria or dysentery; and all were suffering the humiliation of surviving America's largest defeat."

The old General paused his narration long enough to take a strong pull from his glass. Licking his lips, the patriarch of the Philips family stared into the fire.

Hunched forward to the edge of their seats, Philips and McKay took in every word he had to say.

Regaining his composure he began again. "The first thing the Japanese did was make us stand in the hot sun for hours stripped naked. They confiscated everything from money, jewelry, and combs, to extra socks, toothbrushes and wristwatches. After they were satisfied that we had no contraband we were allowed to dress. I was able to hide my wedding ring under my tongue and remember sucking on it the entire afternoon.

For the first couple of days the Japanese employed a strict regimen of constant beatings with a lack of nutrition. Really it was quite ingenious to demoralize us to the point of pacification; we became nothing more than lambs. Almost daily any one of the officers would be called into a hut reserved for interrogations. When you did not provide the expected answers, you could count on a beating to follow. Do you know how the Japanese administered punishment?" the General asked the room.

"No sir, I'm not sure that I do," Philips answered.

"Punishment was almost always in the form of a beating, and the Japanese would never use their hands. Instead they used gun butts or bamboo sticks and kicked the holy shit out of you while you were on the ground. Thumbscrews were another handy device; they would attach the apparatus around your thumb and slowly insert a wooden screw under the nail until you passed out from the pain.

We had one soldier who was constantly drinking water, so the Nips brought him into a hut and held him below a fifty-five gallon drum they had suspended from the ceiling. Attached to the drum was a rubber hose which was fed down his gullet into the poor mans stomach. After a guard opened the tap and he could hold no more, an officer took a sword and split him wide open. Water, blood and guts spilled to the floor with the soldier still trying to scream around the hose.

I can recall helping a disabled sailor get to some water. A short guard took offense to what I was doing and demanded he be made to stand unassisted. The sailor, a petty officer I think, had open sores and ulcers on the insides of his thighs from the heat. He couldn't stand without support but the guard demanded he do just that. After watching him fall on his face I attempted to assist.

All this did was enrage the guard to focus his anger on me. A series of well placed blows from his rifle put me on the ground where he continued kicking until I lost consciousness. Later, I awoke in the hospital tent with several fractured ribs and a deflated lung. I didn't know it at the time but he saved my life by putting me there. I spent the better part of the next three weeks recuperating on my back where conditions were slightly better than what the general population was receiving. By the time I was released, the guards had vented most of their anger. The interrogations had stopped, but occasional beatings continued at the whim of a guard.

While I was in the hospital, the prisoners had constructed barracks and piped running water into the compound. Because the latrines were constantly seeping into our drinking water, I tried to collect water as far upstream as I could, and avoided standing water at all costs. Finally, I took to collecting rainwater.

Food, now there's another story. As an officer, our rations were somewhat better than the enlisted men's. We would get buckets that contained rotten rice, some small vegetables and maybe a little spoiled fish. This watery gruel was served up twice a day. About once a week the cook would put some caribou meat within the mix. I had it on good authority that the enlisted men only got rice and fish, no vegetables.

The death rate had settled down to several dozens a week instead of several dozens a day as it was at the beginning of our captivity. After nine months, approximately 10,000 Americans and 25,000 Filipinos had expired!

When I was released from the hospital, I was asked to join work details that entailed salvaging everything of use from the former American bases. At first I told them all to go to hell but when I discovered it was really not an option, I 'volunteered'. We were trucked to several bases to help clean out offices, hospitals and any officer's quarters that had survived the Japanese bombers. The good thing about these trips was I could get away from the horror of O'Donnell and the guards were usually quite lax. Sometimes we were able to find such things as canned fruits, vegetables and occasionally Spam. One time I found a long forgotten carton of cigarettes under a bunk.

You have to understand about cigarettes, they were like

cold hard cash and we would do anything to possess them. You could trade cigarettes with the guards for almost anything. I used them to bargain for sulfa and quinine pills, as vitamin deficiency was my number one concern. Also, let me add here, my chief concern was surviving. Which meant you looked out for number one first. Sounds harsh but that was reality.

Another benefit to going on these trips was occasionally we would meet up with several Filipina who would pass along vegetables, money and letters to loved ones incarcerated at O'Donnell. It was at this time that I met a very good-looking young female with the prettiest hazel eyes you ever saw. She asked me to pass an envelope to a Remegio Aleta. He was one of the Philippine Scouts formally stationed on Corregidor.

It turns out he was a mechanic who'd been ordered to drive part of our group to the different salvage locations. He was really quite easy to find, a smallish man with thick hair and an infectious smile. I made a point after that to try and always be assigned to Remegio's truck. He was always quite entertaining with stories of his youth. Besides, he would share some of his fruits and vegetables with us. Our friendship seemed to blossom and he always talked about going to America. We would spend evenings talking about the various places I had been, and what we would do whenever we got out of this mess. He was always willing to listen to my problems, and never seemed to let it bother him that I was an officer while he was an enlisted man. Because he lived locally, Remegio was paroled after a short time. He was required to sign a waiver stating he would not raise arms against the Japanese and had to report daily to drive the truck.

Later on, I would be assigned to different construction projects. We were now working as slave labor in fields, repairing bridges, constructing airfields and repairing harbor fortifications. As always, I managed to get assigned to Remegio's truck.

We were all assigned cells of ten persons each. Every cell was responsible for itself. If someone turned up missing, the Nips would shoot everyone in the cell. The members of our cell had decided early on that there would be no attempts at escape. As long as we stayed in line the Japanese paid us no heed but if a guard had a bad day or you disobeyed even the smallest of orders, there was hell to pay.

Our days had become quite routine starting with roll call at sunrise. After standing in the hot sun for an hour and a half, we would breakfast on the same gruel I described earlier. We would then receive our daily work detail. Sometimes, we would be required to work until well after sunset. Upon our return, we ate in silence, and lights out followed shortly thereafter.

Sometime in late '43, I was assigned to a construction detail that had nothing to do with the war. Remegio would always would pick us up before sunrise, and we would sit in back of the truck blindfolded for hours. Security was very tight, even the drivers were required switch out. Wearing blindfolds for half of the trip, they had no idea where we were going. At our destination, each one of us was issued shovels, picks and axes and we were told to clear an area about the size of a football field. At the very center of this cleared area, we dug a pit approximately two hundred by sixty feet. We then constructed a ramp so trucks could drive into the bottom of the pit.

In the pit we constructed a concrete bunker that was about half the size of the pit. The bunker was constructed of reinforced concrete; there were no windows nor doors, just one large garage type door at the southern end of the structure. I was curious as to its use, but knew that it was not my place to ask. Thousand-pound bombs were placed at regular intervals ringing the entire structure. After we finished constructing the shelter and the bombs were set, we backfilled the pit in. The only exposed part of the job was the ramp, which ran down to the door. The only identifying landmark I can remember seeing was a small village or barrio.

It was about this time that I was ordered on another detail, which entailed a trip back into Manila. As always we sat blindfolded. The trip was quite lengthy but when we arrived at our destination I folded up one corner of my blindfold and recognized Nichols field. The Japanese were now using the field as a fighter base and I could see various aircraft parked in the same hangers that had once housed ours.

At Nichols, Remegio negotiated our truck to a warehouse area where most of the workshops had been. Stopping at the only intact warehouse, he backed the truck up to the loading dock. We exited under extremely tight security. About thirty guards were watching our every move. We were cautioned about talking amongst ourselves and any infractions would mean instant death. Inside the warehouse there was a large supply of ammunition boxes stacked at the back of the room. A guard ordered us to form a human chain and move the boxes out to the trucks. I was one of the end men inside the warehouse.

The boxes were approximately a foot thick and two feet long with Japanese markings across the lid. Rope handles were attached to either end. The boxes were unusually heavy for ammunition, so I suspected their contents to be something other than what we was led to believe. After passing on five or six boxes I accidentally dropped my end and the lid came loose. Curiosity overcame me and I asked my partner to keep a look out while I examined the crates' contents. Under the lid was an oilskin wrapper, which protected six bars of gold! I could see bank stamps indicating purity and weights on each bar. No wonder; we had all the security precautions. Carefully I reattached the lid and we quickly passed the box along.

About three-quarters of the way through the stack we grabbed a box that was much lighter. Again, curiosity overcame me. So… I had my partner, Scotty, watch the door. Prying open the lid, I discovered it was full of captured documents. Sifting through the paperwork to see if there was anything interesting, would you believe it? I came across the pouch again! Opening it up, I quickly ascertained the Mills Transfer was still inside. I don't know what made me do it but I slipped the documents back inside, and stuffed the pouch down the front of my pants."

"Who's Scotty?" Philips inquired politely, interrupting his Grandfather's narrative.

"He was a cell mate. An Army Captain like I was. I think... Yes, I believe his name was Konger. He was someone I befriended during my 'stay' at O'Donnell. If I remember correctly Scotty and Remegio were really close before the

Japanese invasion. When the Army mustered him out, after the war, 'ol Scotty stayed in the Philippines. He opened up a restaurant in Manila. Why?"

"I'm sorry, it's just that his is the first name that you have used." Philips offered.

"Well, you never made many friends outside your cell, as they either died or got transferred," explained the old General. "Now let's finish this up. That night, I had a chance to finally read the document to which my name was affixed. Basically, it was a transfer of ownership from the United States to the Chinese people a series of islands known collectively as the Spratleys. Payments of three installments in gold were to be made by Mao Tse-tung's government to the United States by way of MacArthur's command at Corregidor. The second part of the document promised full and complete support, militarily and financially, to Mao Tse-tung with his endeavors against the Japanese and beyond.

Reading between the lines, I understood the document to be an agreement between what was to become the People's Republic of China and the United States. Both countries were to be forever bonded by the Mills Transfer for mutual, social, and economic reasons.

The third page of the agreement outlined a protest by the Philippine government. To satisfy their objection, for the sum of $60 million, the United States would grant sovereignty to the Philippines and recognize President Quezon as their first president. Furthermore, it stated that President Roosevelt would acknowledge the transfer in a speech pledging all the resources of the United States to the Philippines." The General paused for just a moment, maybe for effect, maybe not.

Philips, who had been holding his breath, now exhaled a large volume of air. "You mean the United States sold off a piece of the Philippines to China and then granted them independence to hush it up?"

"Yep, that's what I'm saying."

"What of the payments?"

"Turns out that the first payment by Mao Tse-tung was

what you saw in the photo, it was loaded aboard a submarine and taken to Australia. The second was made to MacArthur just before he transferred to Australia and Wainwright accepted the third two weeks before his surrender. All the gold was moved to the island by submarine. The only bullion removed from the island was the first installment. As to the Philippine agreement the entire sum was brought to Corregidor before President Quezon was evacuated. The Japanese captured the entire cache intact."

"So what you're saying is that the United States pressured the Philippine government into allowing the sale of the Spratleys?" asked Philips incredulously.

Nodding his head, the weary General got up from his chair and walked out of the room. Philips and McKay sat wordlessly looking at each other. The once powerful General returned with a package in his hands; handing it to his grandson he said, "I think it's time that someone else looked after this."

"What is it?" his grandson asked, examining a brown wrapped package that appeared to be a book.

"Open it," the elderly man offered.

Opening the package, Phillips discovered a leather-bound copy of *Treasure Island* by Robert Louis Stevenson. He found upon opening the book, a folded parchment. Carefully unfolding the old document Lieutenant Philips discovered what looked to be some kind of map. Japanese characters ran down the left side and partially down the right, with what appeared to be locations of mountains and a small town indicated. A small stream ran from left to right. There was no notation of compass bearing.

"So what's this?" he asked after a carefully examining the parchment.

"Why, that's a treasure map!"

"A what?" McKay excitedly responded looking over his teammates' shoulder.

"Just as I said. A treasure map!"

"I don't follow," Philips said as he looked at his grandfather quizzically.

"Remember the bunker I was telling you about?"

"Yes."

"Well, about a week later Remegio told me he helped drive the six trucks we had loaded into the bunker. The Japanese then sealed the entrance and planted shrubs and trees over the area to conceal its location. I had no reason to doubt him as the trucks had simply disappeared. The map was made with the intent of coming back after the war and recovering its contents. This was not the only location in which the Japanese had secreted gold and valuables. I heard after the war that there had been a total of a hundred and seventy-two sites."

"So how did you to come into possession of the map?" McKay asked.

"Good question. After Remegio told me about the map, I had an occasion to be working within the commander's office. The guard had left me alone while he went outside to catch a smoke. While he was out, I was quietly going through the commanders' desk looking for some quinine, when I came upon that map. I figured it would be important someday so I boosted it and kept it concealed until my liberation," explained the former POW.

Shaking his head, Philips asked, "So what does all this have to do with the Mills Transfer?"

"After I read the transfer I gave the pouch and its contents to Remegio for safe keeping."

"And?" his grandson asked holding his breath.

"...And, after the war I was able to locate him. He was farming a piece a land on northern Luzon."

Not able to stand the suspense any more Philips asked bluntly, "Did he still have the transfer?"

"No, he had hidden it in a safe location."

"So give, where'd he stash the documents?" McKay jumped into the suspenseful conversation.

The General looked at the two SEALs with sparkling eyes. The suspense in the air was so thick you could cut it with a knife. The only sound was the gentle crackling of the fire. Finally he spoke up. "It seems that to Remegio the only safe place in the fall of '43 was inside the bunker with the gold."

"Where?" Philips asked, not believing his ears.

"The Mills transfer is buried with the very gold that was used to purchase the Spratleys!" Murdoch quietly offered.

"And this is the map to that location?" The Lieutenant was stunned.

"Yep. Now if you'll excuse me it's 5 A.M. and I'm an old man who needs his rest." The General almost whispered as he rose and walked towards the door.

"Oh Grandpa, one more thing. Why didn't you tell someone about this?" Philips questioned.

"No one asked, I didn't offer, I figured it was something best left alone." General Philips remarked as he left the room.

The young Lieutenant stood in silence for several minutes pondering the tale he had just heard. He looked at the map one more time before folding it and replacing it back into the book. Turning to his shipmate he said, "Your room is at the top of the stairs on the right. I will take the one across the hall." Without waiting for a response, he left the room.

Eleven

It didn't take much prodding on Phoebe's part to get the SEALs to stay for a couple of days of relaxation. For Jake, the familiar surroundings brought back many emotions, some good, and some bad. However, on a whole he was able to relax for what seemed like the first time in fifteen years. It was good to be back home.

McKay who always enjoyed a break from military life, was eager for a few days of R&R. The Philips family had accepted Mike within the fold and treated him as if he was one of their own. They spent the days in idle chat with the General, while doing odds and ends around the mammoth house. On their last morning Murdoch was good enough to show McKay the workings of his private distillery.

As the pair walked to the old barn out back, Philips was busy giving his grandmother his final farewell. "You know Gram I'm really going to miss this place."

"Shucks Jake, do you really have to go? It's been so good having young people in the old place again."

"Yes it's time. Grandpa has given us a pretty good lead. So how's 'bout a kiss and this time could we skip the slap?"

Philips poked fun as he stepped forward to give his grandmother a big bear hug.

Responding to her grandson's affection, Phoebe fought back the tears. "Go on, git! You don't need to see an old fool cry."

Separating from the embrace, the Lieutenant left his grandmother in the kitchen and proceeded upstairs to his room to retrieve the package his grandfather had given him.

Meanwhile, out in back of the house, McKay stood in a dilapidated barn, which had a bright copper still dominating the center space. In total fascination he watched the spry General mash sugar cane with an old wooden mallet, from a supply that was standing in an old stall. After mashing a quantity of cane, the General had the young SEAL dump it into the large copper pot. Taking a garden hose and adding about a hundred gallons of water to the pulp, he then lit a portable propane burner under the pot.

"Here, pour one of those sacks into the pot," Murdoch ordered as he pointed to a mountain of ten pound sacks of brewer's yeast neatly stacked against the far wall.

"Yes sir!" the enthusiastic McKay responded as he grabbed a sack and dumped the contents into the cauldron.

When the concoction began to simmer, Murdoch added several spices, then spoke in a hushed tone as if someone was eavesdropping, "The brew will boil off and the steam will be captured within the copper coils you see there." The coils that he referred to hung suspended from a rafter towards the rear of the shed. He then attached an airtight lid to the pot, which looked something like the Tin Man's hat in *The Wizard of Oz*.

"How long does the process take?"

"About six weeks. By allowing the steam to cool within the coils, an amber liquid, which is the rum, will drip off the end of the last coil into the large mason jars I have there." The informative General pointed towards a row of jars. "Later, when the rum has cooled sufficiently, I will filter and transfer the contents into large oak barrels, date stamping each one for aging." He grinned at McKay.

"And how long before you can consume?" the wide-eyed petty officer inquired as he licked his lips remembering the elixir from the other evening.

"After one year I transfer the rum to the Ed Teach bottles."

"Whew! I gotta know, how many bottles?"

"Above a hundred!" was the General's guarded response.

"How strong?"

"Bout 180!"

"Whoa! No wonder that shit choked me the other night. How's the law?"

"For personal use, they don't give a damn. Matter-of-fact I've a buddy on the force who's developed quite a taste for the stuff."

"Boy, if I was to try this, the law would be all over me in a heartbeat," remarked McKay enviously as he shook his head in wonderment. Upon hearing his name called from outside, the sailor exited the micro distillery. In admiration he turned towards the General and added, "That's some operation you got."

Beaming with pride General Philips spoke up, "Coming from you I do believe that's a compliment, and I thank you. If you're ever back this way, just drop by and we'll brew up a batch of some of the meanest rum this side of the Cascades, and maybe do a little fishing also."

By this time Philips had exited the house with his package and was approaching their car. "Well Mike, it's about time to head out. I see Murdoch showed you his little operation."

"Jake, that's not a little operation! It's a labor of love." McKay retorted, as he and the Lieutenant rounded the corner of the old mansion.

"Get in the car!" Philips barked in mock exasperation.

Squeezing into the passenger seat, the reluctant SEAL gave one more wishful look at the Philips property. "I can't believe you deserted these nice folks for so long."

"You know, you don't really know what you have until you lose it," the Lieutenant philosophized. He started up the vehicle and backed around to negotiate the drive back to the main road. As they started forward Philips though he heard a call from the direction of the yard behind them.

"Did someone just call your name?"

"No, I don't think so."

The old General came bounding around the corner of his Victorian home with a large box in tow. "Mike, pull up! Get Jake to stop the god-damn car!"

Upon hearing his grandfather's shouts, Philips stopped the car. Leaning out the windows and looking backward, the guys could hear the old man's panting as he set a box on the trunk lid.

"I-I wa-want you boys to have a little going away present," sputtered Murdoch, trying to catch his breath. With a quick pull on the door handle he deposited the box on the rear seat and bade them farewell. "Now, git the hell outta here!"

Easing the car forward, Philips waved to his grandfather, then picked up speed and headed toward Chuckanut Drive. Looking back McKay thought he'd seen the retired General wipe away a tear as the car picked up speed. "Sentimental old cus ain't he?"

"Naw, betcha he just got some dust or something of in his eye. What's in the box?"

Reaching over the seat, McKay opened the carton and discovered twelve bottles of Ed Teach's Puerto Rican Spice Rum. Grinning ear-to-ear, he held a bottle up for the Lieutenant's benefit. "Why, Jake, I do believe he likes us."

Laughing heartily Philips replied, "You know, you might just be right."

"What's that?"

"He really is a sentimental old cuss," he chucked.

The duo sat in silence as the Lieutenant retraced his route towards Seattle. The Celebrity negotiated the hairpin turns with relative ease. About ten minutes into the drive Philips noticed a dark pair of Ford Explorers that seemed to be following them. The SUVs stayed a respectable distance back. When Philips reached the first straight stretch the SUVs made no attempt at passing the slower vehicle. Five minutes later, the vehicles were still behind them, and they made no attempt at overtaking the SEAL's vehicle. The hair on the back of Philips' neck was starting to stand on end. He had learned a long time ago to trust his instincts, and those instincts were screaming at him right now!

Twelve

"Don't look now, but I think we've got company!" Philips alerted his partner.

"What, you didn't pay the bill?" McKay responded sarcastically as he attempted to look over his shoulder.

"Face forward!" the Lieutenant barked, "I don't want to spook 'em just yet."

"So what's it look like?"

"Couple of SUV's, been with us a ways... They just seemed to be hanging back there, maybe watching where we're heading."

"Well then, call me when our friends decide to drop in and say 'Hi'," McKay replied as he slid down into the seat as if to catch a nap.

As the car rounded a sharp curve the SUV's were momentarily lost from sight. The Lieutenant decided to test a theory and gave the gas pedal another inch; the spirited six cylinder responded instantaneously and opened the distance between the car and the curve. Ten seconds later, their pursuers rounded the corner and discovered they had lagged behind.

The first SUV's driver responded by down shifting and

giving his vehicle plenty of gas. The Explorers began to gain on the SEALs, smaller, lesser-powered rental. However, the car surged ahead again when Philips gave the accelerator another inch of pedal. The two Explorers confirmed the Lieutenant's suspicions as they increased their speed to match the celebrity's. Negotiating another turn, Philips took a quick second to glimpse in the mirror. His pursuers were maintaining a distance of about a hundred yards with no attempt at overtaking them. Taking another hairpin turn, he lost sight of the suspected pursuers until they appeared right on cue.

"What do you s'pose they want?" McKay broke the silence.

"I don't think it's directions!" Philips responded as he turned into another curve. "Hang tight, here comes a really nasty one." The car did a slight fishtail as Philips negotiated the curve thirty miles over the posted limit. "Let's see them do that!"

Their pursuers followed suit. They did not hesitate to take the curve just as recklessly; but the second vehicle lost it momentarily and drove partially off the pavement, sending up a gravel rooster tail. The driver was good; he was able to regain control and direct his vehicle safely back onto the asphalt.

"You'd better think of something else. They can do that!"

"Why do I have to do all thinking?"

"You're the Lieutenant! Remember, I'm low man on the totem pole. If you'll hold'er steady a moment I think I have an idea," McKay remarked as he tore off his jacket and tossed it into the back. While leaning over the seat, the SEAL grabbed a couple of the Ed Teach bottles. "Want some?" He offered a bottle to his friend.

"This is a silly time for a drink," the Lieutenant said offhandedly as he concentrated on his driving. "We're coming into a really nasty section of road. I'm afraid we're about to be out horsepowered and out maneuvered."

"Listen, when you get around the next corner slow 'er down as soon as we're out of sight." McKay instructed as he rolled down his window. Tearing off a corner of his shirt, he opened a bottle of rum, looked at his partner, and took a big swig from the bottle. Taking a strip of shirt, he stuffed it into the bottle's neck. Looking over to Philips with a puppy-dog face, he meekly retorted, "I hate to see this all go to waste."

Philips understood exactly what his friend had in mind. Improvisation was one of the traits that all SEALs must have; the ability to make do with what was on hand. The following vehicles' routine had not varied; they still maintained their distance. When he had safely negotiated the curve, the SEAL pulled the emergency brake and hit the brake pedal as hard as he could. Because of the wet pavement, the car unexpectedly spun around and stopped in the oncoming lane. Swiftly, McKay pulled himself up and sat in the open window. Carefully lighting the crude bomb, he waited for his first victim to round the corner.

The occupants of the first SUV to round the corner got the surprise of their lives. The little blue Celebrity was going no more than ten miles an hour towards them with a figure propped up in the window. As soon as the pursuing vehicle was abreast of the rental, McKay tossed his makeshift bomb over the top of the Celebrity as if tossing a newspaper. Without waiting for results, he screamed into the window, "Punch it!" Working on instinct, Philips had not waited; he'd already put his foot to the floor when McKay tossed the Molotov cocktail. With rubber squealing and the engine racing, the little car shot forward.

The homemade bomb seemed to float in the air forever. In a vain attempt to dodge the inevitable, the vehicle's driver slammed on his brakes and swerved to miss the bottle. McKay's aim was true, his primitive bomb tumbled end over end until it struck the pavement a foot in front of the skidding vehicle. The bottle exploded into a thousand shards of glass, raining flaming rum over the hood of the vehicle. With a whoosh, the Explorers' entire front-end caught fire.

Now, the second vehicle had cleared the corner and just missed colliding with the accelerating Celebrity as it raced back into the curve. Swerving to avoid the stopped SUV, its occupants were in time to see the Explorer catch fire and their teammates bail out. Pausing briefly to pick up their two comrades, the second Explorer pulled a U-turn and headed back into the curve.

"Yah-Hoo!" An elated McKay shouted a war whoop above the sound of the Celebrity's racing engine. "Did you see the expression on their faces when they got my present?"

"Yeah, but mark my words, these guys are going to be mad as hornets now." No sooner had the Lieutenant spoke his prophetic words when the remaining vehicle rounded the corner at a high rate of speed, with the front passenger leaning out the window brandishing what appeared to be an automatic weapon.

"Get down!" Philips ordered, sliding himself down in the seat to make as small a target as possible. "We're in for it now," he remarked grimly as the first bullets struck the trunk, stitching small divots across the lid.

"Why don't these guys pick on someone their own size?" McKay complained as he lit another cocktail. "See how you like this!" he shouted out the window, tossing the second bomb towards the oncoming vehicle. This time the cocktail exploded harmlessly alongside the speeding SUV.

In that same instant another volley of automatic fire struck the defenseless car. With his foot all the way to the floor, Philips was coaxing as much power from the vehicle as he could. He was considering returning to his grandfather's house when another burst struck the car and shattered the windshield, showering the occupants with shards of safety glass. The right rear tire was next, exploding when a bullet punctured the rubber tread. With the car losing momentum and sparks trailing from the missing tire, Philips did the only thing he could think of. He gave the car a hard right onto the logging road that accessed the clear-cut McKay had commented on previously. Knowing their pursuers were only seconds behind, he figured they might have a better chance on foot.

Bringing the car to a standstill at the edge of the clearing, Philips urged his friend to follow as he dashed towards the fallen logs looking for an escape. Following a close second McKay had little time to ponder what the Lieutenant might come up with. The SEALs were forced to weave in and around the fallen logs and large stumps.

Four goons jumped from the Explorer as it came to a halt

behind the bullet-riddled rental. Dashing down the road into the clear-cut they could see their targets halfway across the expanse. Urging his men on, the leader fired a short burst in the general direction of the fleeing SEALs.

"Did you hear that?" asked Philips anxiously as he hit the ground behind an eight-foot diameter cedar log.

"You think these guys will listen to reason?" wondered McKay as he hunkered down beside his friend.

"Not on your life!"

"Then giving up the map is out of the question?"

"Are you daft?"

"Just checking. So what's the plan?"

"We can't stay here. I've got an idea though, follow me," Philips instructed as he moved in a crouched position towards a couple of trucks that were parked at the far end of the clearing.

Having no better suggestion, McKay silently followed. Keeping a low profile, the pair made their way across the clearing. Working silently from one felled log to another, the SEALs closed in on the logging equipment. Occasionally, the Lieutenant would stop to check on their pursuer's progress. Each time he looked back, he observed his adversaries stumbling and swearing over the obstacle course created by the loggers. This gave him some satisfaction, but the goons continued to make steady progress towards the trucks.

The SEALs held up fifteen yards from the logging truck. It was a large yellow Mack with twin vertical chrome exhaust stacks that climbed to just above the cab. The truck was approximately half-loaded with seven large cedar logs. The logs themselves were draped from one u-shaped device just behind the cab, called log bunks, to another set, which sat atop the eight large tires of the rear trailer. The suspended logs were the only things that connected the trucks' trailer section to the cab. A series of cables were suspended from a steel bar or tongue which tethered the trailer to the truck. Black smoke rolled from the exhaust pipes indicating the truck was idling.

Right behind the logging truck sat another large truck. This truck had a thirty-foot tower that was stabilized by guy wires radiating out in all directions. It was used to hoist logs onto the transportation truck. Evidently the loggers had vacated the site upon hearing gunfire, leaving a two-ton log suspended fifteen feet above the ground.

The last ten yards, offered no protection whatsoever. "If only we could get outta here," Philips said aloud. Looking over his shoulder, he could see their adversaries working closer. "Any ideas Mike?"

"What about that?" McKay asked, indicating the idling truck, as he anxiously watched their pursuers move steadily towards their location.

"My sentiments exactly. Think we can make it without getting hit?"

"Just watch me!" McKay exclaimed as he checked in the direction of the goons one last time. Springing to his feet, he sprinted for the truck with Philips right on his heels.

The whine of bullets could be heard striking the earth but the pair had no time to dally. McKay rounded the front of the truck just as a hail of bullets stitched a neat pattern across the dirty yellow fender next to his head. Meanwhile, Philips was busy climbing into the cab as another burst chewed its way along the logs.

Slamming the door shut, the big SEAL was offered some protection within the cab. Scanning the wraparound dashboard, which mimicked the cockpit of a 737, everything seemed to be in order. As he depressed the clutch and gunned the monster diesel, a thick cloud of black smoke belched from the exhaust stacks and shot skyward. As Philips shifted into first gear he shouted above the Mack's throaty roar, "Hang on Mike, I'm getting us the hell outta of here." He mashed the pedal to the floor and popped the clutch.

With McKay still climbing through the passenger door, the big rig's tires dug into the mud and the truck lurched forward. Their pursuers had finally cleared the logs and all four opened fire with a continuous stream of lead. Most of the rounds chewed large splintered craters into the logs but a few managed to strike harmlessly at the back of the cab. Intended to shield loggers from whiplashing cables, the cab was protected by a heavy gauge wire mesh. Philips shifted into second gear as the truck picked up momentum. He pointed the mighty machine towards a second road he had spotted earlier, hoping that it would lead back to the highway.

The Lieutenant's hunch was right. The second road entered the highway about a mile farther down the hill from the first. With the Mack gaining speed on the paved roadway Philips began to relax, as he did not see any sign of pursuit. Grinning to his partner he inquired, "You okay?"

"Nothing that a few Band Aides won't fix," he replied rubbing his elbow. "What about the book?"

Philips reached into his peacoat and produced the bundle for McKay to see. "Too bad about the rum."

"If I ever find out who these guys are, I'll send them a bill."

Rounding a corner, they were surprised to see the still-burning SUV where it had been abandoned. A group of onlookers stood around gawking as several burly men sprayed the fire with portable extinguishers. Passing the scene Philips did not slow down. Instead, he gave the rig more fuel to increase the distance between them and their would-be assassins. When they had reached another straightway, he shifted the truck into a higher gear, grinding them in the process.

"So what's next?" McKay sighed.

The Lieutenant was slow to reply as he concentrated on manhandling the ungainly vehicle through a series of tight turns. "I guess we stop at the first state police station we find," he finally replied as the truck hit another straightway. Double-checking the mirror he was not surprised to see the remaining SUV again. "Mike, they're back!"

"Don't these guys ever give up?" McKay complained as he studied the Explorer through the passenger mirror.

"It appears not," Philips answered, "This looks to be a case of David and Goliath now. All we have to do is stay ahead of 'em. We're bound to find some help further down the road."

"I hope you know what you're doing." McKay responded

with a note of concern in his voice.

"What else can we do?" Philips philosophized as he turned the mammoth diesel into a new curve.

"How 'bout we call in reinforcements?" the petty officer suggested as he unhooked a microphone that was attached to the truck's CB radio.

"Why didn't I think of that?"

"Breaker... Breaker... Is anybody out there? We're being pursued by a couple of guys with some really nasty guns," he shouted into the microphone.

The radio squawked, and a distant voice answered their plea. "This is Washington State Patrol Trooper Brown, how about a location? Come back..."

"We're on Chuckanut Drive heading south..."

"You stay right where you're at. I'll be there in five minutes."

"Are you kidding? This'll be over in two!" McKay shouted.

The sound of gunfire could be heard over the throaty roar of the diesel, the logs still absorbing the brunt of the assault. "You think they'll shoot out the tires?" Philips asked.

"They'd better not, I don't feel like walking," McKay was quick to respond as another volley struck the back of the cab. The lead did not penetrate the protective mesh. As they were rounding a switch back, Philips had to down shift to maintain control of the vehicle. Suddenly, their pursuers put up a wall of lead, peppering the vehicle from front to rear. One lucky shot parted an air hose that ran suspended under the trailer tongue. This one-in-a-million shot hit the rig in one of its few vulnerable spots. The parted air hose gave off a hissing noise that could be heard in the cab. No longer able to keep air pressure to the rear brakes, the tires locked up.

As the tires locked up a bluish cloud of acrid smoke was emitted from between and around the rubber. A high pitched screech could be heard over the clamor of bullets and the throaty diesel as the rear tires laid down a patch of burnt rubber seventy-five yards long. The big Mack was now pulling the dead weight of the logs and the rear trucks.

Endless rounds of gunfire continued to strike harmlessly along the logs, chipping splinters and chunks of bark into the air. One burst stitched a pattern across the driver's door taking out the handle, mirrors and turn signal. "Shit!" muttered Philips as another series of rounds punched fist-sized holes into the left smokestack.

With the Mack losing speed, McKay became concerned and asked, "What's going on? Why we slowing down? We otta fuel or something?"

Tapping the air pressure gauge on the dash the Lieutenant answered quietly, "It appears we've taken a hit to the brake system. I no longer have control of the rear trailer."

"What does that mean?"

"It means this diesel's not strong enough to pull the entire load while the brakes are locked up."

"Is there anything we can do?"

Scanning the dash for answers, all Philips could do was shake his head. The rig was down to less than fifty miles an hour. With the SUV gaining rapidly, the SEAL scanned the dash again for an answer. On the dash's lower right panel Philips spotted a button that looked to be an emergency hydraulic release for the hook. Without a moment's hesitation he disengaged the switch. Nothing happened!

"What's that?" asked McKay inquisitively. Before he could reply, the big truck struck a very large pothole in the pavement. The sharp upward movement disengaged the tongue from its position in the hook. For just a moment the tongue was suspended in air by safety chains designed to prevent a runaway. Because of the tongue's weight, it dropped down to the pavement with a dull thud.

"And, what was that?" McKay asked, as he stuck his head out the window in time to see the rear log bunks starting to slide down the logs. "This is gonna be good!" he urged, "Give 'er all the gas you got!"

"I don't see how it will do any good," the Lieutenant responded as he complied with his friend's order. The truck jerked, as it sprang free of the rear wheels drag. Suddenly the cab jumped ahead as if a gigantic rubber band had launched them down the road. As the rear tires finally blew out from the friction, the trailer totally disengaged from the logs that had been suspended between the bunks. The tongue dug a huge gouge into the pavement, propelling the wheels into the air end over end several times before coming to rest in the middle of the road.

Without the support of the rear bunks, the unrestrained logs vaulted into the air. With loud 'tonking' sounds, the giant tinker toys collided with each other as they unloaded themselves from the escaping truck. Several came to rest cross-wise in the road; while one, weakened by a fire eons ago, splintered in its center. The heartwood was stubborn and still held the mangled ends together; thus, as the once great tree hit the pavement, the upper part of the log came crashing down, almost folding the log in two. With a cloud of splinters, the vaulting pylon crushed the skidding Explorer with a sickening sound of screams, screeching metal and splintering wood. The remaining logs rolled off the road into the bushes.

Philips stopped the truck and ran back to the wreck site. The devastation was total; the log lay lengthwise down the middle of the SUV, pancaking it to the pavement. A hiss of steam was issuing forth from the engine compartment as the remnants of the engine slowly cooled. There was obviously no hope for the vehicle occupants. Philips slowly walked around the scene of carnage wondering if the map was really worth it.

A distant siren could be heard getting closer as a state trooper rounded a curve and proceeded to pull up next to the bullet-riddled truck. Acting instinctively, Trooper Brown drew his weapon and ordered McKay and Philips to lie on the ground. The pair complied, and after they were handcuffed, began to relate their story to the unbelieving officer.

Thirteen

At that very moment Clifford Wardon was having problems of his own. After spending a couple of peaceful days with his parents in Brooklyn, He'd proceeded to Washington as instructed. Instructions notwithstanding, spending several hours in the archives was not Wardon's idea of a good time.

To further his anxiety, he'd been kept waiting thirty-five minutes. The reception area served numerous offices on the fourth floor of the National Archives and Research Administration or NARA, building in Washington D.C. Wardon had been instructed by the Under Secretary to arrive promptly at 3 P.M., and look up a Charlie Lysander, the assistant curator. After giving his name to security, the officer asked the petty officer to make himself comfortable in an overstuffed couch that seemed to swallow him up.

An elderly woman, not too much different from the one that had helped out in Seattle, checked on him once. She announced that Mr. Lysander was preoccupied, but should be free shortly. After staring for some time at the same wall map of Washington DC circa 1850, Wardon let his mind wander over the events of the past two weeks. He didn't notice a short thin person approach him. “Petty Officer Wardon?” The stranger asked with a high-pitched squeaky voice.

Coming back to earth, Wardon looked to see who had addressed him. Before him stood a very short man who was dressed in a blue blazer and tan slacks. The blazer had a pocket protector with several pencils and pens protruding for from it. Perched atop his left ear was an unlit cigarette, while spectacles were pushed up into his brown curly hair. The curator had a stack of computer printouts tucked under his left arm while carrying a coffee cup in his right. The petty officer had seen quite a few “geeks” in high school and this one looked to be president of the club. “That’s right,” he answered, not really believing his eyes.

“Sorry for the delay, some pressing matters in Charlottesville.”

Standing, and extending his hand momentarily, and then feeling foolish, Wardon looked down upon the scholar and asked, “Charlie Lysander?”

“Yes, you’re exactly how Mr. Parsons described you. If you please, follow me.” The little guy showed no sign of intimidation as he turned and walked through a door with a sign that proclaimed, ‘Authorized Personnel Only.’

Not wanting to be left behind, Wardon hustled after the curator. The door opened into an immense room, with row upon row of what looked like bookshelves or stacks from a college library. As Wardon caught up to Lysander, the wiry academic spoke up, “I see you have friends in high places.” In the same breath he continued on, “Here, at the National Archives we safeguard our nation’s history by overseeing the preservation and management of all Federal records. We have thirty-three facilities that hold twenty-five million cubic feet of textual materials, and four billion pieces of paper from the executive, judicial and legislative branches of government.”

Wardon was impressed with the diminutive nerd’s extensive knowledge about the facility. As he tried to express his wonderment, Wardon was cut off before he could speak.

“We not only store and maintain national records, our

private sector contains some 300,000 reels of film and another 200,000 sound and video recordings. With more than nine million aerial photos, five million charts, maps and fourteen million still pictures and photos, we are the largest repository of celluloid in the world." Stopping at a long bank of cubicles, much like the cubbies used in college study halls, Lysander continued, "This is our Central Research Room. From here you can access the millions of data sets that we have stored within our mainframes," the little man paused to catch his breath.

Using the brief interlude, Wardon was finally able to enunciate a thought. "I had no idea of the immense size of the archives," he paused and then continued, "Would I be able to find reference to little-known treaties and such in here?"

"If there's a reference to it, we'd have it," assured Lysander. "What we have here," pointing to a computer within the cubbie, "Is NAILS, which is short for National Archival Information Locator. Once you find what you're looking for, you can print out the reference. Then we can locate the original hard copy, if need be. They're stored in specially built boxes, which are fireproof, waterproof and acid free. Temperature, humidity and light are carefully controlled, you know."

"I had no idea. Was that the rows of boxes we passed through?" Wardon queried.

"Correct, however, we call those stacks." Lysander continued on, "If you need copies of any original document, I will assist you."

"Don't you have an assistant or something?" asked Wardon. "I'm not sure that I warrant the attention of someone of your stature," he continued, not wanting to let on that Lysander's high-pitched voice was a bit annoying.

"I have very concise instructions, I'm the only one to assist you. I don't know who you know, but he sure knows how to pull strings," muttered the assistant curator.

Sitting down at the closest computer, the SEAL asked, "So what do I have to do?"

Setting the computer printouts and coffee cup down, Lysander reached over Wardon's shoulder and hit the enter key, which brought up the main menu. "From here, all you have to do is enter a series of queries or keywords in the search bar. Such as JFK." He said as he typed the letters quickly. Almost instantly, 9862 entries were noted on JFK. "Then highlight any entry you choose and a brief description of the document will appear," the curator instructed as he highlighted an entry halfway down the page. NAILS took all of two seconds to bring up a file that was a reproduction of Kennedy's first inaugural address.

"Impressive, very impressive, it looks like not all our tax dollars goes to waste after all!" Wardon quipped. Pointing to a series of numbers and letters at the bottom of the page, the petty officer inquired, "Is there a particular meaning to the sequence here?"

"That's our in-house reference number. The first four digits signifies year, the next four is month and date, followed by letters indicating the hard copy's location. The document you see here is coded 1961-01-29-WNRC, meaning it is stored at the Washington National Records Center located in Suitland, Maryland."

"And the reference under that?"

"You mean 26A-192?"

"Yes."

"That translates into row 26, north side, bin 192," the curator was quick to point out. "Now, where would you like to begin your search?"

"How 'bout the Mills Transfer?" the black petty officer asked as he started to type. The computer hummed for several seconds and then displayed a couple of entries. The first was coded 1942-02-7-WNRC and the second was 1953-04-19-WNRC.

Excitedly; Wardon double-clicked on the first reference and was presented with a copy of Lieutenant Commander Harold P. Saunders' log entries as captain of the *Sealion.* They detailed acceptance, storage, transportation and subsequent transfer to the United States State Department in Brisbane, Australia, nineteen crates of gold transported under extreme secrecy. The entries were in the typical sterile naval fashion. All Wardon had to go with were date of entry and a brief notation. The crates were loaded between the hours of 0300 and 0500 on the morning of February 3rd 1942. While enroute, a sentry was posted twenty-four hours a day in the aft torpedo room where the boxes were secured. Upon reaching Brisbane, a contingent of individuals from the State Department was waiting at the pier to receive the crates. In Commander Saunders' last log entry dated the 7th, he indicated that Commissioner Sayer was in the company of the State Department when he turned over the shipment.

The next entry was even more ambiguous than the first. Before Wardon was a newspaper clipping from the South China Morning Post reporting on a radio broadcast from North Korea.

Resumption of Korean peace talks possible!

Aberdeen -- A broadcast from North Korea yesterday as intercepted by the BBC International is reminiscent of the 1952 broadcast by General Ridgeway asking the North Koreans to sit down at the peace table. The broadcast aired at exactly 12:01 P.M. local time, and is reproduced in its entirety below.

"Attention! Attention! This broadcast is intended for the United Nations forces currently in conflict with our North Korean comrades. If you please, and at your earliest convenience, the North Koreans would be interested in resuming talks at Panimunjom. The senseless slaughter of innocent civilians must come to an end! We are willing to concede certain issues if the United Nations is willing to negotiate in good faith. America must stand up and be accountable for its deeds within this action. Years ago, with the Mills agreement, America was bold in its leadership against the Japanese. Now we are asking that they use the same leadership and resume talks with an open mind as to the commitment and integrity of the Korean people. Let's end this slaughter and allow our soldiers to go home to their families and loved ones. We will await your response, the future is in your hands."

We may only speculate as to when talks may resume, but this reporter has it on good faith that an American contingent will report back to Panimunjom within a fortnight. There has been no further communication from General Kim Il Sung.
By Slick Thompsen

"So Moe, what does this mean by "Mills Agreement?"" Wardon asked aloud, showing the affection he was starting to feel for the little nerdy curator.

"Who's Moe?" queried Lysander as he looked up. "I have no idea, there's no cross reference," he continued on in obvious frustration.

"Hows 'bout a recording of the broadcast?" Wardon suggested with little hope of success.

"Nope, no recording here," Lysander added, "just the newspaper clipping from Hong Kong."

Typing several entries with no results, Wardon remarked, "There doesn't seem to be a cross reference to the peace negotiations. Am I doing something wrong?"

Pushing past Wardon, Lysander was quick to respond, "Here, let me give it a try," as he started typing keyboard commands at a lightning pace. Screens would pop-up and then disappear as the curator entered and then re-entered information, with no results. "This is really unusual, you'd think there'd be more information. When did you say the treaty was signed?"

"Spring of '42, why?"

"No record of that either."

"How come? Aren't all documents pertaining to our government kept here?"

"Supposed to be, maybe the treaty was never ratified," suggested the curator.

"Wouldn't there still be notes, or something?"

"You think."

"What's next?" Wardon sat back and watched the irate scholar work his magic on the computer. For the next two hours, screen after screen came and went as Lysander worked every possible angle to get more information on the Mills Transfer. Every effort netted the same negative results. All the while Wardon had a growing admiration for the little guy as he began to appreciate the impossibility of the task.

Dusk was falling when Lysander finally looked up from the monitor in exasperation. "I have tried everything I know to find any references or cross references to the Mills Transfer with no luck." The perplexed man proclaimed, then asked. "Could the treaty be logged as something else?"

"The information we have indicates the Mills Transfer, nothing else."

"I-I just don't understand it," said the bewildered man. "Other than the two references here, there is absolutely nothing else. There should be more."

"Well, that's better than nothing. Could you please get me copies of what we have?"

"No problem," commented Lysander as he punched a couple of keys, seconds later the printer began to hum. "It'll be just a sec." A minute later he had reproduced copies of the two references and handed them to Wardon.

"Well Moe, I guess I'll be going. If you think of anything else feel free to give it a try and send the results to this address," Wardon said as he jotted down Philips address and phone number. He tucked the copies into a briefcase. "I thank you for your time and patience." With that, Wardon retraced his steps out of the building and walked towards his hotel. As the SEAL braved the early evening chill for the short walk, he considered what he had learned.

Back in his room, Wardon phoned Philips to check in, but only got his voicemail. Leaving a brief message with the service, the SEAL decided to catch dinner and a movie. Again taking to the streets, Wardon found a cozy restaurant where he ordered prime rib with all the trimmings. He followed the meal with a leisurely stroll down Washington's cherry tree-lined boulevards. Wardon was enjoying himself with the chance to stretch his legs after spending an entire day in the archives.

Deciding to skip the movie, he headed back towards his hotel with the intention of catching the Lieutenant before he turned in for the night. Upon entering his room, Wardon stopped dead in his tracks; something was amiss. He didn't know quite what it was but the room was just too silent. A quick check of the bedroom showed nothing, but a light was visible beneath the closed bathroom door. Quietly opening the door, he was surprised to see a tall lithe blond female dressed in a black leather skirt with long legs sitting on the toilet reading his files from earlier in the day. Stepping into the room, Wardon commented, “Interesting reading, isn’t it?”

The mystery lady looked up from her reading with shock in her eyes, “What! You’re supposed to be...” she hesitated for a moment. Then a seductive smile spread across her face. Before Wardon could question her further, there was a sickening crunch on the back his skull, followed instantaneously by a bright flash before the big man’s eyes as he saw stars. Crying out in pain, he slowly sank to his knees as darkness enveloped him.

Sometime later, a groaning Wardon was dimly aware of bright lights. Slowly coming to, he found himself lying on the bathroom floor with all the lights on. As he tried to sit up, nausea swept over him. Lying back down on the cool tile, Wardon closed his eyes and waited for the feeling to pass. Attempting to stand, he was assaulted by a thundering throb that radiated from a knot just above his left ear. He tenderly examined the spot with his fingertips; and found a knot the size of a silver dollar. “Shit!” The SEAL grimaced as he lay down again.

After a while, he was able to crawl from the bathroom into his bedroom, only to discover the room had been completely ransacked. Working his way to the bed, Wardon was able to make a couple of phone calls. In the first call, he explained to Philips what had transpired. The second call was to room service for an ice pack.

The following morning, Wardon filed a complaint with the local DC Police Department, after which he proceeded back to the archives. Chuck Lysander was dressed in the same suit as his previous visit and was as chipper as ever. After explaining the loss of the documents the night before, Wardon requested new copies. Lysander was more than eager to run off another set.

“Using notes I jotted down yesterday it’s a piece of cake to punch up the articles,” informed the curator as he retyped the codes into NAILS. After a moment’s hesitation, the computer screen began to flash again. When the screen stabilized, they saw the results were different form what they’d seen the day before. A surprised Lysander exclaimed, “No! This can’t be true!”

“What’s up, Moe?” the petty officer asked casually.

“They’re gone!”

“What’s gone?” asked Wardon with a little more interest.

“Why, the articles about the Transfer,” informed the awestruck curator.

“How can that be?” queried Wardon.

“It’s impossible! It’s just impossible, it takes an act of Congress to delete something from NAILS,” exclaimed the panicked Lysander.

“Well, it looks like Congress was up late last night!” Wardon said smartly, as he turned quickly and exited out the hallway.

A further check by Lysander would confirm the hard copies had been removed from the storage trays. All traces of the documents had been eradicated. It was as if the Mills Transfer never existed!

Fourteen

Beijing, China

Premier Xian had a migraine. The aspirin that he had taken two hours previously did nothing to quell the pounding behind his eyes. Migraines were nothing new, he'd had them before, but this one was a dandy, one for the record books. Its onset had been caused by sheer exhaustion. Xian had spent several sleepless nights trying to decide who would replace the slain ministers; migraine or not, he had to appoint replacements. Rubbing his temples lightly, the Premier closed his eyes to try and focus on the task at hand.

Defense Minister Chan had just left his office where he had lobbied for a couple of old party hard-liners who Xian was completely against. Xian enjoyed Chan's visits less and less, and resented the Minister for interfering with affairs that had nothing to do with his post. Lately the Minister had taken to overstepping his bounds on several issues. As long as he held a power base, Xian would have to ignore it, for his time would come.

When Premier Xian had entered politics, his father passed

on a puzzling piece of advice. “My son, keep your allies close to you at all times, but keep your enemies even closer.” With all the political intrigue that governments inherently have, Premier Xian took his father’s words to heart. During the first years of his tenure, Xian gradually brought people that he trusted into politics. He surrounded himself with individuals with whom he could entrust his very life. As ministers retired, he would appoint younger, more energetic people who worked towards the betterment of China. They were not necessarily strong political figures.

Premier Xian had inherited Chan when he took office. At the time Chan was an under Secretary in the Defense Department. Through the years the Premier was forced to tolerate him, as Chan was in political favor with some of the important figures in the Chinese Congress. A couple of years back when the aging Defense Minister announced his retirement, it was only natural that Xian appoint Chan to the post. Though he did not trust him, Xian took his father’s words to heart and decided that the Defense Ministry was the best place to keep an eye on Chan. Besides, all military operations still needed his approval.

A knock at the door interrupted the Premier’s musing. A half second later it was flung open to admit a little girl dressed in the traditional dark green pajama-type garb characteristic of the Communist military, followed by her mother. The strain on Xian’s face suddenly melted away as he stood from his desk and scooped his young granddaughter up for a big bear hug. Reaching out with his left arm he enclosed his only child and hugged the two women in his life. “What brings you two here?” he asked as he released his daughter and granddaughter.

“Mommy said we could stop by on our way to the zoo,” the wide-eyed youngster with ponytails exclaimed.

Showing her daughter to a chair, Hui Woo, the only child to the Premier of the Peoples Republic of China, was a villain in her own right. Within a country with a population crisis, it had been necessary to enact laws allowing only one child per household. Space wasn’t the problem, as China had plenty of that. It had become increasingly difficult to feed its massive population, which was growing by 10,000 people a day. Each year China was forced to import more rice to feed her rapidly multiplying population.

When her first son was born, Hui told her father that, despite the law, she was going to become pregnant again. Against Chinese custom, she wanted a girl! Therefore, without her father's, consent the daughter of the most powerful individual in China had three lovely children, two boys and a girl. Xian was sure this would be an extremely unpopular decision within the Communist Party. The Party however, did an about face and embraced the stubborn Hui for her defiance of her father. He was glad she did so, because his granddaughter had become his prized possession.

Xian always enjoyed any time he could be with his daughter and her children away from politics and the public eye. The first family enjoyed notoriety, which was second to none in an otherwise restricted society. Treated much like the royal families of England, the popular Hui and her family were constantly harassed by the press bombarding them with questions about their daily lives. In recent years it had become necessary to hire bodyguards to protect the family from thousands of fans who waited impatiently for glimpses of the Premier's grandchildren. Their popularity grew tenfold when Xian relaxed the broadcasting guidelines. Now, like celebrities worldwide, China's first family had to steal fleeting moments alone whenever the opportunity arose.

Smoothing out the wrinkles in her suit, Hui stood to face her powerful father, "Papa, I have to give an interview this afternoon. Could you do me a favor and watch Zhang-Mai?"

"What about the governess?" the smiling Premier asked.

Stepping closer to her father, Hui straightened the lapel on his suit, "Why father, you know it's her day off and the boys are fishing with Hung. Besides, she would rather be with you," she said looking deeply into her father's face. For the first time Hui noticed the stress lines across his forehead and radiating out from the corners of his eyes. A clouded look spread across her face. "Papa! Are you okay?" she asked in a concerned voice.

"It's the demands of the office. How long has it been since I've had personal time, six maybe eight months?" Wanting to change the subject, the weary Premier offered, "I'll be happy to watch Zhang for a few hours. We can take a walk in the garden and enjoy ourselves."

Kissing her father on the forehead, Hui cautioned, "You take it easy, China is counting on you. Have one of the stewards serve up lunch and watch Zhang, I'll be back in three hours." Not waiting for a response from her father, Hui exited the executive office.

Taking the opportunity to set aside the duties of state, Xian was eager to take his granddaughter on a tour of the extensive gardens behind the executive office building. Though the fall had been relatively warm there was still a crispness in the air. The elderly statesman made sure Zhang was bundled snugly in her jacket, while donning a greatcoat for himself. Taking his granddaughters' hand, the pair stepped out into the brisk mid-December air.

Cherry, maple, several kinds of pine, and both large and miniature bonsai trees occupied the gardens. A stone walkway meandered through various settings with fountains and goldfish pools. Concrete statues of tigers and pandas stood a silent vigil while mini pagoda lanterns, spaced every three yards or so, decorated both sides of the walkway. Lotus and bougainvillea in their wintry slumber competed with ivy still clinging to the walls surrounding the garden. Stone benches were strategically placed throughout the garden. One such bench contained an effigy of Quan Yin, the goddess of compassion and help for a difficult world. The garden was one of Xian's favorite places. He would seek solace and solitude here whenever the pressures of his position seemed insurmountable.

In the back, farthest away from the hustle of the executive building, stood a round doorway. The doorway was the entrance to an enchanting world. An enclosed grotto depicting various mythological deities from Chinese folklore had been assembled here. Brightly painted tigers and dragons seemed to dance alongside colorful figurines of rulers, priests and human beings.

Miniature pagodas stood atop dwarf mountains populated with several kinds of bamboo. Even tinnier streams ran downhill into a large pond populated with goldfish. The entire hill was covered with Japanese maples, sans their leaves, which gave the shrine a most mystical flair.

The grotto was divided into different dioramas depicting ancient beliefs. Each setting told a tale similar to Aesop's fables. Heaven, the Ten Courts of Hell and the Neptune Palace were recreated in miniature. Tiny mythological figures addressed topics such as virtue, adultery and death. At one time, grottos such as this dotted the Chinese countryside. Their function was to remind the young of the various lessons of life. Slated for demolition, it had taken Xian's power as General Secretary to have the shrine dismantled and reassembled in the garden.

A slight wind rustled fallen leaves about their feet as grandfather and granddaughter proceeded into the monument. It was in such a place, sitting on a similar stone bench, recanting the ancient stories which he had been forced to learn in his youth, that Premier Xian first questioned the legacy that communism was forging for China. With a history so rich in color, why were today's politicians trying to suppress it? It was a pity today's children did not learn of the ancient beliefs, for it was those lessons that guided even the most humble of individuals.

With his granddaughter nestled comfortably on his lap, Xian told the story of how a peasant girl named Mulan helped save China from the Mongol hordes. For twelve years she fought alongside her male counterparts, never exposing her female gender. After the Mongols had been defeated, Mulan revealed her true self and received a heroes' welcome. When he finished, the elderly world leader hugged his granddaughter and noticed for the first time in weeks that his migraine was gone.

"Shi," he thought, *"Like Mulan, he was doing the right thing for China. Timing, Everything depended on timing. It had to be perfect. He finally had the support in Congress he needed. He'd selected Christmas Day, because of its significance to the Western world, to drop his bombshell. Christmas day signified peace to most of the rest of the world. Was that not what he was*

about to do? Bring peace to the rest of the world." Lost in his thoughts, Premier Xian did not notice that he was no longer alone.

"Excuse me, General Secretary, it is time to take your medication." A white-clad orderly stood with his head bowed humbly, respecting the leader's privacy. He held a tray, which contained a glass of water and a small envelope containing a powdered medication.

Standing, the Premier approached the orderly and accepted the glass of water into which he poured the powdered ibuprofen. Drinking the water down, the Premier dismissed the orderly with a wave of his hand. Sitting back down, he took his granddaughter into his arms. He began to recite the poem of the battle for Red Cliffs, a poignant tale of how General Juan Fe overcame insurmountable odds against an ancient enemy along the banks of the Yangtze.

As the afternoon passed, Xian became lost in ancient battles of a bygone era. The message was always the same, good overcame evil. As ancient warriors thundered across the landscape on majestic horses, China would always be saved. The hero would come marching home to a grateful nation. For the moment in Xian's mind, he was that hero. Looking at his granddaughter, the Premier ran his hand through her hair as he hugged her sleeping form. Sometime during the battle of Red Cliffs, Zhang had drifted off. That did not dissuade Xian, who continued to recite the ancient poem.

In the waning minutes of the afternoon, as he was finishing up his last story, the migraine came back. Something new, however, accompanied the blinding pain behind his eyes, and he experienced a dimness in vision. The shrine had an almost mystical haze around it. The Premier tried to focus on one of the larger dragons, but it hurt his head to concentrate. Setting his granddaughter on the stone seat, Xian stood and immediately stumbled back to his perch. The weakness in his right leg alarmed him.

At that moment he could hear his daughter calling from the walkway, but was unable to understand her words.

Attempting to stand again, Xian collapsed in front of the grotto he so dearly cherished. Hui rushed to his side to offer aid. Screaming for one of the security officers, she sat sobbing on the cold cobblestones cradling her father's head with her tears falling onto his face.

Premier Xian stared almost blankly up into his daughter's eyes. He could feel her tears landing about his cheeks. Trying to mouth words that would not come, the General Secretary lay disabled in her lap. As darkness began to creep over the scene Xian felt himself relaxing for the first time in months. He felt himself drifting, the pressures of the office were no longer a concern. As darkness overcame him, Xian felt sorry for the pain he knew his family would endure. Then the General Secretary of the Communist Party and Premier of the People's Republic of China lapsed into a coma.

Fifteen

Manila Bay

Captain Robert Chester Foute sat in his chair on the bridge of America's newest aircraft carrier the *U.S.S. Ronald Reagan*. He loved his job. He loved flying more but being in command of the world's largest aircraft carrier was definitely a rush. He looked on as harbor tugs inched the 105,000-ton leviathan towards her temporary moorings.

The harbor pilot spoke constantly into his walkie-talkie issuing final commands to dock workers on the pier and the Captain of the harbor tug. Captain Foute allowed his capable second in command, or X.O., to bring the mighty warship in. He watched in silence as commands were quickly and efficiently issued between the X.O. and harbor pilot to the third officer of the watch. Who in turn acknowledged the orders and then passed them on to the crew via soundpowered phones. Everything was working like a well-oiled machine.

The *Reagan* was tying up to a pier along Roxas Boulevard four blocks south of the U.S. Embassy in Manila. The usual protesters lined the end of the dock with signs that read

'*Yankee go home*' and *'No imperialism here'*. Ignoring the protesters; dockworkers shored up the spring lines and the ship was moored.

"Commander West secure from docking stations, set the watch and issue orders for liberty." Captain Foute spoke softly. He sighed with satisfaction when the *Reagan* was finally secured.

The X.O., who had been waiting in anticipation on the liberty decision, responded, "Aye Sir." After a second thought he added, "Port and starboard Sir, or just a fire watch?"

The Captain could still remember how much Liberty meant to him when he was a flyboy. The Philippines was always a popular place, lots of cheap liquor and willing women. They could do with just a fire watch, so as many of the crew as possible could get off the ship and let loose a little steam. "Fire watch will do fine, Mr. West. And advise the *Chancellorsville* and *Russell* to do the same."

"Aye Aye Sir." The Commander responded with a crisp salute, anxious himself to lose his sea legs. Moreover, one of the Bosuns mates had given him an address of a little Filipina who knew how to treat a sailor right. "Shall it be a Cinderella liberty?" he cautiously asked, hoping that would not be the case.

"I don't see a need for that. What say 0730 hours?" responded Foute, knowing that reporting at midnight was an unpopular move.

"Yes sir!" came the enthusiastic response.

The Captain left the bridge and retired towards his office, which was attached to his stateroom. "And Mr. West, you have a good time!" He shot over his shoulder as he started down the companionway. Foute didn't have a problem with his senior officers enjoying themselves while on shore as long as they remembered they were officers in the United States Navy. In the privacy of his office, Captain Foute was able to relax a little. Armed with a cup of coffee, he sat down and proceeded to fill out the necessary reports for the proceeding weeks.

The carrier battle group was standing down from its first WESTPAC in the Persian Gulf, when a priority message from CINCPAC changed that. The 'Ronnie', as the crew affectionately called the carrier, and her attending escorts were being diverted into the South China Sea, Specifically, to a series of shoals known collectively as the Spratleys. They were a somewhat rag tag group of islands whose ownership had been hotly debated within the United Nations between China, Vietnam and Philippines. After several decades of bickering there was still no clear-cut victor between the superpower and the Third World states, however, the Philippines did have a physical presence on the islands. Total warfare had been averted several times by the intervention of the United States.

So it was nothing new when the *Ronald Reagan* received orders into the Mischief Reef area, where so much of the action had taken place. It was really the same old story; several Chinese fishing vessels had been seized by the Philippine Coast Guard for illegal fishing, and their crews arrested and transported to Manila to await deportation. China would respond by sending a destroyer group in to ensure the safety of their fishermen and run off the Coast Guard. Once the Chinese destroyer was on station the Philippine government would ask the United States to intervene, while issuing a protest to the Chinese Embassy.

This time though a Philippine Coast Guard cutter was found drifting with its crew executed. The investigation turned up several Japanese vessels that happened to be in the vicinity. Witnesses claimed the cutter had stopped a Chinese fishing vessel and was attempting to arrest its occupants. Never before had either parties in the dispute resorted to violence. Fishermen normally arrested are held for a short time and then repatriated to China. However, in response to the executions, the Philippine Government issued orders to their small Navy to board and confiscate any vessel suspected of illegal fishing in the area. Poachers would then be bound over for trial with the possibility of a death sentence.

When the *Ronald Reagan* appeared on scene, tensions were high. The Chinese government had deployed a destroyer group to the vicinity. The Philippine Coast Guard had been beefed up by the addition of several naval vessels, most notably an aging missile frigate from the Vietnam War era. With the arrival of the *Ronald Reagan* and her escorts, the area was becoming extremely crowded with possible combatants. Finally, ambassadors from China and the Philippines had gotten together and brokered a deal whereupon the Americans would oversee policing actions within the area. The Chinese and Filipinos would back down, leaving one ship each representing their respective governments and fishing would be suspended for the time being.

The American task force had been on station for several weeks now charged with the tedious task of patrolling the waters off Mischief Reef. There were no further altercations between the Filipinos and the Chinese. The Philippines had assigned their largest warship the frigate *Mabini* into the area, while the Chinese deployed the destroyer *Hangzhou* to look after their interests.

Captain Foute found it challenging to keep the Chinese and Filipinos apart. He had to admire the seamanship of the Chinese. Not once did they try to penetrate the American destroyer screen but on numerous occasions the Chinese Captain would bring the *Hangzhou* in close to the Philippine frigate, only to be run off by the *Russell* or the *Fife*. Foute was surprised the Chinese would task their newest destroyer to such a mundane mission.

Six days before Christmas, the *Hangzhou* was relieved by an unnamed obsolete frigate. At the same time, the *Mabini* departed for Manila, leaving a small Coast Guard cutter to look after the Philippine interests. As the foreign capital ships sailed over the horizon, Captain Foute consulted with Admiral Burke, the task force commander about a little Christmas shore leave for his own command. The Admiral concurred, and so the *'Ronnie'* accompanied by the *Chancellorsville* and *Russell* proceeded to Manila Bay. The cruiser *Shiloh* and the destroyer *Fife* could look after things until they returned.

When Captain Foute completed his report, he posted it to Admiral Burke and decided to catch up on some much-needed rest. Notwithstanding the idea of going ashore himself, he decided the best course of action was to stay aboard and get some shuteye. Before he could retire, there was a knock on his cabin door. A young yeoman was standing squarely in the doorway when he answered it.

"A communication from shore, Cap'n," he said in an equally smart voice without waiting for the Captain to address him.

Accepting the message, Foute began to open the small envelope when he noticed the sailor was still there, "You may go." The yeoman saluted crisply and did an about face and left. Opening the envelope, Foute was surprised to see a dinner invitation to the American Embassy on Christmas Eve. "Well, well, well, looks like you're moving up in the world. Dinner with the Ambassador," he spoke aloud, and then headed for his rack to get some rest.

Seaman John Lennon Carter was excited. Manila, the Pearl of the Orient! He could hardly wait. He was the son of Pete and Sarah Carter, a pair of Beatles groupies from Davenport Iowa. As John Lennon lay dying on an operating table from a bullet delivered by Mark Chapman, Sarah was giving birth. She named her only child after the slain rock idol. In school, he had to put up with constant jokes and teasing. Outwardly this made him mad, but secretly he was proud of his namesake.

Stepping from the shower, the redhead donned his dress whites with anticipation of liberty. He wasn't due for watch until 12 P.M. tomorrow and the twenty-four-year-old could hardly wait to get off the ship. Even though her immense size reduced the effects of the sea, the son of an Iowaian farmer was only happy when his feet were on terra firma or rather, his stomach was.

When liberty call finally sounded, Carter was among the first sailors down the gangplank. His first observation of Manila was the protesters at the end of the dock, shouting and chanting, being held at bay by a chain fence. Crewmembers wearing armbands with SP on them stood just inside the fence alongside a small security shack that had been lowered from the hanger deck.

A group of eager sailors had already collected next to the gate waiting impatiently for shipmates so they could be on their various ways. Being somewhat of a loner, Carter passed through the crowd acknowledging a couple of familiar faces as he stepped out onto the sidewalk. The crowd of protesters parted as the sailor made his way to the waiting bus that would carry him to the popular fortress of Intramuros, the Old Spanish walled city district of Manila.

The ride to Intramuros was like a shot into another world. Roxas Boulevard followed Manila Bay northward into the old city. To the right was a modern skyline of high rises, dense traffic and thousands upon thousands of people moving along sidewalks going about their business. An occasional horn blast followed by excited dialogue in an exotic language could be heard at almost every intersection. Seamen Carter took in the sights as the bus lurched along from stop light to stop light.

Strange looking minibuses that remotely resembled elongated jeeps from World War II darted in and around the slow moving bus. Each bus or 'Jeepney' as the locals called them, was decorated to the taste of the driver. Carter spied one dirty blue bus that had five steel miniature horses attached to the hood next to a set of air horns, while sporting a dozen or so orange reflectors down each side. The driver had one leg extended out of the cockpit area, which had no door, while talking excitedly to a passenger in the jeepney next to him. In the back there must have been twenty or twenty-five passengers packed into a space no larger than the bed of a pickup truck. A ticket taker standing on the rear bumper just outside the passenger area collected fares and hung on for dear life whenever the dense traffic allowed the jeepney to proceed forward. The Iowaian sailor smiled outwardly as the vehicle roared by, with the occupants paying little attention to the military bus.

After a forty-five minute ride, the driver announced they were at the main gate of Fort Santiago, the chief citadel guarding Intramuros. For centuries the fort was the center of Spanish rule, and was constructed along the lines of a large star. Now a national shrine to Jose Rizal the fallen Philippine martyr, the fort was a popular tourist stop. Carter, a lover of history, was anxious to explore the old casements, bastions and ruins.

Walking through an area that was once living quarters, the seamen expressed dismay over the deteriorating state of preservation. The massive stone edifice was entered via a drawbridge over a moat that was choked with weeds and lily pads. The aroma of stagnant water permeated the area. The sailor was so absorbed in his guidebook and corresponding scenery where flora and fauna were slowly gaining the upper hand over the crumbling walls, that he hardly noticed the youth following him. Carter felt a tug on his right sleeve just as he was about to enter the fort. Whirling about, he was surprised to see a young boy about nine or ten, standing in tattered clothing. The boy was holding a Sprite can in one hand while extending his other. "Yes?" the naive seamen asked, not quite understanding the boy's intent.

"You GI, yes?"

"I'm a sailor if that's what you mean."

"Want refreshing drink? Twenty-five peso."

Sizing up the situation, Carter was quick to understand the boy's plight. He probably bought the soda for five pesos and now was trying to resell it for a profit. The seaman wasn't sure if the boy's clothing was merely a prop or in fact the youth was down on his luck. Reaching into his pocket he took out a dollar and looked quizzical at the young entrepreneur, "Do you have change?"

Quick as lightning the boy snatched the dollar and dropped the soda. He was off before Carter could mount a protest. The dumbfounded American watched the speedy lad dart out of sight behind some ruins a distance away.

A giggling sound could be heard from the direction of the drawbridge. Casually looking over towards the sound, the unlucky sailor did not want to appear frustrated. Standing in the sentry way was the most beautiful woman John Carter had ever seen. She was adorned in a green and white floral print dress, which fell conservatively between her knees and ankles. Her long black hair fell to her waist, with bangs cut just above her doe shaped brown eyes. This Asian beauty immediately smote the American.

The young woman hesitated but a second before she daintily walked over to the shy sailor. Stopping a respectable three feet apart, the vision of loveliness held out for hand and spoke softly, "Hello, I'm JoAnn. Are you stranger here?"

Seamen Carter did not have much experience with women so he tended to shy away from them. Being at a loss for words, he mumbled, "Yes ma'am," as he shook her hand. The young Filipina put her hand to her mouth and giggled again. Not wanting to be mocked, Carter became slightly defensive, "And what is that supposed to mean?"

"Nothing, I mean nothing. It's just, you cute. Let little boy steal from big strong American." As she said this, JoAnn lightly nudged the obviously empty can with her foot. The giggling began again.

"Well, I could have chased him if I wanted, it's just that I have a limited amount of time and I wanted to see the fort. Besides, he probably needed the money more than I did," he defended himself.

In a move that surprised Carter, JoAnn took his hand and offered, "Come, I show you." Not believing his luck, the American followed without protest. It must have looked a little odd, a six foot American male being led by a four foot-seven inch Asian female but John Carter decided, "*What the hell*".

They spent the better part the afternoon exploring the fort and the old city beyond. As time passed, Carter became comfortable with the beautiful maiden. He found it easier to talk to JoAnn than he ever thought possible. She was inquisitive, bright and witty. JoAnn questioned him about his duties aboard ship while complementing him about how big and strong he was.

Towards evening, she steered him into a small family run restaurant where he was able to sample many items of Philippine cuisine. He enjoyed the pancit and pork adobo best. After the meal was complete, a dessert that JoAnn called hallo-hallo was served. To Carter, it was much like a snow cone with fresh fruit. When dinner was complete, the young Filipina advised Carter that it was time for her to go. At his insistence, she agreed to allow him to escort her home. Stepping out from the curb the young lady hailed a taxi, which stopped with a squeal of its tires.

With darkness creeping over the city, the cab negotiated narrow streets choked with hundreds of children playing various games of soccer and basketball. The children stopped playing and watched the cab slowly drive by. It was almost as though they had never seen a white man before. Stopping midway through a block, the cabby spoke to JoAnn in their native language. She quickly paid him and exited the cab. Leaning through the open window, JoAnn spoke for the first time since they had gotten the taxi, "John, I enjoy today. Could we see again?"

"I'd love to see you again, but may I come in now?" asked the anxious sailor, not wanting the evening to end.

"No, mustn't."

"Why not?"

"No understand. Father, he no like sailors."

"But, I'm not like other sailors. Besides, I'd really love to see you again," he pleaded.

The wide-eyed JoAnn leaned forward and brushed her lips across Carter's. She then turned and walked towards a building that was no more than a shack. It looked to have been put together with clapboards and whatever else its owner had scrounged up. The roof was constructed from corrugated iron and the front door was merely a curtain strung across the opening. Carter called out, "JoAnn," as the taxi began to move away from the curb. The Filipina turned and waved silently as the taxi sped away.

"She pretty. You girl maybe?" commented the rather greasy looking cabbie.

"Naw, she's not my girl yet, but. I would like to see her again, maybe we could work something out."

"Lady pay fare. She say take you anywhere you want go."

"Is there a place where a sailor can get a drink?" asked Carter.

"Me know just a place," answered the cabbie.

For the next twenty minutes Carter sat in silence while the driver negotiated the back streets of Manila until he came to a bar with a large neon sign that proclaimed, 'GIRLS GIRLS GIRLS'. Seamen Carter exited the cab to find loud music blaring from the swanky club. It wasn't exactly what he had in mind, but the sailor wasn't ready to return to his ship yet. After glancing up and down the street and seeing no other possibilities, Carter decided to check the place out.

Inside, the club was crowded to standing room only. Across the back wall was a stage where scantily clad women gyrated to popular American tunes. Finding an unoccupied table was a chore, but the sailor was able to find one towards the back. As he sat down, a young female approached and flashed him a big smile. "You need drink?"

Nodding to the question Carter shouted, "Beer." Momentarily the hostess returned with two beers. She promptly sat down and started to drink from one of the bottles. The amazed Carter watched her for several seconds before he followed suit. In no time flat, the beer was gone and two more appeared as if by magic. He was halfways through the second beer before his companion spoke up; "You want good time?"

With the beer's effects starting to work on his mind, the sailor asked, "How much?" As he looked blearily into the pretty girls brown eyes.

"Bar fine two hundred peso," the hostess replied.

Carter began to lose interest as his head started to spin faster. Looking at his bottle, the drunken sailor thought, *"this Philippine beer is powerful stuff."* Downing the remainder of the bottle, Carter wondered what he got himself into. The officers aboard ship had cautioned everyone about joints such as this, where pretty girls got you drunk and you woke up the next morning in an alley without your wallet.

Carter decided it was time to leave. As he stood, his legs seemed to turn to rubber and he sat down hard into his chair. All the while, the young Filipina continued to smile and drink across from him, as if nothing was going on. When another attempt to stand failed, Carter realized the beer must have been spiked. He laid his head down upon the table in a vain attempt to regain control of his faculties. Within seconds the sailor, who had just met the girl of his dreams, passed out.

His eyes fluttered open. The bright sunlight hurt so badly that he was forced to cover them with his hand. His head felt like there was a runaway locomotive loose inside, while his mouth tasted like a thousand soldiers had tramped through it. Struggling to move, Carter slowly regained his senses and realized that he was lying in a rubbish heap. He could hear the sounds of waves gently lapping against a wall nearby. Sitting up and trying to regain his composure, Carter could see the superstructures of the *'Ronnie'* and the *Chancellorsville* over the top of a nearby warehouse.

Struggling to his feet, the unlucky sailor staggered towards 'Home'. *"Man, I'm fucked,"* he thought as he walked towards the deserted gate where protesters had brandished signs and shouted jeers towards the Americans twenty-four hours earlier. The sentry on duty stopped him and asked for ID. Searching his now soiled tunic, Carter was surprised to find his wallet safely tucked inside where he kept it. Checking through it, he was relieved to find all his money untouched and nothing missing. The Seaman flashed his ID at the sentry and was permitted to pass without comment.

Obviously the sentry had seen more than one drunken sailor stagger in that morning. After what seemed like an eternity, Carter was able to stumble to the compartment, which he shared with four other sailors. Thankfully the space was empty, so he was able to remove his uniform and catch a shower in private. The hot water refreshed him somewhat, and for the first time Carter was able to see the condition he was in. There were three long nail-like scratches down his right cheek. More scratches were up and down his back while his left biceps had several bite marks. "Damn, what happened to me?" he said following his self-inspection.

Quickly donning dungarees, Carter went to check his uniform and was surprised by its condition. The tunic had a pocket torn loose while the ships name patch was missing from the right shoulder. The entire uniform looked as if he had rolled about in a garbage dump and emitted an odor that confirmed it. The puzzled seamen stashed the uniform under his mattress. Checking the time, he confirmed he wasn't due for watch for another hour. Not sure who he could confide in, Seamen First-class Carter reported to the ships chaplain and related the story as he knew it. The warrant arrived three days later.

Sixteen

Vladivostok, Russia

Commander Oskar Petropaulovsk looked nervously to the sky. Threatening clouds once again promised another shower within short order. With the warm Japan Current flowing northeasterly just off shore, such was the order of the day in the Russian Far East. This did provide for an ice-free port even during the coldest of winters, however. Standing on a large pier and watching the dark angry clouds roll across the bay at twilight; Petropaulovsk pulled his hat low and stuffed his cold hands into his pockets. The Commander was beginning to doubt the sanity of his decision.

His current assignment was senior weapons officer attached to the Zolotoy Naval Weapons Depot. His job at the supply center was to ensure that all Russian naval vessels were properly supplied with the necessary armaments prior to sailing on patrol. From 9mm side arm ammunition to the most sophisticated S-10 Granat cruise missile, Petropaulovsk had the final decision as to how much would be allocated to each vessel.

The depot, located at the apex of Zolotoy Rog Bay, was in a state of disrepair. Several abandoned, rusting frigate hulks and a half-submerged harbor tug were tied up to secondary quays. At the end of another jetty was a rusting submarine with water gently lapping at the conning tower hatch; where, in times past, sailors would dash through at the sound of the klaxon. The Russian Federation was so strapped for cash that it could not even salvage the hulks. Gone were the busy days of the Cold War. With the breakup of the Soviet Union, the base was but a shadow of its former self.

In the past, Petropaulovsk would have orders to supply a destroyer or submarine almost daily. Now he and his men spent most of their time playing cards and reminiscing of days gone by. It had been almost four months since his last assignment, which had been an aging destroyer bound on a goodwill cruise to America's Pearl Harbor carrying only light arms.

It was everything Petropaulovsk could do just to keep his men busy with daily work assignments, of ammunition inspection and rotation, and grounds, building and truck maintenance. The morale of the sailors under his command was at an all-time low. With the scarcity of most foodstuffs and heating oil, he was obliged to allow his comrades to spend a good portion of their days trying to provide for their families. To add insult to injury, the cash poor Russian Federation had not paid his command in nine months. Instead, the government issued vouchers that the local business community was extremely hesitant to accept, as the Navy department was more than eighteen months in arrears on paying its bills.

The real demoralizing news came last January when the Russian Duma ratified the S.T.A.R.T. II non-proliferation arms treaty with the United States. In early June, the ammunition center received notice of the first shipments slated for elimination. Commander Petropaulovsk was tasked with disassembling the first shipments of ten SLBM or submarine launched ballistic missiles. Once the hundred-megaton warheads were dispatched to Zaozernyy for storage, the missile canisters were stripped of their guidance systems and propellant, and shipped to Baikonur Cosmodrome for destruction pursuant to the treaty. It wasn't until the second shipment departed that Petropaulovsk came up with his daring plan.

Acting quickly and quietly, he had three of his most trusted comrades manufacture two dummy cruise missiles in the supply depot's machine shops. After an intense week of casting, grinding, painting and labeling, the imitation missiles could be easily mistaken for real ones. Petropaulovsk had his ordinance officer secretly remove the two missiles and exchange them for the dummies. The real S-10's were then stored in an abandoned bunker underneath the main operations building. At the time the Commander couldn't really say why he had the missiles switched. He did ponder the expense, time and energy that was spent developing the weapons system using reverse technology from an American 'Tomahawk' captured in Iraq. It would be a shame to put all that work to waste.

Petropaulovsk's current sense of foreboding had started about four months earlier. One evening after a particularly frustrating day, he had stopped into the Boars Head tavern to relax a little. The place was a dimly lit hole in the wall, which was frequented by local ruffians, longshoremen and other riffraff. The house specialty was cheap vodka and even cheaper prostitutes. Stepping up to the bar, Petropaulovsk ordered two shots of vodka. The first he tossed back as soon as the bartender delivered it, the second he decided to nurse a few minutes. An old jukebox in the corner was playing some old scratchy American tune that was barely distinguishable above the noise of dozens of conversations.

Glancing about the crowded, smoke filled room, Petropaulovsk looked for an open chair. Spotting one in the corner, he grabbed his vodka and took the seat. Sitting quietly and sipping his drink, Petropaulovsk was totally oblivious to his surroundings when his thoughts were interrupted.

"This chair taken, no?"

"I'm alone," the tired commander responded without looking up.

"Let me buy you a drink, yes?" a red plaid arm reached

forward and refilled his glass from a half-full bottle.

"Do you always buy strangers drinks?" Petropaulovsk questioned the dark haired patron who sat opposite him.

"For one of our comrades-in-arms I always buy a drink," the stranger responded after removing the cigarette that was dangling from his lips and crushing it out on the floor with his foot.

Throwing his head back in laughter, Petropaulovsk banged the table with his fist. "Comrades-in-arms, ha, that is a good one."

Extending his hand, the bar patron introduced himself. "Demetri. I'm pleased to make your acquaintance Commander."

"Call me Oskar, I see you know naval rank."

"I used to be in the Navy myself. Submarines!" he stated while shaking his head and rolling his eyes towards the ceiling. "Too many people telling me what to do, so I got out. I'm my own man!"

Raising his glass to his lips, Petropaulovsk studied his benefactor as he drank the clear liquid. Demetri had coal black wavy hair that almost touched his shoulders. With a round pasty face and dark rings around his chestnut piercing eyes, there was a sinister look about him. A scar ran from his left earlobe to the edge of his left nostril. His nose had obviously been broken on more than one occasion. His rough-looking red plaid shirt gave the impression of someone who worked on the docks.

"Another?" Petropaulovsk asked as he sat the glass back down.

"So, what do you do for the Navy?" Demetri casually inquired as he refilled the Commander's glass.

"I baby-sit weapons."

"You what?" the civilian asked in a hushed tone.

"I baby-sit weapons," the Commander repeated slowly as the alcohol was beginning to take effect. "I'm in command of the naval weapons depot, only with this damned government I no longer have much to do."

"Times change comrade."

"Da, that is true. Only last week I sent weapons to be

destroyed. Weapons that ten years ago brought the Soviet Union respect. When I first joined the Navy, I was protecting Mother Russia, now I'm helping to dismantle her military might. And for what you ask?"

"I understand Commander, but you have to learn to change with the times..."

"Change?" Interrupted the inebriated commander. "Under the Soviet system we had respect, my men held their heads high, we were something. Ha! Now, we are nothing. Do you know how long it has been since Russia paid my men?"

"No, you tell me." Demetri's eyes focused on his now drunken companion.

"Five months! Five months, I have used all my abilities to care for my men, for they are all I have now. How are they to care for their families, or provide shelter and heat for the coming winter? How? How...! It's like Moscow doesn't listen or care. Moscow is so far away; it's like we're on the moon!"

"Tell me my friend, would you be interested in helping your command, perhaps?"

"What have you in mind?" the commander queried.

"What say I give you a hundred Eurodollars for, maybe one-hundred rounds of 9 mm ammunition?"

"Are you suggesting what I think you're suggesting?"

"What? You think the government that has forsaken you cares about a few rounds of ammunition? Just look at the rusting hulks in the harbor; they don't even care about entire warships. Why would they worry about a few rounds of ammunition? You could use the money or divide it among your command. In a way, the sale would be your way of providing for your men."

To Petropaulovsk's intoxicated mind this made sense. He could trade unwanted surplus ammunition for much-needed cash. He and his command would benefit from this arrangement, but was it safe? He hesitated for a moment and then asked, "how do I know I can trust you?"

"Comrade, remember I was in the Navy too. I know the pain you are suffering, but think of all the good you can do with the money. Besides, if you can't trust a fellow sailor, who can you trust?" assured Demetri, sensing an agreement was near.

Hesitating, Petropaulovsk drank down the last of the vodka. After several moments of silence he agreed to the trade. "Da, I think we can do business. How will this work?"

"Give me a phone number, something private, I'll call you in the morning," responded the elated Demetri.

In the blink of an eye, the Commander grabbed one of Demetri's hands and squeezed it hard. Drawing his head close to Demetri's, Petropaulovsk cautioned in a low husky voice, "You make sure this gets out to no one. Remember, I have many more weapons that I can personally use." After writing down his personal phone number, the Commander got up and exited the tavern.

Over the course of the next three months, there would be similar trades. Each would be a little more demanding than the previous. Two dozen A. K. 47's, a dozen 5.2-mm shells and five 500-pound depth charges. Each time Petropaulovsk would distribute the money evenly among his command, claiming that Moscow had finally acknowledged their plight.

Finally, Demetri asked for a Granat nuclear cruise missile. Petropaulovsk was expecting the request. It all made sense. Demetri was never really after the small arms or the shells that had just been a smoke screen to ensnare him. Petropaulovsk informed Demetri he would have to think this over, but the Commander had already made up his mind. His price would be twenty million American dollars, not the Euros that made up the previous transactions.

Petropaulovsk let Demetri stew over the proposition for a week. Dodging his phone calls, the Commander had to work out certain details before he succumbed to Demetri's wishes. He made subtle arrangements for his own departure, as Petropaulovsk knew that once he crossed this line there was no going back. When everything was in place, he called Demetri. The Commander informed his associate that this was to be their last transaction, and Demetri was quick to accept.

Petropaulovsk stood in a driving rain awaiting the prearranged signal from Demetri. As their negotiations progressed, he discovered Demetri would have an associate during the exchange; the buyer wanted to take charge personally. This did not sit well with the Commander, but it appeared he had no choice in the matter. In addition, he was having second thoughts. Something was nagging at the back of his consciousness telling him to forget it, but he pushed those thoughts aside. With Christmas less than a week away, thoughts of how his men would benefit clouded his judgment.

Just when the cold Petropaulovsk thought Demetri was a no-show, he observed a blue light blink three times out in the bay. With shaking hands, the Commander returned the signal by lighting a cigarette. He was now past the point of no return. Moments later, the stillness of the night was broken by a muffled splash and the sound of something approaching the pier.

Out of the midnight darkness came an unlikely craft. To Petropaulovsk it looked to be an ancient Chinese junk silently approaching the dock. The craft had a seaman working the main sail, while a dark form was standing in the welldeck area quietly issuing orders. Another was manhandling a large tiller that was attached to an old-fashioned wooden rudder. The rear mast or mizzen was devoid of any sail. Golden Chinese characters were emblazoned just below the forward bulwark. To complete the image, the bow strip was adorned with a roaring Lion. A third seaman forward, materialized out of the mist, and tossed a bowline over to Petropaulovsk.

As soon as the bowline was secure, the man who had worked the main sail jumped ashore and caught another line tossed ashore by the helmsman. A small gangplank was hauled out from the welldeck area and bridged the gap between the obsolete transport and the pier.

Petropaulovsk stood in silence and watched the Crewmembers secure the vessel. A moment later, two figures descended the gangplank and approached him. Even in the dark he recognized Demetri accompanied by a shorter older man of Asian descent, dressed in black.

After a brief hesitation, Demetri approached Petropaulovsk and offered his hand, "Oskar, good to see you again. This is my friend Mr..."

The short figure motioned for Demetri to desist. Stepping forward and speaking in broken Russian, he ordered. "No speak! Have you merchandise?"

"Da, do you have the payment?"

"Yes, I have." The Asian turned to one of his seamen and spoke something. Immediately he disappeared belowdecks and returned with a briefcase, which he handed to Petropaulovsk. "I think you inspect payment now?" his mysterious benefactor offered.

"I'm sure that won't be necessary," the Commander assured him. He handed the briefcase back to his chief machinist who had been waiting in the shadows armed with an assault rifle in case of treachery.

"What's this?" demanded Demetri, who did not like the change in plans.

"You bring this stranger to the meeting..." Petropaulovsk started but was interrupted by a hand signal from the elderly gentlemen.

"This not important. Complete transaction now, time wasting!" the dark figure demanded in a stern voice. "Or shall I go?"

Silenced by the stern rebuke, Petropaulovsk turned and led the duo through the deserted supply base to the operations building. Pointing to the ramp that led down to the old bunker, he said, "I have it stored in here."

"Show me." The stranger demanded.

Fumbling with an old round padlock, Petropaulovsk quietly eased the large garage-type door open on well-greased rollers. Silently the two figures followed the depot Commander to the back of the room where a steel door was recessed into the concrete wall. Disengaging a deadbolt, with a key that he wore around his neck, Petropaulovsk flipped a switch that illuminated a small storage room. The area was lined with metal shelves, which contained various civil defense foodstuffs, canned water and medical supplies. What appeared to be a tarp-covered bench dominated the open space in the center of the room. Pulling up a corner of the canvas tarp and flipping it back, Petropaulovsk revealed the white painted S-10s resting on carts designed to facilitate movement of the two-ton weapons.

Whistling softly, Demetri slowly approached the closest missile and ran his hand along the warhead as if caressing the cheek of his current lover. "Are these for real?" he asked in amazement.

"Da, they're real," Petropaulovsk confirmed. With his back to the door, he did not notice a slight movement made by the stranger. Turning, Petropaulovsk spotted a glint of metal and heard a swishing sound. Before he could react, a sword severed his head in one complete pass. With a surprised expression frozen on the lifeless face, the head hit the floor with a sickening crunch and rolled to the feet of a shocked Demetri.

The Commander's body stood momentarily as blood shot across the room, splattering the occupants and missiles with the crimson life force that once coursed through his veins. Collapsing in a heap at the base of one of the missiles, the grisly corpse would be discovered the next morning when Petropaulovsk failed to show for morning roll call.

The mysterious stranger had positioned himself between Petropaulovsk and Demetri. When he removed his Samurai sword from its sheath, the stranger, in a single continuous movement, beheaded the Commander, and then thrust backwards into Demetri's gut. A look of pure terror overtook arm's dealer face as he tried to call out, but was too late. In a vain attempt to defend himself, the terrified Russian grabbed hold of the razor-sharp blade, slicing his hands open to the bone. He tried to push his way past his attacker and exit the room, to no avail. The stranger pulled up on the lethal weapon, splitting Demetri's sternum and piercing his heart. Death was instantaneous; the entire procedure had taken less than ten seconds. As the corpse slowly sank to the floor, the mysterious figure carefully withdrew the sword and wiped it clean with a white silk handkerchief. He returned the antique weapon to its sheath.

Meanwhile outside, the three sailors had silently located Petropaulovsk's security detail, consisting of the three machinists who had helped fabricate the dummy missiles. Each one crept up behind an unsuspecting Russian, covering their mouths with one hand, and sliced open their throats. The deeds were done silently and efficiently without remorse. Once the Russians were dispatched, a red-haired figure emerged from the shadows and made the sound of an owl hoot. Instantly, more than a dozen men materialized and reported to the missile storage area.

Speaking rapidly, the leader of the mysterious group instructed the men on how to handle the cruise missile. He reminded them of their pressing schedule and urged them along. Within forty-five minutes, the assassins had carted the weapon dockside and loaded it aboard the junk safely. The briefcase was quickly located and returned to the group's leader. Lastly, the bodies were moved into the storage room. Quietly, just before sun up, the small junk slipped carefully away into the December darkness.

Seventeen

The old brownstone for which Rolf Heinrich called home was at the top of Browning Street. It was a narrow affair where all the buildings were alike; wrought iron fences dressed up smallish yards while narrow, steep steps ascended to old faded doors. Heinrich had purchased the house several years' back to celebrate his promotion to Inspector. The brownstone, although old, was quite comfortable with a dining room, parlor and three upstairs bedrooms. The former upper-class neighborhood was undergoing a revival of sorts, becoming quite popular with the new and younger upper middle-class.

It had been a snowy day and was the perfect evening to sit by a fire in the parlor. So with the telly on and the volume turned down, Heinrich was enjoying his pipe while trying to catch up on his reading. For the better part of an hour he'd been sipping hundred-year-old sherry while scanning reports from around the world. The warmth of the crackling fire added coziness to the room as the wind whipped the snow just outside the windows.

Now and then, something would catch his eye, and the

Inspector would stop and carefully read the report. Meanwhile, images would flash back and forth on the telly as various reporters described doings from around the globe. Heinrich was in the middle of a memo on a weapons sale to a Middle Eastern group in Beirut, when something caught his eye on CNN. It was video of a smallish elderly person being removed from a gigantic gray stone building on a gurney. Wanting to hear more, he grabbed the remote and adjusted the volume.

"'…And so Premier Xian will be admitted to Keio University Medical Center where he will undergo tests...'" The picture panned out to reveal a smartly dressed female reporter holding a mike and speaking rapidly as the gurney was loaded into a waiting ambulance with red lights flashing.

"'...to determine the extent of the damage. Sources close to the Premier speculate that he may have suffered a stroke brought on by the long and stressful hours the Premier has been working lately...'" The camera followed the ambulance as it sped away from the building with sirens wailing.

"'...The Chinese Congress will assemble in an emergency meeting to discuss who will oversee the daily operations of the office. They want to assure everyone that calm is needed right now...'" The camera now moved back to the huge monolithic building, which was bathed in dazzling light. Sixteen flagpoles stood silent watch as their red flags with yellow stars were whipped gently by the breeze.

"'...this is Anita Chew reporting from Beijing for CNN International.'"

Heinrich jotted down a few notes on a pad that he always kept on the table next to his chair. "Interesting," he said. Next, the Inspector wrote down Premier Xian's name. He scribbled 'assassination' with several question marks, then circled it. He made a mental note to ask Amanda to retrieve the file on the assassinations of the Chinese ministers.

Returning to his reading, the Inspector continued to wade through the remaining cases. After putting in several hours of reading, his eyes became fatigued and Heinrich decided to turn in. Damping down the fire, the tired Inspector was on his way upstairs when a thought crossed his mind. Retreating back to the parlor, he made brief call to headquarters. Detailing what he wanted, the Inspector hung up and proceeded to bed.

The previous evening's snow had to turned to a light rain. Heinrich had been hoping that the snow would hold out till Christmas, but rarely did it last more than twenty-four hours in London. The light rain was letting up as Heinrich walked to the end of Browning Street towards the underground station. He had to tread lightly, as the street was partially flooded with melting snow and pools of standing water. Finally making the subway, the Inspector shook off his umbrella and proceeded to board the next train for the Kings Cross stop.

Upon entering his office, the Chief Inspector hung up his coat and umbrella and sat behind his utilitarian metal desk. His smallish office was neat and orderly, with a half dozen file cabinets along one wall. The walls recorded his career in crime-fighting, with dozens of pictures of the Inspector and his comrades, and a couple of candid shots of celebrities whom he'd had the opportunity to meet. Fitted into the mahogany door was a frosted glass pane upon which his name was neatly stenciled. In reality, Heinrich was quite comfortable in his private domain.

Setting the stack of reports in the out basket, Heinrich checked with the Records Division to see if his earlier request had been compiled. They informed him it would be noontime at the earliest. Undaunted, he took out the scrap of paper, with his notes from the previous evening. Heinrich again read the notion of assassination. *"Something appears to be rotten in China,"* he muttered to the empty room.

A light knocking at the door interrupted the Inspector's train of thought. He could make out the sexy silhouette of Amanda through the door's opaque glass window. Trying to look busy, the Inspector grabbed the top file from the out basket and sighed to himself, as he called out, "Yes."

"Ins-inspector," Amanda addressed him as she came through the door, "Ho-how are you this fine day?"

"Fine, just fine."

"Good, I have a portfolio for you, thought you would like to take a peek at it before lunch," she said smiling.

Pretending to be deep into his reading, Heinrich discretely watched Amanda's lithe figure cross from the doorway to his desk. "Leave the file, I have plenty to do already."

Setting the folder down, the beauty took a step back and asked, "Well?"

"Well what?"

"See anything different?"

Looking up for the first time since she had entered the room, Heinrich noticed that Amanda was dressed as one of Santa's elves. She wore a red short skirt, green stockings and a white silk blouse. Over the blouse she wore a green velvet vest that had gold chains instead of buttons. The chains held the vest about two inches from being closed. Her tastefully done raven hair, however, had a silly Santa hat perched atop it. The entire look was really rather sexy. "Well, I have to admit you really look smashing in that get up."

"And, I see you wore your rather boring brown tweed again."

"I wasn't aware of instructions to the contrary."

"Don't you remember the memo, silly? The Christmas party, it is this afternoon. I wanted to be in touch with the holidays." Leaning forward, she gave him an unobstructed view of her cleavage and coyly pointed out, "I know where the mistletoe is."

Leaning back in his chair Heinrich lit up a cigarette as if he hadn't noticed. Carefully blowing smoke towards Amanda he inquired, "Is that an open invitation?"

"Ha! You've had an open invitation for a year, and what do I get? Nothing! I'm telling you Inspector Heinrich if you don't start paying a little more attention...Well...I'm not sure...I'm... Oh my gosh! I mean...I don't..." The embarrassed vixen turned and stormed out the door.

For the first time Heinrich saw Amanda in a different light. *"Maybe it wouldn't be so bad to look her up some evening,"* he thought as the manila file drew his attention. When the Inspector went to pick it up, he spotted a red envelope lying underneath. The envelope had his name neatly printed in gold on the outside. Curiosity got the better of him and he opened it. Inside was a very tasteful Christmas card depicting a serene wintry scene. Opening the card, Heinrich read the standard printed Christmas greeting. Underneath, in Amanda's handwriting, was an invitation to Christmas dinner. Closing the card, the Chief Inspector took another drag of his cigarette. "*Blimey, she's really hung up on me,*" he thought guiltily.

Setting the card aside, he opened the folder and dumped it's contents upon his desk. There were a handful of 8 X 10 glossies of what appeared to be a crime scene with an accompanying police report. This was nothing unusual, for he got envelopes such as these all the time. The first black and white photo showed a room about twice the size of a garage. The lower left-hand corner showed shoes attached to legs that went off the photo. In the center in the photo was a long cylindrical object with a tarp partially covering it. What looked to be blood splatters crossed the front of the cylinder. Next to it was a vacant cradle of some kind that obviously had held a similar object. The next photo showed the bodies.

Inspector Heinrich lit another cigarette off the first and inhaled deeply. The second photo disclosed a series of corpses piled like cordwood next to a door. The following successive photographs were of different bodies after they had been removed from the pile. Three of the victims appeared to had their throats cut from ear to ear. One victim looked like he been totally gutted while the last one was beheaded. All of the corpses, save one, were dressed in uniforms, with the headless one appearing to be an officer.

The floor under the bodies was completely covered in blood. The final image showed a severed head beneath a workshop bench. Alongside the corpse was a white handkerchief, stained in blood. When Heinrich finished examining the photos, he leaned back in his chair and closed his eyes to shake the images from his mind.

After pausing a moment, he rang up the switchboard and

asked for Amanda. After a brief wait her voice answered, "Yes Inspector."

"Sorry to bother you, but when did we get this report?"

"No bother, I think, yes, it was yesterday, early, came in with the morning post."

"And I'm just seeing it now?" he asked with a hint of anger in his voice.

"But-but Inspector, Yo-you were busy with the Carlos case," Amanda sputtered defensively. Reminding him that he had spent the entire day going over field reports on the most wanted terrorist in Europe. The thirty-year manhunt had culminated with an arrest in Istanbul

"Right," Heinrich responded. "If you get any more updates, please rush them to me. Now be a good lass and check on a report I requested from records."

"So-so you're not upset with me?" Amanda asked in wonder.

"Why no, whatever made you think that?"

"Well I-oh never mind," she answered before hanging up.

Heinrich just smiled as he sat the receiver in its cradle. "*Let's have a go at that report*," he pondered. Setting the photo's aside, the Inspector took the report and studied it for a whole ten seconds. The report might as well have been written in Greek, as it had been filled out in Cyrillic and Heinrich couldn't make head nor tales of either. Shuffling through the papers, he found a brief translation that detailed the when and how, the grisly scene had been discovered. In addition, a vague outline suggested a possible scenario as to motive. The report raised more questions than it answered and he felt an uneasiness in his gut when referring back to the photo with the empty cradle.

"Inspector!" Amanda, in her silly get up, was at the door again.

"Yes."

"Here's that file you requested."

"Good," half-standing, he motioned towards the vacant chair next to his desk. "Amanda would you care to take a seat?"

"Wh-why, Have I done something wrong?" she asked as

she entered the room hesitantly and laid the folder on the desk before taking a seat.

Sitting back down, Inspector Heinrich took the folder, and put it in his 'in' basket, *"for later reading,"* he thought. "No, nothing, nothing like that at all. It's just, that I want you to take a peek at this file I've been going over," he said, putting her at ease while handing her the glossies. "Tell me, what do you make of this?"

Amanda took the pictures and studied them for several moments, shuffling and reshuffling them. She always returned to the same picture, the one with the empty cradle. "Peers, there's a bit of nasty business here," she concluded with confidence.

"Yes quite, anything else?"

Flipping through the photos again, Amanda stopped at the group photo. "I see some sort of military installation." Setting down the snapshots of the individual victims she added, "a most peculiar business here."

"How's that?" queried the Inspector.

"Wouldn't you say that the choice of murder weapons was most unusual?"

Lighting up another cigarette Heinrich inhaled deeply and blew the smoke towards the ceiling. "Go on."

"Must you continue with that foul habit?" she questioned as she wrinkled up her nose.

"It helps me concentrate. Now, get on with it," he shot back, smiling just a little.

"What bothers me most is not the obvious murders."

"And what, pray tell, is that?"

"You haven't given me the location, but I see a sign on this far wall that looks to be Russian," the young sleuth pointed out.

"And." Another cloud of smoke was exhaled towards the ceiling.

"By the looks of this photo I'd say something extremely important has been nicked and the murders was committed to keep people from talking."

"Loose lips sink ships."

"Something like that. It's what's missing that I'd be concerned about," Amanda finished. She sat silently for several minutes as the Inspector finished his cigarette and crushed it out.

As if coming out of a trance, the Inspector spoke up, "Now be good lass and keep that under your knickers."

"And what makes you think I wear knickers?" she asked mischievously.

"Well I..., What would your mum say?" Heinrich tried to recover gracefully.

"She'd probably tell me not to bother with an old coot such as you."

"Amanda! You should be ashamed..."

Taking the Inspector's last comments as a dismissal, the dispatcher rose and snickered as she walked towards the door. The Inspector went back to studying the photos. Just as she was exiting the room he looked up from his reading and asked, "What kind of pudding?"

"Pudding Sir?" she asked, slightly puzzled.

"Your card, the invite to dinner."

"Rice, rice pudding," she answered with a hint of triumph in her voice.

"Say half past eight?" he came back a little awkward.

"Lovely." Santa's elf acknowledged as she pulled the door closed.

"You know old boy, she's rather fetching in that getup," Inspector Heinrich thought as he went back to his reading. Several hours later, after he had read the report from Records Division, Chief Inspector Heinrich had a grave feeling that something serious was amiss. He made two calls, the first to the Home Secretary, the second to his travel agent.

Part II: Yamashita's Gold

Eighteen

January 2nd 2004
Seattle Washington

For Jake Philips, the holidays had been a bitch. After offering his companions time to go home for the holidays, the Lieutenant went back to his parents' houseboat. He instructed McKay and Wardon to meet up with him shortly after the New Year. Therefore, for the first time in years, he would spend the Christmas alone.

Phoebe had invited Jake over for Christmas dinner but he had respectfully declined, preferring to divide his time between the bottle and reminiscing over Christmas' past. The dreams were back. Each night his mother would assure him things would be all right and each morning he woke up with an overpowering sense of doom. Every day he would drive the depression away with the reassuring solace that only a bottle could provide.

Somewhere between Christmas and New Years, Jake pulled himself up out of that bottomless pit. Philips wasn't sure if it was the motocross bike that was still sitting in the livingroom or the realization that he couldn't bring his parents back. Whatever it was, it probably saved his life.

On that gray morning, the young SEAL got up and instead of craving a drink, he started to tinker on the bike. Even though it had never been ridden, time had not been a friend to it. Gasoline within the fuel tank had broken down and contaminated the fuel system. Most of the rubber hoses were brittle and cracked. Bearing grease had dried up, and the front tire had gone flat.

First, he drained the entire fuel system and tossed the rubber gas lines. The carburetor took him several hours to dismantle, clean then reassemble it. The plugs came next. Opting for new ones, Philips removed and replaced them. A check of the electrical system confirmed the battery was shot and the starter refused to turn over. After catching a cab to the local dealership, he was able to install a new battery and fuel line by late that afternoon. The sky was just getting dark when the SEAL rolled the bike out onto the pier to give it a try.

With the starter out, the Lieutenant was forced to use the kick-start. After a dozen tries, the bike roared to life. With a sense of accomplishment, Philips gunned the engine several times much to the annoyance of his neighbors. Now the only real chore left was to repack the bearings. Shutting the bike down, he made a mental note to try and locate his helmet and boots.

To celebrate, later that evening, Philips made himself dinner for the first time in a week. The meal was followed up with brief phone conversations to Murdoch, Mike and Clifford. Satisfied with the day's accomplishments, he sat in his father's chair and watched a little television. The exhausted SEAL turned in around 11 P.M. That night the dreams did not return.

Philips spent the better part of four days putting the houseboat back in order. It felt odd to call the place his, but, once he thought about it, it kind of made sense. Though the Lieutenant wasn't sure what the future had in store, for the first time he wasn't afraid of it either. Philips celebrated New Year's Eve by sitting on his porch and watching the sky around the Space Needle explode in a glorious display of pyrotechnics. After the show, he toasted the revelry with a soda. Brief phone calls to McKay and Wardon confirmed their arrivals later in the week.

Several days later, Philips had just finished his morning run and sat down to a cup coffee when there was an insistent pounding on the door. Checking his watch, he wondered who would come a-calling at 6:37 A.M. He opened the door to find a little person soaked to the skin and shivering in the predawn darkness.

"Wh-why the h-hell didn't C-Cliff or M-Moe or whatever, t-tell ma-me was a ho-house boo-bo-boat?" sputtered the obviously agitated man.

"What th-?" Was all the response Philips could muster.

Pushing past the dumbfounded Lieutenant, the little man stuttered on, "Ar-aren't you go-going to invite m-me in?"

"Be my guest."

"Ly-Lysander's the n-name, and where's that Wardon f-fellow, I have a bone to pick wi-with him." He continued not giving Philips the chance to respond, "How was I suppose to know this address was a houseboat? Took me two hours to find this ruddy place. In this rain I could've caught my death...Ah-choo." Sneezing, he glanced to the young Lieutenant with the puzzled expression, "You must be Jake. Charles Lysander, just call me Charlie." He took a breath while extending his hand.

Philips didn't know what to think. Closing the door he accepted the extended hand. "Jake Philips." He paused, then added, "How'd you know Cliff?"

"Excuse me. Let me introduce myself properly, Charles Lysander First Assistant Curator, National Archives, Washington D.C.," he spoke slowly so he wouldn't stutter while searching his pockets and finally producing a business card.

Philips expression changed almost immediately as he realized this was the guy that Clifford was sent to see in Washington. "I'm sorry, Clifford's not due 'til this afternoon."

"Figures, that's about the way my day is going," the little man sighed. He looked about the room and then sat down. "He gave me this address, and said if I came across any additional information about the Mills Transfer I was to forward it here, in care of you," the squeaky-voiced Lysander explained.

Lysander now had Philips's undivided attention. "Mills Transfer?"

"Why yes, of course, Clifford gave me this address and told me if I came across..." He hesitated, and then continued, "...I seem to be repeating myself."

"That you are," the smiling Lieutenant agreed. "So let's cut to the chase. Why don't you elaborate on what you found."

Rubbing his hands together, the curator asked, "Got any coffee, hot chocolate, milk; anything warm for a guy who's freezing?"

"Forgive me, I don't have the manners that Mom gave me. This way," Philips excused himself, as he walked from the living room towards the kitchen. The Curator followed and took a seat at the table and sat in silence while the young man prepared coffee for the both of them. "Sugar? Cream?"

"Black please."

"I was hoping you'd say that, I don't have the other stuff." The Lieutenant snickered as he set a cup of steaming coffee in front of Lysander. "Now, what were you saying about the Mills Transfer?" he asked, as he sat down opposite his most unusual houseguest.

Lysander related briefly the events that transpired at the Archives, confirming the unbelievable tale that Wardon had passed on concerning the missing documents. After a brief silence the curator continued, "I was so mad about the missing entries. This isn't AirStrip One in Orwell's *1984,* where you can delete history and convince the populace that it never existed. I know and you know, those references were real. So, I got to checking, same results every time, nothing."

"Doesn't that seem a bit odd?" Philips quipped.

"First, let me say this; nobody, and I mean nobody fucks with Charlie Lysander!" exclaimed the agitated Curator. "When whoever deleted those files did so, he opened a can of whup-ass he'd wish he'd left well enough alone. I'll find out who they are..."

Philips was taken back by the little man's aggressiveness,

and doubted that the implied threat was a hollow one.

"...Enough of that. I got to thinking, only eighty percent of the National Archives is computerized..."

"So?"

"I got to thinking," he hesitated, "There I go repeating myself again. What I'm trying to say is... there's a lot of information that has not been cataloged. Private diaries, letters, minutes from meetings, even phone recordings. Sooo, I decided to do some further investigating."

"Was your search fruitful?"

"To say the least. I wondered who would most likely have information on the Mills Transfer."

"Presidents!" the Lieutenant chimed in.

"Exactly! And where would one find private correspondence from our previous Presidents?"

"The Presidential Libraries," answered Philips, starting to see where the little man was going.

"Right on! So, the closest one to me was FDR's in Hyde Park. Using my status as Curator, I was able to gain access to Mr. Roosevelt's most private letters and communications. For the most part the man's correspondence was rather mundane. I did run across a brief reference to the treaty. In one of the President's personal journals he expressed outrage with General MacArthur..." changing the subject, Lysander inquired. "Have you anything to eat? It was noontime yesterday since my last meal."

"Continue your story, I'll rustle up some chow," the SEAL offered, as he got up to fix something. A brief examination of the fridge revealed the bill of fare would be ham and eggs. Philips' unexpected guest watched as he prepared the pans and cracked some eggs. "Go on," he encouraged.

"The journal entry was dated March 31st 1942. FDR admitted that correspondence from MacArthur had brought on a bout of depression. It goes on to state that MacArthur had accused him of treachery, when in January, the first nations signed the original UN charter brokered by the President. The General further cautions, that by leaving Mao Tse-tung in the dark, and I quote, *"Trouble could be brewing."* FDR finished the entry by questioning MacArthur's ability to dictate foreign policy."

Setting two heaping plates on the table, Philips questioned, "Not much there, but at least it's a start. Find anything else?"

Taking a bite, the famished curator continued. "This got me to thinking, I decided to check with a historian I know over at the United Nations. It was true; the first twenty-six nations signed the UN charter January 1st 1942. General Chiang Kai-shek signed for the Republic of China. There were no protests from the Mao camp. You know, this is pretty good." He complemented the cook while pointing to the ham with his fork.

"How do you screw up ham and eggs?"

"Thought I'd offer anyway. Things remained pretty quiet for the rest of Roosevelt's administration, for the treaty that is. After the war, George Marshall became Secretary of State for Harry Truman. I got to thinking maybe Marshall..."

While Philips listened intently, he was slowly rolling his cup between his hands.

"So I popped over to Lexington, Virginia where the Marshall foundation is located, and spent a couple of days pouring over his personal memoirs. I found a couple of artifacts related the Mills Transfer. First, there was a letter sent to Secretary Marshall from Mao Tse-tung asking for aid akin to the Marshall plan. The letter accused the United States of turning its back on China." Getting up, the curator helped himself to another cup of coffee and savored it as the hot liquid warmed his insides. "Umm, that sure puts a little life back into my weary bones."

"Let me see if I understand this. You're telling me China requested funds to help rebuild the country through the Marshall plan but was declined, am I correct?" Philips asked.

"Exactly. I also discovered a formal protest posted in 1948 which looked to be a rebuke to America's abstention to China's request for admission to the United Nations. This time Mao was extremely upset with Marshall, because our lack of support assured China's denial by the general assembly.

Attached to the protest was a brief handwritten note reminding the Secretary of State of Mao's position. It seems that Mao was upset with the way America's foreign policy was ignoring China. Was it not the Communists who stepped forward in the early days of the war, when America needed help, providing hard currency, intelligence and organization when things weren't going so well?"

"Let's see," Philips philosophized. "If I remember my history correctly, we would only recognize one China, and that was the government of Chiang Kai-shek. Looks like the makings of a political enemy."

"Exactly. The tone of the letter implied America would soon pay for turning its back on their former ally," Lysander sighed.

Shaking his head in disbelief, the Lieutenant offered. "And you came all this way to tell us that?"

"Not exactly."

"You sound like a commercial. What do you mean by, 'not exactly'?"

Getting up and walking over to the window, Lysander stood in silence for several seconds. Doing an about face, he continued. "With my early successes I decided to check other Libraries. In vain I may add. And I checked them all, Truman, Eisenhower, Kennedy, Nixon, I mean all of them. Each time the same results, zero, zip, nada! This was turning out to be a real puzzle, and I can't stand it when there is no obvious answer."

The bemused Philips queried. "You really checked each and every library since Roosevelt?"

"Yep, spent the better part of the last ten days bouncing back and forth across the country," Lysander confirmed. Heading back to the livingroom where he'd left his jacket, the weary Curator sank down on to the sofa. He took a deep breath and continued. "I was rummaging through some boxes stacked in the basement of the Reagan Museum in Simi Valley when I came across this..." He reached under his coat and presented a royal blue book with the Presidential Seal. With this, his mood turned sullen, and he spoke barely above a whisper. "I think this will explain. In light of what happened in Washington, I took precautions. Be advised, I have spoken with no one, other than you. And, I've probably broken several laws, but I feel it's for the best that you have it."

Taking the ledger, Philips read the words "Top Secret" inscribed on a red ribbon wrapped around the book. He opened the document and began to read. Lysander, being somewhat lethargic from all the traveling, began to doze off as the inquisitive SEAL immersed himself in the incriminating file. It took the better part of four hours to completely ingest the sordid details of the past fifty years. When he finished, the Lieutenant's hands shook slightly as he put the document down.

Looking to the sleeping curator, he said, "Now I understand, little buddy..." Philips practically jumped out of his skin when a knocking at the door interrupted him.

Without hesitation, the door opened to reveal McKay and Wardon punching and playfully pushing each other trying to be the first across the threshold. "Jake!" The duo chimed in. "How'd the hell are ya?" they greeted in unison.

He stared momentarily as his two companions entered the room. McKay was first, followed by Wardon. Never was an odder couple. McKay looked the sailor he was, close-cropped hair, Navy peacoat and denim jeans. Wardon, on the other hand, was straight out of an *Indiana Jones* movie. He sported a brown leather bomber jacket, sidearm and an old leather *Indy* fedora propped atop his shaven head.

"Would you git a load of this!" McKay exclaimed, as he shot a glance over his shoulder in the direction of his shipmate. "All he needs is a whip, he's already got the attitude."

Standing, Philips greeted his friends. "Mike, Clifford, good to see you guys." Then, nodding towards the black *Indy*. "What happened you?"

"Well Moe, it's like this. I figures we're going to look for treasure, so might as well look the part," he grinned then added. "Besides, this beats a uniform any day."

"And that?" inquired the Lieutenant as he pointed to the sidearm.

"Jake, I got whacked in front of a beautiful babe. Ain't going to happen again. Besides dad gave me this piece," he commented as he pulled a Desert Eagle .44 magnum from its holster slung low on his hips.

"And just what are you going to do with that cannon?" McKay asked, jumping into the conversation.

"Protection!" he uttered slowly.

"From what.." McKay shot back. "...The little lady that had you bonked on the head? You probably scared her with that shiny noggin of yours. If our paths cross again, I'll offer apologies and ask her out."

"You're not the one getting shot at or whacked," he defended himself, "So, girl or no girl, this time I'm prepared."

"Just like the Boy Scouts." McKay contended.

"Put that away before you hurt yourself," the Lieutenant suggested.

"Yes Sir," he said with obvious disappointment.

"In light of information I have just received," Philips offered, "It's not a bad idea. I hope you brought a little something for all of us."

"Arrangements have been made for a parcel to be delivered to the American Embassy in Manila."

"Good, get everything on the list?"

"Yep, with a few extras," Wardon assured him. Glancing towards the sofa he gestured, "What do you have there?"

"I believe he's a friend of yours." Philips responded.

Wardon went over to the sleeping figure, bent over and exclaimed. "Why, if it isn't my little buddy from Washington!"

"I wouldn't get too close," the Lieutenant cautioned. "I found him in a really ugly mood this morning suffering from hypothermia. He was ranting something about having a 'bone to pick with you.'"

Nudging the sleeping form, Wardon was about to turn away when two small hands reached up from beneath the blanket and surprised him. Before he could react, the hands had encircled the SEAL's throat. The big black man took his mammoth paws and carefully pulled the curator's hands free and held him in a vice like grip. “So Moe, what gives?” he questioned his assailant with humor.

“You! You’re the reason I almost froze to death! exclaimed the pinned Lysander.

“What do you mean, froze to death?”

“I tramp around for hours in the rain and dark looking for a house, when what I really wanted was a houseboat.”

“Now Lookie here Moe, I told you to mail the stuff. Didn’t I?” queried the amused Wardon.

With the release of his hands, the curator sat up and answered. “Yes, you did, but this was too important to be mailed. After all, I saw what happened to you, I decided that I was the only one I could trust.”

Turning to the Lieutenant, Wardon inquired. “So he found something?”

“Yeah!”

“What gives?” McKay added to the exchange.

Philips turned solemn again. He showed his teammates the ledger and explained. “You see, this ledger is really a diary started by Harry Truman. Upon vacating the oval office the diary was passed on to the successor. That is, until Ronald Reagan. I speculate that Reagan’s Alzheimer’s prevented him from passing the document to George Bush.”

“So this is a record of the Mills Transfer?” McKay asked.

“Not quite Mike. What it really is, is a record of requests and payments.”

“I don’t understand,” Wardon put in.

“China and the United States, blackmail,” squeaked Lysander.

“Say again?” McKay requested.

“As our esteemed guest has pointed out...” Philips confirmed, “...For the past fifty-five years the United States and China have been involved in...” he paused, then continued. “...For lack of a better word, extortion! With China doing the blackmailing and the United States paying the tribute.”

“Shit!” exclaimed McKay and Wardon in unison. “Are you sure?” questioned McKay.

Flipping through the blue book, the young Lieutenant showed a page to his comrades. “Check this out. Here’s an entry penned by Truman.”

“Mao Tse-tung has agreed to resume talks upon receipt of $35 million.” McKay read aloud over Philips’ shoulder.

“What’s the date on that?” Wardon wanted to know.

“February 10th 1953. Why?”

“That’s nine days before the article I found in the archives. To think the commies blackmailed us into negotiating cease fire in Korea.”

Flipping to another section, Philips again read aloud, *“Following the transfer of the $100 million required by China, the UN will vote tomorrow for admittance. A seat on the permanent Security Council is assured. A pity about Taiwan.”*

“Who made that entry?” inquired McKay.

“Nixon, October ‘71.”

“That was when the People’s Republic of China replaced the Republic of China in the United Nations. Negotiations for peace in Vietnam followed shortly thereafter,” Lysander informed the group. “And, as you know, a truce was formally signed in the spring of ‘73.”

“There are many more entries.” Philips went on, “The Tet offensive, Free Trade Agreement, China’s abstention to the resolution over the Gulf War, just to name a few. This document is HOT! I think it’s best we find the treaty ASAP and turn it and the journal over to Mr. Kelly.”

“So what do we do next?” Lysander asked, putting an emphasis on ‘we’.

“We, are going to the Philippines, but Moe, its back to Washington for you. Keep your trap shut, and you should be okay.”

Before Lysander could mount protest, Philips added, “You be available, while we’re in the Philippines. We may need some research done.” Turning to his shipmates the Lieutenant ordered, “Pack your trash boys, we’re heading out. And, Clifford, lose the outfit, we don’t need to attract any more attention than we have to.”

Later that day the boys bade their new friend a fond farewell as they caught the flight to Manila.

Nineteen

Bayou Choctaw, Louisiana

Located twelve miles southwest of Baton Rouge is the mangrove swamp known as Bayou Choctaw. Named for the indigenous people, who once called the swamp home, Bayou Choctaw is now home for several endangered species, including the bald eagle, gray wolf and freshwater crocodile. The BLM administers almost one million acres of swampland in the bayou with limited access to the public. The mostly inaccessible bayou has another more ominous role, for it is the location of the nation's first Strategic Petroleum Reserves or SPR facility. Designed in the '70s after the Arab embargo, this is but one of four sites used to store oil for the Department of Energy. In the event of a national emergency America could go without importing oil for six months. Only at the direction of the President can oil be released from the reserves.

The site contains more than three hundred sixty acres of swamps, forests and buildings. Strategically located about the reserve are windowless structures that house the necessary machinery to regulate the flow of oil into and out of the reserve caverns. The entire facility has a capacity of over 76 million barrels that are stored in salt domes deep beneath the surface. Because it is surrounded by one of the largest bayous in Louisiana, the site maintains minimal security. On this particular evening there was but one guard at the main gate, while two more did duty on a roving patrol.

A light mist fell from low-hanging clouds over the bayou as four figures moved silently through an opening that had been cut into the chain link fence. A lone figure sat on a small knoll with his back nestled against a large live oak tree. He quietly followed the intruder's progress as they worked their way across the well-manicured landscaping to the first of six large sheds.

Utilizing night vision goggles, the stranger was able to clearly observe the unauthorized visitors as they split up. The loner enjoyed the last of his cigar as he waited another fifteen minutes. Humming a tune from his distant past, he decided it was time to proceed. Crushing out the stub, he stealthily followed the intrusive figures at a respectable distance. Passing through the breach in the fence, he made his way carefully to the first building. It was a metal structure without windows and only one entrance. Pressing himself against the cold metal wall deep within the shadows, the figure, dressed in combat BDUs, waited momentarily to see if anyone would pass by his hiding place. A few minutes later he stealthily approached the door and turned the knob.

Inside, the brightly-lit room, the intruder had to pause momentarily to allow his eyes to adjust to the sudden brightness. Dominating the room were two large well heads with pipe sixteen inches in diameter exiting their tops. They connected to a pipeline that ran out the end of the building and merged with the Capline Interstate Pipeline. Another pipe of equal size ran down into the floor alongside the well and terminated outside, in a brine collection pond. On the well head labeled *oil* was a large shut off valve with a bright red wheel. Below it was an access plate, which had been removed. Next to the pipe on the concrete floor was a discarded glass capsule. Smiling to himself, the stranger congratulated the interlopers on succeeding thus far.

Exiting the building he proceeded to the next, and was rewarded with the same results. Careful not to disturb anything, he left the shed and retraced his steps back to the oak tree where he had stashed his kit. From a duffel bag the mysterious stranger removed an average-sized attaché case. Snapping the locks open, he revealed the components of a Super Vepr .308. Each piece of the rifle was nestled in its own foam casing. Quickly and quietly without the aid of light, he deftly assembled the deadly weapon, threading the barrel into the ambidextrous walnut stock. Next he snapped a Russian Vomz P4 sight onto the Weaver Rail, lastly screwing on the muzzle silencer. Finally, he loaded a ten round clip and chambered the first round. Lying prone, he made sure there were no obstructions over his field of fire. Satisfied, the mysterious stranger returned to his post by the tree and lit another cigar. All he had to do now was wait.

Two hours later, when the intruders rendezvous by the fence, the assassin sighted in on the farthest silhouette out, and squeezed the trigger. The Kalashnikov coughed a 7.62mm messenger of death and milliseconds later the target tossed his arms up and fell to the ground. Before the others could react, the stranger squeezed off three more rounds in less than four seconds. The results were devastating. The three remaining intruders each took a single round to their heads. In less than ten seconds it was over without a sound being heard. Breaking down his rifle the executioner glanced one more time over the killing field then silently departed the scene without leaving the trace of his presence.

Sixteen hours later...

Washington, D.C.

National Security Adviser Kelly had just finished a superb sea bass dinner at the White House when his cell phone chimed. Excusing himself, he answered. “Yes?”

The voice of Under Secretary Ronald Ritchie came across with a hint of concern. “We have a situation.”

“My office, fifteen minutes,” was his curt reply.

“Right.” Ritchie acknowledged.

Offering apologies to the President, Kelly made his office in ten. His wait was short. Minutes later Ritchie was in the big easy chair opposite his desk. “What have you got?” the Adviser asked.

“There’s been an attack.”

“Where?”

“Bayou Choctaw.”

“Terrorists?”

“Not sure. We’ve got four members of the Philippine Army lying on a slab in Baton Rouge,” Ritchie offered.

“What does Janice say? “ Kelly asked referring to Janice Martin, the Energy Secretary.

“This is very preliminary, but it looks like four members of the Philippine 1st Division broke into the reserve and contaminated the wells with some sort of agent. Afterwards, some person or persons unknown shot the intruders. DOE has fifty FBI field agents working the backgrounds of the Filipinos and a possible identification of the contaminants.”

“Best guess?”

“Not at this time.”

“Okay, I’ll brief the President. Keep me updated. I can be reached in the West Wing for the next two or three hours,” advised Kelly. “Now, if you’ll pardon me.”

Standing, Ritchie allowed the large adviser to pass before exiting the office. Two hours later, Ritchie was in the White House, preparing to brief the President and his advisors in the Situation Room.

Located beneath the White House in a bunker built during World War II, the Situation Room was really a conference room next to a complete communication center. The space had wood panel walls with large monitors for visual aids when necessary. One monitor currently displayed a map of Central Louisiana, while the other had a site map of Bayou Choctaw. A large table dominated the room with a dozen overstuffed chairs neatly arranged about it.

At the head of the rectangular table was an empty chair awaiting the President. Seated around the table were various advisors including the Chairman of the Joint Chiefs of Staff, Secretary of Energy, National Security Advisor, Under Secretary of the Navy, FBI Director, White House Chief of Staff and other staffers whom Ritchie was not familiar with.

"So, what have we got?" came the voice of the President as he entered the room and stood behind the empty chair. Everyone around the table immediately stood. "Please be seated. Janice, have you further information?" the President asked as he sat down.

Opening the laptop in front of her, the Energy Secretary started. "Mr. President, some time between 2200 and 0530 hours yesterday, persons unknown to us at this time infiltrated the Bayou Choctaw facility of the SPR."

A murmur started about the room and was silenced almost instantaneously by a stern look from the President. "Were the perpetrators apprehended?" he inquired.

"Sort of, sir. Apparently the intruders were murdered at the location," she answered.

"Identified?"

"Yes Mr. President. A Lieutenant, sergeant and two corporals from the Philippine 1st Division stationed at Fort Bonifacio, just outside Manila. We recovered ID and personal papers from the bodies."

"Is there a chance the bodies were dumped there?" The President directed the question to the FBI Director.

"No Mr. President, initial investigations indicate they were shot by a long-range rifle on site. Maybe a .308," Director Chance responded.

"What about the reserve?"

"Looks like they've introduced a bacteriophage into the wells," Janice said.

"Bacteriophage?" the President asked with a puzzled look on his face.

"A virus Mr. President. A virus against bacteria, it's called a vector," the Energy Secretary explained.

"Sir? May I interrupt?" The National Security Adviser spoke up.

"What's on your mind, Jack?"

"How much contamination is there?" he asked.

"Good question. Janice?" The President looked to the Energy Secretary.

Checking her laptop again, Janice answered. "Let's see, there are thirty-three million barrels of light sweet and twenty-nine million barrels of sour oil stored in the sites six solution minded caverns. It appears at this time that all six were infected with the vector. The FBI's working that angle."

Speaking up before the President had a chance to ask, Chance continued. "As of this moment, Mr. President, all pipelines into and out of Choctaw have been closed down. These vectors are highly controlled, so it had to come from a government agency. As far as we know, ours are all accounted for. We're coordinating with Interpol, MI6 and the Mossad. We need a couple of hours. My intuition says something's been introduced that will render the oil useless."

"Is that possible?" the President asked.

As if on cue, Ritchie spoke up. "Oh yes sir!" All eyes in the room fell on the Under Secretary. Clearing his throat he continued. "It's quite radical but the vector is like a parasite which introduces to its bacteria host a set of instructions via DNA. They also impregnate the bacteria to reproduce more of the vector." Checking his notes he continued to his captive audience. "Once the bacteria is infected, it will morph into whatever it's been programmed to. My best guess is it's to activate enough bacteria to consume or contaminate the oil."

"How's that possible?" Kelly inquired.

"Quite simple really. Oil-consuming bacteria is already present in limited quantities, but they lack a single important ingredient to consuming large volumes of oil."

"Which is?" the President asked.

"Phosphate."

"Now you're going to tell me there's phosphate in the oil," the President sighed.

"Not enough to do damage," answered Ritchie. In anticipation to the next question he quickly added, "But the geological formation that contains the oil has a lot of appetite..."

"Appetite?" Kelly inquired.

"Yes appetite. It's an insoluble form of phosphate. All you have to do is program the bacteria to create an enzyme that will degrade the appetite into phosphate. Now you have created a bacteriophage that will start consuming oil and reproducing at an alarming rate; possibly doubling every twenty minutes, rendering the oil useless."

"How long?" asked the President.

Checking his notes once again, Ritchie responded. "Seventy-two to one hundred twenty hours on the outside, Mr. President."

"So we can write off Choctaw?"

"Yes Sir."

"What about Big Hill or Brian Mound?"

"No Mr. President, near as we can tell, Bayou Choctaw was the only reserve hit. I have ordered the National Guard to the sites just in case," responded Janice.

"Good." Looking to the chairman of the Joint Chiefs of Staff, he asked. "Where's the Seventh Fleet right now?"

"Manila Sir. They're bogged down with that Carter problem," he answered.

"Put 'em on alert." Turning to the FBI Director, the President ordered, "Find the shooter and the source of the vector."

"Yes Mr. President. Just a matter of time," Chance responded confidently.

The President stood and turned to leave, pausing he looked to everyone in the room and said, "This is a very serious matter. I'm treating this as if we have been attacked." Turning to the Chief of Staff he added. "Get me ambassadors Jakob and Respicio." Hesitating for a moment he repeated, "Very serious matter... Thank you everyone." And exited the room.

After the room had cleared out, Under Secretary Parsons approached Kelly and remarked. “You thinking what I’m thinking?”

“You mean the Spratleys?”

“Exactly!”

“I’ll send a message to the Embassy and have them bring Lieutenant Phillips up to speed in case there’s a tie in,” Parsons offered.

“Good idea. Now, I’ve work to do.” The Security Adviser dismissed Parsons and left the room.

Twenty

The seventeen-hour flight had been tedious. Lieutenant Philips spent much of the time going over copies of the journal and encrypted map he'd made. The originals were deposited in his parents' safe deposit box. McKay and Wardon spent the entire flight sleeping. Philips wondered, with everything going on, how could they sleep so much? Upon their arrival at the Ninoy Aquino airport, the trio was assailed by the oppressive heat and humidity found only in the tropics. Hailing a taxi, the three Americans headed for the Emrita district of Manila.

Emrita is a busy twenty-five square block district just south of Intramuros, next to Manila Bay. Dozens of shops, markets, tailors, and restaurants of all persuasions occupy the area. This tourist paradise is where everything goes, and anything could be acquired for the right price. The still air above the narrow streets was choked with fumes from hundreds of vehicles jockeying for the limited space the pavement provided. Cars of all descriptions crawled from light to light with loud stereos blaring and people chattering while trying to reach their destinations.

After dark, when the shops close down, the area assumes a new personality. Brightly-lit neon signs that hawk girlie bars, swanky hotels, and massage parlors harass the causal passerby. With a bustling nightlife that includes pimps, pushers, tourists and sailors alike, Emrita is a most popular destination for the young, and the young-at-heart. The center of the activity seemed to revolve around Rizal Park, the final resting-place of the Philippine national hero. Nestled between Intramuros and the American Embassy, the park acted as a buffer between the ancient walled city and Manila's tenderloin district. It was in this maelstrom that the Americans had secured lodging.

"Check this out, Moe, looks like mutated jeeps, packed like sardine cans, and painted by a hippie has-been." Wardon commented on the jeepneys crowding the roadway.

"Would you stop calling me Moe!" McKay exclaimed.

"You answered didn't you?" The big blackman smirked.

"Those are jeepneys, the principal mode of transportation here."

"As I have never been to the Philippines how's I s'pose ta know?"

"There he goes with that fake accent again," McKay complained. Pointing to the Bay, he offered, "Look, there's a couple of our ships."

Philips stayed alert while his friends went on.

"How'd you know they're ours?"

"Take a look Cliff, what's that on the mast? It ain't no Philippine flag."

"Gee Mike, who's looking that close?"

"I am," Philips interrupted without explanation. By that time the taxi had pulled up to a red awning.

"City Center Hotel," announced the driver.

After paying the overpriced fare and checking into their rooms, the trio pondered their next move. As it was middle evening and Philips was still cramped from the long flight, he decided to stretch his legs. The others concurred and decided to tag along. Taking the address supplied by Murdoch, the trio decided to try and locate Captain Konger. Pausing at the Bellman's desk, the Lieutenant showed the uniformed man the address, and he was more than happy to provide the trio with directions.

Following United Nations Boulevard a short way, Philips checked the slip of paper where he had jotted down the directions when McKay exclaimed, "Smell that!"

"Smell what?" questioned Philips.

"I don't smell anything," Wardon added.

Grabbing Philips by the arm, McKay tilted his head up as if sampling the air. "Well I do," he said as he headed down the Boulevard sniffing like a bloodhound.

All Philips could do was shrug his shoulders and follow. An amused Wardon was close behind. After several more blocks McKay stopped, sniffed and asked, "How 'bout now?"

Wardon started sniffing at the air also. "Yeah... yeah... I think... I think, ya got something."

"What's a matter with you guys..." Philips started, but did not complete his statement, as he finally caught a whiff of the sweet pungent smell of barbecue.

"...something sure smells good," Wardon offered.

"Pork ribs! Barbecue pork ribs," McKay said slowly as he licked his lips. "After airplane food, I think I've died and gone to heaven. Look!" He nodded towards a five-story brick building across the busy street. The structure housed various offices on the upper levels but there was an eatery on the street level. Above the restaurant windows, a neon cook armed with a cleaver in one hand and a fork in the other was chasing an even larger neon pig. Below, in large red letters the sign proclaimed 'Scottie-Q.' Smaller letters below the marquee promised 'Kansas City Style Barbecue'. A Budweiser sign hung in the window next to an open door where laughter and music drifted out. "My kinda place," McKay boasted.

"Let's check it out." Wardon insisted as he muscled past his teammates.

"I'm game." Philips chimed in, forgetting his mission.

Upon entering the establishment, the three comrades were

assailed by sights and sounds that can only be found in America. Wafting across the room from somewhere in back came the most delicious of aromas. A jukebox played country tunes while busy waiters delivered ranch-sized plates heaped with American-style barbecue. The low mirrored bar that stretched down one side of the room appeared to be stocked with every known beer and distilled spirit. Behind the bar stood a very large white bartender with salt and pepper curly hair. He was entertaining a pair of Filipinas with a tattoo of a Bulldog that appeared to jump whenever he flexed his biceps. A dozen or so booths populated the opposite wall, about half were occupied. Additional tables were scattered about the room with various patrons enjoying their feasts.

The decor was strictly Midwestern with artifacts from America's cowboy days. Plowshares, branding irons and harnesses were affixed to the walls while posters announced the arrival of the Atkinson Topeka & Santa Fe. Next to the door was a pegboard where four six-guns were slung, holsters and all. A couple of Stetsons hung above the hardware. Suspended from thick wooden beams were five wagon wheels with eight hurricane lanterns apiece, which bathed the room in a warm flickering glow. The final accent was the heavy planked floor that was covered with about two inches of sawdust.

Philips whistled and commented as he walked over to the maitre de's station, "I wouldn't believe it if I hadn't seen it."

Stationed behind the podium was a five foot two inch vision of loveliness. The young Filipina wore a white peasant blouse symbolic of Mexico with a long red skirt that went almost to the floor. A slit on the right side stopped modestly between the hip and knee, exposing a sensual amount of leg. "Good evening. Welcome to Scottie-Qs. Three for dinner?" she greeted them.

Nodding, Philips confirmed silently. The little lady led the hungry men to an unoccupied booth. In short order a Filipino came out and took their orders. For Philips and McKay it was pork ribs with all the fixings, while Wardon ordered prime rib. Following one of the most delicious meals to ever grace their palates, the group was involved in an after dinner beer and light conversation, when a hulking shadow crossed the table. "Hey, you guys strangers here?" a husky voice asked while chewing on an unlit cigar.

Looking up, the Lieutenant recognized the bartender, then spoke for the group. "Just tourists. You the proprietor?"

"Yep!"

"This is some place you have here. The menu is first-rate; the ribs are the best anywhere. Where did you learn to cook like that?" McKay complemented.

"I thank you. I'm a six time grand champion for the Kansas City Barbecue Society." He said modestly, while wiping his hands on the apron that covered his huge girth.

"And I had to come halfway 'round the world to find the best barbecue," Wardon complained.

"You know, you could be of some assistance." Philips spoke up, changing the subject.

"I don't know; it's not good to become involved with strangers these days," he answered, sounding like a page from an old dime novel.

"No, No, it's nothing like that, we're looking for a friend. Could you help us with an address?" he assured him.

The big man hesitated, then acknowledged. "I guess there's no harm in that. What do you need?"

"We're trying to locate 1710 Taft."

A strange look crossed the face of their benefactor, followed by a booming laugh. "Surely you jest."

"What's so funny?" asked McKay, wondering if they were the butt ends of a joke.

Still chuckling, their host informed them. "This is 1710!"

Befuddled, the Lieutenant paused a moment, then remarked, "And you're Scott Konger then?"

"At your service. About the friends part, that remains to be seen," the good-natured man replied. At that moment a ruckus erupted at the bar, taking Scott's attention away from the table. A group of eight or ten guys drinking at the bar were starting to get loud and out of hand. Turning back to the table, the eighty-four year old Konger excused himself, then moved across the dining room with the agilely of a cat.

"Wonder what's up?" McKay asked.

"Beats me!" Philips chuckled, "Check this out!" At that moment the crowd started counting at the top of their lungs. When the group got to 'five' they stopped. Someone proclaimed they could do better, and laugher erupted. The cadence was repeated with the count stopping on 'four' this time. Laughter again. As the crowd parted to allow one of its members to stagger towards the head, the SEALs were finally able to see what the commotion was all about.

"Reminds me of my younger days," remarked Wardon.

"You had younger days?" McKay snickered.

At that moment, a one legged, middle-aged American, standing at the end of the bar, had a companion take his prosthesis and fill it with beer. The leg was then passed from patron to patron in a drinking contest reminiscent of college days. Each participant was counted down as to how much beer he could consume. So far a small thin guy with great big hazel eyes held the best time. Another attempt ended with a tie. The skinny guy, obviously showing his liquor, started mouthing off about how good his time was. A somewhat bigger person of equal age took offense to what was being said and hit the loud mouth over the head with the leg, spilling beer the length of the bar.

The intoxicated patrons were like a powder keg waiting for a spark. When the spark was delivered, the rag-tag group paired off and started swinging. To their amazement and delight the SEALs saw bottles fly and fists swing. The dinner customers continued eating as if the display was an everyday occurrence. Wardon started to stand but the Lieutenant grabbed his arm and ordered, "Not our fight my friend, sit, enjoy, and have another beer."

The big brawny bartender jumped into the middle of the fray with both fists a-swinging. In the center of all this, undaunted, the one legged man was demanding another beer. Above the kicking and gouging, screaming and hollering "*A Boy Named Sue*" was playing on the jukebox. One ruffian grabbed a bottle from the bar and was about to smash it across another's crown, when a skinny fellow grabbed the cocktail waitresses' tray and smacked him in the face with it. A crunching sound was heard as the nose broke and blood started to flow freely. Howling, the patron grabbed the tray and saw the impression of his nose and forehead indented in the bottom and started laughing hysterically. Just then someone tossed a chair, but it was deflected and landed harmlessly nearby.

Konger grabbed a couple of the contestants by the back of their shirts; shouting, "Enough of that!" He then walked the hapless customers to the door and tossed them through. It took the bartender four more trips to finally restore order. The remaining combatants high-tailed it out the entrance as the few remaining dinner guests sat back, raised their glasses and cheered the able proprietor. Konger noticed the forgotten prosthesis lying in the sawdust, retrieved, and tossed it after the scrambling drunks shouting, "You forgot something!"

By now even the SEALs were laughing aloud. The entire scene looked as if it had been choreographed for the diner's pleasure. Mr. Konger approached the Americans again and sat down in a chair at the end of the booth. "Sorry 'bout that," he apologized.

"Sorry! That was the best entertainment I've had in years," exclaimed Wardon.

"Does it get this way often?" McKay wanted to know.

"Couple times a month. Bunch of expats letting off a little steam. No harm, no foul."

"Expats?" Wardon questioned.

"Expatriates, you know, former soldiers," Konger explained. Looking straight into Lieutenant Philips' eyes, he questioned, "So, why is it you've come looking for me?"

"The Mills Transfer," Philips uttered as he watched Scotty's otherwise jovial face turn ashen.

Leaning in towards the trio, Konger spoke just above a whisper. "You're not tourists after all. What do you know?"

"Everything."

"Then you know that it is lost and has no bearing today, anyway."

“I beg to differ with you. You’ve heard of the Spratleys?”

“Yes.”

“There are some members of our government who believe that the doings over here have something to do with the transfer,” he explained.

“Still, the treaty is lost,” Konger repeated.

Taking the folded map copy from inside his shirt, Philips passed it over to the wary bartender. “Take a look at this and tell me it’s still lost.”

Examining the map at length, the former Captain remarked, “This is a Yamashita treasure map! There’s only one place this could have come from.” Not wanting to tip his hand, Konger failed to identify the source.

Smiling, Philips continued, “Let me introduce myself; I’m Lieutenant Jake Philips, United States Navy, grandson of General Murdoch Philips. These are my shipmates, Petty Officers Clifford Wardon and Mike McKay.”

The big man leaned forward and shook hands all around. “Pleased to make your acquaintance. Tell me, how’s the old General doing?”

McKay and Wardon watched silently as their team leader went to work. Philips spent the better part of the next three hours going over various intricacies of the case, as they knew them. The former Army Captain sat politely and listened, interrupting the young Lieutenant only to ask pointed questions. He was more than eager to answer the questions put forth by Philips, confirming the existence of the gold and the way in which it had been buried. His memory was sharp and he was able to fill in several of the missing pieces. By the end of the evening the trio had developed a fondness for the old warrior.

When the Americans stood to go, Konger took each one’s hand in turn, shook it heartily, and offered them good luck and good hunting. He politely declined Philips offer to accompany them claiming ‘ill health’ and ‘old age.’ Almost as an afterthought he volunteered to provide a guide to help negotiate the countryside. Following a hearty good-bye the trio set out for their hotel with a sense of accomplishment for the evening.

Twenty-One

The SEALs were up early with anticipation of the day's events. After a hearty breakfast the threesome was standing under the hotel's awning when a bright yellow jeepney with red stripes, abruptly stopped in front of them. The back was empty; but the forward compartment contained a driver and female passenger. Before anyone could react, the passenger exited the vehicle and stepped forward.

"Jake Philips?" she asked. Standing before the Americans, was the same hostess from the previous evening!

"I'm Jake, and you are?" the Lieutenant admitted as he stepped towards the curb and extended his hand.

"Judelyn Garica!" answered the pretty Asian with large almond shaped chestnut eyes. She flipped her shiny waist length hair over her shoulder and accepted the offered hand.

"Judy-what?" He asked scanning the beauty from top to bottom. The petite Filipina was dressed in jeans and a white cotton shirt that was knotted at her waist, leaving her midriff exposed.

"Judelyn," she repeated.

"Jue-what. I'm sorry, I'm having trouble with that," the embarrassed Lieutenant confessed.

"Try dis, Jue-da-lynn," she pronounced slowly.

"Judelyn," he repeated successfully.

"Better. Scotty say you need guide?" she spoke in broken English.

"He did offer. How well do you know the countryside?"

"Me good, driver Billy, better." She pointed to the quiet individual with dark hair and aviator sunglasses.

"Can he be trusted?" Philips questioned cautiously.

"He cousin, bery trustworthy," Judelyn assured him, then asked, "Who dese guys?"

Taking the maiden by the arm Philips walked her over to where his comrades were waiting impatiently. "Judelyn meet Clifford."

The big black took her tiny hand and brought it to his lips, "Charmed, Madame." Judelyn giggled.

"Don't mind him, he don't get out much," the Lieutenant chuckled, "And this is Mike."

"Pleased to meet you," McKay said in a gentlemanly manner.

"Now lets git this show on the road," Philips ordered. He paused, and then asked, "What's first?"

"I've got a little something waiting at the American Embassy," Wardon volunteered.

"The American Embassy it is." Philips said as the trio piled into the back. Judelyn elected to sit up front with her cousin. In short order Billy had parked their transport in front of the Embassy.

The Embassy, located at the intersections of United Nations and Roxas Boulevards, was quite a sight. A remnant of America's colonial past, the building served first as the Lord High Commissioners personal residence. Built of gray sandstone with a red tile roof, the building was blocky with oversized windows that looked out upon the bay. An eight-foot high wall guarded by Marines from the second detachment surrounded the entire complex. Each weekday morning the Visa offices opened at 9 A.M. sharp. On this particular morning, a line had formed halfway down the block from applicants waiting to apply for visas, and it was only 8:35 A.M.

"Jesus, what's this all about?" McKay inquired.

"People wait for bisa," Judelyn explained in her heavy accent. "Sometime show up 6 A.M. only to be turned away."

As the Americans exited the vehicle the Lieutenant asked Judelyn and Billy to remain there. At the main gate, they flashed their IDs and were granted immediate passage. Once inside, Wardon explained that a 'care package' would be in the charge of a Robbie Wells, the Naval Attaché. As Wells was expecting them, the SEALs were ushered into his office without waiting. A plainish guy with brown curly hair, spectacles and pinstripe suit, the Attaché was exactly what one expected to see in an Embassy.

Following brief introductions, he informed the group their package had arrived and was stored in a small warehouse out back. Wells had been briefed on their mission by Parsons and offered any assistance that might be needed.

At that invitation, Philips spoke up. "Will you take a look at this?" he asked, producing the map and sliding it across the desk.

"This is gibberish to me," the Attaché confessed, after examining the map for several moments.

"Same here. We can't make heads nor tails of it."

"I may know someone who can help." With that, Wells picked up the phone and spoke to his secretary. After a brief wait the phone rang. Speaking quickly, the Attaché hung up and said, "It's set, you need to proceed to this address and speak to Daisy Aure." Passing a scribbled note to Philips, he continued, "Now if you'll excuse me I have pressing issues that need my immediate attention."

At their dismissal the trio stood in the hall for a moment. "What's next?" Wardon asked.

"I want you and Mike to get the gear and meet me at the hotel later," the Lieutenant ordered.

"What about you?" McKay asked.

"Judelyn and I will go see this Daisy lady."

"Don't ya know Moe? He gets to run off with the lady, while we gits the grunt work," Wardon complained to his companion.

Walking ahead of his shipmates, Philips smiled and said loudly, "RHIP, my boy, RHIP."

As the Lieutenant turned the corner McKay looked to Wardon and said, "Rank has its privileges, my ass. He just wanted to avoid the heavy lifting! C'mon lets git the stuff."

Philips instructed Billy to stand by and help his shipmates. After showing Judelyn the address, they headed off. Catching three different buses and traversing across town, the pair located the address just before noon. Several times during the ride, when Philips thought Judelyn wasn't watching, he stole glances at the young woman. She was very beautiful indeed. He would have to suppress any carnal thoughts that tried to creep into his head, reminding himself this was business.

When they arrived, a young Filipino answered the door on the third knock. After a brief discussion with Judelyn, the youth admitted them into the residence. The couple was asked to sit and wait, as Daisy would be out momentarily. The only seats available were around an old square kitchen table. After a short time the same individual who had answered the door helped a very frail elderly woman into the room. Escorting her to a chair opposite the couple, the Filipino spoke quickly to Judelyn in Tagalog.

"Dis Javier, youngest grandson to Daisy," Judelyn translated as the young man acknowledged Philips.

"Why has Wells sent us here?" the Lieutenant wanted to know.

The pretty Filipina spoke directly to the grandson. He listened intently for a moment and then answered. Judelyn hesitated a moment, then asked several questions to which Javier replied, "Oo-Oo."

Turning to the American, she explained. "Lola, I mean grandmother Daisy, she bery old. Will help if can. Older sister work at Embassy, Wells knows of Lola's past."

"So Wells thinks she can be of some assistance?"

"Yes."

"What makes her so special?"

Judelyn spoke rapidly again to Javier. He explained something to which the young Filipina's face showed concern and then understanding. When he finished talking, the Filipino took his grandmother's hand in his own.

"And?" Philips asked, becoming somewhat inpatient.

Judelyn very carefully and slowly explained. "During war with Yapan, Daisy was comfort girl."

"Comfort girl?" The American asked, not understanding.

"Comfort girl is lady forced into sex with soldier. For two-year she must live in special camp. An officer, a Colonel Arika like her, so she cooks, cleans and cares for him every day. At battle for Manila she quietly entered sheeping chamber and give Colonel 'Philippine neck tie.' Den goes to mountain and hide in cave. Brothers killed because she do dis."

The old woman sat proudly in her chair unflinching, as the story was related to the American. Looking into the older person's eyes, the Lieutenant asked. "Philippine neck tie, I don't understand?"

"She cut off his-how you say?" The frustrated Filipina struggled for the right words. "She make him sit down to pee."

"She castrated him!" he exclaimed, then added, "No wonder they killed her brothers. That was a very brave thing to do."

The elder now asked Judelyn something, to which she in turn asked the Lieutenant. "So what bisit about?"

"Has she ever seen this before?" Philips asked, taking out the map and setting it on the table. Judelyn in turn translated to the elderly Filipina, who responded with a wave of her hand. The old woman extracted from her pocket an old pair of eyeglasses with one lens missing. She held the good lens to her right eye and examined the map up close as if studying a diamond through a loupe. Her examination took quite a bit of time; she even turned the map over and examined the back.

"Oo-Oo." She answered in a crackling feeble voice.

"Where?"

A brief exchange followed, then Judelyn translated. "She see map on desk in office when she clean."

"Where was that at?"

"O'Donnell!" Daisy spat out.

"Was Daisy confined near O'Donnell?"

"No, she brought by truck once a month to help clean officers quarters," translated Judelyn.

"Does she know where this is?" he asked, pointing to the map. The elderly matron just shook her head sideways.

"Then what good is she?" Philips asked in a sharp tone, allowing his frustration to show.

"She maybe point you in right direction." The Filipina volunteered.

"What makes you think that?"

"See dis symbol?" Judelyn pointed to a symbol towards the middle of the map. "That the Yaps call 'Smoking Mountain'. And dis mean 'conception.'"

"How do you know that?"

After a brief conversation, Judelyn explained. "Daisy gone to camp O'Donnell to work. Master was bisiting. She knows some Yapanese. Other man want translation, ask master about smoking mountain. He write dat symbol. Then he ask about conception and write that symbol."

"Is she sure about the symbols." The Lieutenant asked insistently, "It's been sixty years."

"She remember clearly. As if yesterday. Never forget." Judelyn persisted.

The young Filipino interrupted the session and said his grandmother was growing weary and they should leave. The couple offered their thanks and retreated back to the street. Philips was astonished to see that it was already after four. He decided to catch a taxi back to the hotel. After dropping off Judelyn, Philips pondered the lead. *"Not much to go on,"* he thought.

"Where you been, Moe?" Wardon asked the Lieutenant when he entered his room.

"I spent a pleasant afternoon with a grandmother," Philips

grinned. “What have we here?”

Set up on the dresser was a laptop computer connected to a Globalstar satellite phone. A small scrambler was attached to ensure privacy over the airwaves.

“A little something from my care package.”

“Great! Where’s Mike, and can you get me through to Lysander?”

“McKay went to lay down. Complaining about jet lag. Lysander’s a piece of cake. In addition, can I interest you in a new car?” he quipped.

“Show me, but let’s skip the car.”

Wardon logged onto the Internet and typed in Lysander’s e-mail address. “What do you want to say?”

Philips produced a copy of the parchment. He proceeded to circle the first and fifth characters that Daisy had identified. Writing a brief note he handed both pieces of paper to Wardon who scanned them and sent the information off to Lysander. “We should know something in the morning.” He informed the Lieutenant.

“Good. What say we get some chow?”

“Any place in mind?”

“I was thinking of a place I know which has great ribs,” Philips answered with a smile from ear-to-ear.

“Just what I was thinking,” remarked Wardon. “Shall I wake Mike?”

“You bet your life,” Philips said as he jumped into the shower.

Lysander’s eagerly awaited response arrived the following morning. His detailed report went on about how the map was written in an ancient Japanese dialect called ‘Kungi’. The script had been phased out about a century before with few modern day scholars understanding its phonics. The ancient language was very complex, with a special emphasis on pronunciation. Therefore, the map’s text had several interpretations. The curator sent back a running dialog as to his findings. The map was divided into two sections, the first is what

Lysander called "prominent information." He believed this to be information that was more important, possibly directions or locations. The remaining symbols or "secondary symbols" as he called them could be most anything. Brief explanations followed each symbol giving their possible meanings.

One interesting note; in the prominent character's section were several references referring to an old building named 'Our Mother of Sorrow.' Another interesting puzzle was a series of symbols, which Lysander indicated represented numbers. Each symbol had three probable meanings. Five symbols were written along the top and four down the left side of the map. The first was possibly a one, seven, or nine depending on pronunciation. The same was true for the succeeding eight characters. The final bit of information he passed on was a phrase referring to 'Charles.' This was a rather interesting observation as everything was else was translated from Japanese.

The secondary information all seem to point to related items in the contents of the cache. The symbols seem to denote inventory, as they were written in a fashion consistent to a list.

After reading the report, Philips reread it again carefully. Handing copies to his pals, he asked, "What do you make of this?" After waiting for his friends to read Lysander's report, he went on. "Ain't going to be easy, is it?"

"Well Moe, it goes like this. We find the gold at our Mother of Sorrow..."

"No, silly." McKay interrupted Wardon. "I'd say Charles has something to do with it. All we have to do is find Charles."

"And who is Charles?" Wardon asked.

"A street maybe or a place?" McKay answered with doubt in his voice.

"I think you might be on to something there," Philips interrupted.

Recognizing the look of concentration on his commander's face, McKay asked. "You have an idea?"

"Maybe. Where's the map? What do we know so far?"

"Let's see, your grandfathers POW camp was on the island of Luzon, and the prisoners were trucked to the site."

McKay offered.

"Good. Anything else?"

"The trip was less than a couple of hours," Wardon added.

Taking the map, Philips marked the location of the former camp. Then making measurements from the legend, he drew in a red circle. "That means we concentrate on this area here. And, the Spanish word for Charles is Carlos, so let's look for a town or place with that name."

With enthusiasm the trio poured over the maps. After a time, their search proved fruitless. Throwing up his arms in frustration, Wardon exclaimed. "It's not here!"

"It's got to be," the Lieutenant encouraged. "We just haven't found it."

"Maybe we're forgetting something," McKay said.

"Like what?" asked Philips.

"I Dunno."

"That's it!" Wardon exclaimed. "We're looking in the right place, but, with the wrong map."

"How's that?" McKay asked.

"We've been sitting here wracking our brains out, and straining our eyes, looking for something that's no longer on the map."

"You mean..." Philips started.

"Yea, we need a map from the same era as the Japanese parchment!" Wardon explained as he beamed with pride over his revelation.

Snapping his fingers, McKay said, "You know, you just might be right."

Sitting down to the computer, the SEAL e-mailed Lysander and requested a World War II era map of northern Luzon. The response came within the hour without comment. Within five minutes Wardon had found what they were looking for.

"Lookie here Moe, right there, just as you said! A little to the north of Angeles City is a town called San Carlos. And it's not on the modern map," he called out excitedly.

McKay and Philips were just as excited over the find. The Lieutenant put in a quick call to Judelyn and explained where they wanted to go. She informed him that an excursion to Angeles would take all day, so she would collect Billy and meet them out front the following morning. Until then the threesome could work on solving the remaining characters on the map.

Early the following morning the SEALs were bouncing along what was the Philippine Northern Highway. The National Highway north of Manila starts off as a divided freeway, much like the ones in America but soon it dwindles to a two lane, pockmarked, neglected piece of asphalt. It was constantly choked with various types of vehicles, and bicycles working their way north and south.

"Is it always like this?" Philips asked Judelyn.

"Dis good, should see in middle of day," she promised.

"How much farther?" he asked.

"Little way," Came the same answer she had been giving him for the past two hours. Soon the jeepney came upon the Clark Special Economic Zone just outside Angeles City. The old air base had been converted into a private enterprise after the Americans had abandoned the field following the massive eruption of Mt. Pinatubo.

Following an even smaller jeep trail out of Angeles City, the SEALs were led through dense groves of banana, dates and coconut. Most of the private residences had planted coffee trees. Their ripening red and green beans weighed heavily on their branches. Before long the houses thinned out, leaving nothing but dense jungle on either side of the narrow roadway and almost choking out the sunlight. Suddenly, the jungle cleared out as if God himself had used a sickle mowing down the forests and jungle covering the surrounding hillsides, leaving a landscape void of all vegetation.

To their right stood Mt. Pinatubo with a cloud of white vapor emanating from its still-smoldering crater. The pyroclastic flows had swept down the river valley burying everything within a two-mile swath, leaving a barren, desolate path of destruction that would take a hundred years to regenerate. The gray ash which covered the landscape, gave one the sense of being on the moon.

"Smoking Mountain," Wardon speculated.

"Looks like it," the Lieutenant agreed.

As the pavement abruptly ended, tire tracks went off across the barren landscape. Following the primitive road, the jeepney came to a small stream, which it forded easily. Climbing the opposite embankment, Billy stopped and everyone climbed out.

"You say come to Barrio San Carlos. Dis San Carlos!" Judelyn proclaimed with a wave of her hand.

Before them were the remnants of Barrio San Carlos! The once bustling community was now half buried by mudflows of Pinatubo's most recent eruptions. Crumbling walls and shattered glass littered the hardened flow. Here and there rusting pieces of metal protruded from the ground like bones from a half-excavated dinosaur as light winds blew loose grains of ash about the crumbling walls. "The barangay get covered up by mountain." Judelyn informed the group.

"Looks like we've got the right place," McKay said.

"Not quite," Philips commented. "Now we have to find the exact location. If you ask me, it looks like all the landmarks are now buried."

"I got an idea, why don't you check our GPS location?" McKay asked.

Getting out his Magellan 2000 GPS locator, which Wardon had conveniently packed, Philips repeated the read out. "121 degrees 15 minutes east by 15 degrees 5 minutes north. Why?"

"Gimme the map," McKay said almost as an order. "See here, the characters across the top. The first one could be a one, seven, or nine right?"

"Yea, so?"

"They're map coordinates!" he exclaimed. "I bet that's longitude across the top and latitude down the side."

"Let me see that." After examining the Japanese map,

Philips agreed. “By God, you’re right. Now let’s see, by using the first number of the first character we have a ‘one’. In addition, the second number of the second symbol is a ‘two’; finally the third number of the third character is a ‘one’. That’s the pattern!” Quickly, jotting down the numbers, Philips then entered the first combination into the device. The repeater indicated they were seven hundred miles from the location. “Nope, wrong one.”

He then entered another combination with the same results. The third time was a charm, according to the hand held repeater they were a mere four hundred yards from the location. “Bingo! I think we have a winner,” Philips said excitedly.

“Which way Moe?” Wardon asked.

“Over there, possibly just past the church.” Philips said pointing towards a large ruin.

Leaving Billy with the transportation, the Americans and Judelyn headed off in the direction indicated. About halfway there, the group encountered the old ruined church. The sixteenth century building had been inundated by the volcanoe’s mudflows. The group stopped to explore for a moment. The church had been a modest building made of sandstone. Various statues of Saints stood in niches between the cathedral type windows. Parishioners were summoned to service by a series of bells still suspended in the attached bell-tower, which stood to one side.

“Our Mother of Sorrow, I bet,” Wardon commented.

The mudflows had piled up against the walls, burying the structure almost to the vacant stained glass windows. Standing next to one of the windows Judelyn remarked, “Pity. Most beautiful church. Go inside?”

“Why not,” answered Philips.

The Americans followed the young Filipina into the building by crouching low through the otherwise buried front entry. As the building still had its roof, its large cathedral windows illuminated the large space inside. Sunbeam’s shone down upon the cavernous room where the mudflow had oozed through the doorways and lower windows and buried the pews, confessionals and altar. Arising out of the ash was a wooden spiral staircase that led to the upper level choir, which remained intact. The nave was completely buried under the concrete-like substance. Suspended from the ceiling next to the wall was a battered crucifix. Fresh flowers were in pots at the feet of Christ.

"Looks like people still worship here," Wardon said in a hush tone respecting the church's sanctity.

"People bisit on sometimes," Judelyn confirmed.

"Let's get outta here. This place gives me the willie's." Philips voice quavered.

The group left the building the same way they had entered. Walking around the structure, they proceeded to the spot where the GPS said the bunker was located. Kicking at the earth with the toe of his boot McKay observed, "This stuff is as hard as concrete."

"So we blast," Wardon commented.

"Didn't your grandfather say the site was booby-trapped?" asked McKay.

"Yep, with thousand pound aerial bombs."

"Then blasting is out, we'd blow up the bunker and never recover the treaty," Wardon reasoned.

"Any suggestions? This stuffs impossible to get through."

Judelyn, who had overheard the Americans, stepped forward and put her hand on the Lieutenant's shoulder. "I make suggestion. Come with me." Without further fanfare she walked back towards the waiting jeepney.

"What's this all about?" questioned Wardon.

"Beats me!" Exclaimed Philips, "But if you have no better ideas, I vote we go with the flow."

"I'm with you," McKay agreed.

The Americans followed Judelyn back to the jeepney, where she informed them they would be going on another short journey. After a three-hour ride, stopping only to refuel and eat, the SEALs found themselves on a small bluff overlooking the South China Sea. The sun was just setting, giving a crimson glow to clouds that started to appear on the horizon. The vehicle rolled to a stop in front of a small compound, which had a waist-high fence built from discarded tree branches intertwined with wire.

Passing through a rudimentary gate that Judelyn opened and then secured, everyone piled out of the jeepney when it finally stopped. The flora and fauna about them was entirely tropical. Several coconuts with green unripe nuts were the monarchs of the area, towering over a broad breadfruit, whose fruit was just turning yellow. The broad leaf banana with it's green hands of mini bananas growing upside-down stood next to a coffee tree, whose red and beans made the tree look like Christmas. Amidst this tropical paradise stood a thatched roofed, wooden hut on stilts that were obviously a high tide precaution that only became necessary during the typhoon season. Nevertheless, the cottage stood as a silent sentinel against the relentless onslaught of the sea.

When the group got close enough, Philips could see there was an individual sitting at the top of a short ladder that permitted entrance into the residence. The smallish, frail looking, Filipino was dressed in a white T-shirt and matching shorts. A broad rim hat made from woven bamboo was perched atop his head. His skin had the texture and look of dried leather, while his once black hair had turned snow white. Smiling broadly, he greeted the group. "Ha-low Bing-bing. Come up."

Speaking to Philips, Judelyn said, "Jake, dis my Lolo, Remegio Aleta!"

Twenty-Two

"How could things have gotten this bad?" thought Captain Foute as he sipped his second cup of coffee. In his personal opinion, Seaman John Carter's world was in the downward spiral with no bottom in sight. The trial had started promptly the first week of January with a JAG Corps lawyer representing the accused sailor. Funny thing though, he believed in the young sailor's innocence. The evidence was too neat.

Under the VFA agreement the accused American would be tried by the Philippine legal system. The trial lasted five days; with the prosecution presenting a case that was tough to defend against. The strangled body was found in the Pasg River where she had been dumped, her right hand still clutching a patch with the *"Ronnie"* name on it. A fiber test was consistent with Carter's uniform. Witnesses at Fort Santiago identified the hapless sailor as the person who had been in the victim's company the day she died. The American lawyer was only permitted to assist the assigned Philippine council; he wasn't even allowed to cross-examine the witnesses. Carter wasn't permitted to testify on his own behalf. Subsequently the six-man jury deliberated for an hour before passing down a guilty verdict.

Captain Foute was now, required to hand over Seaman Carter to the local authorities for sentencing, but he was not about to do that. The Captain had a clear understanding of Philippine law and knew that Carter's punishment would be death. Under the Uniform Code of Military Justice or U. C. M. J. he was prohibited from surrendering the prisoner. The code was quite clear concerning the surrendering of American servicemen to a foreign country when the penalty was death. He was instructed by Admiral Burke to have the accused detained in the ships' brig until making port in Everett Washington.

Then there was the alert, which was passed down from CINCPAC. About six hours after the verdict was read, word came down the chain of command that Philippine terrorists had attacked the United States. Was it really an attack by terrorists? On the other hand, could it have been a well-planned attack by the government? Only time would tell. For now, his orders were to put to sea and resume his station off the Spratleys. Until the *Ronald Reagan* could get underway, Captain Foute had suspended all liberty and posted extra Marines at the security shack where protesters had been gathering since Carter's verdict was handed down.

While deep in thought over the current situation, the Captain barely acknowledged Commander West when he entered the mess and sat down. "Cap'n?" the XO addressed him.

"Yes."

"A communication from Manila, and you're not going to like it. Our request for harbor pilots and tugs have been denied," he said.

"What!" the surprised Captain exclaimed.

"Same for the *Russell* and the *Chancellorsville*."

"The bastards, they can't do that," the Captain said, allowing his voice to rise a little.

"They just did. And not only that, all the aids to navigation have been extinguished. Looks like we're stuck."

"We'll see about that. Has the Admiral seen this?"

"No sir."

"You rush this up to him. I'll bet he doesn't take it lying down," the Captain assured him.

"Aye Sir." West acknowledged Captain Foute and proceeded down the companionway.

Anticipating Admiral Burke's actions, Foute proceeded to his office where he put a call through to the U.S. Embassy. After being put on hold for fifteen minutes, he finally got through to the Naval Attaché. "Wells, have you seen the communication from the Philippine Navy?"

"Is this Captain Foute?" Wells asked his unidentified caller.

"Damn right it is, and just what the hell is going on?" the agitated Captain demanded.

"Listen here Mister, just who do you think you're talking to?" Wells angrily fired back, not to be intimidated by Foute's rank. "I'm not one of your toy sailor's that you can push around."

The Captain was taken back by the Attachés sudden burst of anger, and quietly apologized. "I'm sorry Robbie, I didn't mean to unload on you like that."

"That's more like it. Now, what can I do for you?" he asked.

"Have you heard?"

"About the harbor pilots?" Wells interrupted.

"Yes."

Maybe it was because the Captain was speaking to a civilian; nonetheless, Wells winced over Foute's lack of the use of "Sir". "The Philippine Solicitor General will not authorize harbor pilot's or tugs until you surrender Seaman Carter," he told the Captain matter-of-factly.

"Is there anything we can do?" the Captain asked, using all his strength to remain civil. He was definitely out of his element; this protocol shit was better suited for Admirals.

"Surrender Carter," came the answer he did not want to hear.

"You know I can't do that."

"Then I suggest you have Admiral Burke do a sit-down

with the Ambassador.

"I'm beginning to realize that," he said solemnly.

"If you let the politicians work this out, I can't see the Filipinos holding out longer than a week or so. There's much more at stake then Seaman Carter. The Filipinos are a proud people and they just want Justice. We need to let this thing cool a bit," advised Wells.

"Makes sense to me," Foute agreed.

"By the way, the Moro rebels have put a bounty on any American sailor."

"Moro rebels?"

"An Islamic separatist group working out of Mindanao."

"Shit, this thing seems to roll on and on. How high?"

"10,000 American dollars. If I were you, I'd caution your command."

"I've already suspended liberty."

"That's probably for the best. Well, gotta run, feel free to contact me if I can be of further assistance."

"Will do. I'll keep in touch. Call me if anything changes."

"Okay, as long as you promise not to fly off the handle again," Wells answered with sincerity in his voice.

"Thank you. And Robbie?"

"Yes."

"Thanks for the kick in the butt," Captain Foute said humbly.

"Anytime," he said, then hung up.

Fifteen minutes later, the Captain reported to Admiral Burke's quarters. Foute brought the Admiral up to speed on his conversation with the Attaché. The Admiral advised him the *Chancellorsville* and *Russell* were to put to sea, regardless of the pilot situation.

"That's quite a risk the Navy's willing to take," the Captain offered up.

"Well those are CINCPACs orders and the Pentagon must know what they're doing," the Admiral said.

"What about radar?"

"What about it?"

"They could send a cutter to intercept."

"So... to try and stop them would be suicide."

"And the *Ronnie*?"

"We sit. We're to let the politicians hash this out."

"Sir, does this have anything to do with that attack on the American Strategic Petroleum Reserves?"

"You can bet your sweet ass it does," the Admiral assured him.

"What's next?"

"God only knows," Admiral Burke said prophetically.

Hours later, under the cover of darkness, the cruiser *Chancellorsville* and the destroyer *Russell* slipped their moorings and headed out into the bay. Using ship to ship communications, Captain Foute offered good luck and God speed to his fellow shipmates.

"This is a dirty business, and there's going to be hell to pay when the Philippine Coast Guard discovers a couple of roosters have left the roost," he said to his XO, as the dark silhouettes of the American warships slid silently away from the pier.

"Aye Sir, that there will."

Twenty-Three

Philips stood in silence as the old man motioned for them to enter his humble abode. “Are you Corporal Aleta?”

“Yes, yes. Come in, come in.” He beckoned with both arms while smiling broadly, revealing several crooked dark stained teeth. Standing, the little man disappeared into the bungalow.

“We go,” Judelyn urged as she ascended the steps.

“What do you think Moe? Is it a trap?”

Pushing his shipmate aside, McKay started up the ladder. “Where’s your manners. The man said come in.” The other two Americans followed McKay’s lead and were soon standing inside the old man’s residence.

“Humble but quaint,” said Wardon as he scanned the living quarters, which could be no more than twenty square feet. The evening shadows creeping into the bungalow were hardly kept at bay by a bare electric bulb hanging from the overhead bamboo beam. Stretched across the room was a taut wire over which a threadbare white linen sheet was draped, thus dividing the space in two. A Nara or Philippine mahogany table, no more than eighteen inches tall, was the only piece of furniture in the fore part of the room.

Crouched down at the head of the table was Judelyn's grandfather beaming ear-to-ear. "Come, sit. Bing-bing makes coffee. We talk."

"I tell Lolo who you are," the young Filipina explained as she motioned for the trio to sit.

The three Americans sat at the table in an awkward fashion with their long lanky legs crossed, Indian style. Judelyn was busy building a small fire on a clay hearth just below a window, which doubled as a primitive chimney. Once she got the fire going, the Filipina filled a metal pot with water from a large clay jar that sat next to the hearth. Speaking rapidly in Tagalog to her grandfather, she turned and addressed the Americans. "Lolo wants know how Captain Philips doing?"

"He's just fine and sends his regards," Philips said while looking directly at the elder.

"Good, good." Aleta responded. "Bing-bing say you need my help."

"I'm not sure what you can do for us."

"She say you have problem."

"Something like that, it's just I don't see how..."

"I sorry she waste your time..."

"Tell him!" Judelyn prodded her grandfather. He responded with a stern reprimand in Tagalog, while the Americans sensed a disagreement building between the two generations. The old fellow was very animated in his dialogue, his arms making various gestures as he spoke rapidly. Judelyn was not to be held back. She spoke just as rapidly in their native tongue. Finally the dialogue between the two ceased with a stern look on the elders face. The truce was an uncomfortable one, which ensued until the water began to boil.

Judelyn's attention was drawn to preparing the coffee. She delivered a cup to each person sitting around the table. Squatting down across from her grandfather, she threatened, "You tell or I tell."

Taking a sip from his coffee, the family patriarch leaned his head back as if to collect his thoughts. "O-kay, I tell. Many year past I travel by bus." He turned to Judelyn and spoke rapidly again. She encouraged him to continue. "One day I see place I know. It place where I start drive in war."

"You mean this was where you took over driving the trucks?" asked the Lieutenant.

"Yes, yes. So I dink maybe I follow old route. I rent motor bike and try and follow memory. Get lost many, many time. Finally, find place. Very, very beautiful place. Mountains, weaver, pretty church. I know dis place."

"So, you found the bunker's location. Then what?"

"Me dinks I cannot do alone. So I gets Kuya to help."

"Kuya?" Inquired Philips.

"Son-in-law, my father, Ferdinand." Judelyn whispered solemnly.

"Okay, go on," he urged.

"We dinks no share gold, many, many thieves. So we dig like dog alone. Many, many months go by, we work at night. We dig, we dig. After long time, nothing. I dinks we in wrong place. Then, Kuya hit wall with shovel. I check wall, it made of concrete. We at right place. Next day Kuya is making hole bigger next to wall when all fall down."

"You mean the tunnel collapsed," Philips stated.

"Yes, yes. Only at wall," Aleta confirmed.

"Sand trap!" McKay offered.

"Take me two hour to dig out Ferdinand. He dead by dis time." Tears welled up into the old man's cataract-clouded eyes. "Me never go back, no want blood money," he said sadly.

"I'm sorry for your loss," consoled Philips. "You have to understand it's important that we get inside the bunker. Is the tunnel entrance outside the mudflow?"

"Sorry no help. Blood money, no good."

"Mr. Aleta please understand, it's not the money we're after, it's the papers you put in the bunker for safe keeping. Captain Philips' papers," the Lieutenant pleaded.

"You have dat," the old scout said, changing the subject.

"What?"

"You name. You name is key to past. You give name to

children, dey give name to children. It link to past. I have no link to past. Wife dead, Kuya dead. All dead, all I have is Bing-bing and you no have her." The old man rose and spoke to his granddaughter in Tagalog. He then proceeded through the curtain, only to return momentarily with several bamboo mats. "You stay night."

When Philips protested, Judelyn explained that the roads were unsafe to travel at night. Conceding, he tried again to impress the importance of the documents inside the bunker but the elder wouldn't hear of it. So the SEALs got as comfortable as they could and spent a restless night sleeping on the floor.

"It's okay. It's meant to be this way..." His mother said with the sound of roaring air about her...

A hand shook Philips from his nightmare. Opening his eyes it took a moment to adjust to the darkness of the bamboo hut. He could see a person outlined in the doorway as they descended the steps. Following quietly, trying not to disturb the others, the American observed the old Filipino quickly stride down to the beach.

A half moon reflected off the sea's still waters. Stars so large, in a sky so clear, it was hard to imagine how mankind could ever have waged war in such a beautiful place. The sweet fragrance of tropical fruit reminded Philips of a deserted island in a child's fairy tale. He overtook his host and stopped him on the still-warm sand. "Remegio, you wanted to talk?"

"Yes, yes."

"It's so peaceful here."

"Yes, yes bery beautiful. I get dis place from father. Bery special place. Now, tell me, is papers important?"

"Yes Sir, very important. I assure you it's not the gold we're after."

"What do with gold?"

"We have no interest in the gold. I'll guarantee the Philippine government gets it. Maybe some good can come from it," the young American reasoned.

"Come, we walk." The pair walked off into the moonlight chatting as if they were old friends. Some time later, Philips and Aleta arrived back at the cottage. There he promised to abide by the terms, which they had agreed to.

When the Lieutenant shook his companions awake, he explained that they would be heading out when breakfast was complete. Meanwhile, magical smells drifted from the clay hearth as Judelyn prepared breakfast. After eating heartily, the group said their good-byes and watched the old man fade away while he waved from his perch atop the stairs as the jeepney roared down the road.

"What do you think?" McKay asked his companions as they watched the scenery roll by.

"I think we have to reconsider blasting," Wardon answered.

"Maybe not," Philips offered. He leaned forward and tapped Judelyn on the shoulder, "Tell Billy to take us back to Manila," he shouted over the roar of the engine. Eight hours later, the trio was comfortably seated in their hotels restaurant, sipping beers, when the Lieutenant suggested a visit to the embassy was in order.

The following morning found the SEALs in Robbie Wells' office again, where they sat in silence as he brought them up to speed on the recent events, in both the Philippines and the United States.

"That explains the protesters," Wardon offered.

"Can the attacks be linked to the Philippine government?" Philips inquired.

"Near as we can tell, yes."

"U.S. response?"

"We've filed a formal protest with the United Nations. With political backing from Europe, we're now asking for economic sanctions against the Philippines, unless the person who ordered the attack is turned over by 8 P.M. tomorrow."

"Philippine response?"

"They vehemently deny any involvement with the attack on the United States."

"And the *Ronald Reagan*?" McKay chimed in.

"Stuck! The destroyers were able to slip out, much to the dismay of the Philippine Coast Guard. All sailors attached to the *Ronnie* are restricted aboard ship to avoid further irritation with the populace. The newspapers, however, are having a field day. They were stirring up the populace, while demanding the government force America into surrendering Seamen Carter. And, now the United States won't cooperate 'til all details on the attack back in Louisiana are exposed," explained Wells.

"Looks like a Mexican standoff," Wardon muttered.
"My sentiments exactly," Wells agreed.

"Where does that leave us?" asked McKay.

"As of now, you have top priority. Just remain low-key."

"Okay." The young Lieutenant passed a slip of paper to the attaché. "Can you secure these items for us?"

"I don't see why not," he said, scanning over the list. "How soon do you need it?"

"How does 4 P.M. today sound?"

"A little pushy, but it can be done."

"Fine. We'll be back at four." With that the Americans left the embassy, working their way through the protesters who were demanding, "*America go home,* and *rapist Carter must die*."

Once free of prying eyes and ears, Wardon asked, "Lieutenant, how come you didn't tell him about San Carlos?"

"I don't like the guy. I don't know why, I just don't trust him. Call me paranoid. Maybe, it's in his eyes. I just don't like the guy."

McKay and Wardon followed in silence as Philips led them back to Scottie-Q's.

True to his word, Wells had the equipment as requested. After loading Billy's jeepney, the Americans, with Judelyn in tow, headed back out of the city. Just after dark the group arrived at San Carlos. Philips had Billy pull the vehicle up to the old church. In no time flat they had unloaded the jeepney and started to set up a camp inside the church ruins.

"Feels kinda funny pitching a tent indoors," Wardon said.

"I still don't see why, but at least we don't have to worry about rain." McKay criticized.

"This is the dry season, silly."

"I want a perimeter set. We'll do four hours on," the Lieutenant interrupted.

"There he goes Moe, acting like we're in the military again."

"You ARE in the military, so quit whining," McKay advised.

"Listen up. I want that perimeter set, ASAP," Philips repeated. Turning to Judelyn he inquired, "What time can we expect your people?"

"Her people? Are we throwing a party or what?" Wardon wanted to know.

"One hour maybe two. I cook, we wait."

"Cliff, you got the duty."

"That'll teach me to open my big mouth."

After setting up five Coleman lanterns, that illuminated the campground with flickering light, Philips pulled aside an oblong crate. While McKay was busy setting up the site and Wardon was out front watching for intruders, the Lieutenant set about opening the wooden box. Nestled within the packing material was a White model 2001 metal detector.

Lifting the apparatus out of its protective nest, he was pleased to find the batteries completely charged. Flipping the on button, a barely audible low-level hum could be heard through the unit's headphones. A small LED screen glowed green, indicating the device was functioning properly. Grabbing a powerful flashlight, Philips headed for the nave.

Setting the gadget to detect iron, the SEAL went to work. With the round search coil mere inches off the ground, Philips started at a point next to the wall. Working in a straight line, he started across the nave. Walking slowly, the Lieutenant waved the ten-inch coil to and fro, covering a two-foot swath, as he intently watched the readout for contacts. Working his way to the opposite wall, he turned around and repeated the process back again. Back and forth he went for twenty minutes without a contact.

Just as the SEAL was thinking this wasn't such a good idea, the friendly hum in the headphones was replaced by a very faint squealing sound. The readout indicated an iron object a little to his left. Making broader sweeps with the coil, he winced as the squealing intensified. "Gotcha," Philips proclaimed as he marked the spot on the mudflow. "Mike, Judelyn, quick, I found it," he called across the church.

"Found what?" the big American called back.

"You'll see."

Wardon suddenly stuck his head through the door and whispered, "Company!"

The SEALs reacted instinctively. As the approaching headlights grew closer, Philips grabbed a Glock while McKay locked and loaded his MP5; both weapons courtesy of Wardon's 'care package.' "Quick, get the lights!" the Lieutenant ordered.

Judelyn stepped forward and spoke softly. "Maybe my people."

"Better safe than sorry, Ma'am," McKay advised.

Within the darkened church, the Americans and Filipina waited in silence as the lights approached. Momentarily a motorcycle with sidecar, or tricycle, stopped next to Billy's jeepney. Recognizing the tricycle, Judelyn stood and smiled. "It's o-kay."

With a sigh of relief, Wardon stepped from the shadows and greeted the three riders on the motor bike. "Yo' Moe, you got business in these parts?"

"We come see Bing-bing," said the driver as he stepped into the light from the SEALs powerful flashlights. All three were identically dressed in white T-shirts, dark pants and slippers. Each man was unarmed except for the traditional bolo that most Filipinos carried.

Judelyn stepped out into the open and greeted each one in turn with a hug and something in Tagalog. "Lolo send dis cousins, dey no speak American. Will help dig," she announced.

"Help dig! These guys are here to hijack the gold. See those huge knives!" Wardon cautioned.

"Bolos," McKay corrected him.

"They're Judelyn's cousins who graciously offered to help with the manual labor," Philips explained. "I made a deal with corporal Aleta if he disclosed the location of his tunnel, he could send someone to look after the gold."

"And did he?" Wardon asked.

"Do what?"

"Reveal the location of the tunnel."

"That's what I was getting at when our guests arrived."

"You mean...?" McKay started.

"...the tunnel entrance is hidden within the church?" Wardon finished.

"Found it."

"Where?" McKay and Wardon chorused.

"Right this way," he said, leading the group to the location he had marked earlier.

"Check this out Moe, the Lieutenant's flipped. Nothing here but tons of ash."

"Oh ye of little faith," Philips remarked. Turning to Judelyn he asked, "You think your cousins would mind working tonight?"

After speaking to the men, she confirmed, "Dey ready."

"Then let's get cracking. There's shovels and pickaxes with the equipment over there. How's dinner coming, I'm famished?"

"All done," Judelyn answered.

As the Americans ate rice and pork, the Filipinos attacked the hardened mudflow with vigor. After an hour of heavy work, it looked as if they had hardly scratched the surface. With McKay on guard duty, Philips and Wardon stripped off their shirts, grabbed a couple of pickaxes, and joined in. Even though it was mid January, the heat and humidity inside the ruin was almost unbearable, making the excavation an exercise in pain.

With muscles groaning, sweat pouring from their foreheads, and dust clinging to their chests, the men worked through the night. Hour after agonizing hour, the Americans and Filipinos worked side by side chipping away at the unforgiving surface. Progress was slow. Bored, with nothing to do, Judelyn curled up on one of the sleeping bags and drifted off as the men chatted and worked on the ever-larger pit.

Shortly before daybreak, with the last of his strength, Wardon swung his pickax and struck something other than rock. At first he didn't notice, but when he swung again and the dull sound repeated itself, the big man stopped and peered into the hole. At the very bottom was something other than ash, it could only have been wood.

"Hello! I think we have a winner," Wardon exclaimed excitedly.

"Let me see," Philips said, bringing a light closer. In the bottom of the two and a half-foot hole was a hint of dark wood that had been scorched by the mudflow's intense heat. Wiping some of the loose material aside, the American was able to identify the top of the altar!

With newfound strength, the weary laborers uncovered a three-foot square section of the altar top. Taking his pickax, Philips was about to swing it into the wood when Wardon stopped him. "Jake, isn't this sacrilegious?"

"If you know of another way, I'm open to suggestions."

McKay had left his post upon hearing all the excitement and approached the crowd standing around the hole. Even Judelyn had awakened from her slumber and curiously wandered over.

"Go ahead Jake. Think of all the good the gold will do for the impoverished. Besides it's not like this place is used anymore," McKay reasoned.

With that, the Lieutenant brought his pickax down hard onto the altar. The iron tip dug deeply into the weakened wood. When the Lieutenant rocked the pickax on its head, the board groaned and then splintered. With a rocking motion he was able to work the tool free. Another blow and the board shattered across its middle. Now aiming for the board next to it, the American repeated the process until he had a space large enough to squeeze through.

Grabbing his flashlight, Philips lay on his stomach and stuck his head and arms into the dark hole. After several seconds he slid the rest of the way through, being careful not to gouge his exposed skin on the altar's jagged edges. Sitting on what was once a flagstone floor, the Lieutenant carefully examined the space under the altar. Surprisingly, the heavy wood had withheld the mudflow with relative ease.

Able to stretch out on his hands and knees, the eager American searched the edge of every stone until he found what he was looking for. On one side, over by the west corner, was a loose stone. He was able to work it free with his fingers. Several more came loose once the first one was out, exposing a wooden door with a heavy iron ring. Pulling with all his might, he was not able to budge the old door. Several decades of high humidity had rendered the trap door's hinges inoperable. Looking up through the opening, Philips spied the eager faces of his comrades staring back at him.

"Well?" called down McKay.

"Looks like the right place. Toss down a line, door's jammed," he called up. Moments later, the end of a nylon rope came tumbling down. Philips quickly looped it through the ring and called out, "Let 'er rip.

The rope grew taught as everyone topside pulled as if his life depended on it. At first there was no discernible change in the door's position, but slowly, ever so slowly, it started to move. With a screeching sound that doors make only in 'B' horror movies, the trap door slowly opened to its fullest extent.

"Enough," the Lieutenant shouted up as he shone his light down into the void. Again, lying prone, the big American stuck his head into the cavity. Working the light around, he could see a large open space below the stone floor. The depth of the space looked to be fifteen feet or so. An old wooden ladder lay on its side next to the wall. "Looks like we hit the motherlode," Philips called up encouragement. "I need you to lower me down."

Carefully tying the line around his waist, the SEAL leader signaled he was ready. Assuming a position much like a rock climber, he walked down the wall as his companions fed him more rope. Thirty seconds later, his boots touched down on the floor of an ancient cellar. With light in hand, he examined corporal Aleta's underground hide-a-way.

The Lieutenant was standing next to a stone wall that was part of what obviously had been a storm cellar. The wall was constructed of the same stone as the floor above. Philips surmised that the Franciscan monks, who had supervised the church construction, included the cellar as protection from typhoons.

Shining his flashlight about the space, he figured the room measured twenty by twenty. Along one wall was a cooking stove and table. A bunk had been set up next to the table, which allowed the Filipino some comforts of home during his excavation. The stove had rusting pots and cooking implements sitting on its long-dead burner, while the bunk held the last vestiges of a mildewed blanket. Almost half of the area contained piles and piles of dirt excavated from Corporal Aleta's tunnel. The air of this subterranean world carried the odor of damp earth.

Philips did a 180 and spotted an old wheelbarrow still loaded with dirt. A long forgotten shovel leaned against the wall next to a hole that was maybe five-feet in diameter. Two tallow candles inside tin coffee cans sat on the earthen floor next to the shovel waiting for the Corporal to return and resume his excavation.

"Well?" McKay called down.

"Just as the old man said. You guys stand fast, back in a few." With that, Philips aimed his flashlight down the tunnel, took a deep breath, and stepped forward. The big SEAL had to stoop over in order to negotiate the excavation without hitting his head. The passageway was straight as an arrow with a slight decline, but the going was easy. After struggling along for about fifty yards, he came across another discarded shovel. A mere yard past the shovel, Philips came across the cave-in. The area before him was three-quarters of the way buried in loose gravel and sand.

Wiping his brow, the American examined the site.

Though the passageway was almost completely filled in, Philips decided to try and squeeze through. Setting his flashlight down, he approached the obstruction and started to scoop sand from across the top. Within seconds he was able to work an arm through and bring back a huge armful of dirt that he dumped on the floor. Remembering the shovel, Philips hustled back and retrieved it.

Now armed with the digging implement, he was able to work a hole big enough to shimmy through. After clearing the cave-in, Philips stood and gazed further down the shaft. Approximately two dozen arm-lengths beyond the sand trap, was the end of the tunnel. The Lieutenant cautiously approached, wary of other possible booby-traps as he examined the wall.

Putting his hand against the gray concrete, Philips felt elation. He'd made it! With the light, he carefully ran his fingertips along the edges of the tunnel where it intercepted the wall. A metallic object, on the right side, caught his attention. Lightly running his hand over it, he realized it was the center section of a bomb! The bomb appeared to be packed in a thick layer of cosmolene grease and was wedged tightly against the bunker's wall. Philips carefully backed away from the "live" weapon.

Retracing his steps back to the cellar, the Lieutenant reset the ladder and tested it for strength. Surprisingly, the rungs felt secure, so he carefully made his way back into the confining space below the altar. As he poked his head through, fresh air and an eager crowd greeted him. After the underground's stale atmosphere, the sweetness of fresh air was quite intoxicating. Inhaling large gulps of it, Philips spoke between labored breaths, "It-it's there. I've seen it!"

"The bunker?" Wardon asked.

"Yep, it's partially blocked by a cave-in, but I was able to squeeze through," he said, as strong hands reached down and pulled him from the hole.

"Great!" exclaimed Judelyn.

"Will you look at what the cat drug in!" McKay exclaimed, examining his superior from head to toe.

"Looks like ya's from the hood, bro," Wardon commented to the half dressed, dirt encrusted Lieutenant.

"I bet I look like shit," Philips remarked, realizing how ridiculous he must look. "Now, let's knock a hole in that wall. And be careful when you're traipsing around down there, I saw a bomb and I'm not sure if it's live or not."

The Americans spent the better part of the next thirty-six hours clearing the cave-in, moving debris and removing the bomb. With the aid of the wheelbarrow, they carefully manhandled the instrument of death to the storm cellar. Now it was safe to work on the concrete wall.

Here, progress was even slower than on the mudflow. Because of the confining space, Philips divided the Filipinos and SEALs into shifts with McKay and Wardon working one, while the Lieutenant worked with Billy. Each shift was two hours long, with off duty personnel resting as the others worked the stubborn concrete. One partner would hold a steel rod in place against the wall while the other would strike it with a twenty-five pound sledge.

"So tell me, why we doing this by hand?" Wardon grunted as he swung the sledge.

"Because of the bombs. You don't want to blow us up, do you?"

"You think."

The work was dirty, backbreaking and agonizingly slow. Judelyn's cousins were assigned the laborious task of moving tons of dirt, gravel and bits of concrete as it was passed back. In turn, they filled the wheelbarrow and then deposited the debris into the cellar.

It was during McKay and Wardon's shift when the wall was finally breached. Once there was an opening, it became a relatively easy task to enlarge it. After much groaning and grunting, the pair had a hole large enough to step through.

After the last of the debris was cleared away, Wardon peered inside at the total darkness. Stepping back he said, "Mike, you go first."

"What's the matter Cliff? You afraid of the dark?"

snickered McKay.

"You never know what could be lurking in the dark," Wardon confessed.

"Tell you what, let's send one of the guys back for Jake."

"Why didn't I think of that, Moe?"

"Caus you're too busy shaking in your shoes." McKay scoffed.

Twenty-Four

Back in Hong Kong, Captain Tong was concerned over this most recent turn of events. He'd received orders just before Christmas to proceed back to base immediately, no explanations and no details. Upon arrival, the station commander was just as surprised. Nothing made sense. Now, almost three weeks later, he'd finally received a communication from the Ministry of Defense instructing him to await a new weapons system.

The destroyer Captain convinced himself the delay in orders was due, in part, to the confusion caused by the unfortunate Premier's stroke. In fact, he had spent much the past hour watching a news special. The news anchor announced a special committee had been set up and given limited powers by the Chinese Congress. Defense Minister Chan would head up this committee that consisted of various ministry heads. The group as a whole would assist with the day-to-day operations of the government. Minister Chan would have the ultimate say-so on foreign and domestic policy. Later, the Minister appeared on television and made a brief statement. Expressing his condolences to the Premier's family, Chan urged China's populace to remain calm. He issued assurances that everything humanly possible was being done to ensure their fallen leader a speedy recovery.

With the Captain's attention drifting from the television, Tong decided to focus on the job at hand, which was reviewing status reports submitted by his Chief Engineer. He was not surprised to see the evaporators top the list. *"The evaporators again? The damn things never work right."* Tong thought. Glancing down the list, he noted the port diesel was starting to act up and the bearings on the starboard shaft needed repacking.

In reality he was glad for orders back to Hong Kong. It's true, the *Hangzhou* was the most modern ship in the Chinese Navy, but she had sat neglected in Archangel for several years while negotiations with Russia dragged on. Without routine maintenance, the destroyer had fallen on hard times and her state of affairs was most appalling for a modern warship.

After delivery, there had been a two-year refit punctuated by constant delays and material shortages. Finally, in late summer of '03, Tong was able to report to Beijing that the *Hangzhou* was fit for duty. The destroyer was immediately posted to the East Seas Fleet where her primary duties were patrolling the Taiwan Straits and applying pressure to the runaway state of Taiwan. Over the previous six months, the Captain had diligently executed his orders, keeping the *Hangzhou* at sea as much as possible, hence the ship was showing signs of wear.

Because of this, he was very surprised when he'd received orders to the Spratleys. Not that he disliked the assignment; in fact the chance to get away from what had become a boring routine was most appealing. The cruise south was exhilarating, with the *Hangzhou* cutting the opalescent water as Captain Tong pushed the ship to her limits.

When they arrived on station, he was astonished to find an American task force patrolling the waters off Mischief Reef, alongside the Philippine frigate. This was not their affair! Not to be deterred, Captain Tong was able, on a regular basis, to maneuver his agile man-o-war between the islands and the American task force to harass the obsolete Philippine ship.

After being on station for three weeks, the frigate *Hefei* had arrived with sealed instructions. Beijing's bewildering orders recalled him back to Hong Kong. The Captain felt cheated; he'd finally gotten a juicy assignment only to be sent home once things got interesting. He didn't complain however, one of the first things you learned in the Navy was to obey orders without question. This brought him to his present situation. Captain Tong was patiently awaiting a weapons system that had been promised by Beijing. In the interim, he was keeping his crew busy locating and repairing the little problems that had been plaguing the warship.

The Captain was interrupted by a knock on his office door, followed with a loud 'Sir'.

"Shi!"

A third watch ensign entered the close quarters and saluted. "Captain, there's a group of officers and technicians waiting to come aboard."

"Yes, the weapons system. Permission granted. Show them to the wardroom, I will be there momentarily."

When the Captain arrived at the wardroom, he was surprised to see Minister Chan himself.

"Minister, had I known, I would have greeted you personally."

"Not necessary," the Minister replied. "Are you ready for the new system?"

"Shi."

"Good." Walking over to the Captain, Chan continued. "I have some disturbing news from back home."

"Sir?"

"It's about the General Secretary," he paused. "All the specialists agree that his condition is irreversible."

"That bad?" Tong said with a hint of concern. "This Premier is very popular with the people."

"Shi, I know, this is the reason for my visit. With our leader ill, and with little or no hope for recovery, it looks as if

I'm going to replace him." Chan continued, "What I need to know is -- I can rely on you?"

"Of course!" Captain Tong exclaimed, a bit surprised by the question. "What kind of question is that?"

"Even if things get...well, let's just say-interesting." the Minister persisted.

"You can count on me, sir. I've a sworn duty to support our government regardless of who sits in the Premier's office," the Captain reassured him.

Minister Chan sighed. "I knew I could count on you. Now, about the system. The government wants to test fire a new cruise missile. We have chosen the *Hangzhou* to be the launch platform."

"I am honored."

"The technicians will supervise the loading and arming of the weapon. At the appointed time and place you will launch and monitor the missile's progress. Upon completion of the test, you are to proceed to Shanghai, where the technicians will be debriefed."

"When and where will this test commence?" Captain Tong asked curiously.

"On Xing Nian in the Taiwan Straits at noontime."

"Xing Nian." Tong repeated. He was a bit surprised over a test on the Hou Shen holiday.

Sensing the Captains curiosity, Chan explained. "I have sent a demand letter to Taipei just this morning requesting a formal declaration of unity between our governments. As always, they will decline. The missile test will be our protest."

"Don't we usually reserve these types of protests for Taiwan's Election Day?"

"Shi, but in this case I've decided to break away from tradition. Our protest on New Years day will be noticed by the whole world. The propaganda will be most valuable. Will the *Hangzhou* be ready in time?"

With his chest swelling with pride, Captain Tong stood just a little more erect and assured the Defense Minister, "Sir, the *Hangzhou* is ready at your command."

"Excellent, now if you'll pardon me I have a public address to make on our demands." The Minister excused himself. He exited the wardroom and walked carefully down the gangplank to a waiting limousine.

The next two days saw the crew of the *Hangzhou* busy scurrying about the ship, assisting technicians and scientists, as they installed the new system. In short order they were able to convert the aft vertical Moskitt launcher to accommodate the S-10 cruise missile. Tong admired the missile's sleek profile as it was installed into one of the launcher tubes. A technician explained that the device would be remotely launched from the Hangzhou's command center. He further went on to say that the missile had a capability of carrying a hundred-megaton warhead for 2500 miles. Again Captain Tong felt a sense of pride to be included on the preliminary tests. He would do his best!

Early the next morning the *Hangzhou* put to sea. She was about to rendezvous with destiny.

Twenty-Five

Leaving the Filipinos outside to serve as lookouts, the Americans carefully stepped into the bunker. Inside, the darkness was complete! Their flashlights barely gave off enough light to discern details five meters in front of them. Somewhere, off in the darkness, water seeped through the ceiling, causing an eerie dripping sound. Taking a few hesitating steps forward, Philips was able to just make out the outline of what appeared to be a truck. “Let’s fire up the lanterns,” he suggested.

After lighting the lanterns, the sheer size of the cavernous space became apparent. The SEALs had entered the bunker about halfway down its long side. It had an arched ceiling twenty-five feet over their heads, with a steel roll-up garage type door at the far end. Fifteen or twenty paces ahead of them was a relic from a bygone era. The truck was a standard troop carrier with driver compartment followed by a canvas-covered seating or cargo area. Painted olive green, the transport had held up pretty well over the years, as very little rust was apparent. The only outward sign of time was the vehicle’s flat tires and a thick layer of dust, which mantled everything within the confines of the cavern. In the dim light, one could almost hear the soldiers' voices as they loaded the old Isuzu.

The Americans walked carefully towards the deuce-and-half. As they got closer, two more trucks appeared from the shadows. Parked end-to-end as if waiting their turn in a parade, the transports seemed to beckon the Americans on, as the Sirens did to Ulysses and his crew.

"Will you look at that!" McKay exclaimed. He let out a low whistle.

"How many trucks are s'posed to be in here?" Wardon directed his question to no one in particular.

"Six," confirmed Philips.

"You think the gold's inside?" Wardon queried, stepping ahead of the others.

"Stop!" The Lieutenant ordered. The word echoed about the room three times before dying down. His shipmates stopped in their tracks as if playing a game of red light, green light. "Booby-trap!" he whispered loudly, pointing to what appeared to be a bomb sitting between the first two vehicles.

Giving the vehicles a wide berth, the trio carefully circumnavigated the entire bunker. Their close inspection confirmed that all six transports were rigged to blow. Additionally, a large cache of boxes against the wall was similarly rigged. The crude device had trip wires running from the bombs to small wooden boxes sitting below each truck. More wires ran from the box to the vehicles themselves. What looked to be pressure switches were attached to the truck doors and tailgates.

"This isn't going to be easy." Wardon spoke what Philips was thinking.

"We can do it," McKay assured him.

"We're not the bomb squad," cautioned Wardon.

"Wait here," Philips said. He proceeded to the truck closest to the door. After a careful examination, he set his light upon the ground next to the box. Taking his flashlight in hand, the Lieutenant lay prone and shimmied under the vehicle until his nose was mere inches from the box. A close inspection revealed a relay station. He studied the box and its contents for quite some time, as his companions watched breathless from afar. Finally, he reached out and carefully separated the wires. Backing out; Philips stood and crossed over to the tailgate where he tore out the trip wires recklessly. Much to everyone's relief the bomb did not detonate.

Walking over to the bomb, the Lieutenant slid something into an open access plate. A moment later, he walked casually back to his astonished friends. "That's that," he said confidently.

"What'd you do?" McKay wanted to know.

"I figured the Japs were counting on darkness to conceal the simplicity of the system. Basically it's a black on black, white on white, standard wiring system. All I did was disconnect the leads. I also replaced the safety inside the bomb with a steel pin I found alongside the casing," he explained.

The SEALs disarmed the remaining booby-traps, being mindful that a mistake would prove to be fatal. In short order they were ready to continue with their explorations. The six trucks were the sole occupants of the vast subterranean chamber. The bunker was completely void of any personal items except for graffiti found on the walls in various locations. "Must have been put here by some homesick soldiers," the Lieutenant commented.

"No respect for other people's property," McKay offered.

"How times change, how they stay the same," agreed Wardon.

The Americans started with the lead truck and conducted a careful examination of its contents. McKay took the driver's cab and after a quick going-over reported, "Nothing, not even a girlie book."

Philips and Wardon had better luck. They looked under the canvas which covered the troop area, and were rewarded with the sight of wooden crates stacked to the top of the truck side rails. "Let's check it out," Wardon urged.

The two unlatched the tailgate, being on the lookout for any traps they might have overlooked. Carefully and warily, they lowered the gate and pulled themselves up inside. Taking the outermost top box the duo held their breath as they pried open the lid. Within the light of their flashlights was a thick yellow waxy paper. Warden peeled back the paper and spied a glint of gold!

"Would you look at that!" an elated Philips remarked as he hefted an ingot from it's nesting place. Holding it in the air, the Lieutenant tossed the bar to his companion.

Catching the heavy bar, Wardon whistled. "That's about the purdyest thing I ever did see."

The case contained six ingots, just as Murdoch said. Each bar was stamped with a bank crest and purity stamp. Upon further inspection, the two confirmed the truck contained ten tons of bullion.

"You guys find anything interesting?" McKay called up impatiently.

The black SEAL leaned over the tailgate holding the ingot up for his teammate to see. "Naw, just a hundred million in gold," he gloated

"By God would you look at that!

"This is nothing! There are twenty-nine more crates up here all lined up in a row," Philips grinned from behind Wardon.

"Well then, git your butts going. We've gold to move and a treaty to find," McKay chuckled as he encouraged his shipmates on.

The trio went about searching the remaining vehicles. The results were always the same; the cabs empty and the cargo spaces were full of crates, but no sign of any documents. When they got down to the final truck, McKay discovered a toolbox behind the driver's seat, which contained miscellaneous tools. Behind the box he recovered several long wooden-handled objects with metal contacts on the bottoms and a steel crown top that looked like a tin can. Holding them up for the others to see he asked, "Jake, Cliff, know what these are for?"

"Hand grenades, Moe!"

"Think they're any good?"

"See any rust?" asked Philips.

"Nope!"

"Then they're probably live, Moe."

Tossing the grenades on the seat as if they were hot potatoes, he hysterically exclaimed, “Now you tell me.”

The final truck yielded another surprise. Among the gold cases was a different kind of box. It was made of metal and had a lock through its hasp. The two men muscled the heavy container to the floor. The Lieutenant took a swing at the lock with his shovel and popped it open. Inside was a mountain of official looking paperwork. Sifting through the contents, McKay grabbed one document and examined it before laying it back in the box confirming, “Looks like the missing documents.”

“Great! That’s what we’re here for,” exclaimed Philips. “Cliff, get the wheelbarrow, we’ll take this crate with us.”

Before anyone could, move there was a sound at the tunnel entrance. The SEALs turned and made out a dozen figures in various stances pointing automatic weapons in their direction. “We’ll take the case, Lieutenant,” a familiar voice said. Naval Attaché Wells stepped forward holding a gun. “I thank you for doing all the dirty work.”

“I knew it! I knew I didn’t trust him,” Philips muttered.

“This is a fine time to be without our weapons,” McKay complained.

“Not again! If I get out of this, I’ll never be without a weapon again,” Wardon swore.

“What do we do now?” queried McKay in a hushed tone.

“Ideas?” the Lieutenant whispered.

“I’ve got one. When I toss one of those Jap grenades, everybody drop to the deck,” Wardon instructed.

“How do you know it will work?” McKay questioned pessimistically.

“It beats throwing rocks,” commented Philips.

“Here goes!” cautioned Wardon. Grabbing one of the old grenades, he banged it three times on the side of the truck, and lobbed it at the approaching crowd. The SEALs dropped to the ground as the grenade went off. It’s blinding flash and thunderclap, which echoed throughout the building, caught the dark clad intruders by surprise. Screams of agony went up as shrapnel from the antique weapon tore into the crowd, dropping six or seven of them.

Philips grabbed another grenade and was ready to toss it when a burst of automatic fire caused him to seek shelter behind the stack of crates along the back wall. Suddenly a shriek went up. Momentarily puzzled, the Lieutenant realized the voice belonged to Judelyn.

A tall, huskily-built redhead slowly walked from around the from vehicle and ordered, "Now drop the weapon!" Another goon had the young Filipina by the throat with a handgun to her head. "Or shall we see what kind of a mess this pretty little lass makes when I pull the trigger."

Philips and company slowly came out from their hiding places with hands raised in defeat. "What do you want with us?" he asked.

"Why, the Mills Transfer of course." the redhead offered.

"The what?"

"Let's cut the crap. We know all about it." Turning to the remaining mercenaries he ordered, "Take 'em."

The three Americans were immediately surrounded, and were pushed and prodded towards the tunnel. As they passed their fallen opponents, Philips could see the carnage caused by Cliff's bomb. Four individuals lay unmoving, face down in pools of blood, while three more were moaning as they clutched various parts of their bodies. He derived some satisfaction when he recognized Wells. The Attaché was laying face up groaning with his hands holding entrails, which had spilled, from a large cavity in his gut. The American felt no pity for the dying traitor.

"Die, you mother!" Wardon sneered as he was escorted past.

When the SEALs reached the old cellar, their guards struck each prisoner in turn with the butt of their weapons. There was a sharp pain to the back of Philips skull, and blackness overcame him as he fell to his knees.

Twenty-Six

The Russians, as always, were being uncooperative. They had kept the Chief Inspector waiting for more than a week now and Heinrich's patience was wearing thin. *"Isn't the Cold War over?"* he asked himself as he lit up another cigarette. Sitting impatiently in the outer office of Vladivostok's Chief of Police, the smoke did little to mollify his growing frustration. *"Why is it Ivan always suspects hidden motives behind a simple request?"*

The Brit was ready to get up and leave when the Chief rounded the corner and addressed him. "Inspector?"

Standing quickly and dropping his cigarette to the floor, the Inspector crushed it with his shoe.

Watching the move with obvious distaste, the Police Chief indicated towards his door. "Please, follow me." Turning his back on the Brit, the Russian proceeded across the threshold into his office.

In an act of defiance, Heinrich decided to casually stroll in as if he owned the place. Once inside, he viewed the same dingy office with peeling gray walls for the umpteenth time. An even smaller desk dominated the small space, while a couple of metal chairs were squeezed in against the wall. The only other fixture in the room was the solitary phone perched atop the metal desk.

The Chief removed his high peaked hat, dropped it on the desk, and eyed the Interpol Inspector. “You may sit,” he offered.

“Thank you.” Sitting, Heinrich entertained the idea of lighting up again, but pushed the idea aside, thinking the Russian had suffered enough already. “Have the documents cleared Moscow yet?” he queried.

“Da, the permits are here, but there are some conditions.”

“Which are?”

“You touch nothing, you take nothing. All photographs taken must be approved. You leave all negatives.”

“But?”

“You may take notes; you may interview witnesses.” The Russian Chief continued without hesitation. “You may not go unescorted about the depot. Your escort will be waiting at the entrance of the center.” He finished with a sense of satisfaction and control in his voice.

“I have a few queries,” Heinrich started.

Raising a hand, the Chief stopped him.” You don’t understand, these conditions are nonnegotiable.”

“Well then old boy,” the Inspector from Intorpol resigned, “We’d better get cracking.”

The ride from the city center to the weapons depot was uneventful. Heinrich’s driver spoke not a word of English and Heinrich’s Russian was even worse. The sun had broken through the clouds so at least he wouldn’t have to be out traipsing around in the rain. When the car pulled up to the gate, the Inspector was dropped off unceremoniously. His escort was missing and the guards treated him as if he was a nosy tourist.

After several phone calls, a lone figure dressed in a Russian Naval officer’s uniform, walked up to his position and addressed him, in a heavy accented English. “Inspector Heinrich, no?”

"Yes."

"Deter Petrowski, Naval Intelligence. This way please."

The Inspector was led to the storage area where the bodies were dumped. He recognized the place from the photos. The walls and floor were still stained with blood; but the 'other' weapon had been removed. The vacant cradle stood as it had in the photos. "What is this place?"

"Storage."

"The bodies?" he asked, while lighting up.

"Hospital."

"Not the morgue?"

"Nyet morgue. Just hospital."

"Was there anything peculiar about the crime scene?"

"Nyet,"

"Were the victims all stationed here?"

"Da, one victim not in Navy. He discharged six-year ago."

"Peculiar." The Inspector made notes as he continued with his queries. "Could we see the bodies?"

"Da, this way," the Russian replied shortly.

"What's your impression on what happened here?"

As the two men walked casually to a low one-story building which served as the base's hospital. Petrowski philosophized, "Me thinks an arms deal went bad."

"How's that?" Heinrich asked.

"Demetri Jastrow."

"The civilian?"

"Da, the civilian, was black marketeer who sold old Soviet weapons," Petrowski explained. By now the two had reached the hospital. Leading Heinrich to a room down a long corridor, the Russian unlocked the door and ushered him through. Five sheet-covered bodies were laid out on stainless steel gurneys.

The Inspector checked each body in turn, taking notes as he went. In every case the fatal blow was dealt with a sharp instrument. The three enlisted men were dispatched with some sort of field knife, while the officer and civilian had been slain by someone welding a sword. "Most interesting," he spoke after a prolonged silence.

"What?" asked his curious observer.

"The obvious use of a sword." The Interpol agent explained. "Don't see many of those these days."

"Da," his escort agreed.

"Tell me, was there any evidence at the scene that was not included in the brief?"

"Da," he replied, walking over to a file cabinet. Removing a yellow envelope from the second drawer, the Russian produced a clear plastic bag which held a white silk handkerchief stained almost entirely in blood. "This was found under the missile cradle."

Realizing the officer had made a blunder admitting to missiles being in the room, Heinrich decided not to pursue the issue. Instead he took the handkerchief from the bag and turned it over lightly in his hands. The initials H.Y. were easily recognized. "H.Y. mean anything to you?"

"Nyet, does not match victims at scene."

"Lovely, then one must assume this belongs to the bloke who did this," Heinrich summarized. "Tell me, does Mr. Jastrow have a local flat?"

"What flat?"

"An apartment, a room at a boarding house, a house perhaps."

"Da, he have small apartment over druggist, not far." the escort responded, finally understanding the Briton.

"Could you take me there?"

"Da, one moment please," the Russian instructed as the pair exited the makeshift morgue. Several phone calls later, a driver appeared. He escorted the two investigators to a waiting automobile with a red star on the door. The black Russian made, Zil limousine was almost out of place. A holdover from the finer days of the Soviet regime, the car had seen finer days when party members had enjoyed comforts afforded to only the rich. Now, the Navy could hardly afford the fuel and maintenance required to keep the vehicle in running shape. Once inside, Petrowski assured him that the drive was a short one.

Jastrow's flat was in a section of Vladivostok that had obviously seen better days. Junk cars, trash heaps and piles of rubble filled the narrow streets. Large oil drums positioned at strategic corners contained fires where four or five jobless men hung about chatting. It was not the community that Heinrich expected the black marketer to inhabit. He had stereotyped Jastrow's lifestyle as one of extravagance and elegance. By the look of this neighborhood, Heinrich would have to rethink his impressions of Jastrow.

The rundown tenement had all the hallmarks of abandonment, crumbling walls, broken windows and missing roofing shingles. The first floor contained a central staircase that divided two shops, a druggist on one side and a vacant shop on the other. Of the ten flats over the druggist, only two were occupied. The remaining rooms had missing doors, cracked pipes that leaked water, broken windows and rats that scurried about. Jastrow's flat was located on the third floor. The door had been nailed shut and sealed with a sticker in Russian, which the Inspector assumed cautioned against unlawful entry.

Using a crowbar, Petrowski forced the door. Inside, their nostrils were assailed by an overwhelming stench. All the flats' rooms were filled with trash save one. The former living room had been set up as a one-room studio. An iron, pot-bellied stove stood in one corner with rolled up newspapers stacked like cordwood under the window. Jastrow had been burning trash to provide heat.

Ignoring the urge to vomit, the Chief Inspector lit up a cigarette to help mask the odors and went to work. A neatly made bed occupied the center of the room. Next to it was a small valet where a telephone sat. Its lower shelves were stuffed with various papers. Heinrich quickly sorted through them finding nothing of value. He turned his attention to the bed next, carefully patting it down but again drawing a blank. Checking under the frame, he spied an envelope stuffed between the mattress and the metal springs. Glancing over his shoulder to check on his escort, the Inspector deftly nabbed the envelope and stuffed it into his coat.

Giving the rest of the space a quick going over, the Interpol Inspector was satisfied there was nothing more to learn. Informing Petrowski that he was finished, Inspector Heinrich requested to be taken back to his hotel. Once outside his hotel, Heinrich had one more query for the Naval Officer. "Deter, do you know if there was any unusual traffic the night of the murders?"

"Unusual traffic?" Petrowski repeated, not understanding the question.

"You know, reports of mysterious radar contacts, strange ships reported by local fishermen or a lorry running a checkpoint," Heinrich explained.

"Not of my knowledge," he responded, shaking his head.

"How about vehicular traffic?"

"Again, not of my knowledge," Petrowski repeated.

"I thank you. If you find yourself in London, pop in, and we'll go for a spot of tea," the Inspector said, as he shook his escort's hand.

Once inside the privacy of his room, Heinrich retrieved the envelope and dumped the contents on his bed. There were three letters from a lass named Olga, a small address book, and several postcards. Ignoring the letters, the Inspector went straight for the address book. Thumbing through it, he noted the usual entries for relatives, doctors and friends. On the last page was an entire list of numbers without explanation. Picking up the phone, he punched in the first number.

"Da!" said a feminine voice.

"Hello?" The Inspector greeted the unknown party. "Do you, by chance speak English?" His response was a barrage of Russian gibberish. Excusing himself, Heinrich hung up. The next several phone calls had the same results. He was on the last number, with his hopes waning, when he had a stroke of good fortune.

"Hello." Again, another feminine voice.

"Why hello," he responded, using his most charming manner.

"And what may I do for you?" she asked.

"For starters, you may help me by stating the nature of your business."

"Why, Intercoastal Marine."

"And your location?"

"No. 9 Chattem, Wanchi, Hong Kong!" she said.

Heinrich immediately hung up. Glancing at the postcards, the Inspector noticed all were post marked from Hong Kong. On the back of one card was a series of numbers and the initials "H.Y". A further check of the papers yielded little information. Packing his bags, he was on the next plane to Hong Kong.

Inspector Rolf Heinrich felt a little remorse as he stepped onto the curb at the Hong Kong International Airport on Chek Lap Kok Island. The old Crown Colony had gone the way of politics and Britain's two hundred year presence in the South China Sea no longer existed. Catching the Airport Express, Heinrich settled down for the twenty-five minute ride into Hong Kong.

He had secured a room in the old financial district where things hadn't changed much since his last visit. His first order of business was to check in with the South China bureau of Interpol. The Inspector made several requests including satellite photos and radar records for the night in question.

Heinrich was having tea at the Lord Faulkner pub, across from the Intercoastal Marine facilities, when a courier dropped off a packet from the local offices. Inside were a dozen high-resolution photos from a SPOT satellite showing ship positions the night of the break-in. With the aid of infrared photography, Heinrich could trace the courses of several large ships and many small ones. What caught his attention was a small object, which over time appeared to approach, disappear, and then leave Zolotoy Rog Bay.

Aided with a magnifying glass, the Chief Inspector was able to make out the distinct shape of a small boat. Heinrich estimated the wooden craft to be about thirty meters long. Its general course to and from the bay indicated Hong Kong as a point of origin. "Tis Hong Kong," he mused aloud.

Later, he went into the Marina and spoke with the receptionist. A most courteous Chinese female informed him the boat he was looking for belonged to the Carlisle LTD shipping firm and could be found in slip No. 38. She further stated that the junk had been in port for several days. He approached the quay carefully where he found the 19th-century Chinese junk.

Boarding the deserted vessel, the Inspector found a neat and well cared for craft. The teak and mahogany construction of the junk was impressive. Even though the ship was over a hundred years old, she showed little wear. Her sails were carefully stowed and the decks were immaculate. The salon had teak tables set with fine china and white linens, while chairs were neatly arranged about them. The main hold was free from standing water and clear of any dry rot. All in all, a most impressive craft.

The crew quarters were spacious with bunks and lockers. The vessels only renovations appeared to be the addition of a small diesel engine, modern galley and a state of the art navigation system. *"All the comforts of home," h*e thought. Working his way aft, Heinrich discovered recording equipment in the Captains' Quarters. Fiddling with the equipment, Heinrich discovered that the power was cut off. He did not know the purpose of the video gear, but he intended to find out.

With the intent to locate a breaker panel, Inspector Heinrich saw a louvered door closing, down the narrow passageway. Knowing there was no escape, he quickly reached the door and pulled it open. Inside was a small stateroom, which contained a bunk, basin and writing desk. What drew the Inspector's attention though was the tall, leggy blond female standing in the center of the room. Her expression was not of surprise but of amusement. Before he could say anything, two thugs grabbed him from behind and pinned his arms behind his back.

The mysterious female stepped forward and held his chin steady as she peered into his eyes. "It would be wise if you dropped your inquiries," she said in a sultry voice barely above a whisper.

"I can't do that," he spoke defensively.

"Pity! Then we'll have to do this the hard way."

"You don't know who you're dealing with," the Inspector cautioned.

"Give him a friendly reminder as to who's in charge," she ordered as she stepped back.

Suddenly a blow struck him hard in the solar plexus. He grunted as pain shot upward from his side. Another blow landed, this time to his left kidney. Gulping volumes of air, Heinrich buckled to his knees. Looking towards his tormentor the Inspector noticed the beauty hadn't even flinched. In fact she sported a sly grin! Finally, a heavy object struck him behind the left ear and Heinrich blacked out.

Sometime later, the Brit came to, lying on the floor of the stateroom. His head throbbed from the blow but he figured he would live. Managing to stagger to his feet, the Inspector felt something was not right. Quickly retracing his steps to the Captains Quarters, he was dismayed to find the video equipment gone! Nevertheless, that was not it! Something else was amiss. Then it hit him; the deck was sloping downward towards the bow. The boat was sinking!

Scrambling to the ladder, which led above, Heinrich was not surprised to see the hatchway closed. Giving the wooden hatch a not so gentle shove, the teak door refused to yield. This time the Inspector put his shoulder into it and hit the door with all this might. Again the door refused to budge. Now, he noticed water starting to seep into the companionway. Time was running out!

Running slightly up hill back into the Captains' Cabin, Heinrich checked the portholes, but they were too small to crawl through. He searched the stateroom for anything of use to help pry open the hatchway, but to no avail. The rising waters of Hong Kong Bay had now reached the compartment. Looking up, the Inspector spotted a skylight. He grabbed the table to move it under the skylight, but found it was bolted to the floor.

The water was now ankle deep and rising fast! Thinking quickly, he grabbed the leather chair and positioned it directly under the skylight. Stepping up, Heinrich pushed at the glass and felt it give. Elated, he reached up and pulled himself through.

The deck was almost completely awash as the untethered craft drifted towards the South China Sea. Without a moment's hesitation, the Inspector dove into the harbor. The wreck was about three hundred meters from a small island, which he recognized as Stonecutters. In his youth Heinrich had been an avid swimmer. He paced himself well and was able to make the island in short order.

A couple was startled when the water-logged Inspector came ashore. Quickly getting directions to the local police station, he proceeded with all haste to the location. The Englishman calmly explained who he was, where he had come from, and the particulars of the sinking. After a Q & A session which lasted more than an hour, the local police staff was able to confirm his story. The officer in charge shuttled the still-wet Heinrich across the harbor to his hotel.

The Briton made his way up to his room, swearing revenge for his ruined suit. There, he made a brief phone call to Amanda, explaining what had happened. Later, after a shower and change of clothing, the Inspector treated himself to supper. Upon his return, there was a message waiting from Amanda. He was to give her ring.

"Amanda," he said after the line connected.

"In-inspector, you okay?" she queried with a hint of concern in her voice.

"Just a knot on my head the size of Big Ben along with my soiled pride," he assured her.

"That's bloody awful."

"What?"

"Wh-what they done to you," she sympathized.

"How about Carlisle Limited?"

"It's-it's a holding company, wholly-owned by Nipton Foods."

"Nipton Foods?"

"Absolutely. A mega-conglomerate that specializes in the processing, transportation and distribution of seafood worldwide."

"Be a good lass and tell me where they're located."

"Kobe, Japan."

"Do you, by any chance, know who the chief operating officer is?"

"Of course."

"Well?" he asked, growing inpatient.

"Cost you dinner!" she exclaimed.

"Amanda! You know better than that."

"You want the information?" she teased.

"Go ahead love, you've got dinner."

"Heidiki Sawada, kind of an eccentric chap living just outside Nagano."

"What do we know about him?"

"He's kind of a queer chap. Mostly a loner, a war orphan who parleyed his meager earnings into vast holdings around the world. There's talk he wants to expand into super tankers," Amanda explained.

"What's this bit about super tankers?"

"Why don't you ask 'im." she advised.

"I may just do that," he answered, then repeated. "I may just do that."

"Were you able to run down those numbers I gave you?"

"Yes sir, they belong to a bank account with Carter Bank of Switzerland which operates offices in Hong Kong. The bank had no comment about the depositor."

"Thanks, I've got to run along."

"You be careful out there, remember our dinner date."

"I'll do that, love," the Inspector said as he hung up the phone. His next call was to make reservations for Tokyo. "I don't scare easily," Heinrich swore as he began to pack his bags.

Twenty-Seven

Xian felt as if he was drifting weightless through space. Looking down he could see the battlefield below. Two armies were squared off on parallel ridges with an open field between them. Drifting slowly, the disembodied Premier could see cannons mounted on wooden carriages awaiting the signal to open fire.

A General officer mounted on his white stallion stood atop a small knoll. As he surveyed the field, a gentle wind whipped a series of red flags. The General was not alone; a group of mounted advisers accompanied him. From the opposing army, a courier arrived and handed a scroll to one of the advisers. The scroll was then passed to the General, who proceeded to examine its contents. Shaking his head sadly, he tossed the scroll to the ground. Predictably, a multicolored red and golden banner with a dragon on it was waved. At the expected signal, a thunderous roar went up as a thousand cannons belched fire and black smoke, announcing the beginning of the barrage. The battle of Red Cliffs had begun!

Just as the scene had appeared, it started to fade away.

Again, Xian was floating in darkness. Voices were muttering far away, almost too faint to hear. Now they were coming closer. He tried to concentrate on them; but the more he tried, the more the voices eluded him.

It became light again. This time he floated over the garden behind the executive building. He could see an old man and a young girl walking about the gardens' paths. He saw them sit before a grotto and then the old man collapsed. The scene started to fade even though he wanted to stay.

"Xian, Xian," said a voice so far away that he first thought it came from the garden. He tried to answer, but it was too much effort.

"Premier Xian," the voice said. He decided it had a distinctly female tone to it.

"Xian, Xian."

The voice was practically on top of him now. He had to respond, he must. Xian tried to move his hand, to no avail. Maybe, if only he could open his eyes. The lids felt so heavy. He'd try anyway. Not knowing if he was successful, the darkness faded into a very bright light. He could just make out the round face of Hui Woo. Happiness swept over him, somewhere he felt he knew her, Xian knew her name, but who was she? Trying to refocus his eyes, this time the face was not of Hui Woo but a total stranger. He felt sadness sweep over him.

"Premier Xian, I will help you."

Blackness again. He was able to feel an urgency of something he needed to do. Almost as if it was a job left undone. It was so easy to give up. Voices again. This time they were different, male perhaps. As much as he tried, he could not get his eyes to open. Again blackness. He was drifting.

Twenty-Eight

Nagano, Japan

Sawada's chief of security, Ian McKittrick, sat back in his chair and sighed. The demands of his bosses' schedule had kept him constantly globe trotting these past two months. Not that he disliked travel; it's just that the Scot was glad to be finished with the 'dirty' work.

Born to a small fishing village on Scotland's West Coast, McKittrick had been running most of his life. Both his parents had perished in a house fire when he was ten, leaving Ian to be raised by a domineering sister in London Town. The lad was forced to put up with her doting ways for almost seven years. Finally tiring of her nit-picking, he lit out and joined the British Army six days shy of his seventeenth birthday. After two wars, six campaigns, thirteen secret missions and twenty years of loyal service, Sergeant Major McKittrick of the SAS was drummed out of the service. Found guilty of striking an officer who had been accosting a young lass at a local pub, he wasn't even allowed to testify on his own behalf. To the British there was no excuse, he was expected to conduct himself in a professional manner regardless of the situation. Damn them and their class system, McKittrick had lost the only real home he had ever known.

A strong individual of medium stature, McKittricks short cut-flaming red hair and icy blue eyes always captivated the ladies. He enjoyed a daily ritual of pumping iron within the castle gymnasium, followed by a six mile run around the estate grounds, to keep in shape. Once, he'd held the Guinness record for rolling an aluminum skillet into a tube.

The man had a soft spot for fine clothing and liked to conceal his muscular build beneath silk shirts and Gucci suits. Many an adversary had been defeated because they had misjudged the Scotsman's great strength. He'd once crushed a man's windpipe with his bare hands. A foe should never underestimate McKittrick, as he was a great force to reckon with.

It had not always been this good. Following his discharge, the Sergeant Major spent the better part of two years drowning his despair in Scotch. He bounced from town to town doing odd jobs by day, and spending his evenings in various pubs drinking the pain away. Occasionally he'd pick up security work, nothing special, a load of tax-free cigarettes here and maybe a batch of illegal booze there. Now and then a little muscle would be needed and the wayward Scot would hire out to the highest bidder. Most of the time he spent his evenings on cheap liquor and even cheaper women.

On that cold, foggy February night, when he had been on a three-day bender, his drinking came to an end. Through bloodshot eyes, the former Sergeant Major was able to discern an elderly Japanese individual enter the pub and proceed to the bar. Speaking briefly to the bartender, who nodded in his direction, the gentlemen, approached him and offered to buy a pint. He introduced himself and went on briefly about nothing in particular. The one-sided conversation came to an abrupt end when the stranger offered the drunken McKittrick the head security position for his company. The pay was handsome. It offered an opportunity for McKittrick to climb up out of the gutter and prove he could put the past behind him. It had taken eight months for him to dry out and burn off the extra twenty pounds he'd put on due to the lack of discipline he had suffered the previous years. Nevertheless, that was the past, and Ian wasn't someone to dwell on such matters.

Though Sawada was quite secretive with his operations, McKittrick was aware that something big was in the works. Preparations were going better than expected; they were actually ahead of schedule. Leaning back in his chair and blowing smoke rings towards a computer monitor, he couldn't help but to pat himself on the back. His task had been an important one and now it was complete.

Occasionally, the redhead would reach up and twist one side or the other of a very handsome handlebar mustache. The computer console he sat at was within the main surveillance and communications room of the castle. The sign on the door indicated operations, but with all the gadgetry he thought it should say "Houston Control." There were dozens of monitors that watched every aspect of the property. At his fingertips, the Security Chief could eavesdrop on any room or location, about the castle. Computers recorded readings of doors opening and closing, room temperature, and even water pressure. Motion sensors and surveillance radar were everywhere. No one could approach within a hundred yards of the outer wall without setting off an alarm.

He had to hand it to the man; Heidiki Sawada had been meticulous with the castles' reconstruction. From outside, one could see the central keep surrounded by several outbuildings. A curtain wall with six towers encircled the entire complex. The façade was reinforced with apparent courtyard shops such as blacksmith stable, butcher's shop and stonemason workplace. The reconstructed barn served as sleeping quarters for part of the security detail. Able to comfortably accommodate twenty-five men at a time, the structure afforded a prominent view of the entire courtyard and contained a motorpool in back.

The manor house was a typical fifteenth century structure on the outside; however, many modifications had been made to the interior. While the main public areas all looked the medieval part, certain sections of the castle's interior were ultra modern.

One such place was the operations room, located on the top floor of the old Watchtower, where McKittrick was presently enjoying his cigar. Below him on the Tower's middle floor, was a dormitory for seventy-five men of Sawada's security force. Located deep within the bowels of the castle itself, were other improvements. A series of guest quarters, day rooms, cells and interrogation facilities were hidden away from prying eyes. The very lowest level of the castle, which had once contained a dungeon and wine cellar, had been converted into Sawada's gymnasium and science labs.

The science labs that Sawada called "clean rooms" were the most secret and secure rooms on the estate. These sterile labs had temperature-controlled environments that were closely monitored by the operations room staff. Each room contained a refrigerator, plenty of counter space, test tube racks, culture dishes, Bunsen burners, computers and other necessary items with which to do assigned tasks. Some rooms were responsible for growing different types of cultures. Another had an entire wall devoted to glass cabinets that contained rows upon rows of shelves, all containing beakers of oil. Each container had a label that identified the grade and oil field from whence the sample had been collected. The labs, with various ongoing experiments, were rarely vacant. For safety and security reasons each room had a double, airtight, locking set of doors. These rooms, which were strictly controlled, required special identity cards to be worn at all times. The doors themselves could only be opened with an individualized key card.

"If the lads back in the regiment could see me now," McKittrick spoke with his thick Scottish accent to no one in particular. He rolled his cigar between his fingers and thumb and blew another smoke ring at the monitor.

"I wonder how our guests are doing tonight?" he thought. Punching a couple of buttons on the console in front of him, McKittrick was able to access the proper camera for the desired location.

The view before him instantly changed from the clean rooms to a simple bedroom, which McKittrick could see almost entirely. A solitary hospital-type bed occupied the space, which was painted a sterile white. Next to the bed, monitors beeped as a sleeping form rested in the middle of the gurney. IV tubes ran from clear plastic bags, hanging from a stainless steel pole, into the back of the left hand of the patient. "*Nothing doing here,*" he mused, before changing cameras.

This time McKittrick was afforded a view to a dimly lit room with no furnishings whatsoever. The cell's three occupants rested with their backs against the walls as they discussed their predicament. He felt sorry for these men, as their fate was attached to Sawada's whims.

The Security Chief punched a third button and was rewarded with a view of another bedroom. A neatly made bed stood against the center wall, while to the right was a dresser/mirror combination. The left wall contained a fireplace with a crackling fire. The space had been modestly decorated with lithographs depicting Japanese country life. Next to the dresser was a doorway that opened into a small bathroom.

"Come out, come out, wherever you are!" he playfully called. Panning the camera around, McKittrick saw no sign of Sawada's guest. "Where are you Mr. Smyth?" Still not spotting his quarry, the Scot switched to the bathroom camera. "Ah-ha, now I have you," he called out when steam could be seen rising from the shower.

In voyeuristic delight McKittrick watched as Smyth toweled off, shaved and donned a tuxedo.

"Are we having dinner guests?" he wondered aloud.

A moment later there was a knock on the door. Smyth answered and admitted two extremely beautiful women who manhandled a serving cart through the doorway. After a few spoken words, Smyth sat on the edge of the bed and allowed the women to fuss over him.

Expert and adept, a blond dressed in a red evening gown with plunging a neckline, uncovered various dishes and presented them for Smyth's approval. The brunette, dressed in a traditional Chinese silk dragon dress with splits almost to her waist, was busy pouring three flutes of champagne. All the while,

Smyth sat licking his lips in anticipation of what was to come.

Dr. Smyth's passions were women and food, and not necessarily in that order, and it was one of McKittricks assigned tasks to be sure that he did not run out of either. The Security Chief felt a hand on his shoulder. Turning casually while exhaling another smoke ring, he spoke, "Good evening Mr. Sawada."

"So, how are our guests doing this evening?" his employer questioned.

"Our friends from the Philippines are most uncomfortable. The old man is sleeping soundly and it looks like Heidi and Grace are in for a busy evening."

"Good, good Listen Ian, I have to check on some arrangements. I'll be going to Hong Kong for a couple of days, can you check with Jacori and make certain he understands our guests needs?"

"Yes sir," came a hearty response. "Is there going to be trouble?"

"No Ian, nothing as dramatic as that. Could you make sure the kindly doctor enjoys his final evening. Tomorrow take him for a ride, you know what to." Sawada nodded towards the monitor as the brunette slipped her dragon dress from her shoulders, revealing a pleasing hourglass figure and a well-endowed chest encased in a lacy red bra with matching panties and garters. "It looks like Nigel's last night on this earth is going to be a memorable one."

"You can count on it Mr. Sawada, everything will be taken care of," McKittrick assured him. He turned his attention back to the computer monitor in time to see Grace remove her own dress as well, exposing a completely flawless figure encumbered by nothing. He never tired of watching Grace and Heidi perform for the good Doctor.

"Excellent, send for our Philippine guests. Have them escorted to the old dining hall, I'll be joining them for dinner."

"Yes sir," McKittrick responded with a tone of reluctance to his voice. Giving the monitor a parting glance, he showed disappointment at the prospect of missing the show, then switched the screen off.

Sawada silently exited the room to check on preparations and to change into his dinner jacket.

Twenty-Nine

Five short Asians came for the imprisoned Americans. Ordering them off the floor, the armed guards roughly shoved the prisoners down the stone corridor.

"All right, already!" McKay complained.

"Moe, these guys sure know how to show a fella a good time," Wardon chimed in.

"Where we head'n?" McKay asked his guard, who responded with a shove.

"No speak," said the lead goon.

"To slaughter!" Wardon whispered, as his guard jabbed him with the gun butt. "Yo, Moe you wanna watch who you hit with that thing. Someone could get hurt!"

"O.K. guys, pipe down," Philips ordered in a hushed tone, then added, "I don't need anyone getting hurt."

The guards escorted the threesome from the basement up a massive spiral staircase. Their trip ended at an extensive dining hall on the castle's main floor. The room had large stained glass windows, depicting knights riding triumphantly on their majestic steeds while maidens danced before them. Mounted on the walls were hunting trophies of numerous game animals, including stags, elk and moose. In a marble fireplace large enough to walk into, a stack of logs burned brightly.

Suspended from arched Gothic ceilings were two huge gold plated Czechoslovakian crystal chandeliers. Centered below the chandeliers was the longest table Phillips had ever seen. Made of dark walnut, it had a polish so deep that the Lieutenant could see his own reflection as if it were a mirror. Arranged around the table were two dozen high back chairs. A large silver centerpiece held almost every type of fruit, from oranges to papaya, the yellowish star fruit to blood-red grapes.

"You sit!" ordered the head goon, as he indicated place settings at one end.

When the prisoners sat down, the guards withdrew to sentry positions around the hall. Using his eyes to communicate, Phillips indicated there were two vacant place settings at the table. Momentarily, sounds of a struggle could be heard coming from beyond the large, double French doors guarded by medieval suits of armor. Not sure what to expect, the Lieutenant was amazed when a couple of guards hauled Judelyn into the room.

The Filipina's arms were flailing about her captors' heads, as she spat profanities in her native tongue. Smiling inwardly, the American admired the young woman's spunk. At least someone was not taking this lying down. He doubted that they would harm her, but you never knew. Forced to sit opposite the SEALs, Judelyn's guards stayed right with her, and shoved her down roughly whenever she tried to stand.

"I'd do as they ask, if I were you," Philips advised.

With that, she stopped struggling and proceeded to sit quietly, with her arms crossed in defiance.

"You OK?" he mouthed while looking directly into her eyes.

Judelyn nodded.

"Good," he mouthed.

"Yo, Moe! You think someone's gone to great lengths just to have us to dinner?" whispered Wardon.

"Well, if this is their idea of service, I must complain to the management about the accommodations." McKay complained in hushed tones. “My bed wasn’t made up today.”

“Pipe down! We’re not alone.” Philips nodded towards the security cameras mounted on the walls near the ceilings.

Not heeding the Lieutenants order, Wardon flipped the bird to the nearest camera. “See how they like that!”

Settling down, the group waited in silence for their host. Shortly, a demure Asian dressed in a traditional Chinese green dress entered the hall carrying a bottle of champagne. Her dress was embroidered with gold dragons and had a high straight collar, with slits up both sides. She was indeed a very sexy woman.

The maiden greeted the group in perfect English. “Good evening Lieutenant. Mr. Sawada sends his regrets, but pressing matters have delayed him.”

“Nice place you have here, but if you’ll pardon us, we’ve a train to catch,” Philips remarked as he went to stand, only to receive a stern look from one of the guards. “On second thought maybe we’ll stay and have a bite to eat.”

“By the way, where’s here?” McKay asked, as she filled his glass with from the magnum.

“Why Japan, of course.”

“Japan!” exclaimed Philips. “I don’t recall being out that long.”

“Yes, Japan.”

“So tell me, who’s throwin’ this shindig?” asked Wardon.

“Heidiki Sawada. You’re to start dinner without him, he’ll join you shortly.” With that she clapped her hands. On cue, a whole army of servants entered the hall carrying a myriad of trays and platters. They proceeded to serve the prisoners a feast that was fit for a king. The group had never seen so much food at one time. The main course consisted of duck, venison, and roast pork. Mountains of yams, potatoes and noodles, clams, shrimp and sushi were just a few of the side dishes the servants were constantly bringing. The captives ate as if they were attending a Roman orgy.

“Maybe this Sawada’s not such a bad fellow after all,” Wardon mumbled through a mouthful of food.

"Said the spider to the fly," cautioned McKay.

The group enjoyed their meal while conversing among themselves, always mindful of the guards with automatic weapons. Judelyn detailed how her cousins had been overpowered and then executed by Sawada's goons. She explained how upset the red-haired man was when he didn't find what he was looking for. As they were putting the finishing touches on a tasty cherry cobbler, Sawada entered the room.

Philips was first to notice the two men standing in the doorway. As he stopped eating and the others followed suit, a hush fell over the group. "A most tasteful dessert, wouldn't you say, Petty Officer McKay?" their host spoke up.

"You have me at a disadvantage."

"Oh, forgive me. I'm Heidiki Sawada..." he turned to his associate. "...and, I believe you have met my security specialist, Ian McKittrick."

"Our red-haired guy from Seattle." Wardon offered, "Nice stash."

"'Twas I who had the satisfaction of whacking you on the head in Washington as well," bragged the well-dressed Scotsman.

"I owe you for that one," the black man hissed.

"Gentlemen, gentlemen, we're not here to settle old scores," Sawada scolded. Turning to Philips, he continued with acceptable English. "You must be Lieutenant Philips."

"That's correct. You had no right to bring us here. I demand an explanation."

Holding his hand up to stop McKittrick who had stepped forward to strike the American, Sawada spoke in a soft manner, "Lieutenant, let's not be so hostile."

"Why are we here?" The Lieutenant pushed for information.

Taking a sip from his champagne, Sawada studied the group for a moment and then spoke carefully. "I have a little business proposition I'd like to make."

"Which is?" asked Philips."

"You have a piece of merchandise I would be most

interested in purchasing."

"And," McKay urged.

"I'm aware of the Mills Transfer. I'll let bygones be bygones if you turn it over to me."

"What makes you think we have the Transfer?" inquired McKay.

"My men carefully examined the bunker after you were, shall we say, indisposed, and turned up nothing."

"And if I turn over the treaty, what's in it for us?" asked the big American.

"I will let you go."

"And the girl?" Philips asked curiously.

"You may take her with you," Sawada answered. "I have no interest with her."

"How do I know that I can trust you?"

"As a Samurai, my word is my bond."

"A Samurai! I thought they went the way of the dinosaurs." mocked Wardon.

"And if we don't?"

"Then you die!" exclaimed Sawada.

"If I may," McKay interrupted, "What's your interest in the treaty?"

"Good question. As you can see I'm a collector of historical objects. The Mills Transfer is just such an object. I would like to add it to my collection," he lied.

"And you'll kill for it!" Wardon exclaimed as he glared at the shipping magnate.

"Sometimes priceless objects carry high prices," Sawada reasoned.

"And Mr. Wells?" Philips asked solemnly.

"A most unfortunate accident. I left instructions, no one was to be harmed, but in the heat of the moment, Mr. Wells got a little out of hand."

By this time the servants had removed all vestiges of the supper from the table. Sawada nodded and the female server returned and urged Judelyn to follow her. Upon the Filipina's reluctance, Sawada assured her that no harm would befall her.

Sawada rose from the head of the table and proceeded towards the French doors. Turning, he spoke quickly in Japanese to the guards who, in no uncertain terms, urged the Americans to accompany them.

"You've a special treat tonight," McKittrick offered as he led the party down a hallway to a small conservatory, "it's not often we have esteemed guests such as yourselves." He continued, "You must remain absolutely silent and reflect on your well-being." With that, McKittrick turned and left the garden, leaving the guards to watch over the prisoners.

"So Moe, what's with this dude?"

"Beats me." McKay shrugged his shoulders.

Taking his automatic, one guard struck Wardon on the temple, knocking him to the floor. "No speak!" he ordered.

"Sorry Moe, won't happen again," said the dazed SEAL as he struggled to his feet, rubbing the bruise on the side of his head.

Shortly, Sawada reappeared dressed in traditional Japanese garb. His flowing silk gown looked strangely out of place. Without saying a word he led the SEALs to a small hut which had a round opening, no larger than three feet, for a door. Silently, he stooped and entered the hovel, which was completely housed within the conservatory. The guards indicated that the Americans should follow. Once inside, Philips noticed the hut's construction to be completely of bamboo, wood and straw. The floor was hardened earth. The walls were decorated with paintings of birds, flowers and landscapes. Various scrolls with ornate calligraphy also hung from the structure's walls. Next to the door was a sword rack with four very decorative swords.

The smell of incense permeated the room as Sawada lit several sticks. He proceeded to build a small fire in a clay brazier as the Americans sat Indian style on bamboo mats before a low table. Once the fire was started, Sawada placed a kettle filled with water over the brazier to boil. While waiting on the water, their host silently put before each American, a small cup and napkin. Next, he poured saki in each container and quietly lifted his own to his lips. As if in a trance, the SEALs follow suit.

When the water was finished, Sawada offered his guests some traditional sweets in preparation for the bitter tea. With deliberate, paced movements as precise, as a dancer, he mixed a powdered tea into the scalding water. Their host then poured the green beverage into a decorative bowl and offered it to Lieutenant Philips. Taking the first sip, he passed the bowl to Wardon who in turn passed it to McKay.

"Chanoyu, the way of tea," offered Philips, breaking the silence. "And, may I add, the tea was most exquisite."

"I am humbled. You know the ways of our culture," complemented Sawada. "Perhaps now you understand my interest in the treaty."

"Yes, Wa is harmony, Kei is respect, Sei is purity, and Jaku is tranquillity," Philips continued. "We've been through a ritual process of mutual respect. I must, however, decline. The treaty belongs to the United States and I have no authority to barter it away."

"Perhaps we can…"

"Nice digs and I have to admit you have some peculiar ways," Warden cut in, "but let's cut the crap and understand this. The Lieutenant said the treaty's not for sale, regardless of price." Standing to stretch his legs, the SEAL admired the huts construction while Sawada studied his every move.

Sawada stood and bowed silently. He walked over to the sword rack and selected a weapon. "Here, take this. It is a humble gift from a humble man. Perhaps I could change your mind."

"I doubt it," The Petty Officer remarked as he admired the ancient weapon's craftsmanship. Its ivory handle was embossed with flowers and water birds. As he drew the weapon from its scabbard, Philips jumped to his feet and shouted, "Clifford don't! Don't draw the sword."

It was too late! Wardon had already drawn the weapon. Before he could react to the Lieutenant's warning, Sawada was upon him. Drawing a dagger from within the folds of his robe, the Japanese plunged it deep into the SEAL's chest.

"Umph!" Wardon uttered as he staggered backwards,

dropping the sword and scabbard. Looking to his friends in disbelief, he was able to mouth the word, "What?" before falling towards the floor. In less than a heartbeat, McKay caught the big man and eased him carefully down.

Lifting his friends' shiny head and placing it gently into his lap, McKay comforted him. "It's O.K. Cliff, hang on."

"Wh-what hap-pin," he sputtered.

Looking to the expressionless face of Sawada, McKay demanded, "Get a doctor, you piece of shit!"

The Lieutenant had stepped forward to pounce on the preoccupied Sawada, but was dissuaded when McKittrick entered the space brandishing an automatic weapon. "Now, now, now, be a good lad and back off." Realizing, any retaliation at this time would be suicidal, Philips sat down in disgust and despair.

As McKay embraced his teammate, Wardon spoke barely above a whisper, "Mike, don't leave me here," then slowly, he expired.

Once he was gone, thc angry SEAL stood and threatened. "If it's the last thing I do..."

"There's nothing you can do. He insulted my hospitality." Sawada interrupted him. "Ian, escort our guests back to their quarters and get this trash out of here. Maybe in a few days they will reconsider my offer."

"Yes sir." McKittrick responded.

The two Americans were escorted back to their cell, where they were left to ponder the circumstances of Wardon's death.

"If it's the last thing I do…" Philips started.

"You'll have to get in line," McKay hissed, "He's mine!"

"First we have to get out of this alive."

"Don't worry, we always make it out, and when I do, I hope God in Heaven has mercy on that Sawada, for I will not," McKay promised.

The two sat in silence until a fitful sleep overcame them. Later, Philips was awoken when he was sure someone was trying to work their cells lock. Putting his hand over his sleeping partners mouth, he shook McKay awake and held a finger to his lips.

Eager for revenge, the Americans stood poised on either side of the door. As it swung open, a figure slowly stepped inside. McKay grabbed it from behind, as Philips swung hard with his fist to the person's temple. At the last second he realized his mistake and tried to deflect his blow. Too late, he struck the Japanese hostess with a glancing blow that rendered her unconscious.

"That's some way to greet your rescuer," the maiden complained when she came to.

Thirty

Kelly slammed his fist down on his desk and shouted. "Damn-it, Darnel. Where's my boys?"

The Under Secretary stood almost dumbfounded. He had never seen Kelly lose his cool before. Carefully choosing his words, he responded. "Jack, everything's under control. We know they found the bunker, but with things the way they are over there, we just can't go dashing about the country as if we own the place."

"I don't care. Get a squad of Marines from the *Ronnie* and turn that place upside-down."

"You should know, better than most, that I can't do that. The Filipinos will think it's an act of aggression. Besides, with this oil thing I'm not sure they are so innocent."

"It's a set-up, I tell you. There is no way the Philippine government could have developed that vector," Kelly offered.

"The FBI has a different opinion on that subject," Parsons disagreed.

"Don't you think I know that? Still, it's a smoke screen, something else is going on."

"I'm not so sure," Parsons hesitated.

"Listen man! We have the *Reagan* stuck in Manila, the Chinese demonstrating in the Spratleys, the attack on Choctaw, Wells' disappearance, and now economic sanctions against the Philippines. I tell you, it don't smell right. Now I have to go into the Oval Office and convince the President not to expel ambassador Respicio."

"I beg to differ with you. Our people believe that this is not a bunch of hot air." Parsons attempted to reason with the man. "Perhaps, somehow they got a copy of the Mills Transfer, and this is their way of applying pressure."

"It wouldn't be the first time your people were wrong," Kelly answered.

"What do you want me to do?"

"South China Sea, what assets do we have?"

"The *Ronnie,* you know her status. Various-land based aircraft from Japan and Taiwan. Keyhole satellite provides intel every six hours. There are three frigates moving north through the Java straits. And the *Michigan* on station near the mouth of the Persian Gulf."

"What about the rest of the seventh fleet?" queried Kelly.

"On station, off the Spratleys."

"Carriers available?"

"Everything is committed to the Persian Gulf and the Mediterranean. The *Truman* is currently undergoing overhaul in Norfolk, while the *Washington* is in training off San Diego," The Under Secretary stated.

"What about the Chinese?"

"Where?"

"The Spratleys of course."

"One small frigate," Parsons assured him.

"What about the Straits of Taiwan?" Kelly asked.

"Sir?" said Parsons, caught off guard.

"Why don't we send the *Chancellorsville* into the Taiwan Strait," Kelly suggested.

"Is there a need for that? The EP-3 flights report no unusual radio traffic."

"Call it a hunch. Call it whenever you like, I just don't

like being so thin in that area right now."

"But, the Taiwan straits? Everything seems to be quiet there." The Under Secretary questioned the idea.

"Damn-it Parsons, there you go again. I told you, I don't like it. With the Chinese government torn between Minister Chan and Premier Xian, we need a presence in the area. Besides, the Chinese are going to test fire another missile system. I want surveillance on that test. Now, get me some intel on Jake," Kelly ordered with his voice rising again.

"If we go in there without permission, we're asking for trouble."

"Aggression be damned! Get me some answers. Now get out!" the angry Security Adviser shouted to Parsons.

Thirty-One

"What!" Philips exclaimed incredulously.

"Just what I said. I'm a field operative for the CIA. Name's My-Lin. I heard about your friend, I'm sorry."

"He didn't do anything. Sawada just cut him down in cold blood," McKay offered.

"Sawada is an evil man, he must be stopped. Right now I have to get us the hell outta here!" she said authoritatively.

"How?" Philips asked.

"We swim!"

"You're kidding! What about surveillance?"

"Was never installed on the lower levels of the castle."

"Strike one for the good guys," McKay remarked.

"Follow me." My-Lin ordered as she opened the door and checked the corridor. Giving the all clear, the SEALs followed her down the passageway to the gymnasium.

"This is an funny time for a workout," McKay observed.

"I agree, what about Judelyn," Philips added.

"Judah -- who?" she asked.

"The Filipina who was at dinner," the Lieutenant replied.

"Oh, her, I didn't know her name. Sawada has a thing for young females, he won't hurt her," My-Lin assured him.

"We just can't leave her to that animal," McKay added.

"Please understand, my mission is very important and I cannot jeopardize it by trying to rescue her. Time is short; we'll have to come back. Now, we must go before we're discovered." There was a sense of urgency in her voice.

Leading the Americans over to the Hot Springs, My-Lin quickly found a parcel she had hidden beneath one of the benches. Opening the package she pulled out a Neoprene diving suit. Displaying a moment of modesty, the American spy turned her back on the SEALs and shed her silk dress. Philips noticed the agent's back was covered with dull red welts obviously put there by some sort of flogging device. Trying not to be to invasive, he got McKay's attention with hand signals and nodded towards My-Lin.

"What happened to you?" he gingerly asked.

"Sawada! Let's just say his sexual habits are a bit perverse," she answered modestly as she tugged the suit on.

"And you want us to leave Judelyn here?"

"He won't hurt her," the Asian insisted. "Besides, he's in Hong Kong."

"How do we get out?" the Lieutenant asked.

She pointed to the emerald green water, which slightly bubbled. "No way! I'm not a lobster," McKay protested.

"It's the only way," she said. "It's hottest against the far wall. The water is safe here."

"You don't by chance have a couple more suits in that bag of yours, do you?" a bemused Philips questioned.

"Afraid not."

Testing the water with his hand, the Lieutenant confirmed the agents' statement. Sitting, he slipped his feet into the water. McKay quietly followed suit. Slowly the SEALs lowered themselves into the chest-high water. My-Lin did the same. The group made their way towards a far wall where there was an opening.

Philips could feel a slight current to the steaming water,

as it exited the large pool and followed a brick lined tunnel through the castle keep wall. Their way was barred momentarily by an iron gate. Asking the men to step aside, My-Lin deftly opened the unsecured gate and followed the stream into a storm drain. The drain was totally dark for sixty yards. My-Lin negotiated the passage by feel, with the Americans stumbling behind her. Another gate was at the end of the tunnel. As before, the operative opened the barrier and the SEALs could see stars in the ink-black sky. The warm water rushing about their feet poured gently into the castle moat. They were free!

"The moat feeds into a small stream, over there. Be mindful of motion sensors located about the grounds. Also, Ian has installed GSR around the Manor," My-Lin pointed out.

"GSR?" McKay puzzled.

"Where the hell have you been?" Philips wanted to know, "Ground surveillance radar. Spots everything up to ten miles. And I mean everything!"

"Shit! So the only way out, is down the stream?" McKay responded in frustration.

"Correct, and you'd better keep your head down," My-Lin nodded towards the mist-shrouded stream. "We'd better get moving, times a-wasting."

Nodding, the SEALs eased themselves into the tepid water. Now it was the operative's turn to follow. Taking three quick, deep breaths to purge the carbon dioxide from their systems, the escapees ducked under the surface. The group easily swam the thirty feet across the moat to the opposite bank. With Philips taking the lead, they swam along the bank using their fingertips to guide them. The Americans followed the moat until they came to the stream My-Lin had promised.

Pausing, they put their heads together and the Lieutenant whispered, "What now?"

"We follow the stream for about two miles," My-Lin answered.

"Two miles! We'll freeze to death by then," McKay added grimly.

"Not really! Numerous hot springs along the way

constantly feed the stream. The water never really gets colder than it is right now."

"It's easy for you to say. Look whose got a wetsuit," McKay remarked as he started to shiver.

"Let's go," ordered Philips.

Ignoring the cold, the SEAL lead the others into the waterway. Although they were able to stand, as the water was no more than chest deep, Philips and company preferred to swim to avoid radar detection. Even with a frigid January wind, the lukewarm water kept the group from freezing as they headed downstream. Trying to keep the water disturbance to a minimum, the group took only careful and deliberate strokes. Swimming slowly and in single file, the fugitives worked their way further from the castle.

After making a hundred yards, the Lieutenant spotted a sentry smoking on the far bank. Using hand signals, he warned the others. To keep a low profile, Philips almost completely immersed himself by squatting down. Through the heavy mist, he watched every move the sentry made. Eventually the sentry enjoyed the last of his smoke and continued on his rounds.

Letting out a barely audible sigh, Philips waited for the others to join him. When My-Lin was alongside, he questioned her. "I thought you said there were motion sensors?"

"There are. The guards walk a prescribed path that is not monitored by the sensors. They also check in with security at prearranged times," she informed him. "Now can we go? I'm freezing!"

"You're freezing? What about us? At least you have a wetsuit," McKay quipped.

"Enough already," My-Lin threatened as she squared her shoulders towards the SEAL.

"Would you two kiss and make-up? Right now we've got to get outta here," the Lieutenant advised.

"Fine!" My-Lin acknowledged as she shot a stern look to McKay who silently accepted her rebuff.

Taking the lead again, Philips carefully negotiated the streambed, staying as close to the bank as possible. Each time the water became too cold, a hot spring would dump volumes of scalding water into the nearly freezing stream. At these times the Lieutenant would pause to allow My-Lin and McKay to warm themselves.

Progress was slow, but steady. After three hours of careful swimming, they came upon the impressive wall, which surrounded the property. A large, imposing archway allowed the stream to pass through the wall, but there were large iron bars blocking their way.

"You don't have a key, by chance?" the Lieutenant inquired as he pushed heavily on the unyielding bars.

"Nope, never got this far before."

"What do we do now?" McKay asked.

"Is there another way out?" Philips wondered aloud.

"Not that I know of," My-Lin answered.

Diving underwater, Philips checked the barricade at its base. Surfacing, he sputtered. "Th-the b-bars are set into concrete, no way we're going out here."

"How 'bout along the wall? Maybe there's a tree or something that we can use to cross over," McKay suggested.

Scanning in either direction, the SEALs could not discern anything useful from their present location. The only noticeable feature was the mist rising from the stream into the crisp air.

"How far's the main gate?" the Lieutenant quizzed the young lady.

"Not sure. I've never been out here. I think it's in that direction," she said, pointing over his shoulder.

Turning around, Philips tried to see the gate. Unfortunately he was unable to see any changes in the wall that might indicate an opening. "That's it then. We proceed that way until we find the gate. Stay as close to the wall as possible."

"What about the GSR?" My-Lin inquired.

This time it was McKay's turn to instruct. "This big wall sends out a massive signal. If we stay close, our own returns will blend in with it."

"Oh!"

The Lieutenant was the first to pull himself out of the

relatively warm water into the frigid night air. He extended a hand to My-Lin and pulled her up on the bank. McKay brought up the rear. Walking briskly, the group had covered about a half-mile when Philips held his hand up.

"Car!" he whispered. The trio quickly lay prone against the wall. Car lights could be seen through the trees as the vehicle approached them. The lights slowed, then picked up speed and passed through the gate. "Looks like we found it."

"Good, I'm ready for some warm clothes and a hot toddy," McKay complained.

"We're not through yet," Philips reminded him grimly. Getting up, he slowly walked to the gate, hugging the wall to avoid detection. Once at the gate, he tried the bars confirming, they were locked in place.

"Jake, car!" warned McKay quietly.

Moving quickly, the Lieutenant rejoined his associates. "Follow me," he ordered as he hustled into the ditch next to the gate.

The SUV approached the gate and slowed. The Americans were crouched ready to move as soon as the vehicle had cleared the entrance. As the SUV passed Philips, he stealthily darted onto the roadway and quickly ran around the wall. McKay and My-Lin were close on his heels. They ducked into the shrubbery opposite the high wall. Philips waited to see if there would be a response from the manor house. When all appeared clear the escapees negotiated their way down the road towards a small hamlet.

Stopping at the first house they came to, the now-freezing Americans pounded on the door until an elderly man peeked out the partially open door. Speaking in slow sentences, Philips was able to convince the wary homeowner to allow them inside to warm up. Once inside, the SEAL put a phone call through to the American Embassy in Tokyo. He was advised that a car would be dispatched ASAP but would not arrive for a couple of hours. Their orders were to stay put.

Their host, a single man in his 50's, provided robes and coaxed the young people out of their wet clothing. He also produced a mountain of rice and glasses of saki to help warm their spirits. Suddenly, now that they were safely free, the realization of Wardon's demise overcame the SEALs and they sat in stunned silence watching the sunrise over the distant peaks.

As promised, their ride arrived midway through the morning. After bidding farewell to the kindly gentleman, Philips and McKay escorted My-Lin to the waiting automobile. After the three were comfortably situated, she related an unbelievable story that confirmed the urgency of her mission. Six hours later, the grim-faced Americans were escorted past the Marine guards into the American Embassy. Lieutenant Philips had already hatched a daring plan of action!

Thirty-Two

Several dozen cigarette butts littered the sidewalk across from the thirty-story glass and concrete structure that housed the world headquarters of Nipton Foods Ltd. A conglomerate that maintained offices in a dozen countries, Nipton Foods specialized in the export, transportation and distribution of seafood worldwide. As Inspector Heinrich lit up another cigarette, he stood in the bright afternoon sunlight, never taking his squinting eyes from the building's main entrance. "Lovely, just lovely. Wish I'd known. I would have packed the bloody sunglasses," he cursed halfheartedly.

Checking his watch, Heinrich crushed out his cigarette and crossed the street. He had been on the stakeout for over thirty-three hours without spotting the evasive Mr. Sawada. *"When all else fails,"* he decided, *"Go and bash the door in."* Upon entering the building's majestic lobby, the Investigator headed for the nearest elevator.

As he passed a large security desk, which was manned by a very capable looking young man, Heinrich was stopped by the officer's query. "May I help you?"

Not wanting to tip his hand, the Inspector lied. “By all means. I’m looking for the solicitor’s Waki & Inui.”

“Their offices are located on the 27th floor. You can get there by catching the lift over there.”

“Thank you my good man,” he said, then hurried to a bank of elevators. He was impressed by the guards’ observation of his obvious English background. Just as the door was closing, Heinrich squeezed into the car. Punching the button for the 27th floor, the Brit waited patiently for his designated stop. Upon his arrival, the Inspector exited the car and quickly sought out the seldom-used stairway. Hoping the door wasn’t alarmed, Heinrich pushed the handlebar and ascended the steps two at a time. Stopping at the 32nd floor to regain his breath, the Inspector considered his options. To go storming into Sawada’s office and demand the whereabouts of a missing S-10, or to play ignorant and see what developed. *“Some options,”* he thought.

Taking the last few steps in a leisurely manner, Heinrich entered the 33rd floor quietly. His caution had been for naught, as the hallway was completely deserted. Checking the register next to the elevator, he took note of Nipton Foods Ltd. suite number. Heading down the plush carpeted hall, the Inspector paused in front of the office door, held his breath, and stepped through.

A pretty Japanese receptionist stationed behind a rather bland desk greeted him. Stepping forward, Heinrich produced his business card and inquired politely, “Is Mr. Sawada in?”

“Is he expecting you...” she glanced at the business card, “...Mr. Heinrich?”

“I’m afraid not. I was just in the neighborhood and decided to pop in and pay my respects.”

“Mr. Sawada is an extremely busy man. Without an appointment it would be impossible to see him.”

Taking another business card, Heinrich jotted down 8 Hong Kong dollars on the back. “Be a good lass and give him this?”

Not understanding the cryptic message, the receptionist excused herself and entered the elusive millionaire’s office. A moment later she returned with a bewildered look on her face. “He will see you now.”

“Lovely, now be a dear and fetch us a spot of tea,” he ordered, walking past her into the plush lair of his quarry.

The room was large, but not overly so. Expansive, pale green windows offered breathtaking views of the city and harbor. The remaining walls were covered with lithographs depicting Japanese farm life from the not so distant past. A desk made of modern materials, and of modern design, was centered along the back wall. Potted bamboo plants standing eight feet tall were tastefully arranged in the room’s corners.

Centered in the windows looking out over the city, was a smallish Japanese man, maybe in his 50s, judged the Chief Inspector. Heinrich was forced to stand uncomfortably for several minutes, until the receptionist returned with a tea service. Pouring two cups, she silently left without acknowledging her employer.

“What brings you to our fair city, Inspector?” inquired Sawada, without turning.

“As the card says, someone owes me 8 Hong Kong dollars,” he said, quietly.

“And you think I’m that someone?”

“Perhaps. You do own Carlisle Shipping, don’t you?”

“I’m not sure. I own many companies.”

“Let me refresh your memory. Carlisle Ltd. is a shipping company headquartered in Hong Kong. Various container ships and super tankers are among their assets. Carlisle Ltd. is a wholly-owned subsidiary of Nipton Foods Ltd.”

Turning to face the Inspector, Sawada acknowledged, “You are well informed.”

“Then it’s with regrets that I must tell you that one of your boats is missing.”

“How so?”

“I was aboard a certain Junk when she slipped beneath the waves in Hong Kong Harbor.”

“Pity. Was it some kind of accident?”

“I believe the chaps over ta Lloyd’s of London will label

it an intentional sinking."

"Are you implying I had something to do with that?"

"Why, yes, I'm afraid I am!" Heinrich exclaimed.

Sawada was now looking directly at the Inspector. He could not discern how much the man from Interpol knew. "Maybe we could discuss this over dinner?"

Heinrich now knew he had his man. Without so much as blinking an eye he declined. "I don't supper with murderers." Putting his hand into his coat pocket, the Inspector watched Sawada's cold eyes, looking for a chink in his armor. Finding none, he carefully, slowly, and deliberately, retrieved his cigarettes and lit one up. Sawada did not so much as blink. *"What a cold bastard you are,"* Heinrich thought.

"Murder, is such a harsh word."

With his disgust rising, the Inspector became impatient. "Why don't we cut the chit-chat? Grab your coat, you're coming with me."

"It is you who is mistaken. You have no authority here. If you had, you would have notified the local authorities. They would have accompanied you, so I believe no one is aware of your presence here."

At that moment, a hidden panel slid aside behind Sawada's desk and McKittrick stepped forward holding a silenced 9mm. Behind him, dressed in a tasteful business suit, was the leggy blonde from the boat.

"You're the..."

"I understand you have previously met," Sawada interrupted, "My beautiful assistant is Heidi, and this is Ian, my security specialist."

"I suppose you're the bloke l need to see about my cleaning bill," Heinrich said sarcastically.

"I never expected to see you again..." McKittrick started, before Sawada silenced him with a wave of his hand.

"Enough!" he exclaimed, never raising his voice. "Take him to the house, I'll follow shortly."

"You won't get away with this," the Inspector used the old cliché. "My superiors know about Vladivostok."

"My, my, my. Just what do you think they know?"

"The missile! I know."

"The Russians have denied the missile was even on the premises. I know because McKittrick helped write the report with the aid of a few million dollars." Sawada smiled then added, "And, seeing as how you like using lines from old movies, understand this. I have already gotten away with it. Now, get him out of here!"

"Yes sir," McKittrick responded as he escorted Inspector Heinrich from the office.

Addressing Heidi, the Japanese offered, "This could be trouble. Have Ian beef up security."

"What about the Americans?" she asked.

"The local prefecture will handle them. Our plans are in motion and it's too late to stop them," he assured her.

Part III: Dawn Strike

Thirty-Three

Upon their arrival at the embassy, the Americans were informed that the Ambassador was unavailable for at least an hour. Shortly afterwards, a secretary appeared and asked the trio to follow her. She escorted them down to the embassy's lower confines where they could relax after their ordeal.

"Is there a place where I can get a change of clothing?" My-Lin asked, indicating the wet suit she still wore under a jacket she'd borrowed from the old man who had befriended them.

"I'll see what I can do. If you'd like to freshen up you may use these rooms. How about you guys? Like a hot shower and change of clothing?" she asked, indicating small barrack-type rooms on either side of the hall. The SEALs agreed that fresh clothing would help.

After Philips showered and shaved, he was surprised to find a neatly pressed utility uniform waiting for him on the bunk. Donning it, he was equally surprised to find that it fit! Exiting the room, he bumped into McKay who obviously had the same good fortune. Knocking on My-Lin's door they were impressed to see her in a naval uniform that snugly hugged her curves.

"Nice outfit," Philips observed.

Doing a pirouette, she remarked, "It was all they had. Kind of sexy, don't you think?"

"You'd make a perfect poster babe for the recruiting office," McKay volunteered.

"I bet you say that to all girls." she giggled. "I'm famished. Any suggestions?"

"There's a cafeteria one floor up. It's not the Ritz, but let's give it a try," the Lieutenant offered.

After a light lunch, they were shown to the Ambassador's outer office. "Wait here," instructed the same secretary, "Ambassador Wehking will be with you in a moment." Sitting in silence, each one of them had time to ponder the chain of events, which had brought them here. Soon, a head with thick brown hair peeked around the door and invited them in.

"Come in, come in," the Ambassador said warmly. "Please be seated. I'm sorry for the delay. I hope everything was satisfactory," he apologized.

"Everything's top-notch," McKay piped up."

Gary Wehking, a former NBA star, was just short of seven feet tall. His dark hair and piercing eyes were just as intimidating as they were when he played for the Boston Celtics. Several NBA photos adorned the walls of his wood paneled office, while the MVP trophy sat impressively on his desk. "So tell me, what can we do for you?" he asked.

"Lieutenant Jake Philips Sir, commander United States Navy SEAL Team Three on special assignment," Philips offered formally. Shaking his hand, the Lieutenant was not surprised by the Ambassador's grip.

"Pleased to meet you, Lieutenant," Wehking said, and then acknowledged the others as he went on, "Petty Officer McKay and Agent Beaudoin. I've been on the phone all morning with the White House and the State Department. Seems you've stirred up quite hornet's nest. Where's Petty Officer Wardon?"

"He was executed," Philips solemnly replied, as he felt remorse for his absent friend.

"I'm sorry, I didn't know, you have my deepest

sympathies. I hear that you two go back quite a ways," he admitted. After a prolonged silence he continued. "Now then, to the business at hand. Adviser Kelly will be in later tonight and he wants a complete report on your presence here in Japan."

"We don't have a few hours!" exclaimed McKay, then added, "A young lady's life depends on us getting back to Sawadas' castle ASAP."

"Well, there are some complications here. It seems the local magistrate has forbidden us from disturbing Mr. Sawada."

"How can that be? The son of a bitch killed Wardon!" the irate Lieutenant demanded.

"Here in Japan, he is a man of immense wealth and influence. He hides behind the cloak of legitimacy. We have to do things by the book. I have already filed a protest with the Japanese Foreign Ministry. They have requested proof. Until Wardon's body is located there is little we can do."

"Then let me go and retrieve Wardon's body." McKay pleaded, "I won't leave Cliff with that bastard."

"It's not that easy, we have to do things through channels," the Ambassador explained, attempting to remain calm.

"Protocol be damned!" McKay shouted.

"In light of the current situation, I'll ignore your outburst. I feel your pain, but this is the way we have to proceed at this time. You will get your payback, I assure you. The Navy doesn't sit kindly to things such as this. I wouldn't be surprised if the State Department already has something up their sleeves. If you'll excuse me, I have other matters to attend to," Ambassador Wehking stood and motioned for the door. "Oh, almost forgot, My-Lin, it is My-Lin?"

She nodded when the Ambassador spoke her name.

"Some folks from our Tokyo bureau want to have a chat with you."

"Just a minute Ambassador. Before you go shuffling off, there's something you need to hear." Philips stopped the Ambassador in midstride. "Go ahead, tell him," he ordered My-Lin.

"Ambassador Wehking, my position within Sawada's staff was deliberate. I was placed there to investigate possible economic terrorism against the United States," she spoke just above a whisper.

"I don't see what that has to do with..." the Ambassador started, but was cut short by Lieutenant Philips.

"Sir, let the little lady finish!" he said curtly.

My-Lin paused, perhaps for effect or maybe to find the necessary words. Finally she just blurted out, "Sawada has Premier Xian held prisoner!"

"What?" Wehking asked incredulously.

"Just what I said. Sawada has Premier Xian held prisoner," she repeated.

"How is that possible? I heard that he was hospitalized just outside Beijing."

"Not hardly. One night a Chinese man delivered him to the estate in an ambulance."

"Can you ID the Chinaman?"

"I can, but you're not going to the believe it."

"After what I just heard, I think I'll believe anything."

"Defense Minister Chan." She answered.

"Impossible!" the surprised Ambassador exclaimed. "This puts a new light on things. Is the Premier okay?"

"Sawada keeps him drugged, but, I checked in on him a couple times and he seems okay."

Turning to Lieutenant Philips, the Ambassador had a stern look to his face. "Lieutenant, to save time you start working on a plan. I'll make the necessary calls."

"I already have a plan." Jake answered confidently. "Is Seal Team Five available?"

"Not sure. I'll look into it. There's nothing you can do right now, you guys look beat. Why don't you use the rooms downstairs, I'll get back to you in a couple of hours."

Realizing the Ambassador was right, the trio left to get some much-needed rest. With exhaustion finally showing its ugly head, Philips laid down and passed out.

"It's time. Jake it's time," his mother said.

The words were still ringing in his ears as a young Marine shook the SEAL from his slumber.

"Lieutenant? Lieutenant, you awake?" the guard asked shaking him again.

"Okay, okay, I'm up." Philips answered. He sat straight up. The room about him was totally dark.

The Marine carried a small flashlight that shone on the floor as he spoke. "You're wanted in the Ambassador's office."

"Can you gimme a moment?" the still groggy Lieutenant asked.

"As long as it's a moment. You're wanted ASAP," the Marine said, as he exited the room.

Five minutes later the Philips was back in the Ambassador's office. Ambassador Wehking was nowhere to be seen. National Security Adviser Jack Kelly was sitting in the Ambassador's overstuffed chair. The minute the Lieutenant walked into the room, he jumped to his feet.

"Jake, by God it's good to see you."

"Sir?"

"I mean, it's good to know that you're alive." He hesitated then offered, "I'm sorry about Wardon. I know what he meant to you."

"Thank you, Sir."

Sitting back down, the big man offered a chair to the Lieutenant. Getting comfortable, Kelly was the first to break the silence. "Jake, do you believe the young lady?"

"Yes sir," he said with a sour tone to his voice.

"And you say there's someone else you had to leave behind?"

"Yes sir, the granddaughter of corporal Aleta."

"Corporal Aleta?"

"Yes, she helped us locate the bunker."

"I see. Ambassador Wehking says you have a plan to extract them?"

"Yes sir."

"Is that all you can say?" Kelly wanted to know.

"Sir may I?"

"Be my guest."

"Until I have marching orders, there's not much to say." Philips defended his insubordination.

"Well then Mr. Philips, I think this phone call is for you." The Adviser stood and handed him the phone.

Puzzled, Lieutenant Philips put the phone to his ear and listened. "One moment Sir while I connect you," Said a distant voice.

"Ah, Lieutenant, Lieutenant Philips I believe." An unfamiliar husky voice came on the line.

"Yes," he answered.

"This is President Benton speaking, I understand you have firsthand knowledge about a political drama that's beginning to unfold in Japan."

Gulping, Philips meekly answered, "Ah.Uh.Yes sir."

"Well, in light of the situation, I can't drop the entire Recon Force in there, can I?"

"No sir, not really. The loss of life could be…"

"Kelly tells me the situation is most peculiar." The President cut Philips short. "He also informed me you have a plan of extraction already worked out."

"Yes sir."

"I see you're man of few words. Is your plan feasible?" The President asked.

"Yes sir, it can be done with a little help."

"Son, here's what I want you to do. Implement your plans with personnel as you see fit. Nevertheless, understand this, we must keep a lid on this until the package is safely in U.S. custody. Do you follow?"

"Yes sir."

"Mr. Kelly is there to assist you. Whenever you need, whatever it takes. Understood?"

"Yes sir!" Lieutenant Philips said with enthusiasm.

"Oh, and one more thing?"

"Sir."

"Good hunting and God speed," the President offered his well wishes, then added, "I'm counting on you."

"Thank you very much Mr. President," Philips answered before the line went dead. He looked over to the Adviser, who was smiling broadly. "You knew about this?"

"It was the President who suggested we use you in the first place," Kelly responded while rubbing his hands together. "Now, what do you need?"

"I need lots of intel, photos, weather reports, Sawada's background and anything you can get on an Ian McKittrick," the Lieutenant said authoritatively.

"Okay, what else?"

"Eight SEALs from Iwakuni, armed to the teeth, with scuba gear. One DPV..."

"DPV?" Kelly interrupted.

"Sorry, desert patrol vehicle fitted with an M-60, a MK-19 auto grenade launcher and two AT-4 anti-armor missiles."

"Anything else?" the Adviser asked as he quickly jotted down Philips' shopping list.

"One more thing; have an F/A-18 armed with a Tomahawk in the air when this goes down," Philips said confidently.

"So, what's the plan?"

"We're going to ask Sawada to surrender Premier Xian and let the lovely lady go," Philips stated matter of factly.

"I hope you're going to be polite," Kelly snickered.

"Just as polite as he was to us." The Lieutenant chuckled back.

"Almost forgot, here's a package for McKay." Mr. Kelly passed over a large parcel to Philips. "I'm sure he'll appreciate it. It's from Murdoch. What time's Zero hour?"

"We'll do a dawn strike. The team needs to be at the staging area by 0300, muster everyone for a briefing and rehearsal at 2300." The SEAL answered as he left the room to put the finishing touches on his plan.

Thirty-Four

The late January storm was a blessing. Cold rain poured down in sheets as the wind blew harder than expected. Visibility had been reduced to less than a quarter mile, which helped to disguise the team's arrival at the old man's house outside the hamlet. The place where Philips, McKay and My-Lin had sought refuge, was now a staging ground for the assault on Sawada's estate.

"I couldn't have asked for better weather," commented Lieutenant Stephen Bourne. He was assigned to SEAL Team Five stationed at Iwakuni. The short sandy-haired officer was ready for action. He was presently overseeing the unloading of the DPV from a large moving van, which had been used to disguise their movements into the area. As the assault vehicle was backed from the van, Bourne greeted the temporary team leader, Lieutenant Jake Philips.

"I agree with you one hundred percent," Philips remarked. "Your boys good to go on this?"

"My boys were born ready, so let's shove off," Bourne

responded confidently.

"Good. I read the file on McKittrick, and he's one nasty customer, so show him no quarter."

"Piece of cake! We're ready for just about anything, just say the word."

At that moment, several team members approached the officers. "Time!" the first one said.

"Hooyah!" Philips quietly growled, as he extended his hand to Lieutenant Bourne.

"Hooyah, back at ya. Lets get these bastards," Bourne replied as he seated himself into the DPV, which looked like the dune buggies that were the rage in the '70's. His driver slowly backed the vehicle into the shadows next to a barn, where they were joined by a third crew member who manned the rocket station mounted atop the roll cage.

The remaining team members, all wearing wet suits, joined McKay and Philips in the back of a newspaper delivery truck. The truck proceeded down the country lane towards Sawada's castle. Philips put his hand to his throat and spoke softly, "Radio check." McKay answered first, with the remaining members calling out their respective numbers in turn. Bourne was the last to check in. When everyone was accounted for, Philips reminded Bourne, "Remember, I need an hour and forty-five minutes to get to the castle wall. It's four miles from the old man's house to the estate's gate. Punch it at exactly 0605."

"I Roger that. Lieutenant?"

"Sir?"

"Don't get your feet wet!" Bourne chuckled as he settled down to wait for his appointed time.

Aboard the lumbering truck, the team quietly and expertly rechecked their gear for the umpteenth time. Everyone was dressed alike in wet suits. Each member had two air cylinders strapped to their backs with Halcyon rebreathers, which recycles air so a diver doesn't compromise his position with tell-tale air bubbles. Under the oxygen tanks, the SEALs were laced into web belts that held their primary weapons, grenade pouch, radio, spare ammo and K-bar survival knife. Additionally, each member carried a rucksack that contained specialty items, spare ammo clips, grenades, goggles and fins.

After an agonizingly slow ride, the truck stopped. A light tapping on the cab wall indicated they were on target. Saying nothing, McKay opened the rear door and ushered the SEALs into the ditch alongside the road. Using hand signals, Lieutenant Philips pointed out the stream that he had used earlier in his escape. As the delivery truck drove away, the seven silent warriors were already in the water.

Staying close, they swam single file in the chest-high water, to the culvert that cut under the road. Without hesitation Philips led the way in. Inside, the blackness was as dark as ink. The warriors slipped beneath the water and swam to the stream's bottom. Progressing by feel, they continued until the bars in the outer wall blocked their advance. Holding up his hand, the Lieutenant indicated the obstruction. Now it was the Breacher's turn. The Breacher is responsible for forcing his way into closed spaces including obstacles of many kinds. As the others stayed back, the Breacher swam up next to Lieutenant Philips.

Switching on his small penlight, the SEAL was able to appraise the situation. Working rapidly in the light's red glow, he took demolition cord and carefully wrapped it in a continuous strand around each bar about a foot below the stream's surface. Another det cord was likewise wrapped around the bars at their base in the streambed. Breacher now took the trailing edge of each det cord and wrapped them together. Finally he set an electronic detonator to the charge just before the SEALs swam back underneath the roadway.

Counting down the seconds on his watch, the Breacher held up five fingers, then counted them down silently. When he reached zero, a low muffled detonation could be heard upstream.

Spitting out his mouthpiece, Philips cautioned his command, "Remember, from here on in we have to concern ourselves with GSR."

The six men nodded in understanding and followed the Lieutenant back upstream. Swimming under the severed bars, the group made their way slowly towards the castle. With an adrenaline rush pumping up his system, Philips began to sweat. Pacing himself with leisurely strokes, the SEAL Team Leader felt his way towards their objective. After an hour, he paused and checked his position. According to the Magellan 2000 GPS device, they were less than a hundred feet from the moat. Checking his watch, Philips saw the luminous dial indicating Lieutenant Bourne's attack would begin in seventeen minutes.

The SEAL proceeded to swim towards the moat without checking to see if his teammates were following. He knew better. As the stream opened up and the bottom fell away, Philips knew he was now at the moat. Halting, he waited for the last man of the team to catch up. Rechecking his watch, as time was becoming a factor, the Lieutenant led the group around to the south side of the castle. Consulting his GPS again, Philips surfaced just enough to orient himself. The curved wall of the watchtower was no more than four feet in front of him!

Switching on his radio, Philips whispered, "Team Member 2, this is Team Member 1, do you copy..."

"This is this is TM 2, over..." Bourne acknowledged.

"We're in position, awaiting your arrival."

"I roger that, we're about to announce ourselves."

"Roger!" Philips responded. He slipped beneath the surface of the water. Swimming hard, he followed a faint red light to the moat's bottom, where he joined the others who had gathered in a circle. Watching his watch, the SEAL suddenly dropped his hand. Everyone on the team instantly covered their ears with their hands.

First, they heard a barely perceptible thud. Even through the water, they could feel the ground move slightly. Seconds later, a second, stronger whump was heard. This time it felt as if the entire moat convulsed. It sounded as if someone had fired a weapon in close quarters. A second after the concussion had settled down, the group instinctively dropped their air tanks and swam to the surface.

Thirty-Five

When Lieutenant Bourne received the communication from Philips, they were no more than a half-mile from the estate's entrance. Through the pouring rain he could just barely make out the glow of lights mounted on either side of the structure. When he gave the predetermined signal, Seaman Randolph, standing above and behind him, acquired the target and fired the AT-4. The rocket left its launcher with a hiss! Seconds later in a blinding flash, it destroyed the castles ornate portal.

Without slowing down, the DPV shot through the smoldering entrance. Bourne noticed, with some satisfaction, a pair of guards lying prone in a pool of blood. One man's head was at an odd angle, while the other was face up with a frozen expression of horror. Both bodies were seeping blood from wounds too numerous to count.

The Lieutenant had his driver pull up and stop just inside the tree line. Donning his night vision goggles, he scanned the south perimeter. Almost immediately he spotted what he was looking for. Off to his right, flying barely above the ground, was a Tomahawk cruise missile.

Bourne watched as the graceful missile passed over the wall and proceeded towards the unwary castle. Dropping the glasses, he urged the driver to advance on their target. Seconds later, a bright flash lit up the rain-driven sky. A resounding thunderclap followed shortly thereafter, as the concussion reached them.

"Damn, I bet that woke 'em up," commented the driver.

"Git us up there before this is over!" exclaimed Bourne. As the DPV sped into the night he tried to raise Philips on the radio. "TM1, this is TM 2, over..." Nothing!

"TM 1, this is TM 2, do you copy?" he repeated.

"TM 2, TM 1, I copy..." Philips finally answered.

"TM 1, ETA, three minutes, over..." the Lieutenant advised. Across the open line, he could distinguish the distinctive popping sounds of automatic fire.

"Get up here! Could use your firepower," Philips ordered just before the radio went dead.

"Punch it," he ordered the driver. Two minutes later they exited the forest and saw the castle lights situated in the middle of an alpine meadow. In the dawn's early light, a pall of smoke could be seen rising from the far side of the citadel.

Using his binoculars, the Lieutenant scanned the front of the castle. Things seemed to be quiet on this side as the estate's defenders attentions were drawn to the attack on the far side. When the DPV approached the moat, the AT-4 operator announced, "Target acquired, permission to fire Sir."

"Fire!" he shouted.

The last rocket whooshed away! Bourne could easily follow its progress via the red glare of its rocket motor. Less than ten seconds later, the rocket with its seventeen-pound warhead slammed into the citadel's gatehouse destroying the portcullis. In a flash, the doors disintegrated into a thousand deadly projectiles propelling themselves in all directions. Several anguished cries could be heard over the chatter of gunfire coming from within the castle's confines.

Urging his driver across the ancient drawbridge, Lieutenant Bourne used the MK-19 to fire three 40-mm grenades into the gateway, hoping to catch any mercenaries who may have survived the blast on the main doors. As the DPV negotiated the narrow cobblestone roadway between the fighting chambers, the vehicles occupants remained alert.

Above their heads, one of McKittricks' goons was stationed high on the rampart above the gatehouse, monitoring the approaching dune buggy. Witnessing the attack against the gate, he ducked just as the missile struck home. With ears ringing, the guard stood and aimed a LAW rocket towards the place where he knew the strange vehicle would have to pass. The instant the intruders cleared the portcullis he squeezed the trigger that launched his rocket. The missile struck the DPV just forward of it's right rear wheel, tossing the hapless carriage ten feet into the air, spilling its precious cargo onto the cobblestone. The fuel blister went up in a secondary explosion that mirrored the initial blast, spilling flaming gasoline over a wide area that included a parked limousine.

Surprised by the heat from the blast, the thug stood dazed by his handiwork. At that precise moment Lieutenant Bourne crawled from beneath the mangled wreck, sighted on his aggressor and fired a three round burst. The 9-mm slugs struck the guard in the chest, knocking him from the wall.

Checking his teammates, Bourne was quick to discover his driver was dead. Seaman Randolph had a nasty wound in his thigh. Dragging the disabled SEAL to the cover of the north-fighting chamber, Lieutenant Bourne set off to join the main fighting group.

Thirty-Six

The 700-year-old blocks of the Watchtower were no match for the Tomahawk. With the SEALs safely submerged in the moat, the blinding flash and concussion passed harmlessly overhead. The missile actually penetrated the ten-foot thick wall and exploded within the confines of the barracks indicated by My-Lin. In an instant, sixty-five of McKittricks handpicked mercenaries were wiped out. A secondary benefit of the missile attack was the disabling of the control room's electronic surveillance of the entire complex. McKittrick was now blind!

As the concussion settled down, Philips led his men to the moat's surface. The tower had a gaping hole with black acrid smoke belching forth. Discarding their fins and affixing gas masks, the SEALs proceeded cautiously into Sawada's lair. The hardened SEALs weren't prepared for the carnage before them. Limbs and other body parts lay side-by-side with the shrapnel remains of the missile. Several corpses were burning in the center of the room. Forcing the urge to vomit aside, Philips led the way into the room.

Piles of wrecked furniture were scattered about as if a giant hand had indiscriminately toppled them. Amazingly, along one wall a coffee service stood intact, while a beheaded soldier lay before it, cup still in hand. Drawing their primary weapons, the SEALs fanned out and quickly set a perimeter. Several, "Clears," could be heard as the team members reconnoitered the room's expanse. Next they located the spiral staircase which led to the courtyard.

"Air's good," one of the SEALs reported as he discarded his mask. The others followed suit, wincing at the combined stench of death and Semtex.

Posting a couple of sharpshooters in the shattered windows, Philips ordered, "Shoot anything that moves."

Almost instantly the SEALs started peppering McKittricks' security staff with hot lead. Their return fire was sporadic at most, but the Lieutenant knew, given enough time, an effectual defense would be mustered. At that moment he received a communication from Bourne. What Philips needed now was a diversion. With that thought in mind he urged his counterpart forward.

The two seamen Philips had sent upstairs to clear the operations room, reported back, "All clear."

"Way to the roof?" he inquired.

"Negative!"

"Follow me," Philips ordered, as McKay accompanied him down the staircase. When the Americans arrived at the doorway, Sawada's mercenaries began taking pot shots at them. Ducking back into the stairwell, the Lieutenant tried in vain to raise Bourne on the radio. "Return fire!" he shouted.

His men opened fire, keeping McKittricks' goons pinned behind a parked limousine. Exchanging shots, neither side could gain an upper hand. The sharpshooters in the tower had cleared the battlements of any immediate threats from above, but were unable to get a clear field of fire on the thugs in the courtyard.

Just when Philips thought he would have to retreat and find another way across the no man's land, a large explosion erupted from across the courtyard.

"Damn! What was that?" McKay shouted.

"Must be Bourne. Just in time too, we need to get over there without getting our butts shot off." Philips indicated towards the Manor's massive wooden doors.

"Just a sec..." McKay said, as he pulled a leather jacket from his rucksack and put it on. Next, he deftly strapped on a holster with a mean looking automatic. Lastly the big American pulled an Indiana Jones hat from the bag. Removing his watch cap, McKay perched the hat atop his shaven head. Grinning, he commented, "Let's go!"

"What the..." For the first time on a mission, Philips was dumbfounded.

"A little something from Murdoch," McKay explained.

"Wardon's?"

"Yeah, now let's go git that mother-fucker."

The Lieutenant didn't argue. As he stood to dash across the courtyard, he spotted Bourne's DPV clearing the portcullis. Philips also noticed the flash of a LAW.

"Get down!" he shouted, diving to the pavement as the desert vehicle blew up.

The SEALs were fortunate; the doorway shielded them from the blast. Sawada's gunmen weren't so lucky. Several men who had taken refuge behind the limousine now found the morning sky raining flaming gasoline. With their makeshift barricade in jeopardy, the cursing and howling mercenaries scattered in all directions like rats from a sinking ship.

This was the opportunity the SEAL sharpshooters had been waiting for. Without the benefit of the limousine, McKittricks' thugs were scrambling in the open. Lieutenant Bourne was the first to react by dropping the goon who had launched the LAW. As if on cue, all the team members opened up at once. Several unlucky gunmen were dropped on the first volley, while the remaining men were able to reach the old barn and blacksmith stable.

Sprinting across the courtyard, Philips and McKay dispatched several guards who were too stubborn to vacate the Manor house's doorway. Still moving, the Lieutenant tossed a grenade at the barricaded door, thus dismissing any questions as to its defense. With bullets ricocheting off the cobblestones, the SEALs headed for cover. Dashing past the brightly burning limousine, the pair was scrambling for the steps when Lieutenant Bourne shouted, "Over here!"

They quickly joined their comrade who was hunkered down behind the steps. Automatic fire from the two outbuildings was increasing. Philips stood and expended his clip in the general direction of the resistance. Dropping down, he commented, "Great entrance. Any casualties?"

"Yeah, drivers gone, Seamen Randolph is down."

"Serious?"

"He'll live."

"This is taking too long."

"Tell me about it," Bourne agreed. Checking out McKay's outfit he inquired, "What's his problem?"

"Mike has seen too many movies," Philips chuckled.

"So what's the plan?"

"What say Mike and I go inside for a look-see. Can you hold these guys?"

"No prob."

McKay stuck his head up just enough to see if the coast was clear. Spotting one of the Chinese goons reloading his weapon, McKay unholstered the Desert Eagle, took aim and fired. Belching death, the 44-caliber auto mag caught the unsuspecting man in the upper torso. As the projectile mushroomed within his chest, he was propelled like a puppet, backwards over the blacksmith's anvil.

"Damn, would you look at that!" an astonished McKay exclaimed, then added, "No wonder Cliff wanted to bring this thing along."

"Shit, boys and their toys," remarked Bourne as he stood and rattled off several short bursts from his MP 5. "You'd better go find the Premier, I'll handle this."

With that, the two SEALs scrambled up the steps and through the shattered door. Compared to the pandemonium outside, the inside was relatively calm. Glowing embers contained within a large fireplace warmed the air. The pair was in awe of the medieval furnishings of the entryway.

"Check this place out!" exclaimed McKay

"Later. Where do we start?" the Lieutenant asked, looking up the stone staircase.

"Not that way." advised McKay, "Remember the banquet hall was on the main floor and we came up from below."

"Right then, let's go this way," Philips indicated towards the hallway.

Walking carefully and quietly the two warriors guarded each other's backs as they worked their way down the stone corridor. The first couple of doors turned up nothing, they soon came upon a set of french doors. Peering inside, Philips recognized the place where they had enjoyed the monstrous feast.

"Jake, this way!" McKay said excitedly when he spotted the doors. "The stone staircase is just ahead."

Moving quickly, the Americans sought out the staircase without encountering any resistance. Descending the steps two at a time, the pair was as quiet as church mice. From below a scurrying sound could be heard, as if someone was moving about. Putting a finger to his lips, Philips signaled McKay to stay put. Peering around the corner, he spotted a tall blond Amazon pacing back and forth.

Backing up a couple of stairs to where McKay waited, he whispered, "Beautiful blond with a Mac 10."

"O-kay, I know what to do, you wait upstairs."

Understanding, Philips took up a position at the top of stairs and waited. His wait was short-lived, within seconds McKay was backing up the steps with his hands over his head saying, "Listen sister you could hurt someone with that thing."

Like a Cobra poised ready to strike, the SEAL waited for the right moment. When McKay passed his position, Philips sucked in his breath. Finally, the small boxy form of the Mac 10 appeared around the corner attached to a long slender arm. The agile Lieutenant sprang, grabbing the unsuspecting Amazons arm with his left hand and pointing it towards the ceiling. Within the same movement, he pulled with all his might, knocking the female to the floor. In less than a heartbeat he'd brought his right hand down in a karate chop, rendering her unconscious.

After the SEALs had bound her hands and feet with disposable handcuff's, McKay cooed, "I think I'm in loooove."

"You can schmoose later. Right now we've a job to do," Philips grinned.

Throwing caution to the wind, the pair rushed down the stairs into the hallway. They passed Sawada's gymnasium and stopped short at the sight of a dozen closed doors. "You take that side," the Lieutenant ordered.

The first couple of doors on McKay's side revealed curious rooms that appeared to be science labs. On his fifth try, he got lucky. It opened into a hospital-style room with a large bed dominating the space. Even in the low light, McKay could see a form stretched out on the bed. "I've got 'em," he shouted from within the room.

"Great!" Philips exclaimed, just as he saw McKay's heavy oaken door slam shut. Trying the door, the big American realized it was barred from the inside and there was no way he was going to force it. The Lieutenant decided he needed help to gain the rooms entry. "TM 2 this is TM 1 over..." He spoke into his radio.

"2 over..." Bourne responded.

"How's it going up there?"

"We've got about ten guys bottled up in the blacksmith shop."

"Any sign of McKittrick or Sawada?"

"Negative, what's your ten?"

"In the castle's basement. Call for the extraction team. Also I need the Breacher and the corpsman, ASAP," he requested.

"On their way." Lieutenant Bourne advised.

"Roger!" Philips sighed, casting aside his concern for his friend, *"May as well start checking these remaining rooms,"* he thought.

Thirty-Seven

McKay spun about when he heard the door slam shut. McKittrick must have been standing behind the opened door, for now he was bolting it shut. "Well, well, well what have we here?" the Scot queried as he leveled an automatic weapon.

"Your worst nightmare!" McKay growled.

"Come now, that's no way to talk to a chap with an AK-47 aimed at your chest. Drop the kit," he ordered.

Appraising the situation, the American complied and dropped his rucksack.

"Weapon and web gear."

Again McKay obeyed.

"Step back!"

The SEAL took a couple of steps back, watching for an opening.

Setting the assault rifle down and retrieving McKay's gear, the big Scot removed the Desert Eagle from its holster and commented, "A strange weapon for a SEAL."

"Not so strange. Why don't you put the long end in your mouth and pull the trigger? It would save me the hassle of killing you," McKay hissed. "Better yet, just give up and I'll be on my way."

"You know that wouldn't be sporting, but if you think you're man enough."

"Meaning?" questioned the big SEAL.

"I've often wondered who's the better man, your SEALs or the Queens own SAS. Let's have a little sparring match. To the winner goes the spoils," the Scot challenged as he nodded towards the Premier's sleeping form.

"No contest," McKay promised, tossing his hat and jacket to the floor. "I'm going to gouge out your eyes and feed them to you!"

"I think not."

"Try me!"

McKittrick removed his Gucci coat and loosened his tie. Beckoning the SEAL forward with his fingertips, he gloated, "Let's git it on."

McKay was the first to react; putting his head down, he let out a roar and lunged forward, hitting the Scot squarely in the chest with his head. "Umph..." McKittrick grunted. He reacted by wrapping his giant arms around the big man's upper chest. The Scot then lifted the American off his feet upside-down and squeezed with all his might.

"Aagghh," the SEAL grunted between clenched teeth. As his only option, McKay bit his opponent as hard as he could in the upper thigh. Gasping, McKittrick released his grip and dropped the SEAL to the floor with a thud.

Quick as a cat, the American was back on his feet. The two circled each other within the tight confines of the room. Again, McKay lunged, this time encircled his hands around the shorter man's neck and proceeded to squeeze his fingers closed.

McKittrick brought a knee up into the American's groin sending excruciating waves of pain throughout McKay's body. Forced to hold down bile, the SEAL increased pressure upon his opponents' windpipe.

As McKay tightened his death grip, McKittrick's face was turning a deep shade of red. Hissing, the big goon somehow mustered enough strength to strike at McKay's mid section. He rained several blows into his kidneys, forcing the American to release his grip and back off.

Both combatants stood facing each other, and again circled the room looking for an opportunity to strike. "You're good, laddie," the former SAS man complemented. "Very good for a Yank but you haven't seen nothing yet."

"Enough of this bullshit! Prepare to die!" McKay snarled as he regained his strength by taking several deep breaths. "C'mon!" he taunted.

This time it was the Scot who lunged, and the American was waiting. He sidestepped hitting his opponent as hard as he could with a karate chop to the back of the neck. The goon fell to the floor on top of the SEALs web gear.

Instantly, the American was on him with the death-like grip to his throat again. Groping around blindly looking for a weapon, McKittrick found McKay's K-Bar knife, and in less than a heartbeat he slashed upwards. The knife's razor sharp blade bit into the fleshly part of the big man's cheek. With blood flowing freely, the now stunned McKay allowed the Scot to get the upper hand by relaxing his grip. Seizing the opportunity, McKittrick surprised the American by flipping him onto his back and straddling his chest. Before the prone SEAL could react, McKittrick brought the knife down hard.

With a grunt, McKay felt the blade cut a white-hot furrow into his left shoulder, as his opponent withdrew the blade and prepared to administer the coup de grace. The American knew this was his last chance. Using his good right hand and the last of his strength, he stopped the next lunge in mid-blow. As McKittrick leaned into the knife with all his weight, the door blew off its hinges.

Appraising the situation in less than a heartbeat, the Breacher pumped three rounds into McKittrick's back. Surprised, the big Scot sat up with his eyes glazing over and blood bubbling from his mouth. Slowly, he slumped over and onto the floor, dead.

"You okay Mike?" Philips inquired as he stepped into the

room.

"Oh yeah, noth'in a boy from Michigan couldn't han…" he started, then passed out.

Thirty-Eight

As the corpsman rushed into the room to check on the Premier and McKay, Philips realized he was in the way. Backing out into the hallway, he encountered an old man who was trying to escape. "Where's Sawada?" he urged.

The old man just shrugged his shoulders indicating he did not understand. Growing impatient, the Lieutenant grabbed him by the arms and practically screamed, "Sawada, where's Sawada?"

The old man said something indistinguishable while pointing towards the ceiling. Remembering that My-Lin had said something about a study on the second floor, he sprinted for the staircase. Just as Philips rounded the corner, he ran into Lieutenant Bourne.

"The Premier's okay, but Mike's down. I haven't had chance to finish securing the floor."

"What's the hurry?"

"I'm going after Sawada!" Jake shouted over his shoulder while working his way up the staircase. The Lieutenant retraced his steps to the foyer, then bounded up the grand staircase, three steps at a time, to the mezzanine level. There, he discovered several closed doors and another spiral staircase accessing the tower above. The first door revealed the empty library. No threat there.

As Philips entered the second room he stopped in shock. Before him was the master bedroom with a large four poster bed. Bound standing, spread eagle fashion to the ends of the bed, was a totally nude and moaning Judelyn! Her back was a criss-crossed web of multiple flaming red welts. Obviously, the SEAL's attack had interrupted the sadistic Sawada's morning entertainment.

Gently, the big man loosened the bonds that held the tiny Filipina in place. He carefully laid Judelyn down upon the bed and pulled the satin sheets up to cover her exposed body. As she moaned, anger within the Lieutenant, began to rise. Taking her head lightly in his hands, he spoke gently, "Judelyn, can you hear me?"

Mumbling incomprehensibly, Judelyn opened her eyes at Philips touch and recognized him. Encircling her arms around his neck she whispered, "Don't leave me. He monster!"

"I promise he will never come near you again," he assured her. The Lieutenant pried her arms loose and laid them to her sides. "Do you know where Sawada went?"

"He go when big noise happen."

Realizing she probably knew nothing, Philips tried to comfort her, "You stay here. I promise you nothing will happen."

"You stay!" she begged.

"I can't, I have to get this monster before he gets away."

"You keel him?"

"I might," he whispered. Leaning forward, Philips kissed the maiden's brow lightly. "You let me take care of this. Someone will be up here momentarily. Now, you rest."

Picking up his MP 5, the angry Lieutenant left the room. Pausing in the hallway he called Lieutenant Bourne. "TM 2, this is TM 1, over..."

"Go ahead TM 1."

"There's a distraught young lady in a bedroom on the

mezzanine level."

"You would find a damsel in distress in a castle..." joked Bourne.

"You wouldn't be so jovial if you saw what she's had to endure," Philips said firmly.

"Sorry."

"Would you see to her?"

"You can count on it, buddy," Bourne replied, grateful for a chance to redeem his wise crack.

"Good! I'm going for Sawada. Have they found Wardon yet?"

"I've got a man on it. Jake, about Sawada, he's not worth it," Bourne advised. "Save him for the authorities."

"You have a look at Judelyn, then tell me that," Philips shouted into the radio.

Ignoring the rules of search and seizure, Philips kicked in the final door with his weapon drawn. He had been many places and done many things, but none of it had prepared him for the sight before him. He was in a room no larger than the library. The windows had been bricked over so the chambers' only light was the flickering glow of perhaps two hundred candles. On a bamboo mat, kneeling before a life-size portrait of Emperor Hirohito, was Philip's quarry. Rocking to and fro and chanting in Japanese, Sawada seemed oblivious to the American's entrance.

The room contained other curious artifacts. In one corner stood a life size mannequin dressed as a World War II Japanese General Officer. The uniform was complete, with sword, campaign ribbons and small baseball-style cap. Behind him was an enormous flag. It had a large red ball with radiating sunbeams centered over a white background. The walls were covered with hundreds of photos, all of World War II vintage. Philips could see the photographs' main subject was always the same. A smart looking, well-dressed, general officer. A quick glance back to the mannequin confirmed the likeness was one and the same.

"Lieutenant this is my father..." the soft-spoken Sawada said, then continued with pride. "...Lieutenant General Tomoyuki Yamashita, the 'Tiger of Malaya'."

"I'm sure, now get up."

"Did you know he conquered the Malaya Peninsula when others claimed it could not be done?" Sawada asked, ignoring the order. "He forced the surrender of Singapore almost three months before Corregidor fell," Sawada continued in admiration.

Taking a step forward, Philips remarked, "So?"

"And my father refused to surrender the Philippines until the Emperor himself had surrendered."

"So let's give him a medal. It's time to go," the Lieutenant ordered.

"He was executed by MacArthur for war crimes he didn't commit."

"Good for him!" Philips said sarcastically.

"Do you know what my mother did when she heard about my father's execution?" Sawada asked, still not moving.

"She raised a scum-bag like you!" Philips commented.

"She was so brokenhearted that on their 10th anniversary she walked into the Sea of Japan."

Realizing an undertone of hatred was his reason for being here, the Lieutenant reasoned," You could have used your wealth to enlighten mankind on the evils of warfare, but instead you caused the death of a very dear friend. I also saw what you did to My-Lin and Judelyn. If you ask me, you're one sick fuck!"

"Ah yes, and such sweet things they are. You ought to try them, especially My-Lin. She never screamed once."

Reacting with anger, Philips pulled the small man to his feet and slapped his face several times. Drawing his fist back to strike again the Lieutenant checked himself. Clenching his teeth he threatened, "What I should do is string you up, and give you a taste of your own medicine."

"Ian will stop you."

"Hello! Mike kicked the shit out of your McKittrick's ass."

"Ian was a good man," the crestfallen Sawada sighed.

"He was a murderer. He got what he deserved."

"Maybe so, but at least he died honorably in battle. You! What do you know of honor?"

"I know it's keeping the peace and helping those who cannot fend for themselves."

"That's not real honor," Sawada said sadly.

Realizing it was time to go, Lieutenant Philips motioned towards the door and asked, "One more thing before we go. What did you really want with the Mills Transfer?"

"It was my way of bringing realization to as many Americans as possible."

"Realization?"

"Of how Japan was victimized."

"Victimized, what the fuck are you taking about?" Philips demanded, growing impatient.

"How, after our Emperor surrendered, your government took away our religion, way of life, and bestowed the humiliation of defeat upon us. With the transfer I could expose America's treachery over the past sixty years, thus restoring a portion of dignity to Japan."

"It's ancient history. Besides, who bombed Pearl Harbor?"

"It's not ancient history to me!" Angered, Sawada let his voice raise for the first time. "And we did not start it, as you say. So, I have put into motion something, which, fifty years from now the Japanese will remember with pride."

"All well and good. How 'bout you fill me in on your little plan and maybe I won't hurt you, much!"

"I think not, but you will find out soon. It's too late to stop it."

"Fine, then let's go dirtbag," the Lieutenant said as he shoved Sawada towards the door.

In a flash, the little man drew a small dagger from beneath his robe and plunged it into his own belly. Dropping to the floor as blood started to flow freely, Sawada looked up into Philips face with triumph and said, "I won't dishonor my name."

As he went to complete his Hari-kari, Lieutenant Philips moved swiftly. He grabbed the determined man by his right hand and tossed the dagger across the room.

"There's a cell waiting for you."

"You caaaaaaannnn'ttttt..." screamed Sawada just before Philips struck him with a strong left knocking him cold.

"That's for Wardon, dick-head," the SEAL spat, then picked up his unconscious quarry and headed out the door.

Thirty-Nine

The banquet hall had been turned into a makeshift hospital. Sawada was laid out on the table as the corpsman worked to stem the flow of blood from his self-inflicted wound. Sitting at the other end of the table was a now-conscious McKay. He had been stripped to the waist, with a blood soaked dressing wrapped around his shoulder and a large patch covering half his cheek. At the moment, he was enjoying one of McKittricks cigars, which he had nabbed from the fallen Scot's coat. Bourne's injured rocket man was seated next to him, was also enjoying a cigar as the two conversed like long lost friends. China's Premier was resting peacefully nearby on his gurney. Sitting before the fire with a blanket wrapped around her shoulders, was the sobbing Judelyn. Under the windows, along the far wall were three bodybags.

Satisfied with the completion of the mission's objectives, Lieutenant Philips was on the radio coordinating their evacuation. With several prisoners taken, the sounds of sporadic gunfire could be heard as the SEALs mopped up what little resistance remained. As word of Sawada's capture and McKittrick's demise swept the estate, the remaining mercenaries lost their will to resist. Still, several pockets of opposition did exist. Paying little heed to the gunfire, the Lieutenant instructed the Blackhawk pilot to land the helicopter just outside the Gatehouse.

Lieutenant Bourne approached Philips with a man in tow. "Jake, look what I found. Says he's got important information."

"Yes."

Following the SEAL was a Caucasian male in his mid '50s. Lieutenant Bourne introduced him as Chief Inspector Rolf Heinrich from London. "He was locked up in the last room in the basement," Bourne explained.

"So what's your story? A little out of your jurisdiction, aren't you?" Philips commented.

"Quite. Would you by chance have a fag?" Heinrich queried.

"I don't, but I'm sure we can rustle one up for you."

"Jolly good," he said as the Breacher stepped forward with a lit cigarette and passed it to the grateful Inspector. Taking a long drag, he exhaled with a sigh of relief. "Sawada?" He indicated towards the figure on the table.

"Yep!"

"Nothing serious I hope."

"He'll live to stand trial."

"Lovely. That bloke has been up to some peculiar activities."

"What makes you say that?"

"Have you seen this little bugger's science project?" Heinrich asked.

"Not really."

"You should," he stated seriously. Taking another long draw on his cigarette and exhaling smoke rings towards the ceiling Heinrich continued, "Let me fill you in. This chap was doing something with oil. He's got all kinds of samples in those rooms in the basement. There's also a lab where he's been cooking up something."

"I bet he has something to do with the attack on the American petroleum reserves," Bourne volunteered.

"Indeed, my thoughts precisely," the Inspector agreed. "I don't understand the particulars, but his man McKittrick was bragging about setting up some poor Filipinos."

"So we would accuse the Filipinos of the act," Philips acknowledged.

"Quite. I also discovered he has acquired several super tankers and has them berthed in Hong Kong," the Inspector continued. "Any idea what he needed those for?"

"I might," Philips volunteered no information. "What was the nature of your investigations?"

"The extraction team be landing any second now," Lieutenant Bourne interrupted, as the distinctive rotors could be heard overhead.

"Continue, Inspector," Philips encouraged, ignoring the Lieutenant.

"As I was saying, I was investigating several assassinations in Europe..."

"What has that got to do with Sawada and oil?" Bourne asked.

"Well, if you would let me finish," the agitated Inspector complained.

"Lieutenant Philips, the Blackhawk's on the ground," Breacher advised the group.

"Lieutenant, is there someplace were we can converse without interruptions?"

As if on cue, there was a noticeable increase in automatic fire just outside the windows. Philips' earpiece exploded with chatter, most of it warnings about an escaping vehicle. Just outside the hall, shouts and minor explosions followed a loud bang. Several of the windows shattered from the explosion's concussion. Using his radio, Lieutenant Philips ascertained that a couple of goons had tried to escape by automobile. When they discovered their way was blocked, instead of surrendering, they crashed into the side of the Keep. A well-placed grenade ignited the vehicle's fuel tank.

"See what I mean," the Inspector argued, when the American turned his attention back to him.

"Please understand, this is an ongoing operation." The Lieutenant patiently informed him, as he turned to go. "This can wait for debriefing..."

"Stop!" Inspector Heinrich ordered, "You will hear me out!"

Stunned, Philips stopped in his tracks. In fact everyone in the room had stopped what they were doing to watch the Lieutenant's reaction. Turning, he nodded. "Okay, you've got my undivided attention, for two minutes."

"Sawada has an atomic bomb!" the Inspector said slowly.

"Say again?"

"My investigations have led me to believe that Sawada has an atomic bomb," Heinrich repeated solemnly. Not a sound could be heard in the room as its occupants realized the implications of the Inspector's remark.

"Are you sure?" It was Lieutenant Bourne who broke the silence.

"As sure as I'm standing here. He must have it hidden someplace about the grounds."

"What kind?" Philips asked.

"I don't know."

"What did it look like?" Bourne questioned.

"It was long, white with wings, I only saw a photograph." The Brit apologized.

"How do you know it was a nuke?" McKay said from across the room.

Holding his hands up in despair, Heinrich spoke loudly, "Hold it! Everyone just a minute! By Jove, you chap's won't give me a chance to explain."

"Everyone pipe down," Philips ordered. "You may continue, Inspector."

The Inspector left nothing out; he explained his observations with regards to the assassinations in London and Paris and how he suspected a coup in China. Heinrich went on to explain his investigation and reasons for being in Russia, the escort's slip of the tongue and his narrow escape in Hong Kong. Finally he told how, with no cards left to play, he just confronted Sawada in his offices in Kobe.

"You've been busy," the big American observed.

"So you see, I'm fairly certain our Mr. Sawada has a nuclear device," he reasoned, "Otherwise why would he try to kill me, then hold me prisoner?"

The room was silent for several seconds as Lieutenant Philips escorted the Inspector over to the sleeping Premier. "If what you say is true, why haven't we heard about it?"

"I'm not sure. The Russians have denied everything."

"Do you know who this is?" Philips queried as he pointed to the figure on the gurney.

Looking carefully, the Inspector studied the sleeping figure's features for several moments. Finally he exclaimed, "Great Zeus! Is that who I think it is?"

"You tell me," said Philips evasively.

"Premier Xian! I thought he had a stroke and was bedridden in China. What's he doing here?"

"This leads credence to your coup theory."

"Then minister Chan must be involved."

"Perhaps!"

"By God, do you know what this means?"

"Not if we can help it," the Lieutenant responded, grinning.

"I thought I'd never see the day when America came to the aid of Communist China."

"Things are about to change! Do you think that your missing weapon and the kidnapped Premier have anything in common?"

"Could be. Sawada seems to be the common thread." Inspector Heinrich said thoughtfully.

"Right." Hesitating, Lieutenant Philips made a decision. Speaking into his microphone, he ordered, "Listen up, the mission's priorities have changed. We're not leaving! I repeat, we are not leaving. Secure the entire estate. Bring all prisoners to the gymnasium."

"Mike, you okay?" Nodding to McKay, Philips felt comfortable with his decision.

"Never better. Just give the word, and I'll run a marathon," he assured his friend with a weak smile.

"Good. I want you to watch over the Premier and Judelyn." Turning to Lieutenant Bourne he continued, "Let's get several search parties going and let's evac the wounded, Judelyn and the Premier. Sawada stays. I don't want him on the same flight as the Premier."

"Jake, what about the locals?" McKay popped up.

"I'm not leaving without that nuke! Let State handle 'em," Philips said with determination. "Sawada promised retribution and I believe him!" Getting out his Globalstar, Philips punched in Adviser Kelly's number. The call was answered on the first ring. It took all of thirty seconds to bring Kelly up to speed on their current situation. The Lieutenant listened for several seconds then acknowledged the conversation, and hung up.

"Kelly's got backup airborne. ETA twenty minutes. Now, find that nuke," the Lieutenant ordered, as the SEALs scattered to perform their various tasks.

With the intent of loading the helicopter, the corpsman aided by the Breacher negotiated the Premier's gurney out the door. McKay and the wounded Randolph followed slowly as Lieutenant Bourne went to organize the prisoners.

Just as Philips was about to leave the hall, a blood-curdling scream echoed throughout the room's expanse. Rushing in the direction of the moaning Sawada, the Lieutenant saw a bloody Judelyn standing over his incapacitated form. The grisly sight stunned the American, as Lieutenant Bourne came rushing in from the hallway with McKay slowly bringing up the rear. "What happened?" they shouted in unison.

The shocked Lieutenant pointed to Sawada. "Git the corpsman back in here."

Before him lay Sawada unconscious. His silk robe, covered in blood, lay opened. Judelyn had obviously removed Sawada's member with a large piece of jagged glass. Seeping blood dripped steadily upon the floor from the open wound as Judelyn spat upon her former abductor.

"He rape no more," she said triumphantly, before collapsing to the floor, sobbing.

"That's gots ta hurt," McKay snickered. "That's gonna leave a mark in the morning."

"It looks like Sawada's got some serious issues to address when he wakes up," Lieutenant Bourne commented with a straight face.

Helping Judelyn to her feet, Philips consoled her as he escorted the Filipina from the room. "Corpsman!" he called out.

"Sir!"

"Make sure he doesn't die."

The search proved fruitless. They did however locate the missing crates of gold, which Sawada had stashed in the gymnasium. Among the gold crates was the metal document box. The Lieutenant made a cursory examination to see if the leather pouch was among the documents. Striking out, he decided to see if Sawada could be swayed into revealing the weapon's location.

The corpsman informed Philips that as a result of his injuries, Sawada was in a state of shock. With the lack of blood and the influence of painkillers, the hapless Japanese could not be of further assistance. Therefore, the only avenue open for the Lieutenant was to sit down with Heinrich and hope his memory could recall some obscure fact that he may have inadvertently forgotten.

Again striking out, the frustrated American was about to leave the banquet hall when he heard Sawada moan. Looking to the table, the corpsman spoke up, "He's coming to Lieutenant."

"What did you do?" Philips asked.

"I took a chance and gave him a shot of adrenaline."

"Is he able to answer questions?"

"A few, but I'm not sure for how long. He could lapse into a coma at any moment," the corpsman cautioned.

Leaning over the prone form, Philips asked, "Sawada, where's the nuke?"

Moaning and moving his head from side to side, the Japanese fluttered his eyes open and focused on the American. A slight smile spread across his face, "Never tell," he whispered.

"You must!" Philips urged through clenched teeth.

"Too late."

Grabbing the old man by the throat, the big American applied pressure. Drawing his face close to that of his opponent, he threatened. "I'll bring back the lady."

"I never tell, so kill me."

Realizing his efforts were fruitless, Philips decided on a different avenue. He removed his K-Bar knife and gently put it into the Japanese's right hand. Enclosing the old man's hand with his own, the Lieutenant promised, "I'll finish it."

With destiny within his grasp Sawada hesitated, then whispered, "*Hangzhou*!"

Looking up, "Does *Hangzhou* mean anything to you?" The American asked the Inspector, who had been watching the interrogation with curiosity.

"I think it's a Chinese destroyer."

Turning his attention back to Sawada, Philips asked, "Where's the *Hangzhou*?"

"Taiwan Strait's."

"When?"

"Xing Nian"

"That's Chinese New Year," the Inspector offered.

"When's that?

"I think..." Heinrich hesitated, "Yes, today's Chinese New Year!"

"Shit! Lieutenant Bourne, contact Kelly," Philips ordered as he looked deeply into Sawada eyes, realizing he'd gotten the truth. The Lieutenant removed his knife from his quarry's fingers and walked away.

"Noooooooo!" Sawada moaned as he tried to sit up. "You promised."

"So I lied!" Philips responded casually as he left the ballroom.

Forty

After briefing Kelly on the threat of the missile and its possible whereabouts, Philips confirmed that this was indeed Chinese New Year and the *Hangzhou* was scheduled to test fire a weapon's system at noontime! The Adviser ordered him to try for an intercept.

Running through the driving rain, the eager Lieutenant boarded the Blackhawk just after she had disembarked the second SEAL squad. Adjusting the headset, he shouted above the rotor noise, "Take 'er up, we're going for a ride!"

The pilot gave him the thumbs up and replied, "Yeah! I've already been briefed."

As the helicopter flew north over the mountains and out to sea, Philips marveled at how his mission priorities had changed from a simple rescue to saving millions. When the boxy dark green helicopter flew over the Sea of Japan, he noticed how angry the water was. Through the rain-splattered porthole he could see the waves cresting at fifteen and twenty feet.

"Kamikaze," crackled the pilot's voice in Jake's

headphones just as the helicopter hit an air pocket and dropped ten feet.

“Say what?” the Lieutenant asked, a bit perplexed.

“Kamikaze. You know, ‘Divine Wind’.”

“No. I didn’t know. I though it was some sort of suicide pilot?”

“Yeah, but they were named after a storm which saved Japan from a Mongol invasion in the 12th century,” the pilot explained. “It’s their version of a ‘Nor Easter.”

“I see.” Drifting back to his thoughts, Philips realized that it had only been fifty-two hours since the banquet at Sawada’s castle. A lot had transpired. Wardon’s death, their miraculous escape, and the assault on the estate. Realizing how tired he was, the Lieutenant decided to get some shut-eye as the helicopter flew westward towards the Taiwan Straits. As the cabin pitched forward then jerked backwards, the weary SEAL drifted off into a restless slumber.

> *“It’s okay Jake,” his mother said through the confusion within the cabin. Looking over, he saw his parents sitting calmly amid the chaos about them.*
> *“But Mom, I wanted to say I’m sorry,” he replied.*
> *For the first time his father spoke in his deep baritone voice, “Jake I’m proud of you and I’ve always respected your wishes. It was I who was wrong... I never should have second-guessed your judgment, but now it’s time to move on...”*

“But...” Philips started. The scene faded as the Lieutenant felt himself being shaken back to reality.

“Lieutenant, Lieutenant!” the crew chief shouted.

“Okay, okay I’m up.” The Lieutenant remarked groggily.

“We’re here!” he announced, “We’re at the rendezvous, but if you ask me it looks a bit dicey out there.”

Looking out into the gray morning, Philips could barely see the outline of the *Chancellorsville* as her bow plowed deep into a cresting wave. Blue-gray seawater crashed down on the ship's main deck as her screws spun wildly in open air. Her bow shot through the cascading water high into the air as the propellers dug deep into the wave's trough, propelling the ship forward.

"You're going to attempt to land on that?" he shouted.

The pilot turned and spoke in a soft Southern drawl, "Yeah, we'll make it."

"Are you sure?"

"Yeah, no problem! It's just like a hay ride down on my Daddy's farm," the pilot reassured his passenger. "Only it's the Widowmaker pulling the wagon instead of Old Betsy."

Not so sure, Philips buckled his safety harness and awaited the outcome of this madness. "It's not too late to turn back," he shouted as the Blackhawk started its descent.

"Where's yer backbone Lieutenant? Yawl afraid of a little wind?" the pilot chuckled as the helicopter was buffeted by a strong gust.

With seas running between twelve and fifteen feet, the Captain of the *Chancellorsville* braced himself against the steel bulwark as he observed the approaching helicopter. Commander Albert Sidney Johnston was on the cruiser's starboard docking bridge watching as the Blackhawk descended from the gray sky. *"This guy's insane,"* He thought.

It had been a long night with the force three storm. In a timeless struggle as old as man himself, the Americans had fought for sixteen hours against nature's fury and won. The tempest had abated earlier and current wind gusts were only half of what they had been at the storm's height. Still, the conditions had a long ways to go before he would consider them ideal for a landing.

"All ahead one-third," he shouted into his walkie-talkie. The Commander could feel the ship's vibration slow almost to a standstill. He dared go no slower as they needed headway to keep his beloved ship into the wind. "Keep 'er steady, right there." he screamed over the wind.

Johnston admired the pilot's ability to keep the

Blackhawk steady just off his fantail. *"Those wind currents must be hellacious,"* he thought. The helicopter gracefully descended to within several meters of the cruiser's pitching deck. Ground crew members were on alert just inside the closed hanger door, while a lone signalman waved directions to the helo's pilot. As the helicopter made its final approach, Commander Johnston felt confidence in their ability to recover the aircraft.

"Steady, steady, another foot and you're home free," he said aloud, as he mentally coaxed the craft onto the cruiser's pitching deck.

Aboard the bucking Blackhawk, the Lieutenant couldn't bear to watch and kept his eyes clenched shut. Philips had no way of knowing if the pilot would be able to keep the aircraft from striking the pitching and rolling super structure of the *Chancellorsville.* He prayed that the pilot knew what he was doing.

At the moment the helicopter wheels contacted the helo pad, the cruiser was tilted forward into another trough. The deck struck the helicopter with enough force to propel it into the hanger door. The signalman dropped to the deck just as the whirling rotor blades struck the huge door, snapping like balsa wood. A fifteen-foot gash was sliced across the entry, rendering it useless. "Jesus!" the Lieutenant heard over the headset as the craft dumped itself with a bone-jarring jolt onto the deck.

The ground crew magically appeared through a hatchway and was about to secure the battered Blackhawk, when another wave slid the untethered craft into the damaged hanger door. Miraculously the helicopter wasn't tossed overboard! As one of the ground crew pried opened the aft sliding door, Philips quickly unbuckled his safety harness and exited the ship. "Shit, man! What a ride!" he exclaimed.

The pilot overheard his exclamation and offered a bit of advice. "Any landing you walk away from Lieutenant is a good one!" he said smiling broadly. "And that, my friend, was a good landing!"

Watching the hard landing from his bridge wing, Commander Johnston swore as he saw the helicopter lurch forward and strike the cruiser's superstructure. He immediately ordered damage control to the area. As alarms sounded, crewmembers dashed to their assigned positions. Leaving the bridge to his X.O., Johnston raced down the companionways to the hanger.

Upon entering the spacious hanger bay, the Commander noted with relief that his own CH-60 Sea Hawk was undamaged. Johnston marched up to his four unexpected guests and said, "That was a helluva landing. Thanks to you, no one will be lifting off anytime soon."

"Thank you sir," the pilot responded with a snappy salute.

Ignoring the sarcasm, the Commander asked, "Which one of you is Lieutenant Philips?"

Without saying a word, Jake stepped forward.

"Tell me, what's this all about?" Johnston asked as he led the Lieutenant away from the hanger bay. "I get a communication from CINCPAC ordering me to take you aboard no questions asked. Furthermore, I'm to avail myself and my crew to your directives."

"So I've got some powerful friends in low places." The SEAL sighed theatrically.

"I would say so," the Commander agreed, ignoring the young man's attitude. "It would take an act of Congress to get me out in weather like this."

"Is there someplace where we can talk privately, and might I ask, could I get a shower and a change of clothing?" Philips inquired, indicating his wet suit.

"Sure, follow me."

With a steaming cup of hot coffee and a fresh uniform, Lieutenant Philips had a seat in the Captain's wardroom and was ready to talk. "Commander, have you been shadowing the *Hangzhou*?"

"Affirmative, she's a little distant right now. Why?"

"Is she scheduled to test fire a missile system today?"

"Affirmative."

"What time is the test scheduled to commence?"

"According to the test plan filed by the Chinese, she's supposed to launch at 1200 hours."

Checking the wall clock, Philips realized he had just over an hour to stop the launch. "I have it on good authority and the National Security Adviser believes that the *Hangzhou* will launch a missile armed with a nuclear warhead!"

The young Lieutenant's words hit the Commander like a thunderbolt out of the blue. He watched Commander Johnston's face grow ashen.

"What!" he exclaimed.

"Just as I said."

"How can that be?" the perplexed Commander wanted to know.

"We're not sure. We're not even sure if the *Hangzhou's* Captain is aware of this. We suspect the missile, which was stolen from a Russian supply depot three weeks ago, is targeted for the island of Taiwan or perhaps Taipei itself," Philips finished.

"Are you sure about what you're saying?" the Commander asked in disbelief.

"The information is credible, Sir," Philips responded, not telling him his source was an Interpol Inspector who was suspicious about a photograph and a Russian denial. The SEAL continued, "Time is short. I need you to put the *Chancellorsville* in a position to intercept the launch."

"What type of device are we talking about?" Johnston was curious.

"Preliminary reports indicate a Russian made S-10, with a yield of a 100-megatons," Philips responded.

"Isn't that the cruise missile nicknamed the Tomahawkski?"

"Correct."

"Then we'd better get to it," the Commander suggested. He ordered, "Follow me." Walking rapidly, almost at a run, the pair negotiated the narrow passageways and ladders to the

Cruisers Bridge. Their destination was the ship's Combat Information Center, located aft of the bridge. From the CIC the ship's Captain could orchestrate actions against foreign aggression.

In the compartment's low light, Philips could see several sailors at their posts monitoring a whole myriad of radar, sonar and other computer screens. The compartment contained two different plotting stations, a vertical position for tracking aircraft and other flying targets, and a more traditional table for plotting surface and subsurface contacts. An officer was busy, hunched over the table marking off some notations.

"Ensign, location of the *Hangzhou,* if you please," Commander Johnston requested.

Pointing to a red mark on the chart, he replied, "Twelve nautical miles south-southwest, Sir."

"Thank you, Ensign." Retreating back to the bridge, Philips followed the Commander out onto the port-docking wing. Handing the Lieutenant a pair of binoculars, Johnston informed him. "There she is, just below that dark cloud bank."

Scanning the horizon, Philips was able to make out the sleek white profile of the Chinese destroyer as her bow knifed through a wave. "What's the missile's flight time once it's launched?" he inquired while studying the warship.

"Depends. Let's say the target's Taipei. I'd say 19-20 minutes max." At that moment the Commander's walkie-talkie squawked. He had to put the device to his ear to understand the message over the whipping of the wind. "All ahead full! Come to course 030*" he responded.

"What's up?" Philips asked as he felt the ship's screws bite into the boiling sea.

"AEGIS is down! We're blind! I'm going to close on the *Hangzhou.*"

"What do you mean, down?" the big SEAL asked incredulously. Not waiting for an answer he added, "How long will it take to get it back on-line?"

"We've just been through a helluva storm. Somewhere, somehow, some things got knocked about. The chief said he needed twenty to thirty minutes to run a diagnostic and isolate the problem," Johnston explained.

"We don't have thirty minutes," Philips exasperated. Before he could comment further, his Globalstar rang. Excusing himself, the young Lieutenant took the call before the disbelieving Commander. After a brief conversation with McKay, who informed him the Premier was up and talking, Philips gave his friend a brief rundown on his current situation. Hanging up he asked, "What do we do now?"

Disbelieving what had just transpired, Commander Johnston commented, "What was that all about?"

"News from home," Philips replied, grinning.

"I hope it was good news, as everything here sucks," Johnston cracked.

"Never better. As you were saying, Sir?" Philips steered the conversation back to the current problem. "What say we call up our Chinese friend and ask him not to launch?" the SEAL added sarcastically.

"Not a bad idea, but do you think they'll believe your outlandish story?" the Commander reasoned. He ordered the radioman to try to hail the *Hangzhou.* "Listen, I've got another idea."

"Go ahead."

"Let's say we get between the *Hangzhou* and Taiwan and shoot the missile down with the Phalanx," Commander Johnston explained, referring to the six-barreled Gatling gun used for close-in antiaircraft defense.

"I thought you said the radar was out?"

"If we can get close enough I'll just blast in the general direction, it should do the job."

"Will it work?" the Lieutenant worried. "It sounds like it's a bit risky."

"Don't know, there's nothing in the rule book that say's we can't. If you've got another suggestion, I'm all ears," the *Chancellorsville* Captain said as the ship turned towards the distant warship. Ordering all ahead emergency, the Lieutenant watched as the Commander directed the American warship through the angry seas.

In short order the agile warship was alongside the sleek Chinese destroyer. Philips was amazed at how Commander Johnston had orchestrated his ship through a series of maneuvers, which anticipated the Chinese Captain's counter moves. Now, with no more than eight meters separating the two warships Philips wondered what was next. "Is the AEGIS still down?" he shouted above the noise of the wind and waves.

"Affirmative!"

"How long before the launch?"

"Four minutes," Johnston said grimly.

"The radio?"

"They're ignoring us..."

A Chinese officer stepped out on the bridge wing holding a megaphone to his lips. "American warship, standoff! We are in international waters. You have no right to interfere with our test."

"At least we know they're home," Philips quipped.

Cupping his hands around his mouth, Commander Johnston shouted, "Listen to our radio calls. Cancel launch."

"No can do! Standoff!" the Chinese officer said again, before retreating back inside the bridge.

"Commander?" the SEAL shouted, "Remember in the Cold War days when the Russians would bump ships when they wanted to protest?"

"Yes I do," he responded, "You're not thinking..."

"Yes I am. Get us in close, if all else fails, bump 'em." Philips shouted as he headed down a ladder.

"Where you headin?"

"To talk some sense into that idiot."

"If you're gonna do what I think you're gonna to do, you'd better be quick," the Commander shouted down from his perch on the bridge wing. As Philips reached the quarterdeck, he added, "Good luck Lieutenant."

Standing on the quarterdeck, the Lieutenant waited. He removed the safety rail and hung on as the ships crept closer. The faster and larger cruiser narrowed the gap between the two warships until the SEAL could almost jump across the chasm.

Now it was the Chinese captain's turn to effect a series of maneuvers to try to avoid the American warship. For every move he made, the Americans countered, keeping the gap at three meters. Philips was impressed by Johnston's seamanship.

With the close proximity of the Chinese warship, Philips could see numerous sailors in a panic, waving the cruiser off. Ignoring them, Commander Johnston held his ship steady. With the gap narrowing, the Lieutenant heard a loud 'whoosh'.

A cloud of steam was emitted from the destroyer's aft vertical launcher. The Granat exited its tube and hung in the air momentarily. The American hoped it would be a misfire and fall harmlessly back into the sea. His hopes were dashed when the engine fired flawlessly. As the missile acquired its target, it started to gain altitude and arched itself towards the distant horizon.

At that same instant, the cruiser's Phalanx system engaged and launched a wall of aluminum slugs into the general vicinity of the rapidly escaping missile. To Jake's dismay, the cruise missile was already out of range. It had been a long shot at best.

Philips figured that he could jump the gap if the ships closed to within two meters of each other. He would have only one chance. The Lieutenant was not prepared for what happened next. Just as he was about to jump, the Captain of the Chinese vessel decided that if he could not stop the Americans, at least he could defy them. Ordering his ship hard to starboard he bumped into the cruiser just as Johnston turned to port.

With the screeching sound of grinding metal the two ships came together. As the American vessel swept past the Chinese, sparks flew from the complaining hull plates. Seizing the opportunity, Philips leaped! For the first time since World War II an American had boarded a foreign government's warship at sea.

Unable to check his momentum, the Lieutenant hit hard upon a bulkhead fracturing his hip and snapping his left tibia. As Philips crumpled to the deck, the agonizing pain caused him to cry out. Within seconds of his landing, four seamen surrounded the American with sidearms drawn. Holding his hands up, the disabled SEAL pleaded, "Please, take me to the Captain. Urgent, do you understand?"

The sailors looked to each other and spoke rapidly in Chinese. With one man on either side they hoisted Philips to his feet. Half dragging and half-walking, they assisted the American through a hatchway and into a narrow passageway. Forced to walk on his injuries, the Lieutenant endured the excruciating pain until they managed to reach the Captain's wardroom. With nausea rising, it took all the strength he could muster to keep from passing out. Less than a minute later, the Chinese Captain entered the space with a translator. He nodded to the guards, who exited the compartment leaving the three of them alone.

"Sit!" the translator instructed, and Philips was more than happy to comply.

The Captain spoke rapidly to the translator, who in turn spoke to the Lieutenant. "Captain Tong wants to know why you board ship? Why American ship ram us?"

"Really, I can explain but first you need to abort the test," Philips said weakly.

"This peaceful mission. We're in international waters," The translator continued after he spoke briefly with his Captain.

"Abort the test, please!" the American insisted.

Translating, the seamen asked, "Why?"

"Captain, the missile you just launched is armed with a nuclear warhead," Philips said quickly, urging the translator to inform his Captain.

As Captain Tong's eyes got large when the translator spoke, Philips felt a ray of hope. "How you know this?"

"The weapon was stolen from Vladivostok. Minister Chan had it transported and installed aboard your ship under the guise of a missile test. The test is to protest Taiwan's unwillingness to submit to your country's demands." The American spoke barely above a whisper as the pain started to overcome him.

For the first time the Captain spoke directly to Lieutenant Philips. "I'm not believing you."

“Please Captain, you have to believe me, many innocent people will die. We’re almost out of time.” He urged. “Captain please abort the test now.”

“I have orders,” Captain Tong answered back, while shaking his head.

Barely conscious, Philips held up his Globalstar phone and punched in McKay’s number; “I can get you in touch with Premier Xian,” He mumbled.

“Impossible! He’s in hospital, you talk foolish.” the interpreter remarked.

“No he’s not! He was kidnapped by your Minister Chan and we have recently rescued him.” The American took the chance the Captain would believe him. When McKay answered, Philips’ voice was barely audible. He asked Mike to put the Premier on the phone. McKay tried to protest but Philips insisted with all his strength. Finally his friend relented and went to find the Premier.

“I have Premier Xian on the phone,” he said weakly.

“I no believe you, you crazy man,” the interpreter said as the Captain watched wide-eyed. “You have no authority here. You board our ship and order us to stop our lawful business.” The seamen went on.

Captain Tong bent over the barely conscious SEAL and whispered, “Give me phone.”

Handing the phone to Captain Tong, the injured American passed out!

Aftermath

May 6th 2004
Corregidor Island

Security was tight around the hundred dignitaries and journalists who had gathered under the tropical midday sun to witness the historic announcement. A small podium had been set up before the football-shaped white granite monument memorializing America's surrender of the Philippines to the Japanese in the opening months of World War II. Lieutenant Jake Philips was standing at the end of a row of bleachers in his summer white uniform.

Leaning on a cane, the American scanned the crowd for familiar faces. He recognized several by reputation but otherwise there was no one present with whom he had a personal relationship. Addressing the crowd at the podium was the very same Premier whom he had rescued four months earlier.

Crestfallen, the Lieutenant had hoped McKay would be in attendance. He had not seen nor heard from his friend since the attack on Sawada's castle. Furthermore, his inquiries into the whereabouts of My-Lin met with a stone wall. Philips wondered why all the hush-hush when the rescue had made headlines around the world.

Even more interesting was the fact that he had been ordered to leave the hospital and attend these proceedings in the first-place. As he turned to go, a large form materialized beside him and said, “Glad you could make it Lieutenant.”

Turning to the smiling National Security Adviser, who was dressed as impeccably as always, he replied, “This beats therapy any day.”

“I came to personally congratulate you on a job well done,” Kelly offered as he continued to smile.

“Sir?”

“Yes, our goals have been met beyond our wildest dreams.”

“Goals?”

Avoiding the question, the Adviser suggested, “Why don’t we take a little stroll, Lieutenant. Maybe get out of the sun.”

“Why not,” Philips agreed. Using the cane, he walked slowly beside the powerful man.

Observing the Lieutenant’s noticeable limp the Adviser inquired, “How’s the leg?”

“Doctor says I’m making wonderful progress. I’m to be discharged next week.”

“I hear you have your choice of duty stations. Any idea what you want to do next?”

“Well, the teams are out. I’ve been down for the past four months and the leg will never be a hundred percent again. I could never get back in shape, so I figured being a BUDS instructor would be nice,” he explained.

The Adviser nodded as he listened. “Maybe I have something for you, let’s say on a more permanent basis.”

“Can you do that?”

“My boy, we can do many things,” Kelly boasted. Stopping, he turned and faced the Lieutenant. “By the way, you’re out of uniform, Commander.” He produced a small jeweler’s box, which contained two gold oak leaves.

"But-but how?" Philips stammered.

"It's our gratitude for a job well done. I'd say you earned it," the Adviser beamed, "Now, if you please." He motioned for the befuddled Lieutenant Commander to follow him.

The two walked in silence down an overgrown path that led towards the island's interior. In a short time, they came upon the former parade ground that was ringed with ruined buildings. On the East Side was the mile long topside barracks, whose skeletal remains reminded Philips of bleached whalebones. He could only imagine the horrors that had taken place here when the Japanese had bombed the island, night after night.

Behind the barracks, from out of the jungle, a narrow footpath was barely visible. Kelly proceeded down this jungle-choked pathway; past the long-silenced batteries of Crocket and Way. The pair was now making their way down the side of the island towards the bay. Finally the Adviser stopped. He was standing before a huge tunnel with a rusted iron gate that barred their further progress.

Kelly produced a key and worked the lock. Then, with little effort, he slid the big gate open. "Jake, this is Malinta tunnel, MacArthur's headquarters during the Bataan Peninsula campaign." Taking several steps into the cool darkness, Kelly threw a switch that flooded the tunnel's cavernous interior with brilliant light.

"Where are we going?"

"Patience my boy," Kelly responded. After several moments of walking deeper into the complex the Adviser finally stopped before one of the many laterals that intercepted with the main corridor. With the light only illuminating the central corridor, it was impossible for Philips to distinguish any of the lateral's details.

"Welcome to Fort Mills Lieutenant, oh, I mean Commander," a deep voice spoke from within the darkness.

"What the... Hey! I'd like to know just what's going on?" Philips asked startled.

"Understand the information I'm about to reveal is top secret and must not leave this room," the voice said.

"Understood."

Philips could hear the click of a switch and the room was bathed in brilliance. Before him stood General Murdoch Philips!

Seeing that his grandson was astonished to the point of not speaking, the big General chuckled. "What's a matter, cat got your tongue?" he quipped as he exhaled a cloud of blue smoke from his pipe.

"I-I, don't know what to say," Philips stammered.

"I hear you have questions. I'm here to answer 'em. So, fire away."

"Ah. I don't know where to begin."

"Then let me help you along. You see, back in my West Point days I was approached by a young officer to join the OSS..."

"Wasn't that the Office of..." the Lieutenant interrupted.

"...Strategic Services," Murdoch finished. "I was asked to join the intelligence section. Being the young stud I was and eager to serve my country, I accepted. Upon my graduation, I was posted to the Far Eastern division to keep tabs on Japanese saboteurs operating in the Philippines. Of course my timing couldn't have been better, or worse depending on your point of view. Shortly after I got to Fort McKinley, the Japanese launched their attack."

"So.., what does that have to do with..." Philips started.

"Patience my boy, patience, you need to learn to slow down a little. Right Jack?"

"If you say so, Murdoch," the Adviser agreed.

"So when I witnessed the treaty," the General continued his narrative, "There was a young attaché I befriended while negotiations were in progress. It turns out this attaché was Mao's youngest brother."

"Still..." Philips tried to interrupt but was silenced when his grandfather held up a hand.

"I was offered the opportunity by MacArthur to evacuate the island, however, before I could leave, orders from Washington instructed I be taken prisoner. This was a golden opportunity to gather intelligence from inside the enemy's lines."

Starting to understand what had transpired all those years ago, Philips nodded.

"From inside O'Donnell, I set up an information network which encompassed the islands. Remegio Aleta was one of my best operatives. Because he was able to come and go, I would pass vital information to him and he would get it to the coast watchers.

After the war, the OSS was dissolved to form the CIA. By Presidential decree we weren't really disbanded, we just became a separate entity of the National Security Agency. We have the best of both worlds. Officially we don't exist, whenever one of our operations is successful the CIA gets all the credit, and if something goes to hell they also get all the heat. Currently I'm the OSS's Chief Executive Officer!"

Astonished, Philips didn't know what to say. "How did you keep yourself so secret?"

"We maintain cover positions within the government and answer only to the President."

"And you're the head honcho?"

"Yes, but not for long. I'm about to finally retire. I'm getting too old for this shit." The General sighed as he took another long draw from his pipe and watched the smoke spiral towards the tunnel's concave ceiling. "Questions?"

"How long have you been in charge?"

"For over thirty years. I've led a double life for over sixty years. It's good to finally be finished," he said quietly.

"It's hard to believe," Philips responded slowly.

"It's true, my boy," Kelly assured him.

"Did dad know?"

"Your father was one of our better agents. I know this will pain you, but you have the right to know. He and your mother had been in Europe to expose..."

"Mom was involved?"

"You mom and dad met while working for the OSS," the General explained. Dumbfounded, the young Philips could only shake his head as his grandfather continued. "They were in Europe and had exposed a plot to assassinate the Queen of

England. They died on their way home when the airliner was blown up over Scotland."

"That part I know."

"Your father was the terrorists' target!"

Jake could only stare at his grandfather, astounded. "I'll have you know I took great satisfaction in personally slitting the throat of the man responsible for ordering your father's death," sighed the General.

"You could have told me..."

"No I couldn't. Besides you were too wrapped up in your grief."

"Did Grandma know?"

"Phoebe's never known and I'll never tell her. Now let's finish this. Back in '68 when Nixon went to China I naturally accompanied him. While there, I was reacquainted with my old friend from Corregidor. At that time he expressed disbelief and disillusionment with the Communist ways, so we forged a pact that would enable him to become China's Premier."

"You mean Premier Xian?"

The General answered with a nod.

"You helped him get to power?"

"Well, let's just say we fed him the intel which allowed him to ascend the political ladder within the Communist system. And once in power, we gave him enough support to stay in power."

"What about the Mills Transfer?" Philips questioned.

"A member of Premier Xian's cabinet had discovered that he intended to disband the Communist party much like Gorbachev did with the Soviet Union back in '91," he said, avoiding the question.

"What!" the SEAL exclaimed.

"As we speak, Premier Xian is making a public address about the dissolution of the Chinese Communist Party. Furthermore, he is asking the United Nations to enter the country and oversee public elections to be held in August. The United States has also been asked to allow the new China to sign the SALT II arms treaty. China and the Philippines have signed an agreement to allow oil exploration within the Spratleys with all possible royalties being split between the two countries," General Philips eagerly explained. "One last thing, Premier Xian has recognized the sovereignty of the Republic of China and her right to exist as a separate nation."

Philips was absolutely dumbfounded!

"Minister Chan had stumbled onto Xian's plans and took steps to overthrow the General Secretary. In order to strengthen his position within the cabinet, he had several members assassinated. He also took measures to guarantee acceptance within the liberal Chinese Congress."

"Chan was being fed information from a source we could not identify, so we mounted this operation to ferret out the mole. We had discovered early on that Chan had a close business and financial association with Sawada. We targeted Sawada to see if we could find a way to get to the mole."

"My-Lin?" the Lieutenant inquired.

"Yes, it was she who exposed the coup plot against Premier Xian. Sawada had agreed to help Chan in return for exclusive mineral and exploration rights over the Mischief Reef area. Therefore, the issue of the Mills Transfer arose because Sawada wanted proof that China had control over the Spratleys. By the way, it was Chan who provided the vector to Sawada. You see Sawada wanted to monopolize the oil market by contaminating vast reserves throughout the world. He even tested the vector in America."

"So you ordered Kelly to have me investigate the Mills Transfer when you were really looking for the counter agent?"

"Affirmative."

"Why didn't you just come out and ask me?"

"We had to make this look legitimate. We knew Chan's source within our government could possibly expose the existence of the OSS. Besides, in your grief over your parents you had not been home for fifteen years. What kind of red flag would that have been?" the National Security Adviser reasoned.

Turning to Kelly, Philips questioned, "I know about Wells. Was he working alone?"

"Wells got what he deserved but it was Parsons we were after!"

"Parsons?"

"Yes, we arrested him on the day of your assault, trying to leave the country with ten million dollars in negotiable bonds."

"And Chan?"

"He's currently under house arrest, with a heavy guard I might add. He's awaiting trial for treason," Kelly continued.

"So this whole operation was just for show?" Philips sighed.

"I wouldn't say that, I know of a sailor on the *Ronald Reagan* who owes you his life. Your attack on Sawada's castle provided information, which vindicated his innocence. You see Wardon was supposed..."

"What? Clifford?" the Lieutenant interrupted again, disbelieving his ears.

"Yes, Clifford had worked for me for a number of years. Sad thing about his death. Nothing pains me more than loosing a good man. I know that you were fond of him and am sorry it came to this. I placed him within the operation to make sure we stayed on track."

"You mean to baby-sit!"

"Hardly, you made all the command decisions," the General defended himself.

"Were the attacks on the houseboat and Wardon real?" the Lieutenant queried, raising an eyebrow.

"Most certainly," Kelly offered, "It was arranged by Parsons."

"What about the treaty, is it real?"

"Yes quite. Years ago the American Congress determined the treaty carried no substance, and washed their hands of it... it's worthless," The elderly Philips remarked. "We used it as a way to reveal the American agent's identity."

"What about the ledger?"

Chuckling, the General said, "Lysander's best work."

"Not the little guy too."

"He's my best agent," Murdoch admitted. "Cute little guy isn't he? I'm very fond of him."

Shaking his head in dismay, Philips asked, "Who doesn't work for you?"

"You!"

"What about the missing documents from the archives?"

"Those were real. We discovered them in Parson's office, they have been returned." Kelly said.

Looking to the concrete floor, the SEAL kicked at a loose piece of rubble. "How about the nuke, was that fake also?" he almost whispered.

"No, the threat was real. The nuke and the vector caught us completely off guard. We underestimated Sawada's influence. We never believed he could pull off such stunts. Lucky for us Inspector Heinrich followed his hunch."

"How come you didn't just blast the Chinese destroyer?"

"You have to realize the international implications. What if Xian was dead? We weren't sure; besides, do you realize how many ships are in the straits at any one time? The loss of life and material could have been enormous. Therefore, we had to play it by ear. It was ingenious of you to have your phone with you when you jumped aboard the *Hangzhou.* We had scrambled an F/A-18 out of Taipei waiting to shoot the missile down, but Captain Tong aborted the test just before the fail-safe. Hundreds of thousands of people owe you their lives," the General explained.

"And the gold?"

"Returned to Philippines," interjected a feminine voice from behind the young SEAL.

Wheeling about to see who had answered his question, Philips was pleased to see Judelyn. Beside her, smoking a cigar and wearing Wardon's hat, was McKay, with a broad smile on his face. "Good ta see ya Jake," he quipped. "How's the leg?"

"My Lolo say many thanks for what you do," the young Filipina said as she stepped forward and kissed Jake. Standing back, she handed him an old leather pouch. "Dis for you."

"The Mills Transfer?" he questioned.

"You betcha," McKay answered.

"But where, where did you find it? It wasn't in the document trunk."

"I got to thinking about what Corporal Aleta said about a man's name and how it link's the past with the future."

"So?"

"Remember the graffiti on the bunker walls?"

"Yes."

"Earlier today, Judelyn and I went back and discovered her grandfather's signature. We found a false panel where he had carefully hidden the treaty."

"So what now?" Philips wanted to know.

"I can't start you as the department head, but I do have a position for you in our counter-terrorist unit," Kelly volunteered.

"I don't know..." the young man hesitated.

"You think about it," the General advised.

"I don't know about you guys, but I've got ten days leave, with lots of sightseeing to do and the best guide in the whole country," McKay proclaimed as he put his arm around Judelyn's waist and kissed her. "See ya around Jake. When you get back, your desk is right next to mine."

Watching his friends walk off, Philips turned to Murdoch and thumbed towards McKay.

"As soon as he heard about the unit, he volunteered," Murdoch answered.

Looking from his Grandfather to the National Security Adviser, Philips remarked, "Go figure. I save the world and he gets the girl."

Laughing, the elder Philips stepped up to his grandson and said, "We've got some catching up to do. How 'bout you show me that bike of yours?"

"Bike? Instead, how 'bout we get something to eat, I know just the place."

With his eyes twinkling, Murdoch said, "Now that sounds like an idea."

END

Phillip Gothro lives and works in Lacey Washington. When not writing he enjoys long hikes in the Cascades with his son. He is currently working on a sequel to Dawn Strike.

Cover design by Natalie Murray